The Beta Part Three

Avanne Michaels

Black Dog Publishing LLC

The Beta Part Three is dedicated to my wonderful and patient readers. Thank you all for sticking with me throughout this journey. We're not done yet. Put on your helmets and drink your fluids.

This book has been brought to you by the continuous and unending work of my editor. Thank you for not driving over here with a hammer Misery-style.
It has also been made possible by the support of my girls. My bitches. My hookers. I love you and cannot do this shit without you.
And, as always, I couldn't do any of this without my handsome bearded half standing with me.

Things I would like to NOT thank for the production of this book:
Planetary Retrograde – seriously, get fucked.
People Who Don't Wash Their Hands – please, wash your fucking hands. Fn germ-spreading aholes tried to kill me while I was trying to put this out.
I repeat, PLANETARY RETROGRADE. If the universe would kindly get out of the microwave, that would be peachy.

About the Author

I don't like the idea of making anyone feel like they need to read this, but here are the places you can find me:

@avanne_michaels_author on Tiktok

@avanne_michaels_author on Instagram

@Avanne.Michaels on Facebook

I also have an entire website where you can find information about what's going on with me, what I'm working on, what my release schedule is, and even more contact information.

https://avanne-michaels.square.site/

There is also a newsletter, which you can sign up for here: https://subscribepage.io/Q0oYIe

A note about this Omegaverse story:

There are no shifters in this book.

The completely fictional characters in this story live in an alternate universe where there is a biological hierarchical system in place. The alphas, betas, and omegas in this universe have basic human physiology, but operate with some very animalistic instincts.

Alphas in this universe join together to form packs with other alphas, betas, and omegas (if they're lucky); some packs are familial in nature and others are purely functional. Alphas are stronger and are naturally very dominant creatures, and they make up a small part of the population.

Betas in this universe are not typically dominant and they naturally want/long for the security of being accepted into an alpha pack. Betas make up the majority of the population.

Omegas are precious. They are to be protected and treasured. They can be either male or female. Omegas are very susceptible to alpha orders and pheromones, and are slaves to their heat cycles. Male omegas go into heat less frequently than female omegas, but the frequency of the heat cycle of either males or females is completely individualized.

Only omegas can give birth to alphas, but beta/omega pairings are not discouraged. Mpreg is NOT a thing in this universe, not that I have a problem with it, it just didn't fit this story.

Reproductive Pairing:

Alpha x Alpha = Zero offspring. Alphas cannot reproduce with other alphas.

Alpha x Omega = Alpha offspring or Omega offspring

Alpha x Beta = Beta offspring

Omega x Beta = Beta offspring

Beta x Beta = Beta offspring

Omega x Omega = Omega offspring. This pairing is the most rare, and difficult to achieve.

TW/CW:

There are some very intense themes and acts in this story. Some are sexual, others revolve around violence. Proceed with caution.

Playlist for The Beta Part Three

MWTWB – AmaLee

Feast – bludnymph

Flirt - Neffex

DNA – Little Mix

Poison – Rita Ora

Daddy AF – Slayyyter

Red Light Special – TLC

Popular Monster – Falling In Reverse

Undream – Chemical X feat. TIMMS

Rude Boy – Rihanna

U Got It Bad – Usher

Can't Help Falling In Love – Ice Nine Kills

Say Yes – Elliot Smith

Mary on a Cross – Ghost

Animals – Ice Nine Kills

Love Is a Bitch – Two Feet

Big Bad Wolf – In This Moment

You Want a battle? (Here's a War) – Bullet for My Valentine

Alive (Acoustic Version) – Krewella

This playlist can be found on Spotify under the title The Beta Part Three

https://open.spotify.com/playlist/64KP9zQichJoikqG8N0xPB?si=gEtx__4mTDaQlwidkr44-A&utm_source=copy-link

Contents

Chapter One

Talia

If he tries to leave this nest again I'm going to kill him.

Somewhere in the recesses of my mind, a small part of me is screaming that it's irrational; that he's supposed to stay outside the nest to protect the rest of us. That part of me is also screaming that Devon can't have any orgasms. Jasper keeps reminding me, too. It's fine, though. Devon isn't going anywhere so long as I'm holding onto his balls. And I don't mean figuratively as I roll them in my palm.

Reid brought Nathan's desk chair into the nest for me so Devon could sit down. It was a compromise. It really would hurt him too much to get up and down, and I don't want that. What I want is his taste, and he doesn't need to get off to give it to me. All he has to do is sit there and let me lick it as it drips from him like a faucet.

"Talia, baby," Jasper says gently, "let Devon go. He needs to go with Trent to wait for your mom's team. And you don't want to irritate his wounds, do you? Remember? We talked about it."

Jasper is on his knees next to me in front of Devon. I'm stroking Devon's cock and squeezing it so precum gathers on the head. I wait until there's a big drop and offer it to Jasper. I got the last drop, it's his turn to get this one.

He leans forward and sucks Devon into his mouth. I love watching him pleasure our alphas, it makes me throb and ache; especially if they start making those delicious growling noises. I lick up the side of Jasper's neck and whisper into his ear, "he can stay for a little while. I won't hurt him. I'll be so gentle with him. Then he can go."

Jasper pulls off of Devon and sits back on his knees, "so, you want to make him sit here and let you lick him while we fuck you?"

"Yes. That sounds wonderful. Let's do that."

I resume milking Devon's cock. I've tasted all of them but Trent in the past few miserable hours. Devon, Nathan, and Corso make the cramps tolerable. I'm not in full-blown heat yet, but I'm heading there fast. My mind is trying to rein in the chaos, but I've got too many instincts riding me. If I thought I could manage to keep Devon in this chair for the remainder of my heat so I could keep the taste of him in my mouth, I would. Maybe I can tie him to it...maybe there's a belt or something...

"No, we're not tying Devon to the chair. He'd just hurt himself breaking free when he goes into rut. And a belt would never work, anyway," Jasper laughs.

Oh. I must have been thinking out loud.

"You know," Alex sighs, "it shouldn't be cute. It really shouldn't be anything but sexy to watch them take turns like that. And I should probably be jealous. But that's fucking adorable."

"Sharing is caring," Trent says from the doorway. He refuses to come any closer than that. He says he doesn't want to be tempted to abandon his post. It's very unfortunate.

"Was it like this last time?" Alex asks.

"No."

"Fuck no."

Nathan and Trent respond at the same time.

I want to laugh, because the whole exchange is funny, but another wave is starting to burn through me and I end up whining instead.

"Kaleb," Devon calls. His voice is so rough and strained. It makes the heat coiling around me feel better, but also much, much worse.

I'm on my hands and knees now. Just like before, it's nearly impossible for me to straighten my body or do much more than rock back and forth on all fours or lay on my back with my knees drawn up to my rib cage. It really must be some kind of biological, hormonal, bullshit omegas must endure. Then Kaleb is behind me and an almost instant, cooling calm washes over me when he lines up his cock and pushes it into me. I lower myself onto my forearms to give him the best possible access to make me feel better.

Kaleb's hands are gripping my hips so hard that I feel his nails biting into my skin.

It. Is. Glorious.

I thrust my ass back to match his movements, trying to fuck him right back. Every time he pounds into my swollen pussy, I cry out in relief and pleasure. Then Kaleb wraps his hand in my hair and jerks me back up onto my hands. I'm not even mad. It's perfect and feels too fucking good for me to be angry about his rough handling.

"Now," Kaleb grits out. "Reid, come on."

I can't open my eyes or stop them from rolling back long enough to see what he's trying to get Reid to do. I don't realize what's happened until I open my mouth when Kaleb tells me to and it's not Devon's taste I'm presented with. That's something to be angry about. I pull away and snarl up at Alex.

"Sorry, sweet pea. Had to sneak him away before things get out of hand. "

"I'm not out of hand," I growl, but I suck his cock back into my mouth anyway. It would be silly and wasteful not to. Alex might not ease the cramping as much as Devon, but he still tastes wonderful. Then I lose myself to the sensations of being fucked between Kaleb and Alex.

It's the most amazing thing I've ever felt, until it isn't. They're not doing it hard enough. I can feel and hear Alex's struggle to hold himself back from fucking my mouth the way he wants; and that's unacceptable. "Fucking do it, Alex. I can take it," I release him just long enough to hiss at him.

"No, Talia. You'll regret it when you come down from this."

"Please?" I whine, "Alex, please?"

"Goddammit," he snarls, "I don't want to hurt you."

"Please?" I beg again.

Then there's a sharp smack as Kaleb swats my thigh, "no. He's too big for that. If you want your throat fucked, someone else can do it."

I've been with packs before that would have gone straight into a pride-fueled fight to the floor over a comment like that. Not this pack, though. None of them seems to give a single shit that Alex's dick is huge and Kaleb said it out loud. All they care about in this moment is taking care of me. I can feel it in every single one of the bonds I have with them.

"But I want him now. I need him to cum in my mouth." God, I'm so whiny. I hate it, but I can't do anything for it.

A clit-tingling chorus of male amusement circulates, but Alex gives me what I ask for. He manages to cum a few moments after I ask for it, and Jasper takes his place. Jasper has had lots of practice fucking my mouth, and he knows just how to coax his length past my lips and into the back of my throat without being too rough.

I'm humming my pleasure around Jasper when I feel Kaleb start to push his knot into me. My humming turns into a groan and Jasper's hips twitch.

"He's knotting you, isn't he? I've wanted to see Kaleb fuck you like this for months. It's so good, baby. You're doing such a good job taking him."

Jasper's praise makes me clench around Kaleb, and he grunts in response. Jasper leans over my back and spreads his hands around my ass, then he spreads me wide. "Look, Kaleb. Look how she's stretched around you. I've never seen anything like it. I knew seeing how tiny she is compared to you would be amazing. It's so fucking hot."

"Shhhh," Kaleb tries to hush him. My bond with Kaleb feels so intense right now, I can almost feel how hard he's fighting to control himself. But Jasper, being the brat he is, doesn't stop. He enjoys making Kaleb's predicament worse.

"I wonder what would happen if I just..." Jasper stops talking and I feel him touching my entrance where I'm gripping Kaleb so hard. Kaleb's breath hisses out of him. "Did that feel good? Did you like me touching your cock while you're fucking Talia with it?"

"Jasper." Kaleb warns, but I feel him trembling against the backs of my thighs.

"Open your mouth," Jasper tells Kaleb, then he pulls in a slow breath. "You can't see it, but Kaleb is sucking you off my fingers. He's never done that before, I usually do all the sucking."

The image of Jasper on his knees in front of Kaleb flashes in my mind and that's it. I shove Jasper away from me so I can cry out my orgasm without biting him or scratching up his thighs. I saw Nathan's thighs after my last heat. I don't want to do that to Jasper; or any of them if I'm coherent enough to stop it.

I might have pushed Jasper away, but he went exactly nowhere. He tightens his grip on my hair and thrusts back into my mouth just in time to cum all over my tongue. Kaleb's release comes at the same time, I feel his cock jerking deep inside me. "Fuck, if I could mark you again, I would."

"Can't you?" I mumble after Jasper pulls away from me. I don't even try to fight the warm, sleepy contentment wrapping around me. Kaleb gently helps me to lay on my stomach and stretch my legs out between his. I let my head fall onto my arms and close my eyes as he lets some of his weight settle onto my back. Then he starts to purr for me and it feels a little like heaven.

"I can bite you all day long, but it won't be like when I marked you."

"Will you, please? I'll like that." I'm making that omega sound again. And I'm probably going to fall asleep. Kaleb's gentle weight over me feels so good, almost as good as his knot keeping us connected.

I wake up when another hot cramp washes over me.

"Hey, hey, hey, I've got you." Alex coos, and I cling to him. Then I remember that I was full of Kaleb when I fell asleep. I should still be full of Kaleb. My mouth draws up into a snarl and I whip my head around to find him.

"Where did he go?"

"Which he, darlin? Jasper? Devon?"

"Kaleb," I snap. "He was just here." I want to cry as much as I want to shout.

"I'm right here, cupcake. I haven't gone anywhere. I was just getting you a drink."

I don't want a fucking drink. I want to fuck. When he holds the bottle out for me I just look at it. That's not what I need.

"Just three sips. Three sips, and you can decide which of us you want next. Okay?" Kaleb reasons.

"Three," I huff, and snatch the bottle from him. I take exactly three drinks from the bottle, and hand it back. Then something feels off. Maybe something smells off.Clarity comes slow as I scan the room that is so dim that the men not directly near me are mere shadows.

There's something wrong with my nest. It isn't right. The books are straight. The pillows are where they're supposed to be. I have the blankets settled. What's missing? I look at my wrist. No, that's not it, I have two of Nathan's hair ties right where they should be. Trent's bright red boxers are tucked into the corner where I need them. I look around again but I can't see anything wrong. It just feels wrong. It feels almost tight.

Another cramp rolls through me and I go back to rocking on my hands and knees. This is such bullshit. There's something wrong with my nest and I can't fix it because of these fucking cramps.

"Jasper," I gasp, and he's right here beside me. "There's something wrong with it. It's tight."

"What do you need me to do? How can I help?"

"I don't know," I pant. "It's just wrong. It's too tight."

He starts pulling blankets loose and rearranging pillows so that everything is more loosely woven together, that isn't going to fix it, but I think it's a good start. Then a stronger cramp grips me and I can't think about why my nest might be wrong. I fall over onto my side to pant and attempt to ride out the wave.

Corso saves me from it, though. He rolls me underneath him and pushes my knees apart, then presses his palm against my throbbing pussy. "So hot, bella. You're so hot, and dripping for me."

I whimper and grab his wrist, "Corso, please."

He begins to purr, but I don't want that. I don't want him to be soft and gentle. I need him rough and greedy with my body. I need him to take it. But he's touching me so gently, and trying to give me too many, too sweet kisses.

When he brings his mouth back down to mine again I bite into his bottom lip. Not a little nip, a bite that gives me a taste of blood, and I lick at the small wound.

Corso's lip pops out of my mouth when he jerks his head back. "Like that, stellina mia? That's what you need from me?" I rake my nails across his shoulders in answer. I need him rough. I need him to use his body to *take* mine. I need him to prove to me that every part of me belongs to him, and the only way he can do that is if he takes it for himself. And he does.

He snaps his hips, thrusting every inch of himself inside me. The harder he fucks me, the more relieved I feel. I lose myself in the feeling of being split wide open by my alpha for as long as I can before I can't ignore the voice somewhat urgently calling my name anymore. It's Alex, he's telling me to let go of something, but I'm not holding onto anything.

Oh, he must mean my mouth. I growl in irritation, but I release the bit of Corso's chest I apparently sank my teeth into and lick my lips. Corso's knot is lodged inside me, and he's grinning lopsidedly at me as he finds his release.

"I bit you." I can't seem to stop slowly running my tongue back and forth over my front teeth.

"I don't mind," Corso purrs, and kisses my forehead.

"Everything about you is delicious." That's the last thing I say before I succumb to another short nap.

My nest is still wrong when I wake up again. Corso isn't inside me any longer, but he is still laying over me and letting me feel his weight, which would be wonderful if I didn't need to fix my nest before I completely lose myself.

"Jasper," I call out, and he's there instantly, gently pressing a damp cloth against my mouth.

"I'm here, baby. You're alright. We've got you. What do you need?"

"The nest is too tight."

He looks around with his brows scrunched up.

I touch one of them with a fingertip, "you're adorable, princess."

He leans down and gives me a soft kiss, "you're beautiful. I don't know what you mean. What makes it too tight? I loosened the blankets at the edges a little, but you didn't like that. What do you need us to do?"

I lick my lips again, getting the last little bit of Corso onto my tongue, and look around. That's it! It isn't too tight. It's too small. I'll never fit all of them in here if I don't make it bigger. I shove Corso off of me and start pushing and spreading the blankets and clothes and pillows around, pushing the edges of my nest out a few feet into the room. I need another blanket, or two, maybe some more shirts, and quickly, before I get taken by another wave.

"I'm trying, cupcake," Kaleb says, then he yells for Nathan.

Yes, I need Nathan. I won't be able to rest without Nathan. I keep losing track of which thoughts stay in my head and which fall out of my mouth, it's frustrating. I suppose I may have been a little bossy with Kaleb, but Kaleb can handle it. He handles Devon bossing him around well enough.

I smell Nathan's woodsy scent, deepened due to his oncoming rut, before I see him, but he's on the other side of the room, so I can't reach him.

"What's wrong?" Nathan asks, but his eyes are all for me.

"More blankets. Shirts. Fucking towels. Jesus. Get everything. Pull the fucking curtains off the windows. Fuck." Kaleb sounds harried. He'll live.

"Told you," Nathan smirks but disappears back down the hall.

"Hurry!" I call out, and turn my head to find Alex leering at me. I crook my finger at him, "c'mere you."

He gives me a broad, toothy smile and crawls toward me from the corner of the nest where he was sitting, politely waiting. I don't know how polite he has actually been, but he was waiting.

"You're next," I purr.

"Fuck yeah I am. How do you want me?"

I don't know how I want Alex to fuck me, I just know that I need him to do it. I don't have time to mull it over, either. Nathan comes back into the room with an armload of fabric. It smells wonderful. A lush blend of all of us. I start snatching things before he even has time to put them on the floor. I don't mean to be so awful about it, but I need to hurry. I can feel my body winding back up, and I don't think I'm going to be myself for a while after this wave. I want my nest to be right before it takes me.

"Help," I bark, "make it bigger. Everyone has to fit. Hurry."

They scramble to help me push and smooth blankets and sheets and shirts until it's as good as I can get it with their help, and I spend the few minutes I have left of sanity getting every little bit just right before I'm hit with a wall of heat and need that brings me back onto my hands and knees in agony. Alex grabs onto my hips and drags me back against him. His thighs feel so good against the back of mine, warm and strong. He leans over, planting his hands beside mine, hovering over me with his front flush with my back and his hair hanging over me like a curtain.

He growls into my ear, making chills run up my spine, "is this what you need, sweet pea?"

The last thing I register before I lose myself completely to this wave of heat is Alex grunting when I wrap a fistful of his hair around my hand and use it to roll us over. If Alex wants to be on top he's going to have to earn it.

When I come back to myself, I'm sitting on Alex's lap like a throne with my legs spread over his and his knot pulsing inside me as he laughs like a lunatic. I'm out of breath and sweaty, but I feel so wonderful; and I'm making the omega sound. Is it a purr? I don't know.

Kaleb is yelling and cursing. Corso is a wall of protective anxiety holding Jasper behind him. Jasper is a little pale, but he's still got a little smile tugging at the corner of his mouth. Reid is on his knees at the edge of the nest with his hands resting atop his thighs, which tells me exactly how stressed he is. What exactly the fuck happened that would pull this level of reaction from these men?

"Don't do that shit again, Alex. You can't be that rough with her. You could hurt her," Kaleb snarls.

"The fuck I could," Alex laughs, "you saw her throw me all over this nest. Now she's going to blame me for fucking it up."

"Be quiet, both of you," I say, and take a breath. "Reid?"

He looks at me with his eyes only, not moving his body or head.

I need to go to him, but I can't while I'm still knotted with Alex. "Jasper, go to Reid."

Corso relaxes his stance and allows Jasper to move around him, and Kaleb looks mostly confused. He opens his mouth to say something, but I hold up my hand to hush him.

Jasper gets onto his knees in front of Reid and puts his hands on either side of his face. "Hey, alpha," Jasper purrs, "she's alright. You know Alex would never really hurt her. You know she'd never really hurt him. They're okay. It's just her heat. It makes us crazy sometimes."

Reid gives Jasper his eyes and lets out a breath before pressing his forehead against Jasper's.

"It's never been that rough with them before, has it?" Jasper asks, and Reid shakes his head. "Close your eyes," Jasper continues, and waits until Reid does what he says, "can you feel her?" He smiles when Reid nods, "she feels good, doesn't she? Happy?"

"Happy, and worried," Reid says softly.

"She's worried about you. Can you feel Alex? How does he feel?"

"Ecstatic. Proud. Content."

"See?" Jasper continues his purr for Reid, "they're okay. Are you okay, alpha?"

Reid opens his eyes and gives Jasper a solemn nod before he looks at me.

"Come here, Reid," I give him a soft smile. "I need to touch you."

Jasper moves to the side so Reid can crawl across the blankets to kneel in front of me and Alex. Alex was perfect, based on the warm calm I feel, but he may as well be an actual piece of furniture at this point because this moment is all for Reid. I reach up and hold his earlobes firmly between my fingers, not pinching, just a firm hold, and look into his beautiful, dark eyes. I hold his gaze for a full minute before I make the decision to get him out of here. "Will you do something for me, Reid?"

"Anything you ask."

I smile and pull him close enough for the kiss I give him, "will you help Trent and Nathan make sure Devon behaves? And will you keep them from destroying my kitchen? And make sure Jasper doesn't eat too much shitty food?"

He gives me a smile, "I can do that."

"And," I kiss him again, "will you come back to me later, with Nathan?"

"Of course."

"Thank you, Reid. I'm sorry I worried you." I kiss him again. Kissing Reid is the best feeling in the world right now.

"I'm alright," he says between kisses, and I believe him. "I'll go now. I'll bring back some treats for you after I check on Devon."

"You are a treat," I kiss him one last time before I let him go, and nod at Jasper. He leads Reid out of Nathan's room just as I feel the energy drop that happens each time I'm knotted. I know it's an involuntary, biological reaction, but it's still obnoxious. Fuck, knot, sleep, fuck, knot, sleep. Over and over for a whole fucking week. Every month. For the rest of my life.

"What are you thinking about?" Alex purrs against my shoulder and wraps his arms around me to hold me a little tighter.

I blow out a frustrated breath. "I have to do this every single month."

"What? You don't enjoy all this attention?" He pulls a few strands of my hair.

"Of course I enjoy the attention, Alex," I pull his hair back, and more than a few strands.

"Stop it," Kaleb hisses, "don't start pulling hair again. Just stop."

What the fuck actually happened between me and Alex that has everyone so worked up? I feel perfectly fine.

"Why are you so prickly, Kaleb? And why was Reid so worried? What happened? And tell me quick, because I don't know how long it's going to be before I have clarity again."

"Drink this water and eat a cracker, then I'll tell you."

Fine. I down the rest of the bottle of water he offers me, and shove a stupid cracker into my mouth. Alex's knot is still locked inside me and I don't think I'll lose myself again until we're no longer knotted, which I'm grateful for.

"Does he have to fight you every time before you'll let him fuck you?"

"What?" I snap, "no. Alex wouldn't actually fight with me. We might get a little rough sometimes, but we don't fight."

Kaleb's jaw ticks. "Right, well, what I saw just now looked like a fight. Are you hurt?"

"I'm fine. I feel really great right now. I don't feel hurt. Corso? What happened? Was it different from how it usually is with me and Alex?"

"Yes, Talia. It was. When you see Alex you'll understand."

I turn my head as much as I can to try to see Alex, but all I see is a bunch of blonde hair hanging in his face. "What's wrong? Are you hurt?"

The lunatic laughs again, "no, they're all ridiculous. I'm not hurt, and neither are you. Corso's right, though. That wasn't our usual. Fuck, it was amazing." He rolls his hips, making his knot rub and pull inside me, and I groan.

"Mmm, fuck, Alex. Keep doing that."

"See boys? She's perfectly fine."

"But are you?" Kaleb asks, but he doesn't wait for Alex to respond. "Nathan!"

"For fuck sake," Alex grumbles, and rests his head on my shoulder. "I'm good. I don't need Nathan to run in here with an ice pack and a lollipop."

Nathan strolls through the door, but stops dead in his tracks when he takes in the scene. "Jesus. What happened?"

"Alex fucked Talia, or Talia fucked Alex. Either way, come look at his eye and check his shoulder." Kaleb sounds about as irritated as I'm beginning to feel.

That only becomes worse when my body releases Alex and the scent of my slick and his cum permeates the area. I wasn't ready to let him go, I wanted to have a rest with him before the next wave takes me over.

Corso scoops me into his lap and folds me into his warm scent that makes me think of laundry fresh from the dryer. I look back at Alex and gasp. There's blood trailing from the corner of his rapidly darkening eye and the bite mark on his shoulder would make any alpha proud. "I'm sorry, Alex. I didn't mean to."

He growls and glares at Kaleb, "don't you dare be sorry for anything you do to me when we fuck. I like how it is with us. It's fun, and it isn't always like this. They'll see soon enough. We can love easy, too, baby; you know that."

I nod, I do know that.

Nathan wipes away the blood from Alex's cheekbone with the tail of his shirt and shrugs, "he's fine. He just caught the worse end of it. It hasn't even gotten bad yet. She ran through me and Trent like we weren't there. You okay, cupcake? You need me to come look you over."

"I always need you," I say, and reach for him.

He doesn't so much check me over, he looks at and touches every part of my body he can get to without taking me from Corso in a way that's mostly just touching. He tells everyone that I feel fine to him, then he kisses my cheek and leaves.

I feel my body start to heat up, and I know it's beginning again. "It's starting again," I whisper into Corso's chest.

"I know, bella. We've got you."

Chapter Two

Kaleb

Jasper is worn nearly as thin now as he was during Talia's first heat. In a moment of clarity, Corso and Talia convinced him to leave the nest for a few hours of sleep and eat some real food. He slipped out when Nathan and Reid came in to trade places with me and Alex. So far, Nathan's theory that we can take her heat in waves is holding up. Corso, Alex and I took her on during the first, and most brutal, waves. I say take her on because holy fucking shit it was a battle to keep her properly fucked and knotted. Between the bouts with Alex, her trying to crawl inside Corso to keep him from getting farther than a foot away from her, and her apparent requirement that I stay balls-deep in either her or Jasper at all fucking times ... I need food and sleep. And fluids. I need to drink several gallons of water. Fuck.

"You look like shit." Trent was washing dishes, but now he's leaned against the counter, smirking at me like a smart ass.

"I look better than you did after her last heat."

"No, you don't." He's laughing at me now. "Have you taken a look at yourself since coming out of the nest?"

"No. I feel fine, regardless of how I look. I just need some water. And about six burgers." He and Reid kept us functionally fed, but I feel like I haven't really eaten anything for days. I suppose I haven't. "Maybe eight."

"I'll make you three grilled cheese sandwiches and put you to bed for about six hours, then you're on your own."

I only get three of those hours before Alex wakes me up.

"Just checking on you. You feeling okay?"

I groan into the pillow. "I feel fine. What about you? How's the eye? I still say that was more like fighting than fucking."

He laughs. "It was definitely fucking. The eye is fine. And you wouldn't be so critical of my methods if you could see your own. You did your fair share of manhandling. Go back to sleep. Like I said, I just wanted to check on you." Then he leaves.

That's one of the things I've been pleasantly surprised about with our new pack. I very much enjoy being checked on. You'd think it would be obnoxious or grating, but it's the opposite. Corso, Alex and Reid are older than Devon and I by a few years, and we're older than Trent and Nathan by a few. Devon and I are so used to being the oldest and carrying the worries and weight that come with being the oldest. We found Trent and Nathan when we were still in training and finishing up school, and from that moment forward Devon assumed a leadership role, with me in second. It isn't that Trent and Nathan are less than we are, it just feels natural the way it worked out. I was worried about how the hierarchy might change after we joined our pack with Corso's, I thought that Corso and Devon might clash for the lead position. They haven't, though; and I don't think they will. Neither of them seem to need to lead every moment. It's almost like they, and we, already recognize each other's strengths and lean on each other appropriately. It's only been a few weeks and it already feels so right.

Corso spends a third of his time doing distillery-related things. It mostly runs itself, but there is the paperwork and other decision making to be done. I honestly don't know what he does, only that a few days a week he spends the morning at the distillery with Reid. I don't know what Alex does, other than walk around being as obnoxious as Trent.

Actually, that's not true. Alex writes. I've seen him go at his laptop for hours. Talia walked in on Nathan and me speculating about whether he was writing code of some kind or some gory horror novel. Neither would surprise me. She knows. She definitely knows. But all she'd say is 'it isn't code'.

What I know is that he brings in more than his fair share of income, not that we keep up with who contributes what. All our income goes into the same account. That's the first thing we did. There is a separate account for the distillery, but that's to actually run the thing; it isn't connected to our pack's account. I don't know the exact number, but Devon assured me that money isn't something we'll ever need to worry about. Between Corso's distillery, Nathan's tech stuff, our COT salary, and Alex's ... whatever, our pack is financially stable.

Then there's Devon's eventual seat at the council. Eventually his father will step down, and Devon will have to step up. That's part of why he changed so abruptly after we claimed Jasper. We were a solid pack before we claimed him, but once we had an omega, we leveled up. We became responsible for more than ourselves. Our bond with Jasper pushed us fully into maturity, and Devon had to start building himself into an alpha who would be worthy of a seat at the council. So he stopped playing. He stopped letting himself relax. He stopped a lot of things. And he started working. Every waking minute of the day, Devon works toward the goal of being good enough for the council seat, for his father, but especially for us. I know that's what it is more than anything else. His need to be good enough for us.

Jasper is still asleep in Devon's bed when I make my way back to the kitchen for more food and a cup of blessed, glorious coffee. Devon and Trent are already in the kitchen, and arguing, when I get there.

"I'm going in there."

"No, you're not. You said you wouldn't."

"Kaleb's up now. He'll help you if you need help. I'm miserable. And she's been calling for me."

"She's calling for all of us," Devon sighs. "I gave my word that I'd stay out of the nest. I promised I'd be here for Jasper. One of us will always have to remain outside for him. She would be livid if she came out of her heat and we were all in the nest with her and Jasper was on his own. Fucking livid. You said you'd stay out to take care of me, since I'm still so wounded." The sarcasm is heavy in his last few words.

"You're fucking fine. You know you are," Trent huffs.

"But she doesn't. And I gave my word."

"Stop arguing," I cut in, "you sound like my parents. What do you mean, she's calling for all of us?" I would have heard Talia calling my name. Surely I wasn't so exhausted that I didn't hear her calling me.

"You'll see. I don't know how you and Jasper have slept through it. It's taking everything I've got to stay out of that room." Devon is sulking nearly as much as Trent.

I pour my coffee and begin savoring it. "She knows you're still out of commission. Even in her state, she knows."

"She just wants us with her. But I know better than to go in there. My dick's been hard for three days just being in the same house. If I go into that room I know I'll go into rut, and then that's it."

"Well," Trent throws his arms out, "so what? The property is crawling with Elizabet's people. Your father even sent an extra detail based on some information he received from one of the rogues they've got detained. We could just go in there and give her what she wants."

"I gave my word."

And that is actually, truly, that. Once Devon gives his word, it takes a world-ending catastrophic event to make him break it. And even then it's unlikely that he will.

Trent is a good man and makes a platter of grilled cheese sandwiches for the three of us, grumbling all the while about his poor balls falling off without relief. I'm working on my second sandwich when Talia's voice rings out through the manor. First she calls for

Jasper, then takes turns calling for the rest of us. Every time she calls my name I get a little harder. Trent and I exchange a look. I can feel his need to go to her through our bond. Devon doesn't have a bond with Talia yet, but Trent and I do. It physically hurts me to not go to her when she's calling out in such need.

"How long has she been calling for us?" I hope she hasn't been crying out like that for hours.

"Off and on for a couple hours. I went to the door and snuck a look. She was between Corso and Nathan, but she was asking Reid to go get us. She said she just wanted us to sleep with her. She said she made her nest big enough for all of us and everything. I felt like shit walking away when she needed me." Trent rubs his chest. "I'm dreading taking another tray up there. I don't know if I can walk away again."

"I'll take it up." I've already been in there and I didn't give my word about staying out.

When I open the door to pull out the tray of dirty dishes and empty water bottles so I can sneak in the new tray I expect to hear the sound of an omega being taken care of. What I hear is an omega cursing and growling about what horse shit being an omega is, how much better she'd feel if one of us would make her pregnant, and how rude it is that Jasper left her with a bunch of alphas who won't do what she's asking them to do. All while she's thoroughly knotted by Corso, who is completely lost to rut so he isn't hearing much of it. Nathan has somehow managed to stay coherent and he's listening to her with comically wide eyes and pinched eyebrows. Reid is covering his mouth to hide his smile, and doing a shit job of it because I can still see the dimples in his cheeks.

"Kaleb!"

Shit.

"Stay with me, Kaleb." She sounds so pitiful that I'm tempted to do it. But I'm not here to stay with her, I'm here to make sure there's food and water within easy reach of the nest.

"I'll be back in just a little while, cupcake. Nathan's with you. Would you like for me to leave my shirt for you?" Her face drops, but she nods and puts out her hand. When I give her my shirt, she snatches my wrist and looks up at me with these huge, watery blue eyes, "maybe you could stay for just a minute. Just till I fall asleep. It won't take long, I promise."

Shit.

"Stay," Corso growls, his rut and Talia's need deepening his voice.

So I stay. Talia didn't exaggerate, it only takes her a few minutes to fall asleep on Corso's chest, still holding my hand. I grab the dirty tray on my way out the door and almost drop it when I run right into Trent in the hallway. Devon is at the foot of the stairs. I nod at him and Trent to follow me and put the tray on the little table beside the front door. I wait until the door is safely shut before I scrape my fingers through my hair and start pacing the porch.

"Did either of you hear what the fuck she was saying?"

Trent's lips twitch. "Which part?"

"You know exactly which part. Did you hear, Devon? I know you were at the foot of the stairs, but she wasn't exactly quiet."

"I heard." That's all he has to say.

"We just got these things put in," I point at the implant in my hip, "and now she's in there cussing about getting pregnant. Is that what we're doing? Just going to let her start having babies? To avoid going into heat so often?"

"There are worse reasons." Trent's mouth is doing a little more than twitch at a smile. My head might explode.

"That's not the point. She doesn't even have a bond with Devon yet. And this is only her second heat."

Trent looks at Devon and shrugs, "he'll mark her before her next heat. Besides, she hates going into heat. She doesn't like losing herself to it. Nathan's got a sister who's the same way. Becca, right? The one with all those boys?"

"Yes, Becca. I've overheard her say that having kids is a lot easier than going into heat every eight weeks."

"See?" Trent says, "and Talia will be going every four weeks, most likely. That's going to be exhausting for her.

Dammit. It is rough on her. It's been three days, and she's probably got two or three more left. She's finally over the most intense waves that come at the start of heat but she's still got at least a couple more days to go. I can feel how overtaken she is by her heat, and how little she enjoys being overtaken. I just don't know that having babies this soon after becoming an omega and being claimed by a pack is going to be any better. I imagined it would be closer to a year from now before we'd be discussing the possibility of babies. "It's too soon. It's too much. She's only been with us for a few months, and she's only been an omega for a few weeks. It wouldn't be right."

"I don't disagree with you, Kaleb," Devon says, "but I don't disagree with Trent, either. She does not enjoy going into heat, she worries so much about what could happen while she's lost to it. I can tell that even without a bond."

"It's only been a few months, Devon. We can't expect her to have kids with alphas she's only known for a few months."

"She's known Corso for years."

Devon's right. Corso's pack was the first one she was ever with. "But she's only been an omega for a few weeks."

"Doesn't matter. If Talia wants babies she can have them. She wants a baby with Jasper first. They talked about it. Jasper first, then Corso. Then, I believe she said the rest of us could draw straws to see who went next." Alex says as he walks out onto the porch and sits on the swing. "I don't care. I can't wait to see her pregnant. She's going to be so fucking hateful. It's going to be amazing."

"Your idea of amazing and mine are very different," I argue. "Still, it feels wrong to just let her start cranking out kids."

Alex laughs. "Firstly, we don't *let* Talia do anything. If she wants me to knock her up I'll gladly do it, and you'd be stupid to turn down that offer if she gives it to you. Secondly, buddy boy here is right." He motions to Trent sitting on the porch rail. "Talia hates the entire concept of going into heat. Maybe hate is a strong word, but she doesn't look forward to it. In her mind it is a job and a duty that she can't get out of, not something enjoyable. If she'd be happier having one kid after another, instead of having one heat after another then that's what we're going to do. Talia deserves to be happy, whatever that looks like for her. I'm sure she'll talk to us about it when she's ready. Don't fret buttercup, you're probably closer to the end of the line for that, right in front of Mister Poor Choices," he motions toward Devon this time.

"So, we just pretend like we didn't hear her saying any of that until she brings it up?" That shouldn't stay in the back of my mind every minute of the day at all.

"Pretty much," Alex smiles. He knows exactly how we'll be on edge waiting for her to say something.

"She might not even remember saying anything. She isn't exactly herself right now," Devon suggests.

How very optimistic. If she doesn't remember at least a portion of her diatribe regarding her heat I will be completely shocked.

Chapter Three

Devon

Talia's heat lasted for six miserable, torturous, long, fucking days. She and Jasper have been asleep for ten solid hours. Kaleb and Alex look like they've been hit by a truck full of pissed off wildcats. Reid and Nathan are well enough, only a little scratched up; and Trent is sulking while he adds to his list of grievances. I slept in Jasper's bed with him and Talia for the first few hours when she came out of it, but I got a phone call that needed attention so Corso took my place.

He was trapped under a tangle of arms and legs when I last checked in on them. I hope he gets the rest he needs, he looks every bit as rough as Alex and Kaleb, but he carries it differently. I know he's exhausted. I'm honestly shocked that it hasn't occurred to me to be jealous. It's amazing. I'm *happy* that Jasper can sleep next to Corso, even if it's platonic. It feels good in the same way that it feels good to know that he sleeps next to Kaleb, Nathan, or Trent. I'm not bothered by Jasper's bond with Reid, either. I'm so fucking grateful for it. Even in the condition I was in at the hospital, I could feel Jasper slipping away.

Corso looks well enough the next morning. He looks positively perky.

"Good morning, fratello." Yes. Corso is definitely perky. And I don't know what a fratello is. Hopefully it isn't awful.

"Morning. You feeling okay?"

"More than okay. Do you have plans for the day?"

"What do you need me to do?" I don't have plans, but even if I did I would put them off. If Corso needs me to do something for him, it's something for the good of the pack, and that takes priority over anything else.

"You're good with machines. There is an issue with one of the stills. I can usually take care of it on my own, but this one's got me puzzled. Would you mind coming in with me and taking a look?"

I don't know anything about stills, but Corso's right. I am good with machines, and a still is just a machine. "No problem. I'm ready whenever you are."

"Let me get my shoes on. Meet you on the porch."

The days are starting to get cooler. I love summer, but this summer was horrible. It was way hotter than it usually is, and so many terrible things happened. The only good thing that came of it was Talia, and we almost lost her. Mostly to my own short-sighted stupidity.

Corso steps out onto the porch and I ask him which vehicle he wants to take.

"I thought we'd walk, if you're feeling up to it."

"I'm good. I really am capable of much more than they're letting me do."

He hums at me and gives me that crooked smile of his. "They, being our omegas?"

I nod. Jasper would let me get by with a whole lot more, but Talia is strict. "I don't know if she's ever going to be satisfied that I'm fine."

"Then let's get going before she discovers that I'm letting you walk to the distillery."

I can smell the season changing from summer to fall. I can't remember the last time I took an actual walk. When I was younger, my favorite time to be outside was fall. I liked the way the leaves smell when they cover the ground. That's one of the reasons I find Nathan so soothing, he smells like the woods on a fall day. Floating on top of the scent of seasonal change is the sweet, smokey oak of the distillery. The closer we get, the stronger the scent of superb bourbon becomes. I'm pretty sure I love it.

"Do you enjoy your work with the council?" Corso's question is jarring. I don't really want to think about all the stress about the council, the rogues, the betrayal, fucking Seth. I'd much rather walk in this warm sunshine with these smells enveloping me without any of that shit tainting it.

But I blow out a breath and answer. "It has to be done."

He's quiet for a while before he asks his next question. "I understand that. And I don't mean to overstep, but do you have to be the one who does all of it? Is there no one else who could take over some of it? I understand that you will eventually have a council seat, so you will still need to do a fair portion. But I have been wondering if you and the others couldn't do a little less for the council. Surely you can still work toward a solid position without being sent on so many COT missions."

"You aren't overstepping. I've actually been wondering the same thing. My father is trying to make sure I'm prepared for the seat, but he also sends our unit on the jobs that he can't trust anybody else. We're tired, though. We're not yet in our thirties and we're exhausted. Now that we have a bigger pack, and Talia, I want to shift our priorities. I just have to see this shit with the rogues through."

"So," he bends over and picks up a rock from the road, "you're planning to step back with COT duties?"

"I think so. I haven't talked to the others yet, but I know they've had enough. Nathan will still work with the council on the tech side of things, but that's not the same thing as being expected to march into a fight you didn't start every other week."

We walk in silence again for a while, watching the building that is the distillery grow larger the closer we get. My stomach muscles are beginning to ache, but not hurt. Corso keeps glancing at me, studying my face. If he notices my pinched expression he doesn't say anything.

"What if you did some work at the distillery? I can take care of most of the issues that come along with running it, and I'd never ask you to do paperwork or anything like that. But we need someone who we can trust to handle the machinery instead of outsourcing."

I can't believe Corso is asking me to work with him at the distillery. The Zaphir distillery is the best and most successful one in the country. It was passed down to him. It is an actual treasure. And he would trust me to work on the machines, even knowing that I don't know much about them.

"I am incredibly honored. Of course I'll do what I can for you at the distillery. Whatever our pack needs is what I'll do. I already know that our pack needs less COT and more down time to form solid bonds with each other. Kaleb and Trent will be glad to have the break, too. Our future needs us all to be more here and less there. Especially if our kids are anything like their mother."

"I don't know how much of a break they will get. I won't feel comfortable leaving the manor, even to go the short distance to the distillery, unless there are three of us there keeping watch over Talia and Jasper. After everything that has happened so far, I can't help but think we need to be on guard. Not many packs can boast two omegas, and Talia and Jasper have already been the target of so much."

I hate that I have to agree with him. Truly and genuinely fucking hate it. "You're right. Fuck, you're right. I agree with you. And I'm sure Trent and Kaleb will be more than happy to stay home with Jasper and Talia."

Corso gives me another of those sideways smiles, "I might be a little jealous of them."

"I probably will be, too."

"Will your father be upset with you? If you explain the situation to him, I can't imagine he'd find fault."

I feel like he might fault me for making my pack such a priority, but I will just have to make him see. And if I tell my mother that

I need to focus on my omegas, she will do all she can to help me get him to see that is the right thing to do. "I'll talk to him."

Working on a still isn't all that different from working on a car. Well, that's a lie. It's completely different, but a machine is a machine. I don't know what most of the parts are called, but I can understand well enough how everything is supposed to work. It doesn't take long to get the thing running smoothly again, then Corso and I stroll back down the road to home just in time for lunch.

Talia is cussing and scrubbing down the kitchen when we get there.

"Oh, bellissima, Trent didn't leave that much of a disaster. He did his best. Nothing is broken, and there is still food in the cupboards. Let's call it a win."

"I know," she huffs, and wipes her hands on the back of her shorts. "It just doesn't feel right unless I clean it. Trent did a good job taking care of everyone." Then she looks at me with her eyes narrowed, "you walked. Your shirt is sweaty." Then she turns that hard glare on Corso. "You let him walk to the distillery?"

He doesn't bother looking remorseful. "Bella, Devon needs exercise. How will he ever heal if you don't let him get strong again. We didn't go too fast, and I needed his help with one of the stills. He's going to come take care of them with me."

Her eyes shoot back to me, "when will you have time for that, Devon? You already have COT and council duties. You can't overwork yourself."

Over the past few weeks, Talia has gone from a beta with the sole purpose of keeping her omega happy to an omega with her entire pack's well-being in mind, and apparently none of us are safe from her wrath.

"I'm not going to overwork myself by helping out at the distillery. I really enjoyed being there this morning. And I feel really good." Her mouth draws to the side and she huffs a little more, but she stops fussing over me.

Later, before I turn in for the night, I knock on Corso's door frame. He's propped up against his headboard reading. "Sorry to interrupt. Thank you for taking me to the distillery today. I enjoyed it. I needed the walk, too."

"I know you did. I go several mornings during the week. You should come with me, you could get a good feel for it. And the walk will be good for you, too."

"Talia was right about you."

He raises an eyebrow, "what do you mean?"

"You are a good alpha. I'm glad we joined together. I know I have a lot of making up to do before everything is okay with all of us, but I'm glad it worked out this way."

He nods slowly, "yes, you will need to put in some work with Talia. And possibly with Jasper, as well. He and I are of one mind about several things. I like him very much."

"I'm glad for that, too. I looked in on everyone else, they're all fine. I'm going to bed now. Thank you for listening to me." He salutes me and goes back to his book.

Jasper and Talia are sitting on my bed when I get back to my room. When I checked on them a bit ago they were in their own rooms.

"What's wrong?"

"Nothing's wrong. I couldn't decide where I wanted to sleep, with Talia or with you. So, we're invading your bed so I can sleep with both of you." Jasper sounds very pleased with his decision. Talia is sitting on my bed picking at the threads of my quilt.

"Talia."

"Devon."

"You don't have to sleep in my bed just because Jasper wants you to. Just because you've slept with us a few times before doesn't mean you have to every time." I don't know if that's the problem, but it's the only thing I can think of.

"No, I like sleeping with Jasper and you. I enjoy the scent, it's like a freshly trimmed orchard on a sunny day with both of you. There will only be sleeping though," she raises her brows at Jasper. I've apparently missed part of a conversation.

"I know, I know. Sleeping. When will you agree that Devon is well enough?"

"When he is."

"I'm fine. Really. But I am tired, so I agree with Talia. Only sleeping tonight." I wait for the pouting to commence, but it doesn't. Jasper is just happy to be cuddled between Talia and me. It takes him five whole minutes to fall asleep. I'm not so lucky, and neither is Talia.

"I'm worried about you," she whispers so softly I barely hear her.

"I'm worried about you, too," I reply.

"I'm fine," she whispers.

"So am I," I whisper back.

"If you say so," she whispers again, but I don't want to have a whisper-argument with her, so I don't say anything else. She and I will have this conversation in the morning.

I'm worried that she isn't handling all the catastrophic and seismic changes in her life as well as she's putting on. I want to have a really substantial conversation with her about what I can do to make her understand how much I want and intend to make up for all the bad I've caused.

Talia isn't trying to have that conversation the next morning. Talia seems to not want to have the conversation at all.

"I don't need you to make up for anything, Devon. You were only doing what you thought was best for your omega and for your pack. You stayed with him when I went into the woods, which is what I wanted you to do as well. When those assholes dumped me on the porch, you and Kaleb took me to the hospital, then you came back home to Jasper, which is exactly what I would have told you to do. When you took me to a hospital, you didn't alert the entire world about it...which is exactly what I would have wanted. You couldn't have done anything for me at the hospital, anyway. I don't need you to make up for any of that shit. I made my choices, and I'd make them all over again."

"But I was awful to you, Talia. Awful. It isn't right."

"How about you let me decide what I need an apology for." She isn't asking.

"What if *I* need to apologize? For myself?"

She sighs and lays back on my bed that she just made. I tried to do it, I even attempted to tug the blankets out of her hands. But she jerked them away and spread them out before I could do anything else. "To what end? I don't need the apology. I don't want you to apologize for being yourself. For being a good alpha for your pack at the time. There were too many things none of us knew. I was supposed to be a beta."

"It was wrong to treat you the way I did, even as a beta."

"I don't need an apology, Devon. I'm not going to be traumatized or whatever just because you think I should be. I'm fine."

Chapter Four

Talia

They all suddenly expect me to be a nervous wreck, or something similar. Devon and Corso especially. Corso has been watching me closely since my first day back with him. I don't know how to make him understand that I'm alright. I don't need to have a breakdown. I've processed all the shit I've had to handle over the past few months as much as I care to. I have never put effort into dwelling on the bad shit that happens to me, especially if I chose it, and I don't intend to start now.

And Devon. I don't know what to do about Devon. I don't know what he expects. Sure, he could have been less of a dick, but I never expected anything else from him. And to be perfectly honest, I might have been an asshole if I was in his position, too. I essentially came into his pack and swept his omega off his feet. I disrupted everything. It doesn't give him an excuse, but I do understand his reaction to me. People do a lot of things when they feel threatened.

"Why are you mad at the sink?" Alex asks as he comes into the kitchen to dig around in the fridge.

"I'm just cleaning it. Do you want me to make you something?"

"It was clean before you started cleaning it, sweet pea. How about I make you something?"

"Sure. I'll get some plates. Is anybody else coming in?" If they are, I'll probably take over. I don't need the mess that would happen if Alex cooked for everyone.

"I don't think so. And if they do, they can figure out their own food. You're not a short order cook. And you're not a maid. I don't like you acting like one. I don't generally put my foot down about anything, but I've had just about enough of you cleaning up after everyone and cooking every bite of food we eat." He's speaking into the cabinet, and the ingredients for psycho sandwiches start appearing on the counter.

"You guys make a mess."

"And we're more than capable of cleaning it up. Spoon."

I hand over a spoon, and a fork for pickle retrieval.

"When are you going to let Devon out of the box?"

"I don't know what that means, Alex. What box?"

"He won't heal if you don't let him. You need to let him out of the sick bay." He twists the lid off the peanut butter and starts spreading it across the bread on the plates. Only Alex could make spreading peanut butter erotic.

"He walked to the distillery with Corso yesterday."

"Hmmm," Alex hums, and dips his finger into the jar of marshmallow fluff, "he could have come in at the end, you know." He holds his finger in front of my mouth so I can lick it.

"What are you talking about?"

"The tail end of your heat. He's well enough that he would have been fine. Jasper would have kept you from being too rough with him."

That gives me pause. Alex is probably right. Devon could probably handle sex right now. Gentle sex. Jasper has even told me that getting off doesn't bother Devon like it did a few days ago. Why didn't I let him come into the nest at the end? I remember wanting him, especially at the start of my heat. I wanted him in the nest at the end, too. I kind of remember yelling for him. Why was I so bothered by the thought of fucking him last night when Jasper suggested it?

"You're mad at him." Alex spreads the chips out on the peanut butter and mashes the marshmallow half of the sandwich on top. The muffled crunch might be my favorite part of the whole process.

"My dad, Thaddeous, puts lettuce on his peanut butter sandwiches."

"That's disgusting. And you're deflecting."

I blow out a sigh. I am definitely deflecting. "I don't think I'm mad at Devon. I don't know what I am. My pussy wants him, but there's some kind of block when I start down that path. I want him, but... I don't know. It feels like I need to wait for something first before I let *him* have *me*. It's weird."

Alex takes a bite and considers me while he chews, then, with his mouth still full, he says, "you're waiting for him to prove himself to you." That's actually ridiculous. That couldn't possibly be it.

"Devon doesn't need to prove himself to me."

"Well, he sure as shit needs to prove himself to me, sweet pea. Trent, Nathan, and even Kaleb are in the clear with you, but they're still in the shit with me. The fact that Devon is still in the shit with both of us is telling. What are you most worried about where Devon is concerned?"

I'm worried about a lot of things, but mostly about his physical condition. He keeps saying he's healed up, but he's slow when he walks up the stairs and I've seen him holding a hand over his lower abdomen.

Alex hums again, "looks like you've thought of something. I hope it's groveling. I hope you need Devon to beg you to forgive him before you'll accept him."

"You're terrible. I don't want to see Devon grovel or beg. I don't want to see any of you do it. I would hate that." If Devon gets on his knees for me it won't be for that reason.

"That's too bad. I was looking forward to seeing that. It'll come to you, don't worry. You'll figure out what you need from him and then he can do whatever it is and everything will be right as rain. I, however, still think he needs to prove himself worthy of you."

I put the uneaten half of my sandwich on his plate and stand up, "why wouldn't he be worthy? He's always been a good alpha."

"Honey," Alex reaches out and pulls a strand of my hair, "none of us are worthy."

I don't have anything to say to that, so I kiss his cheek and leave for the laundry room. I think I might feel a lot better if I can stress-fold some sheets or whatever else there is to fold.

There is a glorious amount of laundry waiting to be washed, dried, and folded when I get to the laundry room. I put in my ear buds and get to it. I don't know how long I'm at it, probably a couple hours. I've got three stacks going when Nathan comes in and scares the shit out of me. "I'm going to put a bell on you."

He laughs and says, "I didn't mean to scare you. I just came to check on you, you've been missing for a while, and your dad's been texting me. He wants me to draft plans for production of those omega earbuds. He hasn't told me everything, but it's starting to sound like some of the rogues we detained are talking. I think he wants every omega to have access to the ear buds. I think he's planning a shake-up of the registry, the alpha training center, and the omega institute. I think a lot of things are about to change."

Something that feels like nervousness is trembling along my bond with him. "What's wrong, Nathan?"

He shrugs, "I feel like something really big is happening. Like, it's been happening for years. And I'm anxious about the Dennison pack. I know they were there at the compound, and they're supposed to be following up on a few leads, but I don't think I trust them. And their omega is a..."

"Shit," I finish for him, "Danielle is a shit. I grew up with her. She's never been a very good person."

Nathan nods, "I didn't want to say it, but yeah. She used to be after me and Trent when we were younger and had plenty to say about it when we turned her down."

Now, *that* I didn't know. Growing up, I knew who Devon was because our fathers were on the council together, I knew of Jasper because he was a prodigy at the institute. I didn't know Kaleb, and if I was ever around Trent or Nathan it wasn't memorable. I was a beta, so I tended to steer clear of the alphas and leave the omegas to do whatever they were doing with the alphas. None of it affected me and I liked it that way. I don't feel exactly jealous about knowing Danielle was after Nathan and Trent, but I certainly feel something. And that something is causing a sheepish smile and a little blush spread across Nathan's face.

"We never entertained her. She eventually got the hint and started going after older guys."

"Good," I say flatly. I'm sure my distaste is loud and clear on my face.

"How big do you think this thing with the rogues is? Has your mom or your dads mentioned anything?"

I shake my head, "they haven't said anything to me. But I agree with my father, those earbuds are amazing and you are a genius. I think it would be a really good thing for omegas to have access to them. Especially if you're right and things start getting worse. I'm really bothered that nobody's come up with anything to find the omegas that were being held at the compound." I hate mentioning them. Nathan still has nightmares about those omegas.

He reaches out and pulls me into his chest, it's all for his comfort and I rub his back and let the soft purr that always fights to escape when one of them is upset sound from the back of my throat. I didn't know I was capable of making this sound until a few weeks ago, and sometimes I can't keep it contained. I haven't decided if it's a perk or not, but it's hard not to be glad for it when I can feel Nathan's anxiety start to clear from the bond. "Do you need kisses, Nathan?"

He nods and lifts me up onto the dryer. Then I give him his kisses.

I kiss his closed eyelids and his forehead and the tip of his nose. I kiss both cheeks and his chin. Then I put my hands on either side of his face and press several little kisses onto his lips. "It's going to work out. My dads, Devon's dad, and some others are all working on finding them and figuring out what's going on. And they have you to help them. We would never have been able to get you guys out of there if you weren't so damn smart. Everything will be alright. You'll see."

He leans in for more kisses and pulls my legs around his waist so he can scoot me closer to the edge of the dryer. "I like holding you," he sighs.

"I like it, too. I like doing a lot of things with you."

"Will you brush my hair again tonight? We don't have to have sex, I just want to pet you and be petted."

"Okay," I say, "we don't always have to have sex. I want you for more than your dick. You know that, right?"

He laughs softly, "I know. But it doesn't hurt." It definitely doesn't.

I hold Nathan for a few quiet minutes, rubbing his back and combing my fingers through his hair. His hair is almost always loose. Sometimes he wears a backwards ballcap, and even more infrequently he wears it in a bun. The bun is sexy, but the backwards cap is hot. It's hot when I braid it, too.

"Hey Talia?"

"Hmm?"

"I'm pretty sure I love you. Trent does, too. He probably won't tell you, though. I'm the only one of us who really announces things like that."

"I might love you back," I pull his face up to kiss him again, "probably Trent, too. I don't announce things like that, either." The way his eyes light up makes it worth the small awkwardness that usually plagues me whenever I talk about big emotions. I have only told Jasper that I love him a small handful of times; the same with Corso, Reid, and Alex. They know, though. All of them know. I can feel it now that I have bonds with them.

"Do you think you'll be able to love all of us?"

"Of course I will."

"Even Devon?"

I sigh. Everyone is suddenly so interested in making me talk about Devon. "Why wouldn't I love Devon? I'm sure I will eventually. Whether he wants me to or not. I can't see a reason why I wouldn't."

"I can," Nathan says, "he made you leave Jasper. And he didn't fight for you. And he left you alone."

Irritation crackles through me and I have to put genuine effort into fighting it back. "What was he supposed to do, Nathan? He was doing what he thought was right."

"He was supposed to fight for you. I love Devon, but he has a hard time pulling his head out of his ass. The second we knew you were Jasper's, you were ours, too. And he didn't fight for you. I couldn't do much, and I'm ashamed of that, but I at least questioned him. Kaleb did, too. Trent has been angry for months. Devon was the lead alpha in our pack, when he decides something, it's hard to make him change his mind. Especially if he thinks he's doing the right thing. It's just bullshit that it took almost losing you for him to finally understand what he was doing to you, and to us."

"I don't know what I'm supposed to say, Nathan." I really don't. This has been a close repetition of the conversation with Alex, just from a different angle. I'm not irritated with Nathan, just with the situation, and I'm starting to feel a little unnerved. And there's a really good, really fun fix for that. "But I feel very unsettled right now. You know what helps me feel better when I've got too much on my mind?"

He shakes his head. I smirk at him. "Let's go up to your room and I'll show you."

He laughs, a real one. "You're worse than we are." He might be making jokes about my sex drive, but he has zero qualms setting me off the dryer and swatting my ass when I take off for his room.

I'm still a little unsettled, even after I thoroughly wear out Nathan. Usually a round or three with one of them clears my head, but I'm still thinking about what's bothering me with Devon. I think it may have to do with his recovery. I feel like I have to protect him from further injury. That has to be what it is. Maybe Obi can come by and check him out again. Just to put my mind at ease.

He responds to my text while Trent and I are finishing up dinner. I say we because we're both in the kitchen, but I'm browning the baked mac and cheese, and he's ripping small pieces off the roast I have on the counter to settle before he slices it up for easy serving. Either Trent or Alex are almost always in the kitchen with me while I cook. I'll never tell them, but I love it. I love that Trent sneaks bites of everything and that Alex likes to try to add ingredients when he thinks I'm not looking.

I announce in the group text that dinner is ready and wait for everyone to come to the table. When Corso sees the food he grins at me. Roast beef surrounded by cut up potatoes, carrots, and onions, sauteed asparagus, and baked mac and cheese is his favorite dinner. I try to make someone's favorite at least once a week. "Thank you, stellina mia."

I kiss his cheek and order everyone to dig in before I let them know that Obi will be by after dinner.

"You didn't have to call him, Talia. I really am nearly as good as new." Devon doesn't look or sound irritated, but I know he doesn't like being fussed over.

"It will make me feel better if he looks over you one last time. I won't ask him to do it again, I know you hate it. I just," I sigh, "I don't know. It will make me feel better."

"He can look me over every day if it will make you feel better. I don't mind. But he's going to get tired of coming by every week."

"I'll make him some cookies. And I'll send plenty home with him for Jamie."

"Make plenty for me, too," Trent says with his mouth full. "I also require macaroni and cheese like this three times a week. Maybe

Jamison and the rest of them can come over one night. He used to be fun before he got old."

I point my fork in Trent's direction, "Jamie isn't old, he's just older than you. He's only a little older than Corso."

"Yeah," he smirks, "but kids still tell stories about Jamie and the shit he pulled. Corso has always been so... responsible."

"I'll take that compliment," Corso tips his chin. "And I agree with Trent, I would be very happy if we had macaroni every week."

Obi strolls through the door right before we start the movie for movie night. It's horrible horror tonight, "want to stay for a while after you check on Devon? We've got popcorn with all the sides." I actually do like Obi. He's hilarious when he wants to be. I think having him over for one of Jasper's awful movie marathons would be extra fun.

"That depends on what you're watching," he says as he lifts Devon's shirt and pushes down the waistband of his jeans a couple inches. I can't seem to drag my eyes away from the skin above the line of fabric. Devon might actually scar. Alphas rarely scar. The injury has to be very serious before it leaves a scar, and Devon might end up with three circular scars marring his lower abdomen.

"Don't drool all over the floor, it's a slip hazard," Obi jokes.

"That's putting it mildly," Jasper says and puts his arms around me from behind. "Talia could definitely be accused of being a walking, talking slip hazard. We need to put out those floor signs."

I pinch his side, "is Devon okay? It looks like he's going to scar."

Obi hums, "he might, but he earned it well. He's fine, though. As far as I can tell he's healed for the most part. The only thing left is the reconditioning. And that's often the most difficult thing, believe it or not."

Obi ends up staying for the majority of the first movie Jasper puts on. I'm pretty sure the snacks are the biggest draw, though. I make my nightly round before I go to bed after he leaves. I'm almost always the first one to turn in for the night, and I think

Kaleb is usually the last. I've already decided that I'll be crawling into Alex's bed tonight, but it's very likely that Nathan will join us before the night is over. I won't let Trent sleep with just me and Alex. I think too much about what it would look like if they went at each other and it keeps me awake and soaking wet, and then none of us get any sleep. Devon is the last one I check on because his room is next to Alex's.

"Talia."

"Devon."

"Thank you for having Obi check on me."

"I'm sorry. I know you hate it. I'm just worried."

"You don't need to apologize, cupcake," he says, "especially not for giving a shit."

I put my hand on his forehead, brushing his hair back and the other on his chest so I can feel his heart beating under my palm. "I do give a shit. I hope you don't mind."

He looks at me like I've said something utterly ridiculous. "I don't mind. I'm glad you do. I'm sorry you're worried about me."

"Don't be," I say, and run my fingers through his soft, brown hair again. "I can't help worrying. Goodnight, Devon." Then I kiss his cheek and head straight to Alex's room with all his blankets and pillows. His room reminds me of bonfires and burnt marshmallows in the best way, because it smells like him. I'm just dozing off when he comes in and flops onto the bed and I waste no time wrapping myself around him.

"We sleeping or fucking, sweet pea?"

"Hmmm, sleep first. Then we can fuck."

"Let's make love instead. I think you need it."

I nod and put a kiss on his chest. He's right, I do need it.

Chapter Five

Devon

She won't let me apologize. A few kisses and words are fine, but I need to make up for being so fucking horrible to her. For letting her put herself on the line again and again knowing the damage it would cause her. But Talia refuses to let me. She's told me several times that she doesn't need that from me. And I'm faced with the question of what does she need from me? Because something needs to be done.

I thought she was angry with me after her heat because I couldn't come to her, but she isn't angry. She really isn't. Everyone, including her, has assured me that she isn't angry with me for anything. She won't let me do things for her. She's got a whole dresser full of dead and dying flowers that Alex gave her. She has an entire bookshelf full of books courtesy of everyone; I even brought her a book of twisted fairy tales. She accepted it but she didn't read it, she just put it on her shelf. I've tried food. I've tried weapons. I've even tried a playlist of songs that attempt to convey how guilty and regretful I feel. None of it seems to matter. She just smiles at me and gives me the equivalent of a head pat and then goes on with whatever she was doing.

All the kisses have been initiated by me. All the touching comes from me. She doesn't reach for me and I fucking *need* her to. I need her forgiveness. I need it.

I followed her down to the training room in the basement. For a fancy ass manor, this place is very modern. I expected a cellar full of cobwebs and dirt, but here we stand in a brightly lit area filled with equipment and mats. She and Jasper come down here almost every morning to workout or spar. Nathan hinted that most of their sessions usually end with sex. I didn't follow her down here to watch her and Jasper fuck, but I will never be disappointed to find them in the act.

Right now they're flipping and thumping all over the squared off sparring section in the center of the room. I'm sure they know I'm here watching, but neither of them pay me any attention. Watching them go at each other is fascinating. I can see that they're both holding back, trying not to hurt each other. They could both go so much harder.

"Devon!" Jasper yells. "Are you just going to stand around watching?"

And with that, I guess I'm officially healed and deemed ready for business as usual. I was probably fully healed days ago, but Talia was adamant that I needed just a bit longer. A surge of happy adrenaline rushes through me as I realize I'll be cleared to train and build my stamina back up. And fuck. I'll be able to fuck. Not that I'd ever complain about the amount of blowjobs I've enjoyed or the number of times Jasper has made me cum all over his hands... but those things aren't fucking.

"You need to go easy on him," Talia insists. "He hasn't been able to do much more than go for walks in weeks. Be careful."

She starts to walk off the mat but Jasper pulls her back. "Both of us. Even out of shape Devon can handle both of us." Jasper winks at her.

"Don't tease the alpha, princess. I'm not in the mood for a tantrum."

Tantrum. I guess I have had a few tantrums since she's been with us. That's just another thing I need to atone for.

"We're going to do more than tease him."

"No," Talia pops her hip out and cocks her head, "we're not. We can do a couple circuits with him but I won't have him exhausted or hurt. And you're going to be gentle with him or you and I can have a real go."

I'm not really sure which part of what she said bothers me most, that she thinks I'm fragile, or that she's offering to have a real bout with Jasper. It might not be a fair match. Based on everything I've heard from the others, it might not go in Jasper's favor; and if it did go in his favor I'd have to cut in and protect her from him. It would be a shit sandwich I don't want to be in the middle of.

Jasper throws her a sideways grin. "We can have a real go with or without Devon getting hurt. I'll be gentle with you, too." She rolls her eyes.

"Two circuits, and one short, modified bout. If he so much as twitches wrong I'm calling it. Clear?"

"Clear." He's still grinning at her.

"I'm right fucking here," I repeat the words she said a few weeks ago when we were talking about when she might go into heat again. "I can handle the two of you. You don't need to be gentle."

"Don't argue with me, Devon. If I go at you the way I go at him," she tips her head at Jasper, "I could hurt you. You're still not at your best." Then she looks back at Jasper, again like I'm not standing here. "Thirty percent."

"Seventy," he counters.

"Forty-five."

"Sixty."

"I'll leave right now."

"Fine," Jasper huffs. "Forty-five."

"I'm right fucking here," I grumble, "I can take more than forty-five percent effort from both of you. I'm an alpha, for fuck sake."

Talia looks me slowly up and down. "Alright, *alpha*. Seventy-five percent."

I take off my shoes and roll my neck as I step onto the mat with them. Seventy-five percent. Healing or not, I should be able to take two omegas at seventy-five percent. I stretch out my shoulders and swing my arms in a few wide circles, then assume a defense stance.

Talia scoffs and shakes her head. "Negative. Do what we do for two circuits or get off the mat."

"Fine," I say, trying for a neutral tone, but barely managing to not sound pissy. Then they start torturing me. I thought they were going to do stretches or something. No. They're doing full-blown yoga poses that I have no hope of doing, and not because my body won't move that way. The first thing they do is reach straight up into the air and then bend at the waist, presenting me with both their asses wrapped up in tight little shorts and giving me an instant erection. Then they roll down onto their elbows to hold a plank for a full minute before raising up onto their hands and bowing their backs. I have no hope of being as graceful as they are, and I have even less hope of doing it without making an obscene spectacle of myself.

"It's just a sun salutation, *alpha*," Jasper teases, "I've seen you do them before now."

"I can do sun salutations, Jasper," I say, then add quietly, "I just can't do them after watching you and her do them."

He must have heard me because he cackles. Jasper is just full of himself lately.

We run through a few more stretches and then have a round of easy warm ups, then Talia rolls her neck on her shoulders and claps her hands together. "Take your stance. If you lose your feet we'll back off. If one of us loses ours, you can have at the other one until we're both up. You start with three points this time, because you're not at one hundred percent. If you're pinned you lose a point. We get six because there's two of us, and you're an *alpha*. Fair?"

"Fair," I agree.

It only takes thirty seconds for me to regret that. They should have gotten three points to share. It took them less than a minute to put me on my ass. I blink up at the ceiling a few times, then roll back onto my feet. My stomach muscles only protest a little, and I make damn sure there's no trace of that on my face when I turn back to Talia and Jasper. "Again."

It takes them longer than a minute to take me down this time, and I'm pretty sure it's because they let it take that long. I cannot possibly be so out of shape that it's this easy for them to take me to the ground. Neither of them are even breathing hard. I get back to my feet and motion for another round.

This time I manage to get a hold on Jasper and pin him to the mat. He smirks and gives me a quick kiss. "Better not stay down here too long. She's faster than me."

She is, too. I'm barely back on my feet before she's got her thighs around my neck, bringing me back down to the mat. Jasper hasn't even bothered to get to his feet, he's just laying there beside me smiling like he's having the time of his life.

"I thought this was supposed to be seventy-five percent." I'm trying very hard to not sound as winded and pinched as I feel.

"This is a combined seventy-five percent. We work really well together, in every way," he winks. "If Talia and I were both going at you at seventy-five percent each you'd have already tapped out, *alpha.*"

He's got to be joking.

"You've got one more point," Jasper whispers. "You want a go at just Talia? I'd like to see what she does with you." So mischievous, and so damn mean. He knows she's going to wipe the floor with me. Again.

"No, that wouldn't be fair. If you're both at seventy-five together, that would be her giving me just a little more than thirty percent." We're lying here doing math, weighing how much effort it's going to take to let me know exactly how much strength I need to regain.

"I think it would be plenty fair, but she can go at you at whatever percentage you're comfortable with. She's good like that."

I sigh. Do I really want to know what Talia is like at maximum effort? Kaleb told me how she was at the compound, and I saw the aftermath of her work at the farmhouse. Fuck it, why not?

"Give me all you've got," I say, climbing to my feet.

"No."

"I can handle it, Talia. I want to know."

She looks at Jasper. She's really asking Jasper for permission to go at me to the fullest extent. At least he nods. Talia shrugs. "Okay, then. Ready?"

"Ready," I say, and we begin.

I don't think she's actually giving me everything. I've been able to get my hands on her a couple times, I almost got her to the ground once, but she's so damn fast. And she's extremely good at using my size and weight against me. Just when I think I've got her, she'll twist or just slip right out of my grasp and flit away like I never had her in the first place. Meanwhile, I'm sweating and trying to keep either of them from noticing how hard it is for me to keep going. I thought I was stronger than this.

"Is he alright?" she calls out to Jasper.

I don't let him answer. "Ask me, I'm right here," and rush her. I wish I could say I hold back, but it has become painfully obvious that my best effort today is barely enough to keep me on my feet. I also have every confidence that she is perfectly fucking capable of defending herself. Omegas do not get his type of training. Well, Jasper did, and Talia was trained as a beta, but omegas don't typically develop this level of combat ability. They're taught and trained in escape tactics, but my omegas have been trained to make people regret coming after them. After all the attempts on Jasper and my pack, I'm starting to think that all omegas, every single one, should be given the type of training that Jasper and Talia have. If they could actually defend themselves, make themselves really difficult targets, it would be so much better. I don't know if this is something to talk to my father about or Elizabet. She'd probably be all over it, definitely her.

I don't have any more time to ponder it because Talia puts the proverbial nail in the coffin. I might be rushing towards her, but she's the one doing the attacking. She launches herself at me and literally runs up the front of my body, plants her feet on my shoulders, and slams my body to the ground. The end result is Talia sitting on my chest with her feet on either side of my head.

"Three," she says and rolls off me. She starts to walk away, but I grab her ankle and jerk it out from under her. Why the fuck didn't I think to do that sooner?

Talia lands on the mat and glares back at me. "Feel better, cheater?"

She stands up but I keep hold of her ankle. "Why won't you let me apologize?"

"I don't want you to apologize, Devon," she sighs, like she's tired of hearing about it.

"But I need to. You need to know that I'm sorry for everything."

She sighs again and lays her head on the mat, "I don't want you to be sorry. Let go of my ankle." She doesn't try to pull free, she just waits for me to let go. When I do, she slowly stands and leaves the basement.

"Do you remember all the hoops I made you jump through before I let you mark me?" Jasper says. He crawls over and lays next to me.

"You didn't make me jump through hoops."

"Exactly," he says. "You didn't have to because I knew from the first time I saw you that you were my alpha. Remember all those hoops I had to jump through to get Talia to be mine?"

"There were no hoops. She was yours from day one. What's your point, angel?"

"Sometimes you have to earn your omega. Show that omega that you're worthy of them. You have to work for it."

I glance over at him, "I don't mind working to earn Talia. I'll jump through every fiery hoop she puts in front of me."

"That's the thing," Jasper smiles, "Talia doesn't want you to jump through hoops."

"I don't understand, baby. How do I earn her if there are no hoops? How can I prove myself? What did Corso do? Even Kaleb has been deemed worthy. What can I do?"

Jasper sighs, fairly dramatically, like I'm exhausting. Maybe I am. "Did you know that Corso saved Talia from Seth?"

"No, I didn't. Nobody told me."

"He did. Corso, Alex, and Reid went to Seth's place after those motherfuckers raped her and got her out. Corso pulled her out of a fucking holding cell and carried her out of that fucking place in his arms. He saved her. All three of them saved her. They're the only ones who have saved her from anything. Other than them, the only person who ever saved Talia is Talia."

Shit.

"And Kaleb jumped off a cliff."

"He did what?" This is the first I've heard of it.

"After the fight at the rogue compound, we went to a place Talia loves so we could regroup and get cleaned up before we came to see you at the hospital. It's a lake, but to get to it you have to jump off a cliff into it. I mean, there's a little path, but jumping off the cliff is actually safer than walking down it."

"I'm sorry. *Kaleb* jumped off a cliff into a lake? Why?" Kaleb isn't afraid of much, but the biggest thing he's afraid of is heights, and the second or third biggest is large bodies of water he can't see through. The idea of him jumping off a cliff into a dark lake is...this is a big deal.

"He did. He didn't know what she was doing, and he wasn't letting her jump into an unknown alone. So he jumped over the cliff right behind her. Then he marked her. I only got to see the aftermath."

"So, Corso's pack saved her and Kaleb jumped off a cliff to get to her. How did Trent and Nathan earn their places, since you know everything?" I tug on one of his curls.

"They treated her like she mattered."

Oh.

I definitely didn't do that. I did the exact opposite of that for entirely too long. I drove her away, and when she came back I still made it perfectly clear what her place was. Then, after we brought her home from the hospital, I treated her like I'd treat any omega who needed help. That's not treating her like someone who matters. Even now I mostly treat her the way you're supposed to treat an omega, not how you should treat Talia the individual. Fuck me. I've dug myself a hole I'll never get out of. How could she possibly ever think I'm worthy of her?

"It's subconscious to a certain degree. Almost instinctual."

"What is?" I don't understand what that means. I had the same omega courses as every other alpha when I was in school, and then in training, but I don't know what he's talking about.

"Think about it. I instinctively knew you were mine. Kaleb, Trent, and Nathan, too. I felt it from the start that every one of you was worthy and good. It makes me sound arrogant, but I don't know how else to put it. I knew you were mine and that I was yours with complete certainty. It was instinctual. You didn't have to work to gain my acceptance and submission because I already knew I'd give it to you."

I'm nodding, but I still don't know what he's getting at. I'm trying, though.

"Nathan's sister, Lotus, is a good example."

"Oh god, don't make me think about sweet, little Lotus," I interrupt. Lotus is just seventeen. She's not old enough to be officially claimed, and she's certainly not old enough to be marked, but she sure as fuck already has a pack. And they're all older than I am. Nathan was proud of her for making them fight for it, but I was pretty horrified to see three big, mature alphas pin her to the floor during a meet and greet for omegas. I trained under one of them, for fuck sake.

We went because two of Nathan's sisters were there to be introduced to a few packs and we wanted to make sure they would be treated right. Which gives me yet another reason to feel like a piece of shit. If anybody treated one of Nathan's sisters even remotely close to how we treated Talia, they'd have to answer to us. We did the exact thing we were trying to protect Nathan's sisters from. Fuck.

"That's exactly my point, Devon. Sweet little Lotus needed her pack to physically prove that they were worthy of her. She made them *make* her submit. She even broke one of their noses. Some omegas are like that, especially the females. Female omegas can be vicious, a lot more vicious than the males."

"I don't know, Jasper. Don't you think Talia's had enough alphas try to force her submission? I hope that's not what she needs from me because I don't want to do that." Just the idea of forcing Talia to submit to me makes me feel a little sick.

"That's not what I mean. The reason Lotus needed her alphas to make her submit to them is something personal and instinctual. She needed them to prove that they were able to handle her at her most volatile state, which is also, funnily enough, her most vulnerable state. Maybe Talia needs something like that from you. How do you not know this?"

"Alpha training is different from omega training, I guess. We're taught the basics, and that omegas are to be cherished and protected. How their instincts work isn't really addressed." Now that I'm thinking about it, that's pretty fucked up. We're supposed to care for our omegas, and ensure their health, safety, and happiness, but we're not taught about their instincts, or that they need special tea and vitamins. "I'm not making Talia submit to me. I hope that's not what she needs from me. I won't do it." What I don't tell him is that I might not be able to do it on my own. If this afternoon is anything to go by, it would likely take me, Kaleb, and probably Trent to get it done, and we'd be hard pressed to do it. I won't even consider Nathan, he wouldn't force her to do a fucking thing. He had a hard enough time just being rude to her in the beginning.

"No, you're right. I don't think she needs you to force her to submit. But she does need something more from you than she needed from anybody else. You've just got to figure out what it is."

~

"You should take her on a date." Jasper looks so happy with his suggestion, which would be a great one if I thought she'd actually go anywhere with me when he finds me later on that same day..

"Jasper, baby, that is a great idea but I don't think Talia would like that."

"Why not? You can both dress up and she would love a night out."

"She may have wanted me while she was in heat, and she may be giving me small bits of affection, but that doesn't mean she'll let me take her on a date." And then it hits me exactly how long it has been since I've taken Jasper on a date.

I can't believe I allowed myself to be buried so deep in responsibilities and preparations for the future that I let myself turn into the kind of alpha I hate. The kind that leaves the needs of his omega and pack on the sidelines. And then it hits me, I've become my father.

My father is a great man. He holds his position as a councilman based on his actions, not because he inherited the seat. He leads the COT with a level head and heart. It is these things that make him a great man, a great councilman, but a poor father and an occasionally lacking alpha.

He was always working when I was younger. If we had familial problems, we took them to one of my mother's other alphas. Most packs are like Talia's, with every alpha being considered a father figure, but the pack I grew up in was stiff and awkward. I knew from a young age who my father was and wasn't, and that my father was too busy for me or my mother. Sure, he made sure we had all we needed, but he was emotionally absent. My mother's other alphas took her out for dinner or movies; my father only ever attended council functions with her on his arm. I don't remember him sitting on the sidelines for a single ballgame. He was a provider and a protector, but he wasn't a partner or a father. I swore I wouldn't do that, wouldn't be that; but here I am, doing just that.

Kaleb has had to pick up so much of my slack. Trent and Nathan also give Jasper way more of that kind of time than I do. I feel awful enough about Jasper, and now with Talia as a second omega ... I have to do better. I can't be like my father. They have to know that they're more than just a designation, Talia especially.

"I don't know, Jasper. I haven't even taken you on a date in way too long. I'm sorry for that. I haven't been what I needed to be on so many fronts."

Jasper rolls his eyes. "I'm alright. You watch movies with me. And, no offense or anything, your idea of a fun time with clothes on is very different from mine. I'm fairly confident that both you and Talia have the same opinion on what a fun date would be."

He isn't wrong about most of that. Kaleb is very good at taking Jasper on Jasper-themed dates. They enjoy the same things, fancy things. Things like plays and ballets and poetry readings. I would rather go to a loud, dirty bar with loud dirty music, or go to a game or a fight. I've taken Jasper to plays, I've even enjoyed them, but it isn't my natural habitat.

Talia would hate all that too. Hell, she'd probably hate all the fuss that omegas get. The parties, treats, packs vying for her attention. She just isn't wired like Jasper or most other omegas. Talia would have probably done everything in her power to get out of all of it, omega status or not. She has that in common with me. I'll never complain about the fuss or function, though. Not really. If I hadn't attended those functions I wouldn't have Jasper.

"Jasper, I can't take Talia to bars and ballgames. If her parents found out that I was taking their daughter with a brand new omega designation out to rowdy bars and boxing rings, they'd be less than thrilled."

"Marcus would love it. And nothing any of us do, including me, will ever be good enough for Elizabet. She might make a fuss over us and all that, but none of us will ever be good enough for Talia. Well," he looks to the side at the stairs, "Corso might have a shot at being good enough. Maybe even Reid. But the rest of us don't stand a chance at her approval."

"You're wrong. Elizabet thinks you're wonderful."

Jasper sighs. "Take Talia out somewhere. Just you and her. Be charming."

"I don't know. I'll think about it."

Jasper rolls his eyes and clucks his tongue. "If you take her on a date, you can spend time with her, just the two of you. Without me or anybody else around. She's only seen the version of you that is focused on the pack, or me. She needs to see and experience the version of you that isn't that. You need to show her how you can be, how you want to be. Not how you have to be. I think that may be what she needs, to see that you can be more than just an alpha."

He struts off toward the stairs where we've been listening to Corso draw the most wonderful sounds from her for the past hour. The unofficial door-open policy in our pack is both a blessing and a curse. A blessing because open doors are usually open invitations; but a curse because we can't spend our lives fucking no matter how enjoyable that would be. So, while I can sit down here and listen to Corso, and now Jasper, wring pleasure from Talia like it's his mission in life, I'd better serve my pack by calling my father and have the conversation I've been putting off for literal years.

Alex and Trent are in the garage when I get there. It's a big area, big enough for three vehicles plus Talia's *classic*. It will be a classic by the time I'm finished with it. It'll be gorgeous. I started working on it right after Daniel drove it back to the farmhouse when I brought her back. After I sent her away. Jesus, I'll never make any of this up to her. I can restore her car, I can give her time, I can take her on fucking dates, I could worship the very air she breathes for the rest of my life and it still wouldn't make up for how goddamned horrible I was.

"It can't be as bad as all that," Alex smirks. He and Trent are, well, I don't know what they're doing.

"What is all that?" It looks like they've got catalogs for fishing equipment and swimming pools and gardening supplies spread out over the work table.

"We're picking out birthday presents." Alex is very pleased with himself.

"For who?"

"My great uncle Cornelius, and Trent's brother Joe."

"Trent doesn't have a brother. And do you have an Uncle Cornelius? What are you doing?" Whatever it is must be completely ridiculous.

Trent rocks back on his heels, "Talia said we could spoil her on birthdays, just not *her* birthday."

I stare down at the collection of what-the-hell on the table then back at the two idiots patting themselves on their backs. I open my mouth to tell them Talia isn't going to appreciate fishing supplies, but then I shut it. "You know what, good luck. I hope she enjoys whatever this," I motion to the catalogs, "is." Then I sit down in the ratty old recliner in the corner of the garage to call my father.

I decide mid-ring that this is more of a pacing conversation and stand back up.

"Son," he doesn't bother with a hello. He sounds happy enough that this call might not ruin his entire day.

"Father," I reply. "Do you have time to talk?"

"Of course. I'd make time. How are you feeling?" It's quiet on his end of the call. Great. His full attention. I almost wish he was at the office with other people to distract him from his disappointing son.

"I'm alright. I won't take too long. I need to talk about stepping back. At least temporarily. I have neglected some very important things, and I need to get my priorities sorted and back in order. We're going to finish up this mess with Crane and the rogues, but then we're offline for a few months, maybe even a partial retirement. I've let things go that should have never been let go and I have to get myself and my pack back in order."

There's no sound from the other end of the call for a full ten seconds before my father responds. "Good. It's been a shit thing to do to you, son. I've been pushing you too hard for too long. I was going to force a break on you and your boys when you agreed to take in Talia, but then things with the rogues started escalating and your unit was, and still is, the only one I really trust. I've leaned too heavily on you, for that I apologize. I was never the best father when you were younger, and I've just made it worse as you're grown. Now I've got a grown son who thinks his only worth to me is in the job he does. That's on me. That's the downfall of being a father, sometimes you get caught up in building the wrong sorts of things and lose sight of the right sorts of things. I hope to do a much better job of it from now on, or at least fuck it up in different ways."

I take the phone from my ear and look at the screen to make sure my dad is who I actually called. Well...shit. I don't know what to say now. I thought he was going to take it poorly. I never expected this reaction. "I have never said you were a bad father."

"Of course you didn't. You would never say that, you'd just keep trying to be better and let me get by with all of it. Elizabet had a little heart to heart with me after you left the hospital."

Oh my god. "What do you mean? What did she say? I didn't mention anything to her."

He laughs. "Don't be so worked up over it. You were in and out of consciousness for days and you were on quite a few medications. She had a few things to say to me about some things you may have let slip in your semi-conscious state. I'm just sorry it took so long and an ass-reaming by a Graves to get us to this point." I hear an engine start on his end. He must be heading home for the day. "I owe Jasper an apology, as well. I haven't been very fair to him over the years. There's also a project I want him to head in the future, so I'll need to get into his good graces before I can spring it on him."

"Jasper isn't doing missions."

"No, I'd never even attempt to send him out. I'm more worried about what Talia might do to me if I suggested something like that than I am you," he laughs. "It's nothing like that, anyway. No missions. I swear it. I also think a sit down about your team retiring would be a positive step forward. Maybe not Nathan, but no field work for him, just his brains behind a computer, especially after those ear things he made."

I still have no idea what to say.

"Your mother wants you over on Saturday afternoon if you can make it. All of you."

"I'll talk to everyone and see what we can do," I say, then change the subject. I'm much better at talking to him about government espionage and possible treason than what Mom wants us to bring for lunch this Saturday. "Have you heard back from the Dennison pack?"

"Not yet. I'll let you know when I do. Now, get off the phone and go actually enjoy something."

Then he hangs up, leaving me holding the phone to my ear and staring blankly in Trent and Alex's direction.

"Everything alright?" Trent asks.

"I guess so. We're taking a break after we take care of all this shit with the rogues."

"Well, thank fuck for that. I don't like to complain," Trent says, but I interrupt him.

"Yes, you do."

He grins at me, "I'm just saying, we need to regroup. As a pack. I know we have a job to do and all, but we have other things to do, too. Especially now."

"Yes, like Talia," Alex cuts in, with a bigger grin than Trent's. "You'll have to make lots of time to do Talia. There's a line, though. And you're both at the end. I'm her favorite, anyway."

"Jasper's her favorite," Trent argues.

This could go on for a while. They're both so full of themselves that I don't bother getting involved. There's no point, especially when we all know Jasper really is Talia's favorite.

Chapter Six

Jasper

I hope Devon pulls his head out of his ass soon. I don't know what other advice I can give him. I think taking Talia on dates and showing her how it would be to truly be *with* him would go a long way toward mending their relationship and moving it forward in a positive way. Up until now, as far as Devon is concerned, she has been a temporary beta, an omega in need, and my girl; and as far as Talia is concerned, Devon has been an alpha, my alpha, and an asshole. If she could see that he is so much more than that, it would make so many things so much better, and easier.

The thing that has been most surprising, even more than the fact that she's mine in the first place, is how she is with Corso, Reid, and Alex. If she wasn't mine, she would be theirs. Wholly theirs. I think she has always been theirs, but she's been too stubborn and self-sacrificing to realize or act on it. Reid worships her, loves her. I can feel his need for her through the bond I have with him, and it feels nothing like I've ever felt before. He needs her at a different level than how you need to be with and see someone you love. He needs her to function. I can't imagine how horrible it was for him to be without her. Alex loves Talia. He loves every word she says, every breath she breaths, and every dick-move she pulls. I don't need a bond to feel that. As for Corso...Talia is everything to Corso. It's obvious every time he looks at her. I feel guilty for my connection with her sometimes, like I'm taking her from him. He doesn't seem to care that she and I are the way we are, that we are somehow tied together in an unexpected and undeniable way. He's just happy to have her.

Corso and I have come to a silent agreement that she is ours before anyone else's. That isn't *quite* right, but it's the best explanation for the way we are with her. I don't want to take her from Corso any more than she wants to take me from Devon, and Corso understands that without effort or discussion. He and I understand that she is our priority, and that's why it's perfectly acceptable for me to lean against this door frame so I can enjoy watching him give her such pleasure that her voice is echoing off the walls of the manor. The smile he gives me as he plunges his fingers inside her is one that is only ever aimed at me. Because she is ours, and it is our privilege and duty to take her to the point of making those gorgeous noises.

He's leaned against his headboard with Talia facing away from him, hands and knees on either side of him while she licks and sucks the precum that's visibly dripping down his length. Every time he fucks his fingers inside her she cries out or groans around him, and he could do it all day. He likely has, to be perfectly honest. She's been singing his praises for the past hour, at least. I've heard at least four orgasms, but it's probably been more. Corso isn't one of those men who get distracted by his own need, I've seen him hold himself back for hours to ensure that she's been thoroughly fucked and loved. Only then does he work for his own release, and even that is designed to bring her off just one last time. I don't have stamina like that. It's sad to say, but Talia is more than I can handle for very long. She takes me too high too fast, and I can't hang on to save my life.

I walk over to the side of the bed and stroke my fingertips down her spine. Chills break out and she hums a greeting. "You're being a very good omega, Talia. Taking such good care of your alpha's cock." All omegas, even accidental ones, love hearing that they're good omegas. Especially when they're pleasuring their alpha.

She hums again and the corner of Corso's mouth turns up. "She is. And she's so needy, I've already made her cum several times in this position. Can you see the little collection on my chest?"

I take a step back so I can look, and sure enough there is a little puddle on his chest. "You must have been making her feel so good. Did he make you feel good, Talia?"

She softly moans and nods, pushing her hips and ass up, presenting herself to us.

"You see how she offers herself to us? She knows we can take care of her; don't you, bella?" Her body rocks forward as he thrusts his fingers into her again and again, the wet sound of it going straight to my own dick.

I take another step back, far enough that I have almost the same view Corso does. A fantastic fucking view. I reach out and grasp her hip. "What if we swing her around and I fuck her while she finishes you off. We could race, or we could see who lasts the longest. What do you think?"

I can guess what Corso thinks, but Talia's opinion is obvious when she does the rearranging herself. She props herself up on one elbow so she can use her free hand to roll Corso's balls and positions herself on her side. After she's settled, she takes Corso all the way down to his pronounced knot and hitches her knee up, which is also a fantastic view.

Corso laughs softly, but it turns into a rough groan when she starts gently stroking his knot. "I won't win if you do that, amore."

She pulls off of his cock just long enough to tease him. "You'll win if you're racing."

My knees dig into the mattress when I climb onto the bed, and I put my hand on her hip for balance as I pull her bottom leg out so I can straddle it. Perfect. My balls are going to drag across her inner thigh every time I thrust inside her. I glance over at Corso before I push inside her. "Racing or competing?"

He laughs and looks up at the ceiling. "I think I'll win a race before I win a competition."

I line up my cock and brace myself on her hip. "I could probably win a race, too. You've had her going for hours. Everybody in earshot has been hard for half the day."

Corso laughs again but chokes on it when Talia wraps her fist tightly around his knot. They say it's easy to drive omegas to the point of being mindless sex fiends, but all it takes to overwhelm an alpha is a little squeeze in the right place.

"Are you ready, baby?"

When she nods, I thrust inside her all at once, making her gasp around Corso. She feels so fucking good. So wet. So hot. Soft and tight at the same time. I take a few seconds to savor the feeling then I fuck her, setting a steady, firm pace right from the start. She moves with me, stroking and sucking Corso in time to my thrusts. Corso and I are both mesmerized by the way her ass and thigh tremble and quake with every movement. Yeah, I'm not winning a competition. My balls are already tightening up.

"You're going to make me cum already, bella. You're making me feel so good." Corso sinks his fingers into her hair and doesn't look away from her body to say, "do you think we could both cum at the same time, Jasper? I think our beautiful girl would like that very much."

Talia moans, long and loud, and I feel her tighten around me at his praise.

"I think she'd love that," I manage to respond, "I'm ready if you are."

Talia pulls off of Corso again. "I'm ready." Then she goes back to making Corso's eyes roll back into his head.

"Hurry, Jasper. Or I'm winning the race." He might, I can see his toes curling.

I grab a handful of Talia's ass and let it go so I can watch it bounce before I give it a nice swat. It throws her over the edge into the release I wanted her to have before I finish. "Good girl," I purr, the same praise coming from Corso with his deep growl as he finishes just seconds after I do. We're all still breathing hard when Corso decides now is the perfect time to talk about Devon. Talia is going to be thrilled.

"Are you going to forgive Devon?"

She sighs like she does every time someone mentions Devon or forgiving him. "There's nothing to forgive."

"I don't agree," I interject. Devon is in dire need of forgiveness, but it has to be her choice.

Corso's purr intensifies and he combs his fingers through her hair. "Devon needs to be forgiven, whether you feel justly wronged or not. You might not think like an omega, not yet, but Devon is an alpha. He is an alpha who has wronged and hurt you, he feels that even if you don't. I will never push you to do something you don't want to do, or don't think you should. But I would like it if you would consider letting Devon apologize."

Talia rolls around and wriggles until she's on her back using Corso's arm for a pillow and pulls me up to rest my head on her stomach. Once she has us all settled the way she wants us she sighs again. "I don't want Devon to apologize for being what he is. I was a beta, an unaffiliated beta, who came into his pack and essentially stole his omega out from under him. I was a threat, and I brought more threats to his pack, his family. I don't fault Devon for protecting the things most precious to him."

I turn my face up to look at her. She really believes what she's saying. "I don't know how accurate that is, Talia. I'm still angry with him over the way he treated you. I don't care that you were a beta. You were my beta and that made you his beta, too. Corso would never have allowed you to be treated the way Devon did. It's my fault, too." I don't need to hear Corso agree with me, I know he does.

"Nothing's your fault, princess."

"The fuck it isn't. It was almost too late when I finally took a stand. I should have protected you so much sooner than I did."

She starts petting my hair, and the tone of Corso's purr changes minutely in response to our growing anxiety. "Jasper," she says,

"I was there to protect you. That was my job. To help you, and protect you."

"Bullshit, and don't argue with me. Devon treated you like shit, nobody stopped him till you were gone, then he still didn't treat you the way he should have after you came back. It took you nearly dying, Talia, *dying.* We are all at fault. I can't make you understand that you were wronged, and I can't make you understand why Devon needs forgiveness. But I can keep trying, and I can make sure that shit never happens again. You're ours to take care of, ours to protect. And you're going to fucking let us."

Chapter Seven

Talia

I'm alone in the kitchen. I'm never alone, especially not in the kitchen. I intend to take full advantage of it, too. I have a gigantic bowl of cereal and a book, this is just about blissful. I should have known it wouldn't last as Devon comes in and sits down across from me and looks... nervous.

"I want to take you on a date."

"I'm sorry?" I'm talking with a mouth full of cereal and milk, but really, a date?

He looks even more nervous. "A date. I want to take you out somewhere."

"No."

His jaw ticks.

I don't have the energy right now for an alpha tantrum.

"Why not?" he asks, with only a little bite in his tone.

"You don't even take Jasper on dates." I can't go out on a stupid date with Devon when I've never seen him take Jasper anywhere but the bedroom.

"I'm going to. But I want to take you somewhere tonight."

I'm trying to force my face into something resembling neutrality, but I'm pretty sure I'm doing a shit job. "Why?"

"Because I want to?"

"No, you don't." Why would Devon want to take me on a date?

"Yes, I do. What? You don't want to go anywhere with me? I won't let anything happen to you. I'll make sure you're safe. We can go out and do something."

"Like what?" I don't address the part about keeping me safe. I can keep myself safe, omega or not.

"I don't know. Something. We can have fun."

Can we, though? We can live in the same house, we can agree about a lot of things, we can both sleep with Jasper in his bed, and we can certainly fuck if we need to; but I don't know if Devon and I can have fun. I don't think Devon can have fun at all, if I'm honest. The closest thing I've seen him do that looked like having fun is when he accidentally pulled me into the tub, and that made me cry for completely unrelated reasons. "I don't know, Devon. Is everyone going?"

"No. Just us. Come on, Talia. If you hate it, I'll bring you home, I won't even pout about it."

At least he's admitting to his penchant for pouting.

I sigh.

"Fine. Alright. What should I wear?"

Devon's eyebrows draw together, "I don't know. We'll be indoors. There will be dinner that requires forks," he fights off a smile. There will never be a time that the mentioning of forks won't make someone in this pack have a reaction.

"What time should I be ready?"

"Six? That's three hours from now. Will that give you enough time?" Sweet heaven, he can't possibly think I'm one of those women who spend hours getting ready.

"I can be ready by six." Then I end the conversation by shoving another spoonful of cereal in my mouth and my nose into my book. Over the top of my book, I watch him look around the kitchen, then he gets up and walks back out to the garage.

I'm looking through the clothes that have magically appeared in my closet when Jasper comes in and flops on my bed. "The jumpsuit. The black one, with the leg cut-outs. And heels. Tall ones."

"I can't do anything in heels, Jasper. Especially tall ones. But I think you're right about the jumpsuit." The jumpsuit really is great. It's made of a soft, airy black fabric with thin straps over the shoulders and slits running down the outsides of the legs from mid-thigh to ankle, and it's backless. It's sexy as hell.

"If you wear the jumpsuit, you'll have to wear the heels. And your hair up because of the back." He's on his side with his head propped up on his hand watching me. "And no under things. He better not try to take you somewhere ridiculous. If I find out he took you to a wrestling match or something like that I'll never let him take you anywhere again."

So this was Jasper's idea. I smile, but part of me hopes he will take me someplace like that. A wrestling match sounds like way more fun than the stuffy formal dinner I feel like I'm dressing for. I slip the jumpsuit off the hanger and lay it across the bed while I go back into the closet to get the red and black peep toe ones with a very functional kitten heel.

"Those will look just as hot," Jasper smirks at me. "Did he tell you where he was taking you?"

"No," I huff, and pull off my shirt, "did he tell you?"

He shakes his head. "Nope. Better hurry, cupcake. You've got fifteen minutes to be ready to go."

It only takes me five because all I really have to do is step into the jumpsuit and twirl my hair up into a fluffy bun. It takes longer to do the clasps on the shoes than anything else.

Devon is waiting by the door when Jasper walks me down the stairs. He's wearing black slacks and a pale blue button-down shirt with the sleeves rolled up a few inches above his wrists. He looks amazing, and I'm not afraid to tell him. Alex beats me to it, though.

"Well, don't you clean up nice!" he crows as he comes down the hall. Then he sees me, and he whistles, motioning for me to spin in a circle.

"You're ridiculous," I grumble, but I spin for him anyway.

"I might be ridiculous, but you're gorgeous." He turns to Devon, "have her home by midnight or we'll send the dogs after you. She's got brothers, you know, and I think her dad's on the council."

"I think you're joking, but we won't be very late coming home." Devon tends to take Alex more seriously than I ever could, and now is no different.

"Also, keep in mind, Johnson, if anything happens to her you'll have to answer to us. Not a scratch. And no tears. Understood?" Oh. Alex actually is serious.

"Understood."

Oh for fuck sake, "I'm right here, Alex. I'll be fine, and we'll stay out as late as we want."

"Not too late, bella." Corso walks around Alex and sweeps me up into his arms. "And I agree. Not a scratch. Not a single tear." He brushes my cheek with the pads of his fingers like he'd wipe away a tear.

He puts me down and I pull his cheek down so I can kiss it, then Alex, and lastly Jasper. Then Devon and I finally get to leave.

After a drive that lasts a little longer than I thought it would, we pull up to the front door of an extremely upscale restaurant. At least I'm dressed for it.

"Don't touch that door handle," Devon looks at me like he's daring me to open the door. I shrug and keep my hands in my lap while he gets out and rounds the car to open my door for me. Then he hands the keys to the valet and holds out his elbow. So I tuck my hand into it and let him lead me into the fancy-pants restaurant.

Once we're seated at our table I whisper, "have you been here before?"

Devon nods, and whispers back, "Jasper likes this place. Why are we whispering?"

I stifle a giggle, "I don't know."

The menu is in a language I don't speak. Phenomenal. "Whatever you're getting, get me the same thing," I say quietly, "I can't read the menu."

Devon studies the menu, and when the waiter comes to take our order he points to something and says, "we'll have two of those."

The waiter notes our choice and scampers off to place the order. I lean forward and whisper, "what did we get?"

Devon leans forward, too, and also whispers, "I don't know. Jasper always orders for us when we come here. I hope it isn't salad."

The laugh that bursts out of me startles the couples sitting near our table, which only makes me laugh harder. "Me too. Salad at a place like this would be a tragedy."

As my laughter fades, Devon and I fall into an awkward silence. Devon and I don't really spend much time together alone. We don't know what to say to each other unless it's about Jasper.

Then the food comes. I don't know what it is, but it's not a salad. It's not terrible, though, and we're half way through it before I see Seth's father lead his mother to their table. It isn't close to ours, but we won't be able to leave without them seeing us, and any appetite I had disappears.

"What?" Devon asks. "What's wrong? I can smell your anxiety, it's like burnt chicory coffee. What happened just now?"

Devon couldn't have seen them come in from his vantage point. "Behind you to the left, Seth's parents."

Devon doesn't bother looking. "Fuck."

I put my fork down and look at the table. I'm not afraid of Seth's father, but he knew who my parents were and said all those disgusting things to me at the auction, and I blame him for what happened to me with Seth's pack more than I blame Seth. I don't think I can be in the same room with him without either killing him or vomiting.

"Do you want to leave?"

I nod without looking up from the table.

"Don't do that. I don't like that. You don't look down for any-body, understand? Especially not for him." Devon reaches across the table and tips my chin up so I'm looking into his eyes instead of at my plate of beige sauce. "You don't look down. Understand?"

I give him another nod.

"Alright, let's go. They've got my card on file. It'll be fine."

Then we very calmly and efficiently get up from the table and move toward the door. We almost make it.

"Devon!" Seth's father calls out. Shit.

"Shit." Devon speaks my thought.

"Talia, a word, please," Alpha Pratchett says as he weaves through the few tables between us and him.

Devon steps in front of me, blocking me from Alpha Pratchett's view. "No."

"I just want to apologize."

"Unaccepted. Go back to your table, Pratchett."

"Talia," Alpha Pratchett tries again, "I can't begin-"

"No, Jonas, you really can't. Don't speak to my omega again. Don't look at her. Don't say her fucking name. Go back to your table and sit the fuck down."

"Devon, your father will-"

"My father would have already killed you where you stand. The only reason I haven't is because I don't need another mess to clean up because of you. Your time will come soon enough."

"Are you threatening me?" Alpha Pratchett sounds out of breath, like he's struggling to control himself.

"Don't embarrass yourself, Jonas. Go back to your table." Devon sounds perfectly in control of himself. Maybe even a little bored. I'm suddenly feeling so shaky, in a way I haven't felt in years. I don't understand why. I'm really not afraid of Jonas Pratchett. This isn't fear, but I don't know what it is. My teeth are actually starting to chatter.

Awkward or not, marked or not, Devon is my alpha. Alphas protect their omegas. Alphas help their omegas find calm in the middle of the worst situations. That's what the books and lectures say. That's what Corso and Nathan have done for me in the past. Devon is my alpha, and he will help me. I press my forehead between his shoulder blades and tuck my fingertips into the back of his slacks, gripping tightly to his belt. He tenses for just a moment, then he redoubles his efforts to get me out.

"Jonas. We're leaving. I don't care what you think or what you say, but I will not allow you to antagonize or upset my omega any more than you already have." Then he turns away from Seth's father and moves me with him, using his body to block me as we walk out the door.

We don't wait in front of the restaurant for the valet to bring the car. Devon tells them to meet us around the corner, and he grabs my hand to pull me down the sidewalk. My teeth are still chattering and my breath is short. I don't understand why I'm having this reaction. My phone starts dinging notifications right before Devon's rings. He answers it with a gruff, "everything's fine."

I only hear half of the conversation, and I don't want to let go of Devon's warm hand to dig around in my bag for my phone.

"She's alright....yeah....Jonas was at the restaurant....no...I know. ..*I know*...I'll ask." He turns back to me just as we reach the corner, "do you want me to take you back home?"

I hope my eyes aren't as wide as they feel. I don't want to go back home like this. It will freak everyone out and they'll blame Devon. He really didn't do anything wrong, it wouldn't be fair. And the questions and fussing...no. I don't want to go home right now. I shake my head.

He nods once, "no, she's not ready to come home...I don't know, I'm looking at her right now. She's a little shaken up, but she's okay...no, I don't think so." He touches my cheek with his other hand, then my forehead, "maybe a little...I'll keep an eye on it... she's going to be fine...I've got her...yeah, I'll let you know...okay. Bye."

"Reid thinks you're having a panic attack. Corso thinks you're in shock. Alex thinks you need a drink. Jasper, Nathan, and Trent want me to bring you home. What do you want? That's what we'll do. All you have to do is tell me."

I think they're all right, but I still don't want to go home. "I'm fine."

"No, honey, you're not. But you will be. Let's get out of here. This isn't the place for us. I wanted to take you somewhere special and nice, you never got all the omega pageantry and I wanted you to have just a little of that. But you don't like that stuff any more than I do." He wraps his warm, nearly hot, hands around my biceps and holds them firmly, keeping eye contact, until our car pulls up to the curb. Then he puts me into the car. He even buckles my seat belt for me.

Devon pulls into the street, I don't know where we're going. It doesn't matter. My teeth won't stop chattering, and he keeps glancing over at me. This is fucking awful. "I'm sorry. I don't know what's wrong with me right now."

He snorts. Then a laugh barks out of him that makes me jump. "Absolutely not. Don't you dare apologize for this, or any of the other things that are not, in any way, your fault. None of this shit is your fault, Talia. Us treating you like shit when we got you wasn't your fault. Me *continuously* being horrible to you wasn't your fault. You were a perfect beta, you didn't deserve any of that shit. Jonas and Seth being shit isn't your fault. Fucking Jay and Derrick weren't your fault. What those rogues did sure as fuck wasn't your fault. And this reaction that you're finally having because of all of that shit, isn't your fault either. I honestly don't know how you've held it together this long. You might have cried a little bit after I got water everywhere and with the coffee thing, but this," he motions to me in general, "is the reaction you should have had a couple months ago. You scare the hell out of me, you know that?"

"I...what?" I stammer. It sounds like he's yelling at me, but his words don't match it.

"You scare the shit right out of me, Talia. I don't know what to do with you. You can take on any one of us, and I don't mean sex. But you seem so fragile sometimes. You're not afraid of a single fucking thing, but then you have this kind of reaction to Jonas Pratchett trying to force an apology, that he doesn't fucking deserve, on you and all I want to do is wrap you up and protect you from the whole goddamned world. I thought you were going to take Jasper from me, but you were never going to do that, and now I have both of you and I'm fucking terrified. I am unbelievably and incredibly grateful that we have a bigger pack now. You and Jasper are going to need every single one of us to keep you safe. My god, I have no business having you out right now with just me to protect you. I'm so fucking stupid and careless. Jesus. I'm taking you home."

That's a lot for him to unload, and even more for me to process, but I *really* do not want to go home cold and shaky, with my teeth chattering from nerves. "Please don't take me home. Not yet."

He shoots me a quick look then puts his eyes back on the road, "where do you want to go? I'll take you anywhere you want. Just tell me what you need and I'll make it happen."

"Chili fries."

"What?"

"I need chili cheese fries."

I grab onto the door handle as Devon swings us around in an unexpected u-turn.

"And shots. And horrible music."

He doesn't look back over at me, but he does smile and reach over and grab my hand. He holds it all the way to the seedy little bar on the outskirts of the city, then he tells me again to not open the door again.

The music playing in the bar assaults my ears in the best way when I step out of the car and take Devon's arm when he offers it to me. I'm still shaky, but my teeth aren't chattering as much anymore. Someone lets out a whistle as we walk through the door, but Devon glares around the bar, which ensures the end of that. He leads me to a booth and motions the waitress over to order us a truck load of chili cheese fries and a round of shots.

"This music seems horrible enough to me. How about you?"

I nod my head and look around. I've never been here before, but it's obvious that Devon has. He's tipped his chin up at several guys, including the rough-looking bartender.

"I like it," I say. I do like it, and it is pretty terrible. Sometimes you just need a jukebox blaring an awful mix of country and classic rock to help you feel better. The food and shots arrive and I feel even better. These fries aren't as good as the ones at Danny's Bar and Grill, but they're still amazing.

"Do you have any idea what I ordered us at the other place?" Devon asks before he downs his shot.

I shake my head and throw back my own shot, enjoying the burn down my throat. It takes a few minutes, and several fries, for me to realize that one shot is having an effect on me.

"You've got to be kidding me. This is *not* a perk."

"What? What's wrong?" He looks genuinely confused.

"One shot," I glare at the empty glass. "One fucking shot and I'm already feeling it. This is some omega bullshit."

Devon laughs. A full belly-laugh. "I'm sorry, cupcake. Really. I didn't think that would change for you."

"And now I live at a distillery" I whine.

"I don't think I can take it if you pout, sweetheart. Are you feeling any better?"

I nod, "I am. The fries and you helped more than the shot."

"I helped?"

"You did. You wouldn't let him see me or talk to me. I might have puked or passed out or something else equally stupid if I had to deal with him. I don't know what that was, but I hope it never happens again."

He studies me for a few moments, then he says, "you carried too much for too long, Talia. You're still carrying too much. I think

Reid's right, you had a panic attack. Jonas Pratchett's old ass isn't scary, but what he represents, what he's responsible for, is. You're so strong all the time, you're used to just pushing through. But everyone has a limit, and I think you've reached yours. Do you think you can let us take care of you? I know I don't deserve it, but I swear you can lean on me. I'll never be able to make up for what I've put you through, but I can do everything I can to prove myself to you from now on. I promise I can be a good alpha for you."

The thing is, I know he can. Devon is a good alpha. He was terrible to me because he was afraid for Jasper and his pack. He was afraid for himself,too; and I won't fault him for any of those things. I'm not even upset with him for any of it. I make my own choices, and I chose everything I've done up to this point knowing full well what the consequences and rewards might be. I don't regret any of it. I have the pack and the home I always wanted, and Devon is part of that.

"You're a good alpha, Devon. You take care of Jasper the way he should be taken care of, and you take care of your pack. You're a good alpha."

"I can take care of you, too, Talia."

Chapter Eight

Trent

Talia did have a full-blown panic attack while she was out with Devon. We all knew, we could all feel it. Reid and Corso were adamant that Talia would know whether or not she really needed to come home, but me, Nathan, and Jasper wanted Devon to bring her home when the first tendril of fear and anxiety coiled down the bond. I can't imagine how Jasper felt without a bond and having to go on our descriptions.

All seven of us were sitting in the main room waiting for Talia and Devon to get home. Devon was irritated. Talia just laughed and kissed Devon's cheek before she dragged Jasper up to her room.

It's been almost a week and things between her and Devon feel a whole lot easier than they have been. I hope he figures their shit out soon because Jasper is due to go into heat in about three weeks, and it is very likely to align with Talia's next cycle. At the very least they'll overlap. The biggest problem we're going to have is breaking Talia's rule about someone staying out of the nest on guard duty. There's no way in hell any of us are going to volunteer to stay out of the fray when both omegas are pumping out pheromones in waves. I called Marcus myself to ask him to arrange the best and most trustworthy team he can to watch the place. He promised to help with coordinating Elizabet's people with the COTs being sent, so that will help. When I asked him to talk to Talia he just fucking laughed at me and wished me luck.

The second biggest problem is Devon. He hasn't marked her. As far as I know, and I would know because nobody in this house tries to hide anything, he hasn't even tried to fuck her since she came out of heat. He'd never push her into it, but he'd feel like complete shit if he ended up marking her when she's in heat and he's in rut. Consent is everything to Devon, especially with Talia. She's had so many things happen to her without consent, Devon would rather spend the week she and Jasper are in heat in another state than mark her without her consciously agreeing to it. And that would hurt Jasper. Which would hurt Talia. There would be a complete circuit of hurt feelings and unmet needs, so Devon and Talia need to get their shit settled.

~

"Did you call my father?" Devon asks, looking at me over his coffee.

I bite the inside of my cheek and nod. He was my second call after Marcus laughed at me.

"I was going to call him, but thank you. I don't know if he told you, but he got with Elizabet. They are collectively sending three teams here for the alignment, that's what they're calling it. I think three is excessive, but Elizabet wouldn't be swayed. I think she's anxious about Talia and Jasper being in heat at the same time, but I can't see why. She was happy, excited even, when she knew Talia was going into heat the last time. I don't know why this time would be worrisome."

I don't either, but I got the same feeling when I talked to Marcus. "Yeah, I don't know. Marcus said she was worried about something when I talked to him. I'm glad they're sending the teams, though. All three of them. Have you heard anything from Dennison? I want to trust him, but I don't know. At this point, the only people I really trust are us and our immediate families. Well, not mine, because my dad's a dick. But everyone else's."

Devon puts his cup on the counter and takes a breath. "Their beta called me. They've got a lead on the omegas that were at the compound. They're being moved around pretty quickly, probably so nobody can get a fix on them.When Dennison gets a hook in them, they're gone by the time he and the COT he has with him gets to the location. He wants to get Nathan on it. He thinks Nathan can pin them down so we can get to wherever they are and get them out."

"Nathan has nightmares about the omegas. I don't want him touching this." Nathan has slept with either Talia, Jasper, or me since we've been at the manor. He might fall asleep in his own bed, but before the sun rises he's in bed with one of us.

"I don't, either. But I think he might be the best person for the job. He's really fucking good at that type of thing. The best, actually."

"No," Talia says as she comes in carrying a massive basket of towels; obviously having overheard us. "Nathan isn't ready to deal with something like that. I won't let him. If he couldn't find them it would eat him alive, and he's already in bad shape over it."

"What if he's their only hope of being found? Would you really risk thirty or so omegas? To keep Nathan happy?" Devon's expression is neutral, but he's weighing her answer. Devon doesn't like it, but he knows we can help Nathan weather the backlash of a potential failure. What he doesn't know is that Talia's priorities have shifted. She might worry and mourn for those omegas, but Nathan is hers to protect and the rest of the world can get fucked.

I feel her answer pour through my bond with her before she ever opens her mouth to speak it. "I'd risk more than that to keep Nathan safe. And his happiness is more important to me than most things. I won't let him do it. And you better fucking not, either." Then she stomps out of the room with her basket of fluffy yellow towels.

"So much for progress," I say, "but I don't disagree with her. I know Nathan's stronger than he puts on, but you weren't there at the compound. You didn't see what he did, what he was like. And you haven't been waking him up when he's crying in his sleep. If he takes on this job, and he can't find them, it will ruin part of him and I don't think we'll be able to bring him back from it. Think long and hard before you ask him to do this, Devon."

"I know. He hasn't come to me, but I know about the nightmares, Jasper told me about them and you know I weigh all risks. I just keep thinking about how much it would help him if he could help Dennison find the omegas."

He's right, of course. He's as right as Talia is. If he could find anything, pinpoint any solid location in time to save them, I really think it would help him. But if he couldn't...I don't want to think about it. "I don't know what to say. I agree with you. But I don't want him hurt, either. And if you ask him to do it, he will. And if it goes wrong Talia might never forgive you for it. You're already having a hard time with her as it is."

"It's getting better. The date helped. I'm going to take her out until her heat starts to set in." He looks almost hopeful. Too bad I'm going to crush it.

"You've got three weeks before she goes into heat again. She'll start spiking the week before her heat. I don't think you're that charming. And this heat will line up with Jasper's." I rock back on my heels and smirk at him, "what can you accomplish inside of two weeks, Mister Johnson?"

The corner of Devon's mouth lifts, just a bit, "plenty."

Talia is with Jasper in the main room. They're sitting at the piano playing something together, the basket of towels on the floor beside the bench. If she didn't get so annoyed, I'd take a lot more pictures of them than I already do. It doesn't stop me from taking out my phone and snapping a few shots and sending them to the guys to be distributed.

"I don't want him to do it, Trent." And just her saying those words to me, with that worried tone, and her big, blue eyes looking up at me makes me utterly willing to keep Nathan from ever leaving the house again.

"But what if he can help them? And you know he can." Jasper says softly, but I can feel how worried he is.

"Please," Talia says so softly, "please don't make him do it. If you ask him to, he will. Please don't ask him."

"Jasper, listen, I don't think," I start, but he interrupts.

"Do you think I want to send Nathan farther into the dark? I don't. It isn't right. But knowing those omegas are out there somewhere, with who knows what happening to them, is killing him too. He has a better chance at finding them than anyone else, so he should try. If he knew he might be able to help save them and we kept him from doing it, he'd be just as bad off as he would if he tried to find them and failed."

"It scares me," Talia leans her head on Jasper's shoulder and he puts his arm around her.

"He can do it, Talia. We can't protect them from everything."

And that is an eye-opening statement from Jasper. How often has he convinced one of us or all of us to not sign off on a job, or to go to a particular event instead of another in order to protect one of us from one thing or another? I'm having another of those moments where I'm being forced to realize that my designation is not the strong-point I've always believed it is. Alphas tend to believe that they're the strongest, the biggest, the most invincible person in the room, but that's often our biggest downfall. Jasper has probably saved us from our own pride more than any of us realized by just asking us not to do something and making it seem like he's the reason we shouldn't. Like right now, I don't want Nathan to get involved with any of this shit anyway, but Talia admitting she's afraid and basically begging us not to ask Nathan to do it is almost a more convincing reason to keep him from it.

"He shouldn't have to. It isn't fair."

Jasper gives her a squeeze and kisses the top of her head, "it isn't. But it's the right thing to do. He doesn't have to leave the manor. He can stay right here where we can see him. And we'll be right there with him to help him get through it. Then we can be extremely proud of him."

"I'm already proud of him," she says.

"We all are, but Jasper's right," I reach over and tip up her chin, "we'll be right there with him. And he really does have a better chance at finding them than anyone else. It'll be alright."

Talia's mouth turns down in a little frown, but she nods. "I'm going to take these upstairs. Then I'm taking a nap." She kisses Jasper, then me after she picks up the basket. "I don't mind if anyone joins me, just don't flop." That last bit is all for me. I definitely flop. Alex flops, too, but he's not in the room. That's a conditional invitation I'm probably going to take her up on.

Jasper and I watch her walk up the stairs, then he says, "if we're going to ask him to do it, we need to before Talia and I go into heat. It's only three weeks away, and I can feel myself already winding up. He can find the omegas in three weeks, can't he?"

"I'm sure he can, baby. You know how good he is. And this could help him." Jasper is every bit as anxious about it as Talia, which I'm thoroughly enjoying feeling through my bonds with both of them, not. "Why don't we go find him and drag him to Talia's room and we can all have a nap?" That gets me a smile.

~

Devon, always the man with the best timing, brings up the omegas over dinner. Kaleb isn't amused. "Why do you always do this kind of shit over dinner? Especially when it's an interesting dinner?"

"Because we're all together, and" he points at Kaleb with his fork, "you don't give us enough credit. What do you think, Nathan? You can find them, right?"

Nathan doesn't immediately answer, and when he does he's talking to Talia. "I can find them. I'll be alright. Dennison's pack is good, but they're not me. I can find them. You don't have to worry about me, cupcake. Not for this."

Talia doesn't smile, but she gives him a little nod.

"I hope you can find them within two weeks," Alex takes a bite of what appears to be pasta but doesn't quite taste right and talks around it, "I don't know if you'll be able to concentrate with both of them going into heat at the same time, and nobody's very inclined for you to work away from home."

"Three weeks," Kaleb corrects.

"Two. Peaches is going to start having spikes and get all needy in two weeks, and Talia will start soon after. I'm going to have to teach you boys all about omegas, aren't I?" He takes another bite, "what even is this, sweet pea? My eyes say spaghetti but my mouth says salad."

"It is spaghetti. Spaghetti squash. The squash pulls apart like noodles if you scrape it with a fork. Is this a repeat or a dud?" Talia looks around the table. Nobody says anything for long enough that she answers herself. "Dud. I don't like it, but it's what's for dinner tonight."

"It's not that bad, it's just...different." Is Devon really trying to make her feel better about not liking the food? "It's good to try new things."

"Don't worry, Devon. My feelings aren't going to be hurt because the food is weird. I'd rather make things we like," she looks back at Nathan, "I don't want you to do this. I don't like it. But if you say you can do it then I believe you. I just might be a little extra attentive while you're doing it."

"Attentive or distracting?" Nathan smiles at her.

"Both. Definitely both."

Corso pushes his plate away, his empty plate. He'd eat a bowl of dirt if she gave him a spoon. I probably would, too, to be honest. "I'm glad they're consulting you, Nathan. If anyone can find those omegas, it's you. And I'm sure you'll find them well before our omegas need all your attention. I agree with Alex, none of us want you away from the manor without us, and you will most definitely not be able to get anything accomplished with two omegas eyeing you."

"We do not eye him," Talia scoffs.

"We kind of do, though. It can't be helped," Jasper says, "I mean, just look at them." And just like that, everyone feels a little better about things.

Nathan asks me to go for a walk around the property after dinner. It's getting darker earlier, but there's plenty of daylight left for a walkabout. "What's going on with you?", he asks as soon as we're a decent distance from the manor.

"What do you mean?" Nothing's going on with me. I'm actually feeling pretty solid.

"You've been less full of shit for a while now. Since the compound. What's going on?"

I shrug. "I don't know. Nothing's wrong. I think I'm just understanding some things a little differently. I forgot how much of a badass Jasper is. I didn't think about Kaleb being afraid of anything, much less heights, until he jumped off a cliff after Talia. Apparently Devon isn't invincible, and Talia might actually be a little bit fragile after all. She's constantly worried. Do you think she worried like that before she switched to omega?"

"For sure. We just didn't have a direct line to her so we couldn't feel it. She's different than I thought she'd be."

"Softer." I expected Talia to be as snarky on the inside as she is on the outside. I thought she'd be sour and hard, but she's so soft. Alex and I might talk about spoiling her, but if anybody's getting spoiled it's going to be us.

Nathan nods, "we're such assholes. She was taking care of us the whole time and we were assholes. And she's just letting us off the hook like it's no big deal."

Maybe to Talia it isn't a big deal. She doesn't think like an omega, she thinks like a beta. Jasper is all omega. If we do something to upset him, or something that he doesn't agree with, he makes sure we understand exactly why we're wrong. That's good, it keeps us straight. But Talia handles us the way betas handle alphas. They just work with what they're given and somehow things just work out. The only thing she's ever said anything about is Devon's penchant for tantrums, and today when she made it clear that she didn't want Nathan to work on the omega situation. She really does just go along with whatever we're all doing. I've watched Corso and Alex in particular try to get her to make more decisions about things that omegas tend to need to be in charge of, but she's mostly uninterested. She'd rather 'let Jasper handle all that omega stuff' as she puts it.

"She likes to move forward. She doesn't like to dwell. She's been a beta her entire life, betas don't typically like holding onto grudges or carrying unnecessary stress and strife. Good betas, anyway. Talia was a perfect beta. I think she hates being an omega."

Nathan suddenly stops and crouches to the ground. He stands back up holding a crushed cigarette. None of our pack smoke, not even socially. His eyes dart to the trees surrounding us. We're near the main road, close enough that someone could have parked and walked onto the property, but not near enough to the road that it could have been tossed out from a vehicle. Someone has been snooping around. "I'll see them. The entire perimeter is covered, and most of the property. I'll see them. Maybe one of the guys from the details dropped it." He doesn't believe his suggestion, but it makes me feel better to hear him say it. "Either way, I'll see them."

We finish our round and are almost back at the manor when he says, "she doesn't hate being an omega. She just thinks like a beta. She's all omega about some things. Like the kitchen. And the laundry. And us.

Chapter Nine

Jasper

She's going to have to let him mark her. I need her and Devon to have a bond before we go into heat together. I can feel myself winding up to go into heat, I had my first heat spike this morning. It was just a small one, but they're going to get bigger and more intense; and just about the time I'm ready to go, Talia will be, too.

Devon helped me through the little spike this morning. It was such a relief to be able to do more than give him a blowjob or handy. I've missed having Devon. Really having him. I can't wait to tell Talia that he's well enough to fuck. Things have gotten a lot better between them. I hope they get really good really fast because when our heats sync I don't think either of them will be able to resist the other; and I've been looking forward to seeing them together for literal months. It's going to be so amazing. I hope I remember at least part of it.

Talia is outside right now, sitting on the ledge of the empty fountain. She likes to sit there when she's overthinking something. One day soon I'm going to have fish put in it. It's silly that there aren't any in there now.

I've learned that Talia is more cooperative about talking about the things that worry her if she's asked about them in a text. My mother is the same way, so it isn't a huge thing for me. *Hey. What are you out there thinking about?*

She looks over her shoulder and up at my window. I watch her sigh, and then she pulls out her phone. *You really want to know?*

She always asks that question when it's something big. Oh god, I hope it isn't bad. *Of course I do. Tell me.*

I don't like going into heat. It feels like I'm someone else.

Well, fuck. I hope she isn't going to suggest the suppressants again. And I absolutely will not entertain the suggestion of sedation. If she breathes a single word about sedation I will do exactly what Nathan teases us about and put her over my lap and spank her pretty little ass until both it and my hand are raw. *I understand why you wouldn't like it. But you really are amazing when you're in heat. I love you in heat.*

We'll both be in heat this time.

That shouldn't be an actual problem. That should be one of the best times we've ever had as a pack. *I know. It's going to be so good. I can't wait.*

I can't do it, princess. I don't want to go into heat every month for the rest of my life. I've only had two and I'm already dreading the rest of them. I don't want to do it.

I wait for a few minutes before I text her back. I don't want to be angry before I have anything to be angry about. *I can't see a way out of it, baby. You're an omega now.*

Get me pregnant.

I almost break my ankle twice running down the stairs and out the door. Alex yells, asking what's going on and I wave him off as I slam the door behind me. I'm out of breath when I throw myself on the rock ledge beside her. "Are you serious?"

"I think so. I hate how going into heat makes me someone else. It takes me away from myself, and from you. If I'm pregnant I won't go into heat. If I'm nursing a baby I won't go into heat. That will give me over two years without a heat cycle." She's picking at the strings on her cut-offs.

"Do you really want to have a baby? Right now? You've only had two heats, and we only just combined our packs."

She pulls out a string and drops it onto the grass by her feet. "I hate it, Jasper. I hate losing myself. I can wait if you're not ready."

I never thought about having kids until the day I asked Talia if she'd let me kiss her and experiment with her. From that first touch, that very first taste, I was hers. If she wants to have thirty kids with me and our alphas I'll love every single one of them. They'll be the most horribly spoiled children that ever existed. "If you want to be pregnant and have babies then I want that, too. But it can't just be our decision. It has to be a pack decision. Our babies are *our* babies."

"Of course they'd be *our*," she spreads her hands in front of her toward the manor, "babies. Any child I have will belong to all of us. The first one will be biologically yours, then the next one will be biologically Corso's. They can decide the rest of the order. And I don't need to stay pregnant constantly, I'd hate that, too. I just don't want to have more than two or three heats in a row."

"Talia," I laugh, "that's only two or three months between."

"Maybe not. Some women take a few months after they finish nursing to get their cycle back on track. We'll know after the first one. Do you think they'll hate it?"

I roll my eyes. "No, cupcake, they won't hate it. Corso especially. Devon might be a nervous wreck over it, though. I think they're going to love it. But there are other things to consider."

"What other things?"

It's interesting and not surprising at all, at least to me, that she hasn't put it together that our entire pack is waiting for her to have some kind of nervous breakdown over everything that has happened to her. I know she hates the heat cycles, it's completely obvious; and honestly understandable she's been a beta for her whole life. I don't think she hates being an omega, but I don't think she really feels like she's an omega until she has a very omega-like reaction to something. We can have as many kids as she wants, but I don't like the idea of using a baby as a way for her to not have a heat cycle. I want to have babies with her if she genuinely wants them, when she's truly ready for them.

"Please don't take this as me telling you what to feel or how to think, because I would never do that. I, we, worry that you may not be handling things as well as you appear to be; and part of that has to do with telling Devon he doesn't need to apologize. I don't know, I know you don't enjoy going into heat, but if you have kids with us, I want you to have them because you want them, not just because having kids will keep you from going into heat."

She's silent. She doesn't say a single thing for so long. Then she tucks her hair behind her ear and starts talking without looking at me. "I would never use a child like that. Never. I *want* a baby with you, Jasper. I want a baby with our pack. I think I need to word how I'm feeling a little differently. I don't like going into heat because I don't like the loss of control; but I don't hate being an omega, which is what you guys probably think. I don't hate that I'm an omega. I have been prepped to be an omega since I was young. It just never happened and I feel and think more like a beta, regardless of how much I've prepared or how things have changed biologically."

"I'm sorry," I say, taking her hand. "I shouldn't have presumed. We can't help it, things were starting to change within our pack before you became an omega, but since you've become one, the changes have become more pronounced. They need to take care of you like you're an omega, but you're a prickly sort of omega that doesn't enjoy being taken care of. And you say things like 'omega bullshit', and you keep track of the perks and downfalls of being an omega like Trent keeps track of things he deems as sexual slights against his alphaness. But if you say you don't hate it then I believe you."

She lifts my knuckles to her mouth and kisses them. "Change is hard, but I'm alright. Going into heat and being overly emotional at times is annoying, but I can deal with it. And I really do want a baby with you. I don't want to wait until things are settled, because things will never be truly settled. If we wait to have a baby until our lives are calm enough, we'll never have one. I don't think our lives will ever be calm, but we can be happy and live."

That's good enough for me. "Okay. I can agree with all of that. I'm glad you don't hate being an omega. I think you're a wonderful omega. I just want you to be okay."

"I am okay, princess. I really am. And as far as having babies goes, I think now is as good a time as any to have them. And we're young enough to really enjoy them. Does the Johnson half of our pack even want kids? I know the Zaphir half does."

"Let's find out. Call a pack meeting."

"Now?"

"Yes, now. I had a heat spike this morning. If you want a baby with me this round we need to make sure everyone is on board."

She reaches over and tugs my earlobe. "You're sure?"

"I'm as sure as you are, cupcake. Come on, let's go make the day interesting."

It takes all of three minutes for everyone to get to the kitchen table after I send out the words *Pack meeting in the kitchen* to the group text. I don't wait for them to start asking questions or making jokes. "Raise your hand if you do not want to help me get Talia pregnant in a couple weeks."

Nobody raises their hand, but Corso's face splits into the biggest grin I've seen from him. Nobody says anything either, and after a few seconds anxiety slams into me. It's straight from Devon, and I shoot him a look, silently daring him to make this awkward, uncomfortable, or awful.

Devon shakes his head. Talia's shoulder's slump, and Alex narrows his eyes. Actually, everyone at the table other than Talia glares at him.

"No, listen. Just wait. Talia. Do you really want to have a baby right now? Really? Or do you just want to avoid going into heat so often? Please, listen. I'm not being an asshole. Think for just a minute while all of us are sitting here together. Please. Close your eyes and think. Do you want to have a baby right now? With us?

It's okay if you do, and it's okay if you don't. We'll give you as many babies as you want, I just want you to be sure you really want that."

Talia holds his gaze for a long moment since she just had this same conversation with me just moments ago, but she does close her eyes. And we all hold our breath while she thinks. A few seconds pass, then she does something unexpected that causes a few of the alphas at the table to purr. Talia's head tilts to the side and her hands slowly raise up to her chest to mimic holding a baby against her. She pauses like that for a full minute before the corner of her mouth turns up, just a tiny bit. "Yes. A baby would be good. We can have a baby here and love it. Not having a heat cycle would be the perk, not the other way around." She opens her eyes and looks straight at Devon, "I know it's soon, and I know you're worried. But I feel I'll be happier and less stressed with a ton of kids oddly. And I want them while everything is fresh and new with us. Do you hate the idea?"

"No, cupcake. I don't hate it. I don't know if you'll be able to live with us once you're pregnant, though. And that poor kid is going to be such a spoiled brat."

"Okay," she smiles at him, a genuine one. "Jasper first. Then Corso."

"Then we draw straws," Alex says, but he's completely serious. He isn't teasing or trying to bring some humor into the situation. Alex wants kids with Talia as much as Corso does, I don't need a bond with him to understand that. I can feel Nathan's gentle excitement. And Trent's horrified joy, that's the only way to describe the way he feels right now. Devon is worried but content. Kaleb is the same. Reid is ecstatic.

"I don't think I've ever heard of an omega-omega reproducing couple. I'm sure there have been plenty of them, there must have been. Wait till Elizabet finds out you're pregnant.. She's going to be over here all the time. We'll have to make her a room." Trent rocks back onto his heels and grins at Devon, then Talia. They have the exact same look on their faces, and it isn't a happy one.

"Let's hold off on telling Elizabet, if that's alright with you?" Devon asks Talia.

She nods emphatically. "Yeah, I'd really like to wait to tell my mother until, I don't know, never."

"Oh, hush," Alex laughs, "Elizabet is a wonderful grandmother. She can have Trent's room. It'll be a good time."

"We're not telling her until around fifteen weeks, when I'm half way through the pregnancy. I mean it, Alex."

"Don't worry, sweet pea. I'm not going to say anything. This is our pack, our life, and our baby. If you want to keep her a secret until she's born, that's what we'll do."

"She?" I ask. In my mind, I was imagining a little he. A little he, with big blue eyes and dark hair. I don't know why a boy would be less stressful than a girl, but the idea of having a tiny little girl of our own is terrifying. I catch Trent's eye. "A she sounds a lot more scary than a he."

He is positively jangling with nervousness. "A she would be terrifying. Please, cupcake, for my sake, try to have a he."

"Keep whining and I'll put all my effort into having one of each." Trent pales a little, but I think that might be perfect.

"Now," I say, and wait for everyone to give me their attention before I finish, "I'd like to address something else. We've all been waiting for Talia to have a breakdown or some sort of emotional reaction to all the bullshit she's been handed. Tell them what you told me, Talia. Say it just like you did outside."

Talia takes a deep breath and looks each of them in the eye. "I don't hate being an omega. I have been preparing my whole life to be an omega, but I have always operated as a beta because I wasn't an omega. Now I am. Again, I do not hate it, I'm just still a beta, internally, in my head. You're all walking around on eggshells, waiting for me to have some kind of episode or breakdown, and I'm not going to have one. Because I'm okay. I had a thought when Jasper and I were walking inside just now. If I talked to that omega psychiatrist that took care of me at the hospital, just as a check in, and she agrees that I am not on the verge of a breakdown and that I'm as solid as I feel, would that make you feel better? I don't think counseling is a good fit for me, and I don't think it will be particularly helpful, but I am willing to try it if it will make you all less worried. I don't mean to brush everything off, but I don't think I need to try to feel or be more traumatized than I am just because other people, including my well-meaning alphas, think I should be."

Corso tucks his hair behind his ears and actually looks a little sheepish. "Talia, none of us wants you to be traumatized, but you have been through so many things. I can't speak for everyone, but I would like it if you checked in with the doctor. If you tell me that you're alright I will believe you, always. Never doubt that. I do think it would be good for you to have something like a check up, like anybody else who has been through some of the things you have. It would make me feel a lot better."

"Okay. I'll call her in the morning. She gave us her contact information with my discharge paperwork. Maybe we can do a virtual appointment. I'd really rather not go to her physical office, wherever that is. Does anyone mind if it's a virtual appointment?" Talia asks, unphased by the varying degrees of worry and relief flowing through the bonds. If I'm feeling it, I know she's feeling it.

"I'm satisfied with a virtual appointment if the doctor can do one. Corso?" Devon is filling his bond with relief.

I don't have a bond with Corso, but even I can feel relief coming from him as he nods. "Thank you for appeasing us, Talia. Please don't think we don't trust your feelings about yourself, it isn't that. We just worry, and we all want to know that you are truly as well as you say you are."

She goes over and kisses his cheek. "I know. That's why I'm calling the doctor."

~

Devon and Kaleb come to my room that night. They're both very serious. "Who's in trouble?"

"Nobody, angel," Devon sighs. "We just need to talk to you. About Talia."

"You should probably be talking to Talia about Talia." They really should, too. I can give my input on all things Talia until I run out of breath, but that's all it would be. Input. I can usually talk her into seeing things from a different perspective, but nobody really makes Talia do anything she really doesn't want to do. And I sincerely hope none of them ever use an alpha command on her outside of a legitimate life or death situation.

"We need to talk about you, too. In relation to Talia," Kaleb says, and sits down on my bed.

Devon sits down in the chair by the window and begins what feels like negotiations. "I don't have a bond with her yet, so I can't feel her. Kaleb does, so we're running with his perception and understanding. She's solid with her decision. And I meant what I said, we'll have as many kids as she wants, so long as she's having them for the right reasons. I know she doesn't like going into heat, it's obvious. Kaleb says the way the bond felt earlier when she had her eyes closed was perfect, like her entire being changed when she imagined holding a baby. That's good. Everyone but Trent is pretty happy about it."

"I think Trent is terrified." I'm trying to keep from laughing because they're so stoic. But Trent being this nervous about the idea of us having a kid is phenomenal.

"He is, but that's not a bad thing," Devon takes a breath, "we never talked about actually having kids because, well..."

"Because I'm a male omega. It doesn't bother me. It only bothers me when I think I'm keeping the four of you from having something you want. None of you ever made me feel bad about it. Really."

"When I was younger," he continues, "I always thought I'd find my pack, claim my omega, and have a bunch of kids. That's what my brothers did. It was expected. Then I found you and I didn't give a single shit about having kids. I wanted you, and that's it. I was content. We were content. We would still be content, even having Talia with us, if you didn't want to have kids. But there are nine of us now, and I just...I don't want... Is this what you truly want, Jasper? For your own life, and for our life together? If it isn't we can find a compromise, just like we found one when Corso marked Talia. We'll find a way for it to be okay."

If I didn't already love Devon I would fall in love with him right now. I fell a little more in love with him when he talked Talia through really thinking about having an actual child instead of avoiding the *omega bullshit*. And I love him a little more now for making sure this is what I want. "I never thought about kids before Talia. Not once. I was never interested in females, alpha, beta, or omega. I'm still not. Talia is the exception, and I can't explain it. It's horrible and maybe immature, but the idea of touching any other female makes me feel, for lack of a better word, gross. Maybe wrong is a better word. Either way, I don't want it. Just Talia. I can't explain it."

Kaleb interrupts, "it's the mates thing. It happens, but it's rare. And people don't truly understand it unless they actually experience it. You want Talia because she's always been yours, ours too, but your actual mate. I cannot express how happy I am that you have that and that we get to be part of it. We can feel it when you're together, in and out of bed. It's so damn beautiful."

"I want everything with her. I want it all. I want this pack with her. I want to take her places. I want us all to have a life together. And I want kids with her. I want to see her carrying them. I want all of it."

"Alright then. That's that," Devon says, and stands up. I don't know where he thinks he's going. After a heavy conversation like this we both need the reassurance of physical attention, preferably in the form of intense cuddling.

"Hey," I say quickly, "stay. Both of you." And that's how I end my night. Warm and snug between Kaleb and Devon.

The next morning is problematic. I wake up alone, climbing a heat spike, with the sound of Talia being fucked in the next room. The scent of golden toasted marshmallows tells me Alex is with her. I'm not in agony yet, but I'm working toward it. I roll out of bed and make my way through the bathroom and into her room. Usually it looks a lot like Talia and Alex are fighting each other for dominance when they have sex, but this morning is different. It's slow, gentle, easy. And I get the distinct feeling that it's supposed to be between just the two of them. As delicious as their combined scents of campfire and coffee are, I don't want to take something from her that I think she might rarely get, so I turn back toward my room. There are five other alphas in this house who will help me if I need them to, which I definitely do.

"Get back in here, peaches." Alex's rough voice calls out, stopping me at the door. "Come on now, come back. You're partially to blame for this anyway, we've been waiting for you to wake up. You smell so fucking tasty."

Turning back around, I find two sets of eyes eating me up. It makes me hurdle head first into the spike and I grab my stomach when it cramps.

"Go help him, Alex." Talia says gently.

Within seconds I'm surrounded in a cloud of the scent of roasted marshmallows. Alex comes over and wraps his arm around my waist to help me cross the room to the bed where Talia is waiting. God, I hope he tastes the way he smells.

"I've been very curious about this, Jasper. I hope you'll indulge me at least a little," Alex purrs into my ear, making me shiver. I'll indulge him as much as he can stand it if he'll make me feel better. He helps me onto the bed and Talia immediately folds me into her arms and covers Reid's mark on my neck. I make a strangled sound, somewhere between a groan and a hiss, and she turns it into a moan when she wraps her hand around me over my boxers.

"Keep doing that, sweet pea. That's a fantastic sound for our little peach to make." Alex lays on the bed beside Talia and runs his hand over my hip. I'm straddling her like I'm going to ride her, my knee is trapped between their bodies, and their hair is mingling in a pretty cloud between them. Talia moves her mouth to the next mark and starts to suck and gently bite, every time my arms start to tremble or my hips start grinding against her she moves to another mark. Always moving, never staying long enough for the pleasure of it to roll me over.

"Does it hurt, peaches? Is it too much?" Alex asks and grips my hip.

"It hurts a little. I'm so hot. And so hard. My balls feel so heavy. They ache." I don't mention the cramps that are burning through my stomach.

"His stomach is cramping. It does fucking hurt. Get up on your knees, let us suck your cock. We're very good at sharing. You don't mind, do you, Alex?" Talia asks very sweetly, still rubbing her palm over my throbbing erection. My heart is pounding in my chest, and I can hear my blood rushing past my eardrums. I hope Alex doesn't mind. The things most likely to help me through a heat spike are an alpha's precum or his knot. And Alex and I have never discussed him knotting me.

"I absolutely don't mind. Best start to a day I've ever had," Alex says, and kisses Talia's shoulder before he raises up onto his knees. "Would it be more comfortable for you if I sat or if I was on my back? I'll do whatever you want me to, just tell me what you need."

So accommodating. So helpful. "Get on your back."

"So bossy, peaches," he smirks, but rolls onto his back.

I don't really need Alex to do anything but lay there and let me lick the precum dripping from the head of his dick. Maybe one day I'll spend some time getting to know Alex intimately, and I'll take my time doing it. But not today. Today I need him to be a good alpha and make me feel better.

Talia holds the base of Alex for me so I can lick up the side of him. Alex doesn't exactly taste the way he smells, but he still tastes wonderful. I lick and suck until someone's hand in my hair pulls me away from what I need and I growl in frustration. I look up to find it was Talia.

"Why did you do that? He tastes so good." I'm trying not to bark at her, but I was just starting to feel better.

"Sorry, princess. I was just torturing Alex. You're going to make him cum before you want him to if you keep going like that," she says, but she pushes me back down over him. "Does Jasper's mouth feel different than mine, alpha?"

Alex growls and I grow impossibly harder, I can feel slick start to drip from me. The front of my boxers will be soaked by the time I'm finished.

"Yes," Alex grits out, "his mouth is more...firm. Hard. He pulls harder than you do. Fuck."

I won't make it if I have to listen to him describe the differences between my mouth and Talia's. I'll beg to be knotted.

"How much of him can you take, Jasper? He won't let me have all of him, he pulls me off before I get as much as I want," Talia pouts, and I roll my eyes up to Alex's. An absolutely rotten look crawls across his face and he smiles down at me.

"Go ahead, peaches. See how much you can take. I'll let you try."

"Alex," Talia cautions but there is still a little pout in her tone.

"It's alright, honey. Jasper knows his limits. And you know I won't let him hurt himself. Besides, he sucks Kaleb's dick all the time. Can you take all of Kaleb, peaches?

I hum in affirmation. I can take all of Kaleb. Especially if I'm in heat. I wouldn't let Talia, though. She wanted it badly enough but I was too worried about her hurting himself; and I definitely wouldn't want her to try to take all of Alex.

"See, baby. Let him try. Come up here and watch him do it. Have you ever watched him give a blow job from this angle. Fucking magical."

"If I watch, I'll want to help."

I groan and let Alex go with a pop. "Fuck yes. Help me. I want to do it together." Then I go back to working Alex's length down my throat.

She snuggles against Alex's side and reaches down to touch my cheek. "See how much you can take first. If it looks like it's too much, you stop. Understand?"

I nod.

"Then," she smiles, "we'll make him cum for us."

Alex is long and so thick, but I know I can take most, if not all of him. After a few minutes of work, there's only a little of him left exposed between my mouth and his base.

"Fuck that's so hot. Jesus," Talia whispers, "I'm fucking soaked just watching. Keep going, princess. You're almost there."

Alex and I both groan at her encouragement.

I'm trying, but I can't quite get the last bit of him when I suck him down. I flick my eyes up to theirs to convey my need for a little push. They both look like they want to devour me. That single look makes my hips jerk and I feel a torrent of slick dripping from me. Talia understood, though. She threads her fingers into my hair and firmly pushes my head down until my lips touch the very root of him. Then she helps me bob up and down a few times before she pulls me off, breathless, with a trail of spit and precum connecting my mouth to Alex's cock.

"Do you want me to help you finish him, or do you want me to make you cum while you finish him?" She doesn't understand how impossible her question is.

"Take care of him, sweet pea. I can smell his slick, and yours. Fuck. Finish me off, Jasper. It'll make you feel better. Then I want to watch you fuck Talia. I want you to fuck her the way you did when she was in heat. I want to see you make her scream for you when she's fully aware of herself."

"You're not being very clear, alpha. Do you want me to jerk him off while he finishes you, or do you want him to finish you and then fuck me while you watch? This sounds like an unending cycle, if you ask me," Talia teases.

"Too much thinking, omega." The way he says omega draws a purr from me. The way he, Reid, and Corso say omega when they're talking to or about Talia is delicious.

"I need to finish him. I feel so much better than I did before, but I need it. Then I'm going to fuck you, just like I do when you're in heat." I wrap my hand around Alex and suck him back into my mouth while I brutally pump my fist up and down his length. I don't have to be gentle with him. My rough treatment makes his back arch and he sinks his hands into my hair.

"God," he gasps, "it's so different, but still the same. And I can smell you both, I want you both. Next time I'm doing the licking. I want to taste everything." Just as he finishes the last word he starts to jerk in my hand, releasing into the back of my throat. I pull back in time to catch a bit on my tongue so I can really taste him. He does taste as good as he smells, just in a different way.

Alex took the edge off, but I'm still so hot and aching. I need to fuck and to be fucked. Badly. I grab Talia and haul her up onto her hands and knees over Alex. I'm already on my knees between his legs; this position is going to give him an amazing view, and lots of access to Talia's body.

I don't know what either of us would do if she ever needed me to press her for dominance when I fuck her. I'm fairly certain it would be an even match, but right now, this moment, if she tried to push me away I'd probably handle her more harshly than I've seen Alex or Kaleb handle her. We'd likely destroy both our rooms and half the manor, and it would still end up with me slamming my cock into her from behind like I'm doing right now.

It feels so good to be inside her. The only thing that could possibly make this better for me is if I was also being fucked. That night with Kaleb was one of the best things I've ever felt in my life. I passed right out with the intensity of my orgasm. We are definitely doing that again.

Alex pulls her to him for a kiss and she moans into his mouth. I'm fucking her so hard, I hope neither of them chip a tooth. She breaks away from the kiss and drops down to lick Alex's chest. "I wish you could see this from my view, sweet pea. You're both so gorgeous. I could get off again right now just watching you," he says. Then I slap Talia's ass and he yelps.

I spank her again. "Did you just bite your alpha?" I ask through my teeth. "After he made me feel so much better. Terrible girl." I give her another swat. She just pushes her hips back at me and giggles. "And now you're laughing at me," I cluck my tongue. "Such a rotten girl." The dynamic between the three of us is all over the place. Talia told me sex with Alex is always fun, no matter what it looks like, and she was absolutely right. I might be working through the end of a heat spike, but I don't feel like the needy, whining omega that I usually feel like during spikes.

It goes on like that until I'm trembling, with me fucking Talia as hard as I ever do, Alex encouraging me to go harder between kissing her and teasing her nipples, and Talia shoving herself against me spreading bite marks all over Alex's torso. When I finally reach my end, I lean over her, wrapping my arms around her middle, and bite into her shoulder, catching the edge of Corso's mark, and drag her over the edge with me.

"I love being knotted," I say breathlessly, "but one of the best parts about not being knotted is the ability to remain conscious after a good fucking."

Talia agrees. "Yes. Knots feel so good, and I love the intimacy, but falling asleep immediately after is not a perk."

"Hey, I like it when you fall asleep on me. That's the only time you're cuddly. And if we're knotted you can't get away," Alex argues. "But now we can all walk down to the kitchen together and I can gloat that I got to have both of you to myself all morning."

Chapter Ten

Reid

Jasper's heat spikes are as intense as Talia's, but they don't feel as violent. Whereas Talia's spikes are like a kick in the chest and a knee to the groin that leave you gasping, Jasper's are like an ache that coils tighter and tighter until you can't breath without relief. And I only feel them second-hand through my bond with them. Jasper has been having spikes for a few weeks, and Talia started having them last night. Between the two of them I am exhausted and thrilled. I don't know how else to describe it. I am miserable. I am elated. I am full. But Devon needs to get his shit together.

He's been taking Talia out almost every other night for the past several weeks. She comes back happier with him every time they go places, but she's going into heat in a week. Regardless of the fact that Jasper is going to try to make her pregnant, they will both be in heat and it is going to take all seven of us to tend to them.

Both Talia's and Devon's parents are sending additional support for the week. Elizabet seems especially anxious about it, and her anxiety is making Talia even more anxious about going into heat than she already is. Corso called Elizabet this morning to carefully and politely ask her to talk to Talia about anything other than her upcoming heat. That went over exceptionally well. Elizabet has now directed all communication anywhere but toward Corso.

Devon is nervous about this heat. He has assured me that he's worried for Talia, and her potentially coming out of it pregnant. I think he's nervous because he still hasn't marked her, and he needs to get on with it. I don't necessarily think he should physi-cally force a submission, I would quickly put a stop to that myself, but he needs to do something. And he has a week to do it.

I have accompanied Talia on a walk through the grounds. She said she wanted a walk, but I think she's doing a walk through for Nathan's cameras. She's very protective of her pack, and especial-ly of Jasper. I don't think we'll ever be able to convince her that she needs protecting as much as he does, but we will continue to try.

"Talia, I think we've gone past every camera. They're all where they're supposed to be. Are you finished checking them, or are you still avoiding something? Either is fine, but if we're avoiding something I'd like to know what it is."

She looks back over her shoulder and smiles at me. Every time she does that my breath catches. I'm sure I'll always have that reaction to her smiling at me like that. "I wasn't very stealthy about it, was I?"

"No. Were you trying to be?"

Talia reaches back and pinches the inside of my arm. "Of course I was trying to."

"What are we avoiding, beautiful?"

She wrinkles her nose at the compliment, but she doesn't argue with it. "I don't know what to do about Devon."

"Neither does he."

"I know. It's very obvious. He says he's afraid of me."

"He's terrified. What are you waiting for? He's yours if you want him." He's made that very obvious, as well.

"I'm worried that he isn't properly healed and strong like he was before. And I don't like that he's afraid of me. He kissed me on the table a few weeks ago and I thought everything would just fall into place, but then I went into heat, and when I came out of it everything was awkward. I don't know why. Probably omega bullshit."

This is the one time I'll ever agree that it is omega bullshit. I've been brushing up on my omega knowledge base. My hypothesis is that Talia subconsciously feels that Devon is too weak to take care of and provide for both her and Jasper, so she's taking herself out of the equation without realizing she's doing it. It is most definitely omega bullshit, because Devon is as strong as he ever was, is fully healed, and is perfectly capable and willing to take care of both of them. Best not to tell her that, though. It's never good to try to tell a woman what she thinks, my mother taught me well. "Talia," I pause to look at another tiny camera wedged into the vee of a pine tree, "I know the premise is that the alpha is to claim and mark the omega, but when have you ever done what makes sense?"

I watch realization and understanding settle over her in stages. "Do you think that would help? If I went after him?"

I shrug, I don't know for sure, but at this point it couldn't hurt.

"I think Jasper should help. He keeps saying he gets to pick the place where Devon will put his mark."

I try to keep the grin from my face when I tell her that I think Jasper would very much enjoy helping her claim Devon.

I know the moment Talia and Jasper discuss the matter of Devon. We've just cleaned up dinner and she and Jasper have disappeared upstairs. There is raw, primal excitement and lust flowing freely down the bond. Trent and Nathan are still in the kitchen with me and we all exchange a smirk.

"Are they going after Devon?" Trent asks.

I nod.

"Does he know?"

I shake my head.

Then we make a very calm and collected mad dash to Nathan's room so we can watch the security feed.

Chapter Eleven

Devon

I'm laying across my bed with my ankles crossed, trying to decide if I want to go down and get a snack before I go to bed, when Jasper slinks into my room and leans against the door frame.

"Getting ready for bed?" Jasper asks.

I've felt a buzzing along my bond with him since this afternoon. I assumed it was the same energy that comes along with him working up to going into heat. It feels almost the same. But the look he's giving me is predatory. He generally saves those looks for Talia.

"I, well, I was thinking about it." Why the hell am I stuttering? "Are you getting ready for bed?"

"Nope."

Talia, dressed in dark leggings, a snug thermal, and running shoes, prowls into the room. There's no other way to describe her movement. She is prowling around my room, touching and rearranging my things on top of the dresser. I take another look at Jasper. He's dressed to go for a run, too. It's too fucking dark for them to go for a run. I open my mouth to inform them of that, but Talia tilts her head to the side and asks Jasper, "he's good? You're sure?"

"I'm sure."

"It's too late for any exercise or drills or whatever you're planning outside. It's dark. It's dangerous."

They carry on like they didn't hear me.

"Hundred hundred?" She asks, assessing me from my socks to my eyebrows.

"All the way."

They both look at me then, and I get the feeling this is what a mouse must feel like when faced with a cat.

"Where are your shoes?" Talia asks me.

"What? Why?" I really am stammering. My heart is starting to beat fast. All they're doing is looking at me while wearing running gear. What the entire fuck is wrong with me?

Jasper reaches down and picks up my shoes and carries them across the room to place them very firmly next to me on the bed. "We agreed to give you sixty seconds to get ahead of us."

"What are you talking about?"

"Hurry, Devon." Talia urges.

"Where do you want me to go?" I ask, rushing to get my feet into my shoes. Thank fuck I'm too lazy to untie them when I take them off.

"It doesn't matter. Just go fast." Jasper grins at me.

"Or don't," Talia hums. "We'll get you either way."

"What is happening right now?" I finally get my shoes on and stand up. Why do I feel like I actually *do* need to run?

"Better get going, alpha." Jasper says. He's not smiling anymore.

"Talia?" I think my eyes are a little too wide. How have they reduced me to feeling like prey?

"Run, Devon."

They said I had sixty seconds, how much time do I have left? I launch myself out the door. I rush down the hall and take the stairs two at a time on my way to get to the back door through the kitchen. I'm running for my life and I don't even understand why I'm doing it. I actually feel anxious, for fuck sake.

Corso is walking out of the garage when I skid into it.

"Why are they chasing me?" I ask breathlessly.

He just smiles and looks toward the manor.

I hear Talia's sing-song voice calling my name. Shit.

"If you're going to hide, fratello, I would find another place. This is the first place I'd look for you."

He's right. Where can I go? I don't want to run aimlessly. Do they want me to hide? What is even happening right now? Just a game of chase? In the dark? At close to midnight? For what purpose?

"Deeeevvoooonnn," Talia calls again.

Alex appears out of nowhere and grins at me. "Run, rabbit, run."

I take off towards the back of the property, in the direction of the distillery. I run through the trees, trying to decide which direction is the best course. What if I climb up one of these trees? They could run right past without ever seeing me. No, that's what I'd expect someone to do if I was doing the chasing. I chance a look behind me to see two silhouettes moving faster than they should be able to, closing the distance between us.

I'm being hunted. Really, truly hunted. They move through trees and brush like a unit. Then they split apart and disappear in two different directions. Completely vanish. The small part of my brain that was enjoying the thought of being caught takes pause, and in that pause some very instinctual part of me jumps to the forefront and urges me to run faster. I *am* being hunted. I *am* their prey. And they *will* catch me if I don't run.

I decide to change course. I've been heading toward the distillery, so I take a sharp turn and run in the direction of the main road. God, why is this property so spread out? We had a fairly large stretch of land at the farmhouse, but this is ridiculous. I'm starting to get genuinely tired from running and I'm nowhere near the manor or the main road yet. I have to slow down before I get a side stitch. Slowing my pace enough to allow me to start catching my breath a little, I look behind me again and to the sides. I don't see anything. I don't hear anything. I slow even more and listen even harder. I'm not afraid of the woods or the dark, but nobody, alpha or otherwise, is immune to being uneasy in the woods alone at night when you know you're not alone, when you're prey.

I'm running and contemplating my life choices that brought me to this chase, straining my ears and eyes for any sign of either Jasper or Talia, when something barrels out of the brush right behind me. I completely embarrass myself by yelping. I glance behind me to see which one has caught up to me, but it's just a fucking deer. I keep running.

I'm officially winded, my side is beginning to pinch. I change directions again, toward the back corner of the property. This course will take me past the manor, maybe I'll get lucky and I can get there before they catch me. For some reason, I feel like I'll be safe if I can just get back inside the manor.

I can't make it. I'm going to have to hide. I'm ready to start limping and I've been pressing my hand into my side for what feels like miles. Twenty more feet, I can make it the twenty or so feet to the main path that leads to the manor. I put on my last-ditch, last resort burst of speed and count the inches between my feet and easier terrain, then I feel something wrap around my calves and I plunge to the ground like a fallen tree.

I don't have time to turn over and sit up, Talia appears in front of me like a damn ghost and loops a cord around my wrists before I realize it's even happened. Then Jasper is standing over me and flipping me onto my back. Neither of them look like they're playing, they look like I'm in a lot of trouble.

My arms are stretched above me and I look up to watch Talia secure them to the trunk of a skinny tree. She joins Jasper at my side and looks down at me. "Pants."

Jasper nods. God, I hope I'll enjoy whatever they have planned for me. My heart is racing and my mind is still completely convinced that I'm in danger.

Talia crouches down and starts working my sweats down my hips.

"Wait a minute," I say. "Just wait. What are we doing?"

Jasper stops unwinding the cord from my ankles long enough to give a brusque reply. "We're securing you to a couple of these trees so you can't get away." Then he helps Talia wrestle my sweats off my legs. They leave them gathered around my ankles and Jasper wraps the cord back around. "Do I need to secure the end of this to a tree? I don't think he'll try too hard to get away, do you?"

Talia's lips twist to the side as she considers me. "Hmmm, I don't know. Are you going to try to get away from us, Devon?"

Is that a real question?

"Do you want me to?"

She smiles. "Not really. But you're welcome to try."

"You didn't need to run me down. I'd do whatever you ask me to do."

"Oh, but we did," Talia hums. "You need to understand the dynamic alpha. You aren't in charge right now. If you don't want something, you can of course say no; but you're ours now. And we want to play with you."

Talia pulls out a knife and slips it under my shirt so she can slice through the fabric, it's so sharp it doesn't cut so much as slide apart the fabric while Jasper crawls up to whisper in my ear. "You've taken too long. She's tired of waiting. You might do the marking, but she's doing the claiming." Then he licks the shell of my ear and nips the lobe, "and I'm going to help her do it."

The sweet scent of their arousal hits my senses like a truck, and my poor, confused dick finally gets the message that we're happy to have been caught. Jasper reaches down and grips my growing erection, slowly and tortuously stroking from root to tip while he watches Talia pull off her shoes and leggings. "The shirt, too. I want to watch your breasts when you ride him."

"How will I mark her if she's riding me?"

"You're a smart, resourceful alpha. You'll figure it out," Jasper says, not taking his eyes off Talia. The dynamic is most definitely different from what it usually is. Jasper isn't acting as my omega right now. His eyes are eating Talia up the same way Corso's do, the way Alex's and Reid's do. Like she is his sun. In this moment, she is our omega, his and mine; and we are here at her service and pleasure.

Talia sinks to her knees by my side and licks across the head of my cock while Jasper holds it for her. "You taste so good, Devon. Licking you makes the cramps better. Don't you think so, princess?"

"Yes," Jasper breathes against my neck.

"I'm going to fuck him now. We'll have to let him sit up when he's ready to put his mark on me."

"Wait," I say. "We're moving too fast. I wanted more time with you before I marked you. I wanted it to be special for you."

Jasper nips my earlobe again. "You've already spent too much time worrying about making it special. She just chased you through the woods, and now she's got you trussed up nice and pretty. Just let her take what she needs."

"What do you need, Talia?" I ask, but my voice sounds almost choked. Between the physical exertion of the chase, the realization that I made her wait so long that she lost patience with me, and their attention to my dick, I'm spinning.

"Just you, Devon. Just you, you're enough."

When she goes to swing her leg over my hips, Jasper stops her again. "Let me get behind him first." He picks up the knife Talia put on the ground and pins me with a look. "I'm going to cut the cord loose from the tree, but I'm keeping your wrists restrained. You're going to lift your arms back over my head and put your hands behind my neck. Then you're going to lean against me while she fucks you."

I start to argue that I'm too heavy for Jasper to support, but Talia reaches down and covers my mouth with her hand. "If you can't lean on Jasper now, then you won't let yourself lean on him in other situations. Make the choice, Devon."

They're really taking on my internal hang-ups one after another tonight, aren't they? I don't give Jasper enough credit, I try to keep everything even remotely negative or difficult away from him, and

I'll just end up doing the same with Talia. Part of what's happening right now is to force me to understand that they're more than I let them be, and that they're more than capable of handling me and holding me up, I understand that now. I've done them a disservice. "Okay," I say, "I can do that. I'll be better, I promise."

Talia smiles at me and strokes my jaw. "Good enough."

Jasper gets behind me on his knees and I do exactly what he said to do. I let him guide my hands up and over his head and around his neck. His soft curls are damp with sweat when I twist my fingers into him. I can smell his orange scent, it's always sharper and a little spicy in the week or so before he goes into heat, and it immediately starts wreaking havoc on my senses. Talia's sweet cinnamon latte scent is also spicier than it usually is, between the two of them I'm in a cloud of pheromones that make me think of every wonderful thing I associate with fall and winter.

It is a shame that I won't be able to touch Talia, though. I was really looking forward to putting my hands on every inch of her skin.

"Why are you pouting?" She asks as she settles herself over me.

"I'm not pouting," I argue, but she leans forward and sinks her teeth into my bottom lip for half a second then pulls away to raise an eyebrow at me. "I wanted to touch you."

"You've had plenty of time to touch me and you haven't. I'm in control now and we've got a whole life ahead of us, Devon." She gives me a quick kiss.

I can't process that she's claiming the rest of her life with me with Jasper licking up the side of my neck and Talia lowering herself onto my cock a fraction of an inch at a time. She's so wet, so hot, and so mean. She stops moving with just the head inside of her and circles her hips exactly one time before she lifts herself off. She does it over and over, taking just the head and circling her hips and raising up, until I'm ready to scream. Then she does something worse, and I don't know how she has the stamina for it. She fucks the head just like she would fuck my whole cock. Never taking in more than just a bit more than that. I'm curling my spine, using every muscle in my stomach to try to thrust more of myself inside her, mostly unsuccessfully because she's keeping herself just out of reach and Jasper has me pinned against his chest.

"Are you frustrated yet, Devon?" Jasper whispers.

"Yes," I grit between clenched teeth. I need more than what she's giving me.

Jasper kisses my cheek. "You'll feel better soon."

Soon is now. Talia slides down slowly, fully impaling herself, biting her lip and moaning the whole way down. "You're so thick, Devon," she hisses. "When you fucked me before, I was over-whelmed by the heat spike. I just needed you to fuck me and make me feel better. This time," she rolls her hips, grinding against me, and lets out a breathy moan. "This time I still just need to fuck you. I'm sure we'll be able to fuck like normal people eventually."

She keeps rolling and circling her hips, keeping all of me inside her. I can feel her muscles fluttering around my cock as she moves. I'm groaning and growling, even purring. I'm making so many different sounds, all in a conscious and unconscious effort to get her to give me more than this torturous stirring motion she's enjoying so much.

Talia lifts off of me, exposing my throbbing, hot length to the cool night air, then lets herself fall back down again. I dig my heels into the soil to gain some traction so I can raise my hips to meet her. Jasper leans against me, providing me with more leverage. I can feel his erection pressing into my back and it only adds fuel to the fire we're building. Talia and I fuck each other like that until we're both breathless and even sweatier than we were to begin with, only slowing down when my knot starts swelling.

"I want to feel it get bigger while you're inside me," she pants, and she sinks back down to my base, over my growing knot. Fuck, it's perfect, it feels so good to feel it swell, filling her fuller and fuller.

"Where do you want her mark, Jasper?" my words are barely more than a guttural, choked groan.

Jasper stretches his arm to push his fingers into her hair. He pulls, tilting her head back, exposing her throat. Then he angles her neck to the side, presenting the front of her shoulder, the same shoulder that carries Coro's mark. "I already told you. Right there, opposite of Corso's. Then, when we fuck her together, we can make her cum so hard she passes out. It's the most amazing thing in the world."

I bank that information. I've utilized the marks I and the others have put on Jasper many, many times, but I didn't know it could feel good enough to actually make him lose consciousness.

Talia grinds against me even more urgently. She's gripping me tighter and tighter, I can feel slick dripping down between my thighs and over my balls, and I can't pull my eyes away from the place on her shoulder that Jasper is so perfectly displaying. "I need my hands. I can't mark her with my hands behind my head."

Jasper lifts my arms up and over our heads, then he cuts through the cord around my wrists. I fight every instinct in my body to not flip Talia under me and fuck her into the ground. I want to bite into her shoulder and use that hold on her to keep her still while I drive my cock into her as deep as it will go over and over again until I feel a solid bond form between the two of us. I don't, though. I don't do any of that. I can't help the brutal way my fingers sink into her hair and jerk her head to the side, but when I put my mouth over that perfect place on her shoulder I'm so gentle. I run my lips back and forth over her skin and take in her spiced coffee scent. She almost tastes like a cinnamon latte. I grab her hip with my other hand and push her down, thrusting up as hard as I can manage in this position when I feel my release racing up from my balls.

Then I sink my teeth into her shoulder and let the taste of her wash over my tongue. She sighs my name and wraps her arms around my neck, holding me to her, and rocks her hips while my cock pulses inside her. I lick over the mark for a long while until I don't taste anything but her skin. Jasper is still behind me, but he re-positioned himself so that his legs are stretched along the outside of mine. He's the one holding Talia's waist and stroking her back while I enjoy listening to her soft purr as she sleeps. My knot is still lodged inside of her, and the bond is already twisting its way around my heart.

"I'm jealous of all of you," Jasper whispers, "I can feel her, but it's faint, and muddy. You can all feel everything she feels through your bond with her."

"We could feel her through our bond with you. Very, very faintly, just a little, and not all the time. We realized it after Corso marked her and we were trying to figure everything out."

"What does she feel like?" he asks, placing a kiss between my shoulder blades. My shirt is hanging off my shoulders, and my pants are gathered around my ankles. I don't even care how ridiculous it might look, I can feel two bonds inside me, tying me to both my omegas. What I am and am not wearing doesn't fucking matter. I am glad that Jasper has his clothes on, though, and I'm starting to worry about Talia getting cold.

"She feels like rough water, when the river is choppy and too high after a storm. Water that's angry on the surface but so calm once you go under. She's sharp and sour and loves all of us so much it probably hurts sometimes. Even me. And especially you. She's perfect. Perfect for you, perfect for us.

Chapter Twelve

Talia

Doctor Cortez agreed to have a virtual appointment with me. It helped that she's an omega and is just coming out of heat so she's not really trying to go to her office to meet with clients. It helped even more when I told her that one of the reasons a virtual appointment would be better for me is because I'm due to go into heat in about a week. It's a win-win, really. Can't all appointments be done virtually?

"I'm so glad you wanted to see me, Miss Graves. You look very well." The good doctor is wearing a pretty fuschia blouse under her crisp, white medical jacket. It looks amazing with her skin tone, but she's sitting at a desk in her bedroom, so I'm very curious about what she *isn't* wearing under the desk. She's probably far more professional than I am, because I doubt I'd be wearing the full doctor ensemble. I'd be wearing leggings or nothing underneath that desk.

"Thank you. I feel very well. Much better than the last time you saw me."

She looks down at some papers in front of her on the desk, likely my file. "And you have a pack now?"

I smile. "I do. They're terrified of me, but they're doing a good job not showing it. That's why I wanted to talk to you. Corso is happy about it."

"Corso?"

"Corso Zaphir." She must not know about our combined packs.

"You left the hospital with the Johnson pack. Is the Zaphir pack a better fit for you? You were very concerned about the Johnson pack's omega when you were under my care."

"I'm still with the Johnson pack. The Zaphir pack joined together with the Johnson pack. Corso marked me during my first heat, and it turns out that Jasper and I are mates so we couldn't be parted. So, we decided to combine our packs in order to keep everyone happy, calm, and well taken care of."

Silence. And a struggle to keep herself from dropping her mouth open or gawking.

"It's alright to show a genuine reaction, Doctor Cortez. It isn't exactly typical. But it's the best thing for us."

She squares her shoulders and shakes off her initial response. "So, if I'm understanding correctly, both packs live together peacefully in order for their omegas to maintain their mates status?"

I smile again. "Something like that. I have bonds with every alpha, and Jasper has bonds with all the Johnson pack alphas as well as with one of the Zaphir pack alphas. All nine of us all bundled up nice and tight."

"You have bonds with seven alphas?" she asks, scribbling onto the papers on the desk.

"I do."

"How do you feel about that?"

That is exactly the type of question that keeps me from being a good candidate for counseling. I know she wants me to go into a huge overture about how horrible or wonderful it is, or about how wretched I was until the bonds were in place, but that's not how my brain operates. I work through things step by step until I clear the table, and it isn't a huge or dramatic process. I've disappointed more than one counselor over the years thanks to the center's training requirements and I'm sure I'm about to disappoint Doctor Cortez.

"It feels right. And settled. I've been a beta my whole life, Doctor Cortez. I act and think like a beta. I also, very genuinely, do not feel traumatized by my life; and if I did feel traumatized I have every confidence that my alphas would help me feel more stable."

Her mouth shrinks into a tight, little line and she raises an eyebrow. "You were fairly traumatized when you were at the hospital. I can see that you are no longer in that place, and I'm happy to see it. I'd like to talk with you a little longer, but I know, first hand, how much bonds help omegas; even omegas who can be too headstrong for their own good."

I grin at her. Headstrong is a nice way to say stubborn asshole. "We can talk as long as you like. Thank you for taking time with me."

Then we talk. We talk for over an hour and a half. She gets a full summary of everything that has happened since she last saw me, and by the time she asks me to call in my pack I think I've found an actual friend.

"One last question, just for my own curiosity, and possibly paperwork purposes, if you don't mind."

"What would you like to know, Doctor Cortez?"

"Will your new pack be the Zaphir-Johnson pack? Or some other combination of names?"

We prepared for this question, because it will be asked many, many times. "Since Devon will have a council seat, and because Corso doesn't want anything to do with politics, we will be the Johnson pack."

"And what about kids? Their last names?"

"We will cross that bridge when we get there."

Doctor Cortez nods as she scribbles on her pad.

"Talia, would you mind stepping out of the room? I'm sure you'll hear all about what I'm about to tell your pack, but I think they'll feel more free to speak to me if they're not worrying about offending you or hurting your feelings."

"I absolutely agree. Let me get them in here." I put the text out and am not at all surprised when it takes less than ten seconds for them to file into my room.

"She wants to talk to you guys. I'm going to go make some lunch." I distribute kisses and cuddles on my way out the door. I even wink at Corso and tell him good luck. He's not in trouble, but his face takes on this adorable expression whenever he thinks he is.

Chapter Thirteen

Corso

"Good afternoon, Doctor Cortez. It's very nice to speak with you again."

She looks at me over the rim of her glasses. "Alpha Corso Zaphir?"

"Yes. This is my pack, Reid Scott and Alex Rosen. I'm sure you remember the Johnson pack."

The doctor looks at each of them in turn, then glances down at her paperwork. "Who had the idea to combine packs?" I can't decide if she's angry with us or if something might be wrong.

"I did." Reid waves.

"I see. And Talia and Jasper are mates? Surely you'd know. You'd feel it in your bonds with them."

Jasper steps forward, in front of me and everyone else. "Talia is my mate. They don't need to feel it because I do. Is there a problem we need to be made aware of?"

"No, Mister Nattier. There's no problem. I'm happy you and Talia have found each other. It's rare to find one's true mate. Even more rare for an omega to find her mate in another omega. How's that going? Within the pack dynamic, I mean."

Jasper shrugs. "It seems to be going very well. Devon? Corso?" He and Talia both reference Devon and I equally as lead alpha.

I open my mouth to answer, but Devon clears his throat. "We're very happy with our dynamic. I realize my pack was completely irresponsible and disrespectful of Talia when she first came under your care, but we are trying to make up for that."

"So she says," Doctor Cortez hums. "She and Jasper are on equal ground as omegas in your pack."

I start to answer again, but this time Jasper interrupts. "Of course not. I may be an omega, but Talia is my mate. Her needs come before mine." He gestures toward Devon. "They've already adjusted their actions and reactions accordingly. I don't think they even realize they've done it."

Kaleb's head jerks to the side. "What do you mean, Jasper? We would never put either of you to the side in preference of the other. Is that what you think is happening?"

"It's natural, Kaleb. And it's what I'd ask you to do even if you weren't already doing it. And I'm glad Talia isn't here to hear this conversation. Honestly, what do you learn in your alpha classes? Don't they teach you anything about omegas? Beyond the most basic basics." Nobody has an answer for that, but we all have the grace to look at the floor. The only reason my pack knows as much about omegas as we do is because we sought the information when Jasper chose us. None of our teachers or trainers taught us about the more minute needs and mannerisms of omegas, we learned on our own. But maybe we need to go back and reeducate ourselves on female omegas.

Jasper continues his scolding, with the doctor nodding from her side of the screen. "In an all male alpha pack like ours with two omegas, if one of the omegas is female she is the priority. She will grow our pack, I'll just help her do it. She is my priority, and because of that she's your priority. Your instincts know that even if your minds don't."

"You are a priority, Jasper," Kaleb says, but Jasper waves him off.

"I know that. And I love you for it. But she's the bigger priority and we all know it. That's how it's supposed to be and how I want it. Look at how much things have already changed for us. I know

I'm your omega, nothing's going to change that or lessen it. But Talia is *our* omega."

"That's a good way to explain that," Doctor Cortez breaks in. "Now, I have another question before I get to the business of telling you all off." She looks at each of us in turn again. "Talia would like to have a baby. I'm going to assume you all have implants, with the exception of Jasper, of course; you know omegas can't get implants, the hormonal cocktail is disastrous to an omega's system. Don't tell me if you don't, that's your business; but keep in mind that if you don't have an implant you will likely get her pregnant now that her system is clear from the suppressants she took before. Since alphas are notoriously under-educated about omegas, I would like to remind you of some omega reproduction facts. Omegas are only fertile when they're in heat, both male and female. It is incredibly rare that two omegas come together in the first place, but I want you to be mindful that their heats will sync up and they will both be fertile during that time."

"We're aware of that, Doctor Cortez. Thank you. I think we're ready to be told off, now, if you don't mind." I know about synced heats and when omegas are fertile, but I don't know why we need to be told off by a doctor on a laptop. We've been doing everything we can to take care of Talia and make sure she's alright.

"Talia Graves is an omega, there is no denying that. But an omega designation changes her physically, and possibly, on some level, mentally. You need to remember that she has been a beta for too long to change too many things. She has always considered herself a beta, and it will take more than a new designation to change that. She isn't going to start thinking like an omega just because her designation has changed." She waits until we all acknowledge what she said, then she continues. "You can't expect her to have an omega reaction to trauma when she's been thinking like a beta for her whole life."

Nathan raises his hand. "That's not what we expect from her. It isn't about designation. Talia has been through so much horrible shit, Doctor Cortez. She hasn't had much of a reaction to all of it. The most she did is freak out about Jonas fucking Pratchett trying to talk to her at a restaurant. Even Seth is doing a bunch of counseling at the facility he's at."

"Why do you need her to have a reaction?" Now she's looking at him over her glasses.

He opens and closes his mouth a few times, but manages a response. "I don't *need* her to have a reaction. I don't want her to have one, either. It was horrible when she had a panic attack. I don't want that for her."

"That's good to hear. I'm glad you don't want her to feel that way. So why are you all so bothered by her lack of measurable negative response to her trauma?"

Trent answers this time. "She can't really be okay after everything she's been through. Hell, a whole lot of it happened because of us. She's walking around here like she's unaffected. It's not normal."

"And you're the pinnacle of normalcy, Mister Lancaster?"

"Well, no, but…"

"Did you know, any of you, that people are completely capable of handling their trauma and stress differently than they're expected to? It doesn't matter that Talia's coping mechanisms, which are some of the most successful I've seen, by the way, are not the same as yours or the same as what you've seen from others. Talia is very structured. She handles things very objectively and she is very capable of reaching out for help if she needs it. She is also a very good judge of whether or not she needs that help. I don't mean to speak about stereotypes, and there are always exceptions, but betas are better at working through trauma than either omegas or alphas because they think differently. They work through things step by step and process their reactions quietly and move on. They don't tend to dwell on things once they've finished processing them. Talia is also very strong willed. She decides what she's going to do, then she does it."

I tuck my hair behind my ear and meet the doctor's eyes. "What are you getting at, Doctor Cortez?"

"Leave her alone. She's not going to be a nervous, timid, trembling wreck just because you expect her to be. She's stronger than you are. Be careful of her, obviously, and don't be stupid, but don't treat her like she's broken or fragile. It's one of those situations where you prepare yourself for a potential outcome without expecting to have to experience it. Does that make sense?"

I look around at my pack, exchanging a nod with each of them. "Yes, Doctor Cortez. It makes sense. Thank you."

"Good, good. Talia has an appointment to check in with me every month until and unless that needs to change. Do any of you have any questions?"

We don't have any questions, and we end the call with polite goodbyes. We're all awkwardly silent, then Reid breaks it with a sigh. "So, we just let her be and help her if she needs help."

Devon nods. "Yeah. I'm glad she's checking in monthly, though."

"So am I," Jasper says. "Do we feel a little better now?"

I suppose we do because we all give him a nod.

"And I'm cleared to knock her up next week?"

Alex laughs. "Like you need our permission."

Chapter Fourteen

Nathan

I can't find anything in a week's time. And a week's all I have before Talia and Jasper go into heat. I've got a few decent trails going, but I don't think I'll get anything solid before their heat comes. If I'm having this difficult of a time finding anything, I can't imagine the Dennison pack having any luck at all. I traced the omegas from the compound nearly to the northern territory before they just disappeared.

The digital logs are all over the place, too. I followed one trail down a very scientific path until that shit stopped making any sense at all to me. I called Thaddeus, that's more his speed. Strangely enough, he had me forward everything I found to Elizabet. Then he told me that it would be better if I didn't mention anything I saw in those records to anyone at all, ever. That should be easy because I don't know what the hell I saw, just a bunch of formulas and charts and words that probably mean something to somebody who isn't me.

I don't care about any of that science shit, all I care about is finding those omegas. I have thought about them every single day. Especially the girl who begged me to do whatever the rogues wanted. I've had so many nightmares about what could be happening to her.

The lead I'm currently chasing is interesting, though. It looks like a fuel log. Like what you'd find in a tour bus record. This has got to be important. It doesn't look like anything but stops on a road to refuel, but why would you try to make it look like a cargo van delivering furniture instead of a much larger vehicle that would need a lot more gas than a van would. Then there's the other record. It's a pet delivery service. Tails and Scales Pet Transport. It looks innocent enough until you look through the stops that the GPS recorded. I charted the course. The pet transport vehicle doesn't get as much gas as the other vehicle, but it consistently stops at every single place the other vehicle stops, only about ten minutes later. That's got to be something. If it's the omegas, I might not know where they're going, but I can find out where they've been. I'm digging into the security systems of each of the fueling stations; maybe I can catch sight of the omegas, maybe get a vehicle ID, maybe catch a glimpse of a driver. It shouldn't take too long, but it will take longer than a week to siphon through all those feeds.

It's so frustrating, but I refuse to let that frustration take away from my anticipation and excitement about my omegas' heats. I don't know if they're going to want two separate nests, or if they'll build one huge one. I have a secret hope that they'll use my room. Talia has built her nest in my room twice now at this point, and it might be one of my favorite things in the universe. I love that she feels like my room is the most comfortable and safe place in the manor. I hope every nest she ever builds for the rest of her life is in my room.

I look back to the monitors in front of me. I need to try to get into the system records for the stops the smaller vehicle made. It's just too strange that they're stopping behind the larger vehicle so consistently, and at such regular intervals. Either both vehicles are heading to the same place or the smaller one is following the larger one on purpose. The most recent stop was at a truck stop on a long stretch of road, it's not even part of a town. There are eleven minutes between the stops. Getting into the system is so much easier than it should be, but these types of places are usually only concerned about having camera systems in place as a theft deterrent. Half the time the 'cameras' are just hollow, plastic shells that are supposed to make someone think twice before snatching a bag of chips.

I've got the feed sped up a little so that I can work through it in less time and move on to the next. I started it about two minutes before the larger vehicle arrived. Jesus, it's going to take forever to work through all these stops. I'll have to work every second I'm not sleeping until next week.

A quick flash of something catches my eye in the window of time before the second vehicle's stop. What was that? I back the feed up and show it down so I don't miss whatever that was. I don't know why it caught my attention, but I've learned to trust my gut.

There!

I click pause and play it backwards one frame at a time until I see what caught my attention.

Fuck me! There they are!

A curvy little blonde with purple streaks in her hair, looking straight at me through the security camera in a shitty gas station two hundred miles away. There are a few more, but they're keeping their eyes on the ground as they file into the store. It's a short line of women and girls, most of them look to be teenagers or in their early twenties, being led through the store by one man and another guy closing them in at the rear. This little blonde is still fighting. Keep it up, baby. I'll find you. I get Marcus on the phone, and start yelling into it before he gets out his usual greeting.

"I got them. In a gas station. A couple hundred miles northwest. The feed is from this morning, around ten."

Marcus lets out a long and very loud line of curses, then yells for Elizabet. "Nathan found the omegas," he says, carefully *not* cursing or screaming at his omega. "Two hundred miles away, this morning. Do we have anybody close?" I listen to her muffed answer while I save several copies of the security feed and location information so I can send them out. You can never have too many backup copies of something like this.

"Nobody close enough to catch up by morning, but if Nathan's got the projected course then we should be able to get some teams caught up with them soon enough. I hate to leave them with the rogues any longer than necessary if we know where they are, but it would be good to track them to whatever location they're being taken to. I want to find them and get them safe, but we need to find whoever is over all this mess."

Marcus agrees with her, "I don't like it, but you're right. If we can catch up with them, we can follow for a bit to attempt to get them to lead us where they are heading. Then we'll get them out of there. There are probably more omegas to be found, as well. If we can just get our hands on one of the rogues who has them and get him nice and talkative...and where the fuck is Dennison? Shouldn't he be all over this?"

I cut in. "The Dennison pack's omega is coming off of her heat. I spoke to him last week. He feels like shit over it, but she was very insistent that she needed him home. I can't say anything bad about it, either. Talia and Jasper are both going into heat next week. I'm not going to be able to get shit done until it's over."

"Excuse me?" Elizabet says very clearly. I must be on speaker now. "Both Talia and Jasper are going to go into heat next week? I thought we had more time to prepare?"

"Yes, ma'am." I reply.

The line is very quiet for a moment, then she says, "where is she now?"

"Downstairs," I answer, "it's movie night."

"Please have her call me as soon as she can. It's important."

"I'll tell her," I say, but I don't get why she's so worked up about their heats syncing up. You'd think she'd be excited about that like she was excited when Talia had her second heat.

"Nathan, you're amazing. We wouldn't have gotten this close without you. Don't worry about the Dennison pack. And don't worry about being out of commission next week. I'll keep you updated. Let me know if you find anything else. There are bound to be more than just the omegas that were at the compound," Marcus says and ends the call. I'm going to hold a phone etiquette class one day. Nobody answers with hello anymore, and the only person who actually says any form of goodbye at the end of a call is Reid. Bunch of rude asses.

I can't wait to tell the others. I run down the stairs and into the main room where my pack is spread out over a couple couches and the floor watching whatever horrible thing Jasper picked out. "I found them!"

Everyone jumps up. "Where?" Talia asks, already heading for the door.

"No, no," Corso catches her by the elbow, "even if they were a mile away you wouldn't be going after them, bella. It would be dangerous and irresponsible."

She jerks her arm away and snarls. "I'll argue with you about that later," then she asks me, "where are they?"

"Two hundred miles northwest."

"Shit," Alex rakes his fingers through his hair, "did you call anyone yet?"

"I called Marcus and Elizabet. They're sending teams. He said he'd keep me informed."

Trent almost knocks me over when he hugs me, lifting me off the ground, "you did it! You found them! The teams will get there and get them home. You did it, Nathan." I think I might cry, I'm so overwhelmed now. I wasn't when I was talking to Marcus, but now that my pack is around me, telling me how proud they are of me and so happy that I got a solid location on the omegas my eyes are starting to sting. I think I need to sit down.

"Put him down, Trent," Jasper orders, then grabs my wrist to lead me to sit on the couch. He climbs into my lap and presses his forehead against mine. Talia comes to sit beside us and begins to purr the way my mom always used to purr for us when we were upset or hurt. Even though I am emotionally overwhelmed and about to cry my eyes out, I know how big of a deal that is, how amazing it is that she's making that sound for me.

"I'm sorry," I whisper, "I'm alright. I'm just overwhelmed. I'm so glad I got a location on them. I don't know why I'm upset."

"You don't need to explain anything," Reid's deep voice rolls over me as he sits on my other side, "you're relieved, Nathan. Incredibly relieved. You've been worrying about those omegas since the compound, and you've just found them."

"Sorry I got so excited, I just know how big this is. I'm so happy and proud of you," Trent says.

Kaleb sits back in the chair he was in when I came running down the stairs. "This is amazing, Nathan. We knew you'd find them. Did Marcus happen to say when teams would be deployed, or who they might send?"

I shake my head. "No, I'm sure they'll get it worked out. But Elizabet was pretty insistent that you call her Talia."

"Why? There are several things I'd rather do tonight that do not involve a phone call to my mother."

"I don't know. She got really quiet after I told her you and Jasper are supposed to go into heat next week, then she asked me to have you call her."

"I'll text her later," Talia grumbles, and pulls my arm around her shoulders so she can lean against me.

"Are you feeling more settled?" Corso asks, touching my forehead and cheek with the back of his hand. Corso is always checking on one of us, always using touch to try to help ground us or to just try to give comfort.

"Yeah, I'm good now. They help a lot," I nod at Jasper and Talia.

"They certainly do," Corso says, he runs his fingers through Talia's hair and squeezes Jasper's shoulder.

Jasper leans forward to brush his lips against mine then he asks, "are you still working, or are you going to hang out with us for a while?

"Will you be upset with me if I keep working? I don't know how many days I'll actually have before you and our cupcake are going to need all my attention."

"Of course not. Go do what you need to do," he kisses me again. I even get a kiss on my cheek from Talia.

I've gone back to every logged stop and the blonde with the purple streaks has deliberately faced every security camera she notices. She's a smart, brave girl. And she'll be home soon. Marcus sent me a text a bit ago. They've already got COTs on the ground headed that way. I think it's heavily ironic that a couple of them are driving pet transport vans. I don't want to set myself up for disappointment, but I'm so hopeful that we're so much closer to getting those omegas safe.

Chapter Fifteen

Alex

I don't know what Elizabet wanted to talk to Talia about, but my girl has been pissed off about it for two days. She says she isn't angry with her mother. She claims that she's not angry at all. But she is very definitely pissed off about whatever it was. Jasper is in a bit of a funk, too. The two of them being pissy and pouty isn't stopping either of them from having heat spikes, and a lot of them.

Talia is spending every moment that she's not sleeping or fucking in the kitchen trying to put together foods that we'll be able to dish out without much effort. Corso and I feel fairly confident that between the two of us, Devon, and Kaleb we'll keep everyone fed. Talia is mostly coherent for at least the first day of her heat, and they say Jasper is in and out for the entirety of his, so hopefully between all of us we won't starve to death. We're putting several cases of water near each of their nests for easy and quick access, as well as a bunch of easy to eat snacks.

I think they're going to build a nest together. Reid and Kaleb think so, too. Corso thinks they'll be more comfortable in separate nests. Trent thinks they're going to start out separate and end up together. Devon says Talia might abandon her nest for Jasper's, and he didn't sound happy about it. He would rather they be in the same nest from the start because he thinks they'll be happier together throughout everything. Nathan is just happy to be anywhere they are.

Kaleb built a bit of a bonfire in the back tonight because Talia mentioned s'mores. He didn't get the joke. She wants to have a playdate with me and Trent and that was an invitation, but she thinks too much of Kaleb to tell him she didn't want to actually roast marshmallows. She's watching me try to keep gooey marshmallow out of my beard right now. She's been trying to keep up with the demand for chocolate and graham crackers, but I think she's given up so she can watch me eat this marshmallow; and I'm going to eat it as obscenely as I possibly can.

I waved Trent over a few minutes ago and I just now handed him the bar of chocolate I've been holding for the past few minutes, "open that for me, will you? I've got troubles here, my fingers are sticky."

He caught Talia's intention about four seconds after I did when the words 'I could really go for s'mores right now' came out of her mouth. He looks down at the mostly melted chocolate I handed him and smirks as he tears open the wrapper.

As expected, the chocolate gets all over his fingers. "Oh look, now we've both got sticky fingers." He begins the lewd task of licking melted chocolate from his fingertips.

"Is this what we're doing, then?" Jasper asks, coming to stand beside Trent. He grabs Trent's wrist and brings his fingers to his mouth and licks up the side of one of them. Talia's eyes are losing more and more blue as they dart from me to Trent to Jasper. She's likely to leap through the nice fire Kaleb has built to get to us.

Part of me wishes she would, but most of me knows I wouldn't be the only one who'd lose my shit if she did. The vein in Devon's temple that starts pulsing anytime she starts talking about doing dangerous shit might actually explode if she jumped over the fire. Hell, it might explode if she walks too close to it. She still hasn't told him everything that happened at the compound and it's been well over a month. At this point, I don't think he really wants to know anymore than he already does.

Jasper is sucking on one of Trent's fingertips now and eyeing one of mine. I made a pretty big mess of it on purpose. My plan was to lick it off myself, but it would be a lot more fun if Talia got to watch Jasper lick it off. If she likes what she sees enough, who knows how this night might end? As far as I know, she's only had one spike today, and it was way earlier. It might not take much to nudge her into another one. When I stretch my arm across Trent to offer Jasper my fingers, he happily sucks one into his mouth and closes his eyes as he swirls his tongue around the tip.

Talia's pupils are blown now. Yes, I think we have pushed her right into her second spike of the day. She's got her bottom lip trapped between her teeth and her eyes are focused on Jasper's mouth. He makes a show of licking my finger when I pull it away, and Talia stands up. Excellent. Maybe all three of us can have a go at her. I reach down conspicuously to adjust myself.

She tilts her head to the side and twists her lips into a smirk. Then she walks around the fire and grabs Kaleb by the shirt and heads back inside. Well...fuck.

"Plan backfire?" Devon teases.

I shrug. "It was worth the effort. She wants to see me and Trent together. Jasper was going to be the ultimate bonus." Then I look sideways at Trent, "I don't know about letting you fuck me. She wants to see it, she even thinks I'd like it. He wants to see it, too," I nod toward Jasper, "but I don't know if I'd like it or not. I like that they'd like it. Maybe we can put on a show for them one day." I look back to the manor and nod. "Eventually."

Trent laughs at me, and Devon looks like it pains him to imagine any of the things I just said as he tries to scrub from his mind

~

Two days later, I'm standing behind Nathan's chair looking at four different monitors and agreeing with Marcus Graves. Nathan is a goddamned genius. "She's still there. I think she's got a bit of a shiner now, but she's still showing us her face, still leaving breadcrumbs." I don't mention the split lip, or the tiredness I can clearly see despite the grainy quality of the security feed.

"And Marcus said the COTs have closed in on them?" Corso asks from beside me.

Nathan sighs. "Yeah. Not too close, but close enough. They're still heading northwest. Devon's dad thinks they're trying to get to North Wisen up there. He says a lot of territory meetings are held there due to being neutral ground, and that could be part of all of this. We won't know till they get wherever they're going."

"I've been up there," Corso says. "We deliver to several restaurants and hotels, and quite a few bars there. If it's territory-related, it's likely that any meets could happen at one of the more upscale places. I have connections that could help you get into the systems, if that would even be helpful."

"It might be, I'm just terrified of trusting the wrong people. I've been a server, and Trent had a run as a shitty bartender, so we could go undercover if needed. People who need money can be bought almost as easily as people who don't," Nathan says, then he clicks on a few more things and different windows show on the monitors. "These are all the places they've stopped along the way," he points at a map, "and yesterday I noticed these three vehicles," he clicks on something else and two SUVs and a minivan appear on another monitor, "are following the same path. They're stopping at the same places at about half hour intervals. And look at this." He clicks again, and on a third monitor a group of presumably omegas shows on the monitor. One male and four females. The male looks rough and the females are doing their best to keep him in the center of their huddle. "That could have been Jasper and Talia."

Corso and I both put a hand on each of Nathan's shoulders. "But it isn't. Don't dwell on the things that could have happened, Nathan," Corso says gently, "our omegas are safe here at home with us."

"What if someone else comes for them while they're in heat?"

I give his shoulder a squeeze, "we won't be so far gone that we would let anyone take them. And Elizabet has already assured us that the entire property will be crawling with her people. Do either of you know why she's so worked up over it? By all accounts she should be throwing a party instead of sending half her detail to watch over us."

Corso shakes his head.

"No," Nathan says, "but it might have something to do with all the science stuff I found on one of the servers linked to Crane's bullshit."

Fucking Crane. I could have kissed Reid right there in that office, blood and all, after he killed that asshole; and I may have asked both Talia and Jasper to recount the demise of little Mitchell more than twice.

"Well, whatever the reason," Corso pats Nathan on the back, "I'm grateful for the extra support. I am very much looking forward to this."

~

He doesn't have long to wait. Jasper's heat hits him the next evening, and Talia is only a few hours after him. We kind of knew it was coming because they started gathering things the night before and carrying them from room to room. Nobody got much sleep. They were talking to each other, using actual, real words, but it was only pieces of sentences and mostly facial and bodily expressions. I loved every second of it. They wanted Nathan's room, but Jasper remembered at the last second that all of Nathan's work was spread out in there and he didn't want to chance anything getting ruined when Talia and I get going. Ultimately, they ended up claiming Corso's room; which I'm sure he will be crowing about for the rest of our lives. Omegas are creatures of habit. Talia will most likely build every nest she ever makes when she's the only one in heat in Nathan's room. We don't know what Jasper will do, this is his first heat with all of us. And every collective nest they make from now on will probably be in Corso's room. I'd brag about it, too.

Right now, everyone is upstairs in Corso's room. It's a sexual anarchy. Only Kaleb and I are holding ourselves back from going into rut, and we're hanging on by a bare thread. Well, I am. I don't know what he's over there doing, but I can see his erection straining against his pants. The urge to rut was bad enough with only Talia in heat, but with both of them going it's taking all I've got to maintain a level head. The very second the last of Elizabet's teams pull into the driveway I'm jumping dick-first into the center of that nest.

A SUV turns down the driveway and Kaleb lifts up the binoculars to his eyes. He thought I was ridiculous for breaking them out, but it makes seeing who is actually in the vehicles as they pull in so much easier. And there are quite a few vehicles. Our lawn looks like we're either throwing a party or being raided.

"Thank fucking christ," Kaleb mutters and discards the binoculars on the table by the door. I double check the lock and security system. Then Kaleb and I race up the stairs. We actually race, too; each of us trying to get to the top first. He wins, but only because I tripped over my stupid pants. I was trying to get ahead of the game by taking them off as I ran, but I wasn't successful.

The sight that greets me when Kaleb opens the door is fantastic. Just fucking gorgeous. Talia and Jasper are riding Reid like he's a fucking carnival ride. Jasper is riding his cock, and Talia is riding his face, and they're in the center of the nest. Jasper starts groaning about Reid's knot while simultaneously barking at Devon to move his ass so he can take care of Talia once she cums all over Reid.

"Not until she tells me to, baby. Let's let Corso take care of her this time," Devon reasons. Jasper pouts for half a second, but then Talia starts moaning out an orgasm, and he hisses at Corso to hurry the fuck up. Corso is more than happy to lift Talia off of Reid and lay her out beside him.

"Nathan," Corso purrs, "if you would?"

Nathan crawls over and offer's Talia his dripping cock while Corso slides his into her.

This is going to be one of the best things that has ever happened to me.

Chapter Sixteen

Devon

The past several hours have been eye opening, and there are some very hard lines being drawn right now in the middle of this heat. The first one was clearly put down when Corso and Jasper worked Talia through a particularly violent wave a few hours ago. Corso and Jasper will never have a sexual relationship, ever. Even in the middle of his own wave beginning to crest, Jasper's focus was still completely on working with Corso to coax Talia through a series of orgasms before Corso knotted her. And right now, Talia is squaring off with Kaleb because she feels like he's handling Jasper too roughly. The size difference between her and him is more apparent when we are all naked and hyped on hormones. She's only semi-aware of everything happening around her and the things we're all saying, but that didn't stop her from yanking Jasper away from Kaleb and passing him off behind her to Nathan.

"You hurt him," she's glaring at Kaleb's hand. There are strands of Jasper's hair still trapped between his fingers. It isn't a lot, literally just a few strands, but she is *pissed.* Anger and orgasms show the same on Talia, a gorgeous, full-body blush, and right now she's very pink. Jasper has tried twice to tell her that he likes Kaleb's handling, but she isn't having it. She may not even hear him at this point. The problem is that Kaleb is in and out of the thrall of rut, himself. He's lost to it right now, and he's having a difficult time processing that his omega has been ripped away from him by his other omega. If another alpha had pulled Jasper away from him, pack or not, it might have ended in a fight. But Kaleb isn't dealing with another alpha. He's dealing with Talia. And that just might be worse.

"He's not hurt." The restraint in Kaleb's voice makes my own throat feel tight.

"You were holding him down. I don't like that. Don't do that." Her voice is just as strained.

"You hold him down when you fuck him." His reasoning isn't doing anything for him. The amount of offense Talia takes to that statement, no matter how true it is, sours the air.

"He's mine to hold down. You were doing it wrong. You hurt him. Look at your fucking hand. You hurt him."

"He's mine, too," Kaleb growls, and takes a step toward her. It is officially time to intervene.

I plant myself between them facing Kaleb. "I've got her, Kaleb."

He nods and retreats to the corner of the room where we put all the water. I'm very glad he listened, Corso and Reid both stood up from where they were resting when he took that small step toward her. *I* know that Kaleb would never, under any circumstances, hurt Talia; but instinctive behavior is rampant right now, and his little step could have been perceived as a threat, even though he was likely about to snatch her up and fuck her the way he was about to fuck Jasper.

"The nest is ruined," she snarls, looking down at the wrinkled blankets and things that make up the nest she and Jasper built together.

"I know, honey. We can fix it."

Then she looks back at me and I watch as her anger towards Kaleb, and then the state of the nest, switches to focus solely on me. I can see my faults and transgressions building behind her eyes. "I'm really fucking mad at you."

I have never been so goddamned happy to have someone be angry with me in my entire life. Talia hasn't shown the first hint of anger in all this time, and she should be extremely angry with me.

I have learned from my years with Jasper that being in heat often brings out the same blunt honesty that being intoxicated does. I'm so fucking relieved that I could cry. "Lay it on me, cupcake. Tell me why you're mad at me."

"You treat Jasper like an omega."

I nod, "he is an omega. Of course I treat him like one." This is not what I expected her to start with.

"He's more than an omega. You coddle him when he doesn't need it. You don't let him be what he's supposed to be. You hold him back."

The room is suddenly very quiet.

"He's more than just an omega. He's just as strong as you are but you treat him like he's weak or fragile. I don't like it."

"Noted," I nod. "What else?"

"You don't rest. You let the council and your father, fuck, even *my* father, tell you what to do. This is your pack, not theirs," she's seething now. "Jasper is not their omega. I am not their omega. They," she waves at the rest of our pack, "are not their pack. We are yours, and you allow other alphas and entities to dictate our lives. It's bullshit. We should be your priority."

That...that's actually hurtful. "You are my priority. That's why I listen to the council and our fathers."

She shakes her head, "you know what we need. Not them, Devon. Not them. We are yours. Just yours. Do better. Be with us. *Really* with us, not in the background working toward a future that you're outside of. You are ours. Make them understand that."

I blow out a breath. She isn't wrong. Nobody but Talia would scream at me over any of it, though, and she's working toward some screaming. "Understood. What else?"

Then every drop of anger leaves her in the span of a blink and it's replaced with complete and total gut-wrenching heartbreak. Her eyes flood with tears that don't fall and her mouth turns down. "You made me leave," she says so softly, "you left me."

Here it is. The thing I think we've all been waiting for. Kaleb would have stayed at the hospital with her. Nathan and Trent would have never let her leave in the first place when we got those horrible pictures. It's all on me. I didn't take the obvious and not so obvious opinions of my pack into consideration. I was too worried about Jasper to see what was looking me in the face. "I know," I fall to my knees. "It was wrong," I fall forward into the deepest position of submission we recognize. "I should have stayed. You were my beta. I don't know how to be sorry enough," I say with my forehead pressed to the floor at her tiny feet.

"Get up, Devon. I don't like that." Now she's crying in earnest. "I'd rather be mad. I don't like that." Then she hugs her arms across her stomach and lets a whine escape. "Get up," she whispers, "I don't like that."

"What would you have me do, Talia?" Another wave of her heat is crashing into her. Heat cycles are cruel. It doesn't matter that she is finally allowing herself to feel the things that she should have been feeling all along, her body is forcing its needs on her. I never envied omegas, but right now, at this moment, I hate that she's an omega. I hate that she has to feel the way she feels and still have to bend to her body's will. It isn't fucking fair.

She drops to her hands and knees beside me, rocking back and forth, already beginning to pant. "Be a good alpha. Take care of us the way we need you to." A choked, pitiful sound comes out of her, then she says, "make this feel better. It hurts so much."

I can do that. I know how to make her feel better right now.

It's still painfully quiet, but it doesn't matter. Talia asked me to help her, that's all that matters. The rest of the pack can be as quiet or as loud as they want. Grabbing hold of her hip and shoulder, I roll her onto her back. Her legs are drawn up to her ribs but they spread wide for me when I cover her body with mine. I want to hold her. I want to give her the tenderness and gentle attention that she deserves. But her need is crashing through me, battering my bond with her, and I don't think I'll get to do it. She's still only hours into the beginning of her heat. Regardless of the emotional turmoil, she doesn't need sweet or gentle.

"Ready, pretty girl?" I push her hair back off her face. She's burning up, damp with sweat, and no matter how many times Reid or Corso re-braid her hair strands and tendrils keep escaping.

Talia grips my forearms and nods. "Yes," she groans, "please."

"You don't ever have to beg me for anything, Talia. Never." I touch my forehead to hers and brush the tip of my nose against hers, then I push my cock inside her. I give her long, firm, heavy strokes until she's making these short, high-pitched little cries with every impact. The red-tinged haze of rut that usually clouds my peripheral vision is starting to swirl around the edges of my consciousness, and I have to put effort into not growling at Corso when he so very gently pries Talia's hands away from my arms. I can smell the blood and feel the sting now, she must have dug her nails into me. I'll be wearing her marks down my arms and back, hopefully for days.

Talia doesn't put any effort into holding back her snarl, she puts her effort into trying to pull her hands away from Corso. "Shhh, bella," he hushes, "we don't want blood all over this nice nest. And we don't want to send Devon away to get sewn up, do we?"

She shakes her head, but her face is still sour. "Would you like to hold my hands while he gives you what you need, tesoro?"

Talia squeezes Corso's hands and grits her teeth. "Harder, Devon. More."

I give her more. I give her everything. The only things stopping me from fucking her across the floor to the other side of the nest are my own arms braced above her shoulders. The thick, solid slap of our bodies meeting when I bottom out might as well be the only sound in the entire world. My knot is beginning to swell but she hasn't come apart for me. She's lifting her hips, meeting me thrust for thrust, making the most desperate sounds. Somehow, I fuck her even harder and she starts struggling against Corso's hold, tossing her head from side to side, begging me over and over to make her cum.

"What do you need, baby?" I purr, but it sounds more like a growl.

"The bite," Jasper says from somewhere. "She needs the bite." His last word cuts off in a gasp. Someone must be taking very good care of him.

"Is that what you need, cupcake? You need me to bite you again?" Her entire body convulses under me and she throws her head back, arching her neck beautifully. This is what I wanted the first time I touched her. I wanted to drive my cock into her as hard as I could, over and over again, and sink my teeth into her when she gave me her neck. I clenched my jaw so fucking hard to stop myself from marking her that I tasted blood and my teeth hurt for days afterward. I don't need to do that now. I can take what she's offering me now, and I'm fucking going to. It doesn't matter that she's already wearing my mark, if she needs the bite I'll give it to her. Every single time she needs it.

I run my nose across her shoulder and up her neck, taking in her spicy scent, then I slowly, deliberately, set my teeth right over the mark I already put on her, biting deep, then I push my knot past her tight entrance and groan when I feel it lock us together. I rock my hips, giving her small thrusts as her orgasm finally takes her. She's almost screaming with it, and it's so damned wonderful to hear.

When my cock stops jerking inside of her with my own release, I carefully relax my jaws and lick at the bite I've left and lick at the wound. It isn't another claiming mark, and she isn't bleeding much at all, but it was so fucking satisfying to be able to give her the bite the way I wanted to. Corso let go of her hands right before I bit her, I have newly dug furrows down my sides from where she raked her nails into me when I bit her. I'm glad for that, too. It feels better to have my own taste of pain, Corso must understand that. Talia is right. I already knew it, but even in the middle of a heat like this Corso is a good alpha.

Talia's already asleep, her body loose and warm when I maneuver us into a better position for rest. She doesn't like going into heat, I understand that and I understand why, but I love her like this. Her guard is completely down, she's the truest version of herself. She doesn't hold anything back or separate.

Outside of heat, her focus is fully centered on how she can best care for her pack. She keeps herself held so deep in check that we'd never know how she's feeling or what she might need without having a bond with her. I've only had a bond with her for a few days and it's like the entire world is a different color. I've been trying so hard to not compare anything between her and Jasper, but they feel so different, and their bonds touch completely different parts of me. Everything about having a bond with both of them is so, so good. Even if Talia had never switched over to being an omega, she and Jasper would have still been a mated pair and it was a total dick move on my part to try to keep her separate. We were going to bond her into the pack eventually, I just needed to pull my head out of my ass. We would have been a pack of alphas centered by an omega and his beta mate and it would be just like it is now, just without the double heat factor.

"I don't think you're any worse off than the rest of us, but I'll help you get cleaned up, anyway. You handled her well, Devon." Corso touches Talia's cheek, then my shoulder, and gets up to get a cloth. My blood is all over this section of the nest. I don't think Talia will mind, I actually think she might enjoy it; Jasper, however, will not. He likes his nest neat and tidy. Talia seems to need it mostly unwrinkled and full of the scents she likes. I'm sure she and Jasper will rearrange and straighten everything when they rise to the surface of this wave of their heats in a little while, and I'm more than sure we'll be helping them.

Corso brings more than a damp cloth. He puts two bottles of water and a small bowl of sliced cucumbers beside me and begins wiping off my arms. "She will remember what you did, fratello. That was the best thing that you could have done. She didn't like seeing you do it, she needs you to be her alpha right now, strong and dominant. But when she comes out of heat, she will remember what you did and she knows how important that is."

"It isn't enough."

"Some things I know about our Talia, without any fraction of doubt, is that she doesn't partake in risks if she doesn't understand the potential outcome, she doesn't do things without knowing exactly what she's doing, and she is more strong-willed than all of us together. And one thing I already know about our Jasper is that he will scorch the earth for her, and this pack. I am very happy to be under their care, you should be, too." Then he goes over to take water and crackers to Nathan and Jasper. Corso just says things like that, just drops huge epiphanies on you, then goes off to deliver snacks.

He's right, though. We will need to change our thinking about our pack, and likely society as a whole. When you think of packs and omegas, you think of the omega or omegas being cared for and under the care of the alphas, but that's completely inaccurate. Talia and Jasper are the center of this pack, and she is very quickly becoming our sun.

That's the best way I can think to describe it, but I feel it in every bond I have with my pack. I feel it inside of Jasper, and in every other alpha. Jasper will be our omega, always; but he has a new position in this new pack. While he is our omega, and an omega in this pack, *she* is *his* omega.

And that changes up the hierarchy. She is now our ultimate priority, and he loves it that way. I can already feel him thriving in this new life in a way that he never has before. I can feel the tide turning inside of Talia in very small increments as well, after just a few days. I don't even think she realizes it's happening. She is very slowly starting to think differently about herself. She becomes less rigid every day. I don't think she will ever be a soft, gooey omega, but she might eventually get to a point where she will let herself be cared for the way omegas should be. I hope she will, anyway.

Chapter Seventeen

Kaleb

This is hell. I am actually in hell. When we all agreed that we wanted to bring a baby into our pack and that it would be biologically Jasper's I had no idea it would launch me directly into hell. The last time I was with Jasper and Talia it was in a very similar position, but it didn't have me questioning my control. Talia and I were focused on Jasper and it was completely blissful.

This time there's still plenty of pleasure, but there are a few other intensely overwhelming sensations happening in the undercurrent of it. Sensations like feeling Talia's slick drip onto my abdomen and trail down the outsides of my hips. Sensations like her teeth biting into my chest again and again as she sobs in pleasure and unmet need. Sensations like my blood boiling inside my skull as I listen to Jasper beg her to hold on just a little longer as he rides me to completion. Fuck, from my viewpoint they're both riding me.

"Hold on, baby girl. Just a little bit more. We're almost there. Almost, baby, almost. I can feel his knot, then I can cum for you. You want my cum don't you, cupcake?"

He's drenched in sweat and his thighs are trembling with more than the need for release. Any other time I would have flipped us over and put us all out of misery, but it's important to do this the way we're doing it.

Jasper's riding me, but he's also fucking her. Talia's braced on her hands and knees over me while Jasper takes her from behind.

She needs a knot so badly, and he doesn't have one to give her. He won't cum until I knot him, then we're passing her to Trent, who is on his knees beside us working his own cock while he watches. If we were any other pack, this would be uncomfortable or even ridiculous, but we aren't and he needs to be able to knot her the very second Jasper and I hand her off to him.

Talia is beyond the ability to coherently respond to Jasper's encouragement. She's running on pure instinct now. She is the epitome of a female omega in heat and we are making her wait for what she needs. I'm lucky she's not doing more than just leaving bite marks, and I'm extremely glad that she can't get her hands on Jasper. So far she's done really well to not touch him aggressively in any way, but this is very obviously testing her limits.

"Almost, fuck, almost," I grunt, then she gives me an especially vicious bite and that's all it takes to throw us over the edge. I thrust my hips and shove Jasper down on me as my knot fully expands and I feel him clenching around me when he releases into Talia.

"Thank fuck," Trent grits out and pulls her from between Jasper and me without waiting for us to help him.

Talia's cries are ringing in my ear. Trent didn't even attempt to move her to a different part of the nest, he slammed inside her right beside me. Their bodies are so close to mine that I can feel every thrust Trent makes into her.

"Are you ready for my knot, cupcake? I'm ready to give it to you."

All Talia can manage is a long, breathy moan.

"There you go, darlin. God, you feel so good." His southern accent is thick as he comforts her.

"That's it, baby," Jasper slurs, "such a good girl. Letting all of us take care of you." He coaxes her hand out of Trent's hair and links his fingers with hers. "This is it, you know," he sighs, "I can already feel it." Then he lays over my chest and kisses a few of Talia's bites while we wait for Talia and Trent to finish.

By the time Trent rolls them onto their sides, Jasper is mostly asleep. A combined heat has had unexpected results. Talia was pretty far gone after the first day of her last heat, but she has been mostly overtaken by her heat after the first few hours of this one. But Jasper hasn't lost himself for the first time. He's almost always in and out the entire time he's in heat, but for some reason during their shared heat Jasper has remained fully in control of himself. He's still navigating the waves of heat and his intense need, but he has remained completely conscious of everything happening in the nest. The only time he has been unaware is when he falls asleep after being knotted. He's showing signs of exhaustion, but nothing like when he was helping Talia through her heat. It's the damnedest thing and I can't wait to discuss it with him after it's over with.

"I don't know how many more times we can put her through that," Alex says quietly. "It shouldn't be this damn hard to get cum into an omega. She's only been able to take it, what twice? Maybe three times?"

"Three times. It hurts her to take him when her body craves a knot so badly," Corso answers, and lays back against a pillow. "I agree with you, Alex. I don't think I can take denying her again. I'm barely above rut as it is. I won't be able to hear her make those sounds and not give her what she needs once I'm gone to it."

"Three times is enough." Reid's decree is barely more than a rolling growl. He is further gone than the rest of us, and the strain to maintain control is obvious.

"We all agree," Devon says from across the room. He went to heat up some real food. Talia definitely won't eat it, but the rest of us, including Jasper, are starving. "If she isn't pregnant after this, she'll need to decide if she'd like to wait until their next shared heat to give Jasper another chance, or if she wants to let one of us try again during her next heat. Whatever she wants is what we'll do."

Nathan goes to help Devon put what smells like chicken into bowls to be passed to the rest of us. We learned early on with Jasper that any food needs to be eaten in small amounts and should be given out in bowls instead of plates. We have also learned that any form of spaghetti, or anything with sauce, is strictly forbidden from the nest. Easy to eat, mostly dry foods are what works best.

"We don't need to try again," Jasper mumbles, "it's done. Eat your chicken and try to rest. Her body will need a couple days to catch up, and she's still going to need you. Me too. This has been a completely different heat than any I've ever had. I'm so tired."

I was already purring steadily, but as the words leave his mouth the others begin purring, too.

"Oh my god, thank you. This is one of the things she calls a perk. This is a perfect sound" Jasper groans, then he's asleep before Nathan ever makes it over with food.

"Do you think it worked?" Nathan whispers when he hands me my bowl.

"Jasper thinks so," I whisper back, "I hope so. It's what she wants. I don't want her to be disappointed."

Chapter Eighteen

Corso

Jasper was right. Talia is pregnant. I can feel it and smell the change in her scent. It is altered in a way that seems to be a blend of her and that of the baby she carries, making her notes richer, reminding me of the simmer pots my grandmother and mother kept on the stove when I was still at home. I don't know if any of the others have noticed yet. Jasper will certainly know the moment he comes out of his own heat.

Talia's first heat was a disaster, shortened due to the trauma of me not being able to resist what I always wanted and would have probably lasted the same full week as her second. This heat cut off abruptly at five days, almost twenty-four hours after her last time with Jasper. Which is what happens when an omega becomes pregnant. Symptoms of pregnancy tend to come on quickly, as well. And most females are visibly pregnant by the halfway point at fifteen weeks. We should have a baby to hold and lose sleep over by the time spring sets in.

I'm not sure if it is possible for me to be much happier than I am right now. I have been dreaming of a child with Talia for years. I begged her to consider it before she left us for good, but she wouldn't. She said she couldn't take that away from the omega my pack would eventually find. It was incredibly frustrating for me because she has been all my pack has ever wanted or needed. Her being a beta was never an issue for us, I just wish it hadn't been an issue for her.

She doesn't want to leave the nest, which is also understandable. It's very possible that she will keep restructuring this nest for the entire thirty weeks until the baby arrives; which would be more than okay with me. Then again, it's just as likely that she will claim Nathan's room like she does during her individual heat. It's also possible that she will build her maternal nest in Jasper's room since the baby will be biologically his. Anything she does will be perfect. I want Talia to be wherever she is happiest.

"Is she alright?" Alex whispers as he stretches out on the other side of her. "Now that she's through it, Jasper is starting to wind down, too."

I nod, "she's alright, Alex. She's just very tired. I think it was more intense for her since they were both in heat." I'm not going to bring up the change in her scent. I want to see how long it takes the others to notice.

"Reid went down to take care of the kitchen. We've all been cleaning up when we leave, but he wants it to be perfect for when she's ready to leave the nest. How long do you think it will take the rest of them to notice?" He flicks his eyes down Talia's body and I fight back a smile.

"Not long, but they might not know the difference as quickly. Don't say anything."

"My bet is on Jasper first, then Reid. Then Kaleb. Then the rest of them all when they figure out the rest of us know something." Alex always enjoys being in on a secret.

Jasper whines at something Nathan is or is not doing and Talia stirs. "Do it right, or I'll do it for you. Don't make him whine," she growls without opening her eyes. "Fucking drawing it out. He doesn't need that. Just fucking give him what he needs, for fuck sake." Then she goes right back to sleep. Alex chokes on his laughter and it takes a few long moments for him to collect himself.

When he can manage it, he whispers, "you know, I'm half tempted to buy her a strap and see what happens."

I thought she was back asleep. Her sour little tone is tinged with a bit of her own laughter, "I just need a new harness. Jasper would love that. And you'd love to see it. Now be quiet."

"New?" Alex whispers, "what do you mean new? Why did you have an old one? What did you get up to while you were away?"

She shrugs and pulls his arm around her waist and across mine, "I spent some time with a pack that didn't know how to properly treat their omega. Omegas shouldn't have to suffer because their alphas are assholes."

"You rotten girl," Alex continues, trying to sound scandalized, "I didn't know you enjoyed females."

"I don't. Not like that, anyway. But I was there more for the omega than the alphas. She needed something and I did my best to give it to her. With minimal success, but it was better than being left to suffer alone. Bianca gave me the most ridiculous toy, by the way. It's got a fake knot at the base. It definitely doesn't work for a heat, but I think Jasper would enjoy the change in pace. It's fun to throw him off balance."

Everything she just said is complete news to me. I had no idea Talia tried to help an omega like that. One day, I might take the time to fully enjoy imagining her with another female. I'm not so noble that I don't like the thought. And the knowledge that she has a fake cock somewhere in her room, complete with a fake knot, is incredibly sexy for some reason. Then the thought of her dominating Jasper in that way... "Black leather? Nylon? Something more sturdy?"

She pinches my side, "pervert. You've got the rest of them fooled, but I know how lecherous you can be."

"It isn't lecherous to enjoy beautiful things, bella; and Jasper on his hands and knees with you behind him would be exquisite."

Alex groans, "shut up, Corso. My dick is sore and I need more fluids than I think we have."

Jasper's heat lifts completely by nightfall. He has been asleep for a few hours, tucked between Nathan and Reid. Talia has continued to be reluctant to leave the nest, but her stomach growled so loudly that Devon threw her over his shoulder and carried her down to the kitchen. The aroma of something delicious is drifting through the manor, and now I'm experiencing my own reluctance to wash the scents of my omegas off of me so I can go out and release the security details of their duties. I could easily send a text, but they've done such a service for us that I want to thank them in person.

"She's making beef stew," Trent sighs. He crawls out of the nest and walks out the door with his nose in the air. It's possible that he'll discover the difference in Talia's scent before Jasper simply because he's a bottomless pit.

I go to Reid's side and touch his shoulder, "I'm going to speak with the people Elizabet and Anthony sent over. I'll make sure Trent leaves some food for the rest of us."

He nods and curls his body more closely around Jasper's.

The shower leaves me feeling cold regardless of the temperature I set. Talia's reaction to my shower is even colder. "Is there a reason you don't want to smell like us, Corso?" She isn't looking at me at all, she's stirring the huge pot bubbling on the stove top.

"Not at all, bella. I just didn't think it would be appropriate to speak with the men outside carrying the scent of your and Jasper's heat."

"Why would it be inappropriate? We are your omegas. We've just come out of heat. You washed our scents off to go outside and speak with people we don't know. They should know who you belong to."

"I..." don't know what to say. I look at Devon and Trent for a sense of comradery but all I find are two men with spoons in their hands smirking at me. Devon is at least trying to hold his back, Trent is practically grinning. "I didn't know it would bother you, bella. What would you have me do?"

"I'm not telling you what to do. I don't know why it bothers me so much, but I'm fucking furious," she clips, then goes back to stirring the stew; leaving me standing there with furrowed brows and a slack jaw.

"Here," Devon says, and starts stripping down to his boxers. He hands me his shirt first, then his jeans. "Change into that, it might be an odd fit, but it'll work. I'd go out instead of you, but I'm enjoying someone besides me doing something wrong way too much."

As I'm changing Trent chimes in, "the absolute worst thing you can do after a heat is remove your omega's scent. The first punch Jasper ever threw at me was when I left the house to go get Chinese food freshly showered and in clean clothes. He was mad at all of us for a couple days because I did that. Lesson fucking learned." He's smiling so hard, thoroughly enjoying my plight. "And good luck getting back in her good graces. This is a huge offense, Alpha Zaphir." Smart ass or not, Trent's mirth is infectious.

"I hope I'm not out of your good graces for too long, stellina mia," I whisper against her neck when I walk by her on my way to the back door. "I didn't want to broadcast your scent to the outsiders. I didn't enjoy washing it off and I hope you'll give me the opportunity to replace it after you've eaten some of this stew." Then I nip her shoulder between the marks Devon and I left on her and head outside.

The men who meet me outside are not the ones I wanted to find. I don't know them, but two of them smell heavily of the same scent permeating the rogue compound. I stop a good fifteen feet away from them and pull out a phone from the pocket of my borrowed jeans. I dial Alex, he answers before the first ring finishes, and I say very clearly so there are no misunderstandings between myself and Alex or the men standing around the trucks in my driveway, "outside now. Bring everyone but Reid and Devon. Move quickly." I don't end the call, but I lower the phone and keep it in my hand. If something is said, I want someone other than me to hear it.

"Alpha Zaphir," a tall, lanky beta drawls, "is everything alright?"

"Yes, thank you. I came out to express my gratitude for you men standing guard. Have you been with the agency very long, or are you COT units?"

"Oh," he pauses, "we're not with the agency or the COTs. Alpha Smith sent us over. The others left a few hours ago and we wanted to stick around until someone came out to relieve us."

Lies. Complete lies.

I hear the back door slam on its hinges. Good. I'm not so heavily outnumbered. I hope some of the others thought of grabbing a weapon. "That is much appreciated. Do you mind giving me your name, so I can share my appreciation with Thaddeus. He likes handing out bonuses to good men."

The beta smiles at me. "Tandy. Jacob Tandy."

Another lie.

"What's going on?" Kaleb asks, sounding every bit the arrogant prick he usually does. He's staring down every man in the driveway, glaring at each one until they drop their eyes.

"Jacobi Randy," I purposefully misname the beta, "was just telling me that Thaddeus sent this specialty team over from the institute." I am giving Kaleb deliberately incorrect information. If the beta corrects me, then there's a small chance that Thaddeus may have actually sent these men. If he doesn't, then the beta is throwing around any name he thinks will convince us that he isn't a threat; which makes him an absolute threat.

"Jacobi Randy," Alex hums, "I think I trained with your older brother. How is Parker doing?"

"Oh," the beta stutters, "he's doing alright. Everything alright in there with your omega? It got kinda loud for a while there."

Trent growls low in his throat, and is joined by both Kaleb and Nathan.

"What an inappropriate question to ask us. You should know better than to ask an alpha about their omega in this situation," I say, looking down at my phone as if I'm checking it. I send a text to Nathan, *How fast are the drones? How far can they go?*

The beta tries to backtrack. "I meant no offense, I just heard a lot of noise. I'm just trying to show concern, that's all."

"They're really fast. And can go very far," Nathan says, not bothering to text. That's good enough for me.

"Your job is done here. Get off my property."

"Alpha Smith wanted us to make sure-"

"Get the fuck out of here," Kaleb orders, and takes a step toward the beta who has been speaking.

They pile into their vehicles and Nathan heads back into the house, moving quickly but not running. I want to follow them as long as we can without them noticing, I hope Nathan understood that.

"Why didn't we beat their asses and take them in?" Trent seethes. "We should have killed all but one and taken him in for questioning."

"But what if we left the wrong one alive. Just because that beta was speaking doesn't mean he was the one with the information," I reason. "We need to follow them, see where they lead us. They're bound to have a check in point somewhere close."

"Okay," Trent growls, "we follow them. But then we catch them and kill them and anybody they meet up with. They were here for our omegas. That can't stand."

"Agreed."

The trucks are half way down the drive when Nathan walks out with a box. "Who's driving?"

"Kaleb," I say, and head for the garage. I make it three steps before a shot rings out. I instinctively turn back to the trucks. They have stopped. Another shot comes from somewhere to the left and the back glass of the lead truck shatters. A third shot destroys the driver's side window of the second truck. The men in the vehicles are killed one by one as they frantically leave the vehicles trying to take cover.

"Where are they coming from?" Trent barks, his eyes darting from the roof to the surrounding trees. "They're on our side, right?"

"They appear to be. We're not dead yet, and those assholes are." Alex's eyes are in the trees behind the garage.

Once the cacophony of gunfire quiets, a female with a long black braid wearing tight black clothing drops from the apple tree beside the garage holding a gun that's almost bigger than she is. She takes one look at my pack coming together in a defense formation and drops to the ground, turning her head to show her neck. She's got a bronze skin tone, much like mine and very similar to Trent's. "I'm here at Missus Graves' order. Call her if you need to."

"Where is the rest of your unit?" Kaleb asks brusquely.

"In the trees."

"Why did the rest of the units leave with those pricks in front of my fucking house?" Alex barks.

"The COTs are on the road, waiting to follow the assholes. My people were instructed to remain on the property until Missus Graves gives the order to stand down."

"So, you've all been, what? Standing around waiting for those assholes to do something before notifying us that there was a threat?" Trent is working up to a rage. I can smell his anger on the air between us, sharp, like bitter cocoa.

"No, Alpha Lancaster. We we're waiting for them to get a safe distance from the manor before we acted. We've already gotten into their communications. Alphas Graves and Johnson have the information. We were to take them out as soon as they were far enough away. Missus Graves ordered us not to contact anyone inside the manor unless we needed to get you out."

"How many of you are still on the property?" I ask her. She isn't lying. She's not afraid of our questioning. She's as calm as any good beta would be. She is here to do a job, nothing more. I wave Trent and the others back.

"Twenty-six."

Twenty-six. Twenty-six of Elizabet's people in combination to however many COTs Devon's father sent. I was expecting a much lower number, maybe eight or twelve, and one COT. Why so many? That isn't a question for this beta, however.

Then Talia stalks out of the back door and marches across the lawn with her eyes trained on the beta in front of us. Devon is close behind her, still in just his boxers, looking every bit as angry as Talia feels through the bond.

"Why is there a," she sniffs the air behind the female, "beta on her knees in our driveway?" She turns her head slightly as Jasper and Reid step around the corner of the house coming from the front porch.

"She is one of your mother's people, bella." I don't think Talia would take out her anger and fear on the beta, but she's only just come out of heat and she is very newly pregnant, which is a very intense combination of hormones raging inside her.

"You look like me." Of all the things Talia could be upset about, that isn't one that I'd expect her to address first.

"Yes, omega. That was why I was sent. The plan was for me to be a distraction if we needed to get you out."

"Are you shitting me?!" Trent yells. "Is that what Elizabet does? Teaches females to run around serving themselves up as decoys?"

"Yes." Talia, Jasper, and the beta answer at the same time.

"That's horse shit," Trent rails. "It's irresponsible and unethical. That's why you did it, isn't it? Why you didn't give running through those fucking woods a second thought? Because you were trained how to do it. Get her on the fucking phone. This can't go on."

"Trent," Talia's tone changes completely from cagey and accusatory to utterly soothing, "I would have gone into the woods anyway to save Jasper. I just had the stamina and balls to do it right because of my training. All female betas get that training, and all omegas are taught to deal with it."

"It is bullshit. We hate it. We don't want betas sacrificing them- selves for us, but training is training," Jasper adds. "I agree with Trent, though. It needs to change." He reaches down to offer his hand to the beta to pull her to her feet, but Talia slaps it down and pulls the beta up herself.

"I don't want to be a dick to you. You haven't done anything wrong. Everything you've done has been the right thing. But I am only a day out of my heat," Talia takes a long breath, "so please put some distance between you and my pack. I will be more relaxed if you back away."

The beta backs up several feet as other members of her squad start gathering around us. She holds up a hand and barks an order. "Fifteen feet. No closer."

No one encroaches on the fifteen foot boundary, but not all the gathered men and women are betas. There are several alphas in the mix, and I'm not the only one of us to notice their nostrils flaring as they scent the air. I put my body in front of Talia and catch Jasper's eye. "Take her inside. Don't let her come back out. There are too many alphas."

He nods and scoops her up into his arms, despite the exhaustion he must be feeling, and carries her back inside through the back door. I watch the door close behind them before I turn back around to address the people scattered across my lawn.

"I came out here earlier to thank you all for standing guard. Now I am doubly grateful. What can we do to assist you?"

The beta shakes her head, still not meeting my eyes. "Nothing, Alpha Zaphir. We've got it covered. We'll get everything cleaned up and be gone before sunrise."

"That's good enough for me. Thank you again. I will be contact- ing Elizabet about your good work."

We don't go inside immediately. We're all a little too keyed up. So we sit on the porch for a while watching the vehicles and bodies get cleared from the driveway. When we do go inside and head back to the kitchen, we are greeted with a truly lovely sight.

There is a large cast iron pot in the center of the table alongside a basket of biscuits, with each of our place settings laid out. Jasper is seated in his usual seat with Talia cradled on his lap and feeding her spoonfuls of stew from his bowl. He barely takes his eyes off of her as he feeds her. I've never heard the sound he's making. It's a cross between a purr and a growl that makes warmth curl in my belly.

We all sit around the table and Devon takes it upon himself to fill everyone's bowl. He flicks occasional glances at Jasper and Talia, as we all are doing. It's almost like they are completely unaware of our presence. None of us speak at all for several minutes. We all seem to be under the same spell.

The quiet is destroyed in a very dramatic way whenTrent jumps up from his place at the table, his chair chattering to the floor behind him, and he points at Talia and shouts with his mouth full, "it worked! Jasper did it! Fuck yeah!" Then he loses most of his color and starts rubbing his chest. "Holy fuck. We did it. She did it. It's happening," he almost whispers.

Every one of us slowly turn our eyes from Trent's panic to our omegas. Jasper puts another spoonful into Talia's mouth and smiles. "I told you," he tells us without stopping the sound reverberating from his chest. He feels so much larger than his physical presence all of a sudden. He feels like the most dominant person in the room. I'm half tempted to offer him my neck, and I find myself wondering if the others are feeling the same things I am.

Alex flicks his wide eyes at me and I raise my brows.

"Does he feel different? Am I being stupid? Are you alright, Jasper?" Devon asks in a hushed voice.

"I'm wonderful, Devon. Are you alright? You all look like I've doused you with ice water."

"I'm good. What's wrong with Talia, Jasper?" Talia does appear to be in somewhat of a trance. She hasn't looked away from Jasper at all this whole time, not even when Trent's chair fell to the floor.

"Nothing is wrong with Talia. She's perfect. She was just very agitated when we came inside, and she's starving."

"No offense, baby," Devon says, "but I'm going to need her to tell me that."

Jasper nods, turning his gaze back to Talia, and stops making that sound. "Talia?" he gently calls and strokes down her jaw, "Devon needs to know if you're alright." He strokes her jaw twice more before she shakes her head and pulls away from him so violently that she falls to the floor.

When she stands up, she is seething with anger. She slaps Jasper faster than we can jump to stop her, causing his head to snap to the side. This is the first time she has ever been remotely aggressive toward him. "Don't ever do that shit again" she snarls then stomps out of the room.

If everyone was under a spell of calm before, they are dumbfounded by shock now. "She slapped me. I was just helping her calm down." He looks just as bewildered as the rest of us.

"What was that noise you were making?" I ask him. "Can you make it again?"

He shrugs, "I think it's just for her. I've never done it before."

"Yeah," Alex says, taking a bite of food, "I definitely wouldn't do that again."

Jasper looks down his nose at Alex. "I'll do it again if I need to."

Alex smiles and takes another bite. "Oh peaches, I hope you do. I can't wait to see what happens."

Chapter Nineteen

Talia

What the hell was that sound Jasper was making? I remember coming inside the house angry because Corso made me come in, even more so because some assholes were shooting guns in the middle of the night when Jasper and I had just come off our heat. Then he started making that strange growly purr noise and the next thing I know I've got a mouthful of stew and Jasper's petting my face. Whatever he did took me completely out of it long enough that the alphas had time to come inside and start eating. I don't even remember setting the fucking table.

There's a soft knock on my door. Fuck the mostly open door policy in this pack, I locked it right after I slammed it shut. I locked the door on my side of the bathroom, too. I know it won't do a thing to actually keep any of them out, but it makes me feel better. The soft taps sound again and I huff out a breath. It better not be Jasper. I'm going to be pissed at him for a while longer.

"Talia," Kaleb calls, "I just want to check on you. You don't have to open the door. I'd just really appreciate it if you'd let me know that you're alright."

I remind myself that I'm not angry with Kaleb and I unlock the door to let him inside. "I'm fine. Just pissed."

"Yes," he hums, "you certainly are. But do you feel alright?"

"I'm fine, Kaleb. What was that sound he was making? It feels like when Alex made me sit, except worse." I sit down on the edge of my bed, but then stand up again almost immediately. I'm too upset to sit.

"I don't know, cupcake. I've never heard him make it before. It did have a similar effect on you as an alpha command would. Is that what you meant? When did Alex tell you to sit?"

"When Devon was in the hospital. I needed to know what it would be like for me now that I'm an omega. It was just a teaching moment. What Jasper did wasn't teaching me anything. He took control of me." Oh no. I think I might cry. Jasper actually took me away from myself with that sound, I don't know how long I sat on his lap letting him shovel stew into my mouth. My stomach is almost overly full of food. I might cry while I throw up.

"He did. I don't think he knew he was doing it. He's never made that sound before tonight. That being said," he pauses and takes a breath and gives me a look, "he doesn't feel overly bad about it. It's the wrong time to laugh, but I think it's funny that he knows how it feels for us. To know exactly what to do to help our omegas but also know better than to do it."

"I guess that is funny," I concede, "I just don't want him to do that again."

"Do you think you'll be angry with him for very long?"

I blow out a breath, "no. But I am angry right now. And I might be pissy for a few days. That's not what I wanted. I wanted cuddles and horrible movies and shitty food."

He grabs my hand when I pace past him and pulls me into his arms. "You can still have those things. Do you really feel alright? Not sick or anything?"

"Why are you so worried, Kaleb? Why would I be sick?"

His hand drifts down to my stomach and he holds it there.

Oh.

Oooooohhhhhhhh.

"You can tell already? I thought it would be a little longer before we'd know."

"We can smell the difference. I will personally try to keep my smothering to a minimum. I know you don't like it. I think the only ones who might not give you room to turn your head are Trent and Devon. Trent is already anxious, and Devon has a difficult time handling things that he has no control over. They may be a bit...intrusive."

"You mean obnoxious," I sigh. "I can't complain, though. If I was in their position I'd be a nervous wreck. I'd check on my omega every few minutes and probably drive her insane."

He chuckles and kisses my forehead. "Are you happy, cupcake? Saying you want things and getting them are sometimes two different things."

I take the time to think about that. I don't feel pregnant, not yet. But if Kaleb says he can tell a difference in my scent then I believe him. I tick through the next thirty weeks. That's roughly seven heats I will not be having while I'm pregnant, then another twelve to twenty that I shouldn't have while I'm nursing the baby. And I get to hold him and watch him grow and be loved while I enjoy my alphas and Jasper without any of it being ruined by a heat cycle every few weeks. I'm fucking fantastic.

"I'm happy. I'm going to get fat, though."

"God, I hope you do. You're beautiful as you are, always, but with a little belly, then breasts full with milk, and the extra weight you'll need to put on..." he trails off and I feel his hand twist between us to adjust himself.

"Pervert," I giggle. "You say that now, but when I'm big as a house and trying to ride you, you'll – "

He covers my mouth and growls into my ear. "Don't say it. You really are exhausted and my cock has been fucked raw. If I let myself think too long about that scenario it will lead to worse conditions."

~

I am significantly less excited three weeks later. I am sick as fuck. I can't keep anything down. I want to cry every four fucking minutes. And every breath anyone takes pisses me off. Nothing is clean enough, but I can't clean for longer than about ten minutes before I'm sprinting to a bathroom to puke. Alex says I should just carry a bucket around with me, but I already feel so disgusting that carrying a bucket of vomit around everywhere I go is more than I can tolerate even thinking about.

And Nathan and Trent keep having to leave. They're working closely with my fathers to find the omegas, which should be a good thing. But I hate it. I want them home with me where I can see them. Corso, Reid, and Devon are spending most mornings at the distillery, too. I hate it all. I'm glad Jasper, Alex and Kaleb are at home so much, but I'd feel so much better if everyone was here.

"How about some chili fries?" Kaleb asks as he comes into the kitchen carrying a paper bag.

My mouth waters in the worst possible way. I can't even eat chili fries. And now I'm going to goddamned cry again. Over fucking chili fries.

"Shit," Kaleb says and goes to throw the bag in the garbage. "I thought you might be able to eat them. I'm sorry, cupcake."

"No! Don't waste them," I sniff, "Devon will like them."

"Okay, honey. We'll save them for Devon." He reaches into a cabinet and pulls out a plastic container big enough to put the entire bag in and puts it in the fridge.

"I know it's just temporary, but I can't wait until this part is over. I'm sick of being hungry and sick of being sick. And I've never cried so much over so little in my whole fucking life. It's ridiculous." I wipe my eyes and go back to folding the basket of laundry on the table.

Kaleb sits at the table across from me. He knows better than to try to help fold anything at this point, but he still eyes the basket like he wants to. Occasionally I'll give him a pile of washcloths or dish towels to fold, or the rare basket of socks to help pair, but that's the extent of the help I want from any of them with the laundry. The only reason I let Jasper help is because we need it to be done exactly the same way and he's the only one I trust to do it right.

"Your mother called again," he says very carefully.

My mother. She has called every other day since I came out of heat. Nobody has told her anything, but she is being extremely tenacious. "I'll text her later. Thank you for being a buffer."

"When are you going to tell her?" Kaleb asks, again very carefully. "We can't tell anyone else until she knows. There isn't a universe in which Elizabet would keep that quiet. And I know Devon wants to tell his father."

"I know, Kaleb. I'm sorry. I just want to wait until after Obi does the first scan."

"You've told Obi, then?"

I bite my lip. "Not yet. I've been putting it off. I don't want Jamison to weasel it out of him. I'll tell him in a couple weeks. I just want to be a little less sick. Is that okay?"

"Talia, anything you want to do is okay. Of course we want to tell our parents, but we won't until you're ready to tell yours. If you never want to tell them and we just show up somewhere with a baby in tow and that's how everyone finds out, that's alright, too."

"Thank you, Kaleb." I fucking hate crying and am so glad that his idea makes me want to laugh instead.

"I know," he taps the table. "Would you like to walk down to the distillery and take Devon and the others some lunch? He texted to let me know they were going to be a little later in the afternoon coming home. It's so much cooler outside, you may even need a sweater."

I nod my head, "I'll make up some sandwiches and things as soon as I finish this laundry."

The walk to the distillery is glorious. Kaleb was right, the days are getting much cooler. It's almost chilly, and I'm glad I tied one of Trent's flannel shirts around my waist before we left. Jasper and Alex came, too. This is the best I've felt in days. The only things missing are Nathan and Trent. I have two of Nathan's hair ties on my wrist, it makes me feel better to bring them to my nose when I start missing them too much.

"They'll be home soon, sweet pea," Alex says and takes the basket of food from me. "We should get some cows."

Jasper tosses a rock into the field on the right side of the narrow road. "Why would we want cows, Alex?"

"Because burgers are delicious, peaches," Alex answers. "Besides, they're fun to look at. Aren't they sweet pea?"

"I don't think we'd enjoy taking care of cows, Alex. I definitely do not want to clean up after them," I tell him, "but they would look pretty grazing."

"But the smell!" Jasper argues and picks up another rock. It goes on like that, discussing why cows would be a disaster, and why any other farm animal would be just as awful, until we get to the distillery.

Reid is at the front entryway when we get there and he leads us back to the meeting room across the hall from Corso's office. Corso and Devon walk in, wiping their hands on cloths and talking about something regarding one of the stills. They both give me kisses on the cheek and Devon drops a kiss on Jasper's cheek before perching on one of the rolling chairs around the huge table. "How are you feeling this afternoon?"

"I'm good. Alex wants cows." Then the livestock debate starts all over again and Devon laughs the entire time.

"I would rather not have cows, or any other farm animals, if that's alright with everyone," Corso says at the end of it. "Thank you for bringing lunch today. I didn't realize how much I needed to see all of you until you got here. My day has greatly improved."

"Mine, too." Devon agrees. It's time to go back home. It feels like we only just got here. I know they have work, and there is literally nothing I can do here but get in the way, but it feels horrible to leave them. There's nothing for it, though. They have work to do, and we need to go so they can do it.

Trent and Nathan get home right before dinner. Trent is adamant that they are not to be late for dinner. Ever. He has ruled that dinner is our sacred time together as a pack and has a complete pout if anyone Missus it or is late. He also added an additional movie night to the week, wherein he or I chose the movie. He says Jasper can keep up the awful junk he calls quality cinema on his night, but on our night we'll watch action movies or the occasional romantic comedy. I told him not to bother with the latter for my sake, but action movies are great. The more explosions the better.

Things settle down into a fairly decent pattern for a few weeks, and the longer it goes on like that the better I feel; both physically and emotionally. I don't know what feeling like an omega is supposed to be like, but I am beginning to enjoy being pregnant. I didn't think I'd actually enjoy being pregnant, I just knew I'd enjoy the relief of not worrying over a heat cycle every time I turn around. And I have the smallest, little bump above my pubic bone. Devon made that discovery when he had me spread out on his bed this morning. He was smoothing his hand down my stomach on his way to my pussy and stilled the moment his palm slid over the bump. Of course, he immediately called for Jasper and Corso and they were equally happy about it. So happy that I got a round with all three of them before lunch.

That is something, though. I am trading in constant sickness and emotional and physical exhaustion for an intense increase in my sex drive. My breasts and pussy feel so swollen and sensitive, I need to seek relief several times a day, from either my pack or my own hands. It's still better than losing my mind to heat. The only problem is that every time I think about it, or notice how long I've been able to go without needing to cum, I immediately need to cum. I don't know if it's something worth complaining about, though. Especially when it's such an easy fix.

Jasper is on his bed reading a book. Sometimes I feel guilty for interrupting his reading, but most of the time I don't mind because he doesn't mind. He smiles at me when I enter the room. "How's my girl?" I push my pajama pants off and crawl between his legs to start undoing his pants. I think the sound of a zipper being dragged down is one of my favorites. "I see," he says and puts his book on the nightstand. "Tell me what you need from me, sweet girl."

"Make me cum, Jasper. I don't care how."

"I want to taste you. I want to make you cum with my mouth until you're begging for my cock."

I moan the word please and let him position me over him backwards with my calves tucked under his shoulders. "You can take out my cock, baby. But we're making you cum right now, not me. Maybe if you're good you can help me get off after, or maybe you'd like to watch Kaleb fuck me while you play with your pretty little pussy? How would that be?"

"Fuck, Jasper. Yes. All of it." He said I could get out his cock, so I do. He's already hard and starting to leak. I lick the head, and groan as the taste of him spreads across my tongue.

"Careful, Talia. Just lick it, we don't want to get too carried away. It would be terrible if you made me cum and we didn't get to do all those other fun things. Wouldn't Kaleb be disappointed if he didn't get to fuck me while he watches you work yourself over? He'd be so sad to miss that."

"So sad," I agree and give him another lick. Then I'm moaning as he drags his tongue from my clit to my entrance and back. He swirls his tongue around my clit in slow circles and makes an absolutely delightful sound against me when I do the same to the head of his cock. We tease each other like that for entirely too long, with gentle licks and him sucking bits of me between his lips until I've had enough. I was already needy when I came in here, now I'm ravenous. "Jasper," I say with my lips against him, "I need more than this."

"I know," he purrs, "such a needy, achy girl. Here, is this better?" I whine when his mouth leaves me, but the whine turns to a groan as he thrusts his fingers inside me.

"Again, please, again," I hiss, and he gives me what I need. He's fucking me so hard with his fingers that I'm rocking on my hands and knees. It feels so good, the orgasm I desperately need is finally starting to crawl through me.

Jasper pushes his fingers inside me and leaves them there, like he did the first time he ever touched me. "You're so wet, Talia. You're dripping down your thighs and onto my chest." I'm right on the brink of cumming and he's torturing me.

"Jasper," I gasp, "if you don't keep going I'm going to bite you."

"So mean, so bossy," he teases, and presses his fingertips into that place inside me that makes my eyes roll back, over and over again. I want to suck every bit of him right down my throat, but I don't trust myself not to bite him. "You ready to cum for me, baby? I'm working so hard for it."

"Yes," I gasp, "almost, almost." I swipe my tongue across his cock to collect the big drops of precum gathered at the tip, then I take him completely into my mouth and he grunts in pleasure.

"Hurry, baby. Don't make me finish before you do."

I pull my mouth off of him almost violently, "don't you dare! You said Kaleb!" I can't even form the full complaint.

"Then be good and do what I say. You're almost there, cupcake." Then he goes back to fucking and twisting his fingers inside me. It doesn't take long for him to push me over the edge, and he laughs at me when I cry out Kaleb's name instead of his.

Kaleb comes into the room with a smirk all over his face and leans a hip against Jasper's dresser. "You need something, sweetheart?"

I crawl away from Jasper to sit on the foot of the bed and point back at him to tell Kaleb what Jasper signed him up for. "He said I could watch you fuck him while I get myself off?"

Kaleb's eyes slide to Jasper. "Did he, now?"

"He did," I confirm, and get up to move over to sit on Jasper's desk.

"Did he say when?" Kaleb asks, crossing his arms over his chest.

I shake my head. "He didn't. But I vote for now."

He smiles at me and takes off his shirt. "If you want a show now, cupcake, I'm happy to give you one."

Chapter Twenty

Jasper

I'm getting more used to Elizabet Graves having a permanent and glaring presence in my life. The pedestal I had her on is slowly transforming into a more normal throne, but if she keeps upsetting Talia I will have no trouble giving her a cracked stool on the porch. She's in the main room right now with all four of Talia's fathers, sitting on the couch and demanding Talia's presence. Talia wasn't quite ready to tell her mother that she's pregnant, no matter that we're almost at the halfway point; and now it looks like she's going to have to because it is going to be very obvious the second she walks down those stairs. Her little bump is less little by the day and her already delicious scent is twice as sweet with her pregnancy.

"If she isn't feeling well, I can just go up to her room to speak with her. There's no need for her to come down. She's so rarely ill that I'd like to look in on her, anyway."

"No, no, that's unnecessary," Reid says, "she'll be down in just a moment. She just wanted to change her clothes. She was meal prepping for the freezer this morning. We're trying to prepare for next week." He thankfully doesn't mention that I'm due for my next heat next week and I say another prayer to anybody who might be listening that I won't have a spike while she's here.

The air goes as sour as Elizabet's face, which is something Talia has definitely inherited. "That doesn't sound like my daughter at all. Talia doesn't, and has never, given a single shit about what outfit choice is the most fitting for an occasion. She has a minute to be down those stairs before I go up them. Something is wrong, you're all hiding it, and I've had enough."

"My apologies, Elizabet. I mean no disrespect, but I cannot allow that to happen. Talia will be down when she's ready," Corso says very cooly, then to Reid he adds, "please go check that she's alright. If she doesn't want to come down she doesn't have to."

Elizabet's ability to chill a room with her anger is another trait Talia inherited. Reid is two steps up the stairs when a door creaks open upstairs and Talia calls out, "I'm coming. Just give me a minute, for fuck sake."

"You've had forty-five, my darling. Kindly bring your ass down the stairs before your mother starts setting things on fire," Marcus laughs. I really like him.

Talia trots down the stairs and kisses first Reid, then Corso before coming to stand beside the chair I'm sitting in. Everything is quiet for a few seconds, then Elizabet jumps up from the couch laughing and shouting and crying, "I knew it! I just knew it! Oh! How wonderful! Are you alright, sweetheart? Do you need anything? How far along are you? Fifteen, eighteen weeks? And the nursery! Have you started the nursery? Can I see it?"

"Jesus fuck. Take a breath, mother. Please." Talia takes her own breath and starts answering questions. "I feel great, really great. I thought I was dying for the first few weeks, but now I'm good. I don't know if I need anything or not, I assume I don't. I'm only eleven weeks in. We haven't started the nursery because I can't decide where I want it to go. I have two nests, though; one in Corso's room and one in Nathan's. You and Jasper can decorate the shit out of it once I figure out exactly where it will be, there are two rooms upstairs to choose from. Or I can remodel that ridiculous closet."

When Talia says she's only eleven weeks along Elizabet's eyes drop to her stomach and stay there. She reaches over and puts her hand in Alpha Reyes's. "Eleven weeks? Are you certain?"

"Yes, mother," Talia sighs so deeply even I can hear the eye roll contained in it. "It happened during my, our, last heat."

"Our?" Elizabet sits back down, "Talia? Our?"

Talia looks at me with her brows drawn together. I shrug. I don't understand Elizabet's reaction any more than she does.

"Yes. Our. Jasper and I had a synced heat almost twelve weeks ago. You knew that. What is the problem? Why are you so upset? I thought you'd be happy about me being pregnant. You've been thrilled with all the other omega developments."

Trent stalks across the room and wraps his arms around Talia. I can feel anger crackling off of him despite the purr he's trying to use to calm Talia. "Why is this a problem? What could be awful about our pack having a baby that it requires upsetting Talia like this?"

"They don't know my love," Alpha Smith says softly. "There's no way for them to know."

"Know fucking what, Thaddeus?" Devon barks. "She's afraid and angry, and that's unacceptable. Tell us what we need to know before things get any more disrespectful."

Marcus laughs again. "Oh, Talia, dear. I cannot imagine you with another pack. I was worried for a while, but this is the best thing that could have happened. Elizabet, my darling, my love, I know you're upset, and you were hoping it wouldn't happen, but they need to know everything. All of it. Nathan, do you have tea here? The good omega stuff? I know there's booze in the cabinets. Can we get some things started in the kitchen while my love collects herself? She has a lot of things to share and most of them are shit."

Marcus and Nathan go to the kitchen for whatever they'll come back with, and Elizabet starts apologizing. "I'm sorry, Talia, Jasper, all of you. I am happy. So very happy. I'm just also very nervous. Did you...is there a chance that the baby is biologically Jasper's?"

"The baby is absolutely biologically Jasper's," Talia drops that bombshell in retaliation to her mother's hedging. Her hands are covering the swell of her stomach, and one of Trent's hands is covering hers.

"Oh." Elizabet says, and looks down at her lap. Her worry is so thick we can all smell it.

Thaddeus knocks on the table. "We're not worried about the baby being alright, kids. She's likely to be the healthiest baby to ever cry."

"He," Talia quietly corrects.

Alpha Colton smiles. "Whatever you have in there is going to be perfect, there's no doubt about that, honey."

"And you really feel alright? Nothing strange?" Elizabet asks.

Worry and irritation is thick in the atmosphere, but Talia answers, "I feel fine. I'm finally able to keep food down, and I can do more than sleep and cry. Things are good."

"And they're taking good care of you?"

"Of course we're taking care of her. We learned from our mistakes, and we're going to continue making up for them. And if you have any doubts about us, Corso, Reid, and Alex are here to keep us in check." Kaleb is losing his patience faster than Talia and Devon, and that's saying something.

Corso unfolds from the wall he was leaning against and sits on the couch, right beside Alpha Colton. Corso, as always, exudes a level of calm that most people could never reach. "Talia's mother meant no offense, mio fratello. She's only very, very concerned. Everyone here knows that Talia would never have accepted your marks if she didn't think you would care for her." He's so smooth that I'm not sure anyone but Talia and I realize exactly how offended Corso really is. He may have far more patience with Talia's parents than Kaleb does, but he isn't any more tolerant than Kaleb. And he is incredibly protective of both Talia and our pack.

"Back with tea!" Marcus chirps, pushing an honest to god tea cart. It's absurd. So absurd that I can't stop a snort.

"Why in the world do we have a tea tray?" I laugh.

"It came with the house," Alex says as he pours three cups of 'that omega stuff' and stirs a heavy spoonful of honey into each before he distributes them to Talia, Elizabet, and me. I feel a little silly drinking tea when the other men in the room are drinking beers, but I'm a week away from my next heat and I actually need the tea.

"Now," Talia says over her cup, "spill it. Why are you so upset that I'm having a baby with Jasper?"

Elizabet takes a steadying breath and begins. "I was only twenty-seven when I took over the institute. There was so much work that needed to be done, we had to physically gut the building. After most of the work was finished, I did a final walk through to make sure nothing was missed before the crews left out. In the basement I found a little locked door that everyone assumed was to access the pipes, or something. I didn't give it a second thought the first few times I passed it. I don't know why I felt the need to open it during that walk through, but I did. I found boxes and boxes of old files and paperwork. Lots of pictures. And an overwhelming number of charts. I was curious and started going through it. It took me three weeks of solid combing and organizing to come to understand what it was all about."

She takes a sip of her tea and gives Talia a tight smile before she continues. "All the files belonged to a Doctor Gordon Cabbott. He was a geneticist, and an omega. I won't get into all the details of the files, it's all very tedious; but long story short, Doctor Cabbott was researching the origin of the decline of the omega population. What I read was disturbing, and somewhat disgusting. Many generations ago, the omegas were so much more plentiful than today. There were never a large number of male omegas, but there were significantly more than there are now. The packs were different, as well. They were larger. It was almost always a collection of several alphas and betas clustered around a pair or sometimes a trio of omegas. Not every pack had a male and female omega, some only had females, but it was almost always a large pack and more than one omega. There were omega-omega pairings that resulted in omega-omega offspring. With that number of reproducing omega pairs, the population of omegas was growing steadily. The reigning alphas at the time became threatened by the increasing numbers of omegas and started putting out propaganda about omega-omega children being prone to disease, that they were weak and would weaken the population as a whole. They started openly discouraging omega-omega pairings, even going so far as to forcefully separate packs.

"It became taboo to have more than one omega, and socially forbidden to have a male and female omega in the same pack. Right about that time, there was a dramatic decrease in what we call true mates. Doctor Cabbott hypothesized that there were fewer mated pairs because there were fewer omegas. He thought that the ability for us to have a true mate was essentially being bred out of us all in the name of population control. But nature will always find a way, and-"

"Stop," Trent interrupts, "just wait a minute. That's all fine and good, but what does it have to do with now? You said yourself that was generations ago."

"How many packs have more than one omega, Trent?" Elizabet asks. "How many people do you know who have found their true mate? Have you ever seen or heard of an omega-omega reproducing pair in your entire lifetime?"

"No."

"Exactly. It's still taboo. And there are so few omegas that it's nearly impossible. Doctor Cabbott guessed that a perfect pack would consist of one male omega with one or two female omegas surrounded by five to seven alphas and however many betas that pack felt they could support. Not every child would be an omega because the male omega would only be able to impregnate a female during his heat."

Talia holds up her hand and stops Elizabet's explanation. "What do you mean, not every child? Why would that even be a concern?"

Elizabet smiles at me and pats Alpha Colton's knee. "This is probably what those alphas found the most unsettling. Doctor Cabbott found that male omega sperm are thousands of times more dominant than alpha sperm. That's why male omegas are able to impregnate female alphas, why they're able to produce so many omega offspring with beta females even though the alphas in their pack are also having sex with those same beta females. Even if you all didn't have implants, a tablespoon of Jasper's swimmers would out-swim gallons of your alphas' swimmers."

"Darling, please. Let's not include gallons of sperm in a conversation with our daughter," Thaddeus sighs.

Then Alex's obnoxiously loud laugh echoes off the walls. "So what you're saying," he says, "is that Jasper is the dominant species?"

"Yes."

Alex laughs again, like this is the best thing he's ever heard. "Absolutely fabulous. That might explain that sound you were making, peaches."

I drag my hand down my face. I was hoping nobody would bring that up. Talia was angry with me for days, and still gets prickly whenever someone mentions it.

"What sound?" Elizabet asks. "Can you make it again? What was happening when you made it?"

I groan and explain the whole thing. Elizabet is enthralled by the end of the summary.

"How did you feel when he was making the sound, all of you?" she asks my pack.

Reid answers for all of them. "Like we were under a spell. Warm, well, content. Quiet. Like he was big, bigger than all of us. Then we started to notice that Talia was completely lost in it and it scared us. Devon asked Jasper to pull her out of it so we could see if she was alright."

"It's because she's pregnant," Elizabet is working through the information and connecting things so fast that her eyes glaze over a little. "It was mentioned twice in Doctor Cabot's findings. The sound, he called it reverberation, affects the entire pack, but most strongly the female. It's something that other male mammals are able to do for their packs. He never made it before because he didn't have a pregnant mate to care for and protect. That means..." she smiles a little, "Alex is more right than he intended to be. Maybe you are the dominant male of our species."

"That's ridiculous," I scoff. "That's completely ridiculous. I can't even function when I'm in heat, let alone dominate anything; and I can hold my own well enough, but I'm shit without my pack. Anyway, someone would have publicized a study or something."

Elizabet deflates and folds her hands in her lap and says very solemnly, "Doctor Cabbottt tried. He was silenced."

"Silenced how?" Talia asks. "There is no mention of this in any of the history books. None of the training or workshops."

"When he presented his findings to the council they had him separated from his pack and jailed. He didn't live very long."

Talia puts one hand over her throat and another over her stomach. "What happened to his pack?"

"They were broken, but they had to manage because they had another omega to care for, a female. Doctor Cabbott found his mate during his research and studies, and they had a set of twin boys. There is no record of those boys other than the fact that they were born to that pack. They appear to have vanished alongside their mother just after Doctor Cabbott was taken."

Nathan comes over and stands at my other side. He rubs my back between my shoulder blades and says softly, "no more, Missus Graves, please. Talia and Jasper are at their limit. Can we see the doctor's findings? Do you still have them?"

"Of course, Nathan. I don't mean to be dramatic, but we need to discuss one more thing. This baby," she glances toward Talia, "is the first omega-omega baby that we know of in generations. There are still policies on the council's books that dictate that any omega-omega offspring be tagged, monitored, and tracked for the rest of their lives. The council, as a whole, would likely want to keep this baby as secret as possible to avoid the general public discovering that omega-omega offspring are generally more ge-netically stronger than their more common counterparts."

A growl rips out of Devon. "Our child will not be tagged. Or monitored. Or tracked."

"Of course not," Thaddeus says. "We've been working toward fixing this mess for years. We're sure there are more omega-omega children in the world, they're just afraid to come out into the open."

"Okay, enough. Really, that's enough," Nathan orders. "No more questions. No more anything. There are too many omegas in this house that are too anxious. I'm going to take two of them outside to put their feet in the grass. Elizabet, you're welcome to join us, but no more serious-talk. Talia, Jasper, let's go."

Nathan would never use an alpha command on us outright, outside of a dire situation, anyway, but there's just enough of an undercurrent of one in his voice that we both follow Nathan out the front door without another word.

"The ground is cold," Talia says blandly, but her toes are digging into the grass just as much as mine and Nathan's are.

"It's going to be alright, honey. I promise. The baby will be healthy. You're going to be just fine. We won't let anything happen to either of you."

She pulls him down for a kiss, "I know you won't. I'm glad you brought us out here. The grass does help."

I can feel Nathan's anxiety and worry more acutely than my own. Part of it is worry for Talia and the baby she's carrying, but a large portion of it is a trauma reaction to what happened at the compound. Nathan is so much better than he was, even his nightmares have dramatically decreased; but if either Talia or I get overly upset he's quick to try to help us get to a place of calm. I think he's so overattentive with us because he couldn't do anything to comfort the omegas at the compound.

Elizabet walks outside and leaves her shoes on the porch to come join us at the fountain. "Why aren't there fish in here?"

Nathan shrugs.

"Will you let Obi take care of you and the baby? Would you be uncomfortable with him helping you through the delivery?" Elizabet says and drags her toe across the top of Talia's foot.

Talia links her ankle around her mother's and says, "I wouldn't trust anybody else. Secret omega baby, or not. I'll call him in the morning."

"I didn't mean to upset you."

"It's alright, mother. You're upset, too. The grass helps."

Elizabet lays her head on Talia's shoulder and agrees. "It does."

I lean against Nathan and breathe him in for a moment, then I sigh, "I don't think male omegas are the dominant male of our species. I need my pack too much to be considered dominant. It has to be something else, like a form of population control. I only go into heat every twelve weeks, and I'm only reproductively potent during my heat. Talia goes every four to five weeks, and the alphas are potent all the time. It's just a control to keep the population balanced. That's all."

"Baby," Nathan kisses the top of my head, "alphas are selfish, prideful dicks. If the wrong one found out that his virility was threatened by a male omega he wouldn't like it. He'd feel threatened and do exactly what those old assholes did. You've said it a lot of times. Alphas are stupid and selfish and ruin perfectly wonderful things by trying to control them. I don't want to think about it, but I think you're right. Nature has its own way of controlling the population, and some douchey alpha felt threatened by a week of not being the strongest and has destroyed our balance. There are so few omegas now, and even fewer males."

"Hey," Talia says, reaching over to tug on Nathan's hair, "you are not selfish, prideful, or a dick. You are a good alpha, Nathan."

"And you're a good omega, cupcake. Try not to worry, okay? Nobody's getting their hands or eyeballs on our kid. We just won't tell anybody it's Jasper's until it's safe. That's shitty, but it's safe."

"He," Talia corrects.

"He," I repeat, "will be all of ours. I don't care if anybody ever knows he's biologically mine. He's our kid. That's all anybody needs to know."

Elizabet is smiling now, "I knew sending you to this pack was the right thing to do. I just knew it."

I don't see Talia's eye roll, but I feel it just the same.

Chapter Twenty-One

Alex

I did not expect Jasper's heat to affect me the way it has. I knew it would, obviously. He's an omega, of course his heat would affect me. I just thought that it was so intense last time because it was Talia, too. But this...this is completely different from what I expected. And, for all my banter and bullshit, I don't know that Jasper and I really want or need to take our relationship to the level that me climbing into his nest without a clear goal would elevate us to. I like Jasper. I might even adore his cute little ass; and it is cute. I definitely enjoy looking at him, no doubt. But enjoying the scenery and talking about it are not the same thing as taking a trip through the mountains.

Talia wouldn't mind. Jesus, she's basically encouraging it. Her hormones are wild right now. She's going in and out of the nest a few times a day. She needs to check in on him as much as he needs to see and smell her. Kaleb says this is a normal heat for Jasper, not like the synced heat where he was completely coherent the whole time. The waves seem to be hitting him harder this time, whereas during the synced heat Talia was battered while he was coasting above them.

Corso has steered completely clear of Jasper's room. Reid has been in and out of the nest due to the bond he has with Jasper. I asked him if it felt different than it did with Talia and he said, and I quote, "Jasper is a softer pull, but no less intense. His need calls to me at a different frequency". That makes perfect sense, and at the same time sounds like some high-quality bullshit.

"How much longer do you think he'll go?" I ask Talia when she comes out onto the porch and sits next to me on the swing.

"Two days, tops. He's over the worst of it. How are you handling it? Corso seems to be immune, for lack of a better word. Reid has a bond so he needs to be with him."

I set us to swinging before I answer. "My balls hurt and I want to fuck. I don't want Jasper to feel like I, as an alpha, don't want to care for him; but I want to care for him in different ways. And when I went in to check on him earlier he was more concerned with bitching at me for leaving you alone than my dick, so there's that."

Talia laughs at me. Laughs her ass off. "I can help with your poor balls, and we can definitely fuck. You and Jasper might eventually have a sexual relationship and you can fuck him, too. But in the meantime, he's happy the way things are. And I don't think helping him through a heat spike like you did is the same thing as helping him through his actual heat."

We listen to the swing creek and the crows yell for a while. The sun is shining and it isn't cold, but it's heading that way. The leaves have all changed to oranges and reds, and a lot of the trees are bare already. "I think it's time to bring the quilt back out for when we sit out here. Especially at night." That brings back memories from when she was here before. One of my favorite things was to get handsy underneath the big, thick quilt that we keep folded on the swing in the colder months. I liked the way the sounds I could get her to make echoed off the manor. If the others were out with us, it was a game to see how long I could play with her under the blanket before it was glaringly obvious.

"You just want to finger me on the porch. You don't need a blanket for that. I'll start wearing skirts, you know, just in case."

I pull a few strands of her hair and turn her so that she's leaning against my side and I have full access to the front of her body, which I take full advantage of. The first thing I do is reach under her sweatshirt, actually I think it's Trent's sweatshirt, and run my hands across her breasts. They're already swollen and sensitive, and her nipples are almost always drawn up into hardened peaks. "I love your tits. I can't wait to see them full of milk, and dripping."

"How very taboo, Alex."

I purr, fuck that's going to be so sexy. "It isn't as taboo as you think. I love the idea of seeing milk dripping from your nipples. I hope I get to taste it. Just a little."

"My sister says that her breasts leak milk like a goddamned faucet when she fucks her alphas. She says she has to wear a bra with pads every second or it's a huge fucking mess."

I'm going to have to stop wearing jeans altogether. If Talia starts leaking milk everywhere when I'm fucking her I don't think I'll be able to control myself. "No bras. I want to see it."

"You don't have to do the laundry," she gasps when I push my hand into the waistband of her leggings to rub her clit in little circles. It's swollen, too. And she's so wet. So wet all the time. It's almost torture to know she's walking around so puffy and soaked and needy.

"You like doing the laundry," I kiss her temple as her hips start moving with my fingers. "You know what else I was thinking about?"

"Hmm?"

"Remember when I said I could get you a strap and you could fuck Jasper?"

"Yes," she answers, but her eyes are closed, chasing the orgasm I'm slowly leading her towards.

I dip a finger inside her and bring it back to her clit, changing from circles to slow back and forth strokes. "Do you think he'd like that? I think I really want to see it."

"Don't stop, Alex, please," she sighs, and grabs hold of my wrist. "Just like that, fuck, that feels so good." She gets lost in her pleasure for a minute before she remembers to answer my question. "I think he'd like almost anything I did to him. Too bad I don't have one now, I could go give you a show."

Groaning into her hair, I push two fingers inside her and pump them in and out a few times, intending to keep building this until she cums all over my hand. Then I'm going to lean her over the banister and fuck her good and hard. I want to hear her cries bounce off the trees. But she suddenly jerks my hand out of her pants and stands up. "Come on. Let's go."

"What? Where? I had a plan. You're ruining my plan."

She smirks at me and says, "you can fuck me later, I'll definitely need you to. We're going to see exactly how much Jasper would enjoy me fucking him like that. It'll just be a visual, but it's going to be so fucking hot. And now's the perfect time because the guys aren't completely gone to rut. God, I can't wait to see how they react."

"Wait!" I call, but she's already through the door. "Wait a minute," I hiss, chasing her up the stairs. "Is this a bad idea during his heat? What if Devon or Kaleb get pissed off?"

"They won't. And if they do, you'll be right there to save me."

Well, at least she knows I'll protect her if this goes badly. I could stop it right now, but I'm enough of a pervert that I really want to see what happens. "Should we get Corso?"

"He went to the distillery this morning. We can take some pictures. He's the one who was ready to buy the harness, after all." Then she opens Jasper's bedroom door and steps inside.

Reid, Trent, and Nathan are laying along the sides of Jasper's nest resting. Kaleb is sitting in one corner drinking water, and Jasper has Devon on his back, stretched down the center of the nest. Jasper must be climbing up a heat spike because he's licking at Devon's cock like it's the best thing in the world. Hell, it might be. Talia went after Devon the exact same way.

"Raise your hand if you might be too far in rut to play with me," Talia chirps. Reid doesn't hesitate, his hand shoots up. Kaleb's hand fluctuates from being all the way up and half way up. Trent speaks for him and Nathan, "we're not in rut, but we're too tired right now to be of any use to you." He looks really disgusted about that fact, too.

"Devon?"

He looks at her for a few seconds, then back down to Jasper. "I'm not too far gone. I can be easy with you. Jasper? Talia's here."

"I know," Jasper purrs, and looks over his shoulder to eat Talia alive with his eyes. His pupils are so huge that there's hardly any green left in his eyes. "Take your clothes off. Come help me be a good omega."

She strips off her shirt, but that's it. "Did you know that Alex is a massive pervert?"

Trent laughs. "Yes. We're aware."

"Well," Talia toes off her shoes and starts slowly lowering her leggings, "did you know that Corso's just as bad?"

"Corso might be worse," Reid says, his eyes on every inch of skin Talia reveals.

"Did you know that I might be worse than any of you?"

Nathan lifts his head, and assesses her. She's just in her lacy gray panties. Her breasts are significantly larger than they were before and her nipples have gone from the rosy pink they were to a darker, dusky shade. "I have an idea. What are you getting at, cupcake?"

Talia crawls over the wall of pillows and into Jasper's nest and looks like she's going to join Jasper in making a meal of Devon, but she stops between Jasper's ankles. He's laid on his stomach, propped up on his elbows, with his legs spread out behind him. Talia runs her fingertips up the backs of his legs and very loudly whispers, "Corso offered to buy a harness so I could fuck you with that ridiculous toy Bianca gave me."

"Fuck yes. Go get it," Trent hisses.

"He hasn't gotten it yet," Talia bends down and licks the back of Jasper's knee, then keeps crawling up his body to press her bare torso against his back. "I wanted to know if Jasper would even want that. Why in the world would he want me to fuck him when he's got all of you?"

Then she rises to her knees and taps Jasper's hip twice, signaling him to get up on his hands and knees. I've seen him do it to her enough times. He gets into position without seeming to think about it. "Keep licking your alpha, Jasper. Be a good omega."

Oh my fuck. She's going to fucking dominate him.

AND I GET TO WATCH IT HAPPEN!

I might do a fucking cartwheel. Trent's eyes are about to pop out of his head, and Nathan is just smiling away.

"Reid, will you please sit with Kaleb? He might not understand." Talia strokes up the backs of Jasper's thighs again and he sighs around Devon's cock. Lucky fucker, he's going to have the best view of all of us.

"He understands," Devon purrs, "I promise he understands. Do *you* understand, Talia?"

She smiles, but Reid is who answers. "She understands."

I jerk my head to look at him and pull in a breath when I see his expression. Jasper might be the one in heat, but Reid is on fire.

"This," Devon slowly drags his eyes down Talia's body and across Jasper's, "will be the beginning of something. If we," he tips his chin toward Kaleb, "see this once, we'll want to see it again, and again, and again. My dick feels like it's going to explode right now and you haven't even gotten started. If you had that harness, would you want to fuck him?"

"I want to fuck Jasper every way I can, Devon. I've been jealous of you for months because you can fuck him in a way I can't. If Jasper wants me to fuck him the way you do, then I'm going to." She lightly places her hands on Jasper's hips, "it's just too bad this is only a visual experiment." Every one of us groans; me, Devon, Jasper, all of us.

"Do it. Fuck, I want it," Jasper whines.

Talia grins and leans over his body to wrap her arms around him and kiss his back. "Of course you do. You're such a rotten boy."

"Wait!" I yell. Yes, yell. "Wait a fucking minute. I want a better view. This was my fucking idea in the first place." I jump into the nest and sit my ass right behind Devon's head. "Continue."

Talia rolls her eyes. "You're as rotten as he is."

"You gonna fuck me, too, sweet pea?"

"Do you want me to?" She bats her eyes at me, and my dick twitches.

"Shit," I laugh, "maybe."

"Rotten," Talia smirks, then pushes up off Jasper. And with that, the show begins.

The combination of shit talking, moaning, and purring in here is dizzying; and I'm pretty sure most of it is involuntary. Well, the moaning and purring is, Talia knows exactly what she's saying and how it's affecting all of us. She's rubbing her palms over Jasper's ass and lower back while she thrusts her hips just enough to have him gently rocking back and forth on his knees. Every now and then she switches to a grinding motion that makes him whine and beg her to give her more of something she doesn't have. Yet. I'm getting her that harness, and a shiny new rubber dick to attach to it, in purple. Even if I just get to look at her wearing it, it'll be worth it. Fuck, she's so much fun.

Jasper is licking at Devon at irregular intervals, he's too caught up in the things Talia has been saying.

"You're so wet, Jasper. You're soaked all the way down to your knees. You must want a cock pretty badly." She drags her nails down his spine just hard enough to leave marks but not actual welts.

He nods his head and makes a sound that sounds like an agreement.

"So, wet for me, princess. You do want me to fuck you, don't you?"

He groans in response.

"You want to be fucked so bad, such a needy omega. You want it rough?" She grabs his hips and thrusts hard against him a couple times. "Or do you want me to be so easy, and take it nice and slow?" She goes back to the grinding motion, and he fists the blankets that make up the base of the nest as he whines.

I'm about to start whining, too. This is one of the hottest things I've seen, and she's just playing, just pretending.

"Hard. Need it hard. My dick's so hard. Can you touch it?" The scent of his slick is heavy and intoxicating. I'll bet he's leaking all over everything.

"Why would I do that?" Talia teases. "If I have to bend over to touch your dick then I won't be able to give our alphas this show. And that would be such a shame." She looks down at his ass and licks her lips, "I was right to be jealous. Seeing you from this angle is so fucking sexy."

Jesus, she looks like she really is fucking him. She's looking down at the exact place where she'd be fucking into him if she did have a cock and biting her bottom lip, she's imagining how it would be and doing a damn good job if the look on her face is any indication. What makes it even hotter is when she gives his ass a little slap every few thrusts. Yeah, I'm going to revisit this memory often.

Jasper's mouth is hovering over Devon, like he forgot what he was supposed to be doing. Talia going through the motions of fucking him from behind is probably more than enough to make him forget what he was supposed to be doing. It takes a minute, but when she notices she leans over him again and puts her hand into his curls, she pulls his head back just enough that Devon's cock is just out of reach. "You stopped pleasuring your alpha. That's a no-no, princess. I was going to reach around and jerk you off, but now... I don't know if I should."

Jasper makes a truly desperate sound and tries to lower his head.

Talia holds him firm. "It's too bad I don't have a way to really fuck you right now. You'd make the best sounds for me."

"Fuck," Devon grunts.

Jasper groans and rocks back against Talia.

I'm so fucking glad I moved up here, I can see everything happening so much better. Jasper's lips are swollen and pinker than their usual color, and his eyes are so dark and hooded. And Talia is so beautiful from this vantage point that it's hard to look at anything else.

"This won't do," Talia purrs. Then she taps Jasper's hip again and straightens back up, keeping her hand in his hair to pull him up with her. She looks up at Devon. "On your knees, alpha."

Devon obediently rises to his knees. Now she and Devon have Jasper between them in a mimicry of how Kaleb and I, then Kaleb and Jasper, had her during her last heat alone. "Open up, princess."

Devon isn't the only one who growls when he slides inside Jasper's mouth, and I'm not the only one palming my cock. I could probably fuck a hole through the floor right now.

"You need a knot, don't you, baby?" she says in a syrupy tone that goes straight to my balls. "You need a great big cock inside you, then a great big knot, don't you?"

Jasper moans an agreement.

"I know, maybe Kaleb could come fuck you. Then you can keep Devon in your mouth, and I can make you cum all over my hands. Would you like that?"

Jasper makes a sound that sounds like a sob and a growl. It goes straight to my balls, too.

"Jesus," Nathan whispers, "this is..."

"Hot as fuck," I offer. I look over in time to see Trent cup his balls and nod an agreement.

Kaleb comes over, his hand's tightening into fists at his sides over and over. Talia releases Jasper's hair and slides over to let Kaleb get into position. Then she sits beside Jasper and reaches under him and whatever she does has Jasper moaning and choking on Devon's dick. "Ready?" she asks, glancing at Kaleb. When he nods, she says, "Devon, Jasper, you."

"Got it," Kaleb puts his hand on Jasper's hip and pushes inside him.

Jasper's rough groan is cut short when Devon thrusts forward into his mouth.

Nope, I need a better view than Devon's ass. I crawl around and sit on the other side of Jasper's body. Front row seating for this debauchery.

"Sit on your hands, Alex," Talia says in that sugary tone. She and I may have to do a little exploring of our own if that tone is going to affect me this much. I do sit on my hands, though. "You can't see it, Jasper. But you're leaking a puddle underneath you. And you're so, so hard," she whispers.

I can tell from the way her shoulder is twisting that she's not just stroking his cock, she's milking it, just slowly coaxing the cum out of him. His stomach muscles are bunching and trembling, and the noise he's making when Devon lets him up for air...fuck. "I need you to do that to me, sweet pea."

"Only if you're very, very good." She's talking to me, but she's teasing Jasper. Between every word she gives him a downward stroke that causes his spine to bow.

"Easy, Talia. He's going to finish before Devon if you don't scale it back," Kaleb's voice is harsh. His expression is an exact copy of the face Talia was making when she was pretending before.

"Well, should we slow him down, or speed Devon up?"

Kaleb laughs, throws his head back and laughs right in the middle of pounding the sense out of Jasper. "Oh, cupcake, I like this. Speed Devon up."

"Asshole," Devon mutters, but it turns into a gasp pretty quick when Talia circles his balls.

"I know you're pretty far gone, princess, but listen. We're going to make Devon cum really fast. Can you hold his balls just like this?" He whimpers, but reaches up to do what she says. "Such a good boy. Now, pull down, just a little, every time I do."

Then she works Devon's knot in time with the down strokes she's giving Jasper, and it only takes a moment for Jasper to keep up good enough to have Devon's eyes rolling back in his head. "Fuck, fuck, fuck," he chants.

I'm so jealous, so unbelievably jealous. "I need you to do that to me, Talia. Will you? I'll be good, I promise." She smirks and shakes her head at me.

"Almost there, baby," Talia leans down to kiss Jasper's cheek while he's got his mouth full of Devon. The growl that tears out of Devon when he cums actually rattles the window. Motherfucking jealous.

Jasper jerks away from Devon and lowers himself onto his elbows. "Please, oh god, please."

Talia starts praising him, telling him what a good job he did, how gorgeous he looks, pleasing his alphas, all kinds of shit. She's using one hand on his cock and another on his balls, and he's making these strangled sobbing sounds. Kaleb grunts and changes his angle just a bit and Jasper's done. He's all but screaming as his stomach clenches almost violently with his release. I'm so caught up in Talia's soft praising and Jasper's hoarse groans that I don't notice Kaleb has Jasper knotted until he starts rearranging people.

Devon is the first to move; and Reid, who is too quiet for his own good, scares the shit out of me when he hands Talia a couple towels to put over the puddle of Jasper in the middle of the nest. Then Kaleb gets Jasper, who might be mostly a puddle himself at this point, onto his side in little spoon position. He reaches for Talia's hand and kisses her knuckles before he quietly starts in on Devon. "When this is over in a couple days, I'm going to take you out in the yard and we're going to have a go. Then we're going to let them," he points at Nathan and Trent, "have a go at us."

"Why are we having a fight?" Talia asks, her alarm obvious.

"Because, sweetheart," he says solemnly, "we could have had that all along. And instead, we let this asshole let us believe that we didn't fucking need you. And I backed him up. We were

202 THE BETA PART THREE

goddamned stupid, and we almost lost everything. You, him," he motions at Jasper, "everything. We deserve to have the shit kicked out of us."

"No one is kicking anything out of anyone, Kaleb. I won't have it," Talia kisses his cheek, and stands up. "Besides, if anybody gets to kick your asses Alex, Reid, and Corso should get shotgun. And that's not happening, either. Nobody in this pack is allowed to kick anybody else's ass. It would bother me too much."

"Notice," I shoot every one of them a smile, "that she didn't say you didn't deserve it. Just that it wasn't allowed."

She doesn't bother putting her shirt or leggings back on, but starts gathering empty water bottles and dishes to take to the kitchen. Then she walks out the door, calling over her shoulder, "come on, Alex. After that little show I need to be fucked."

"Yes, ma'am," I say and touch the back of my hand to Jasper's forehead before I stand up. Clammy, but I guess he earned it. I catch Trent's eye. "Extra water. He needs it. I'll bring some fruit up in a bit. And I'll kick all your asses if I want to, we just won't tell Talia."

"I'll tell her," Jasper grumbles, "then you'll be in trouble. You'll all be in trouble. No fighting. Fucking alphas."

Chapter Twenty-Two

Talia

"No."

"Absolutely not."

"Fuck that."

"Out of the question."

They all speak at once, and they all say the same thing. None of them want me to go to the facility where Seth is to see him. And I can't even argue with them about it. I wouldn't want me to go either. It's a stupid fucking idea. But that doesn't mean I don't feel like I should. Like we should. "I won't try to convince you that it's a good idea, because it isn't. But he stood with us. He helped us kill his pack. Regardless of the fact that they were utter bastards, they were still his pack. He severed those bonds, very fucking violently, to get us out. He's been in treatment for a few months. I want to go check in on him."

"It's reckless, bella. I can hardly tolerate you leaving the manor to go to the shops, or even be out on the lawn without us surrounding you. I know we're smothering you, but I don't think I can stand you going all that distance to visit with a man who hurt you so badly. And then we have to take it into consideration that you're fourteen weeks pregnant with our child. La mia bellezza, mia tesoro, be reasonable."

"I am being reasonable, Corso," I tuck his wavy brown hair behind his ear and sit down at my usual place at the table, "I'm not demanding to go. And I won't go if you say I can't. I'm not so stubborn that I'd fight to go when you all don't want me to. I also have no intention of going alone. I wouldn't feel safe unless you all were with me. I feel safe enough going to get groceries with just a few of you, but this is a completely different situation. I don't know, it just feels wrong to let him sit in a facility alone after he went through all that with us." I sigh and look down at the table.

Devon tips my chin right back up, "what did I tell you, cupcake? You don't look down for anybody, not even us. I don't want you to go anywhere near there or him. It's a horrible fucking idea, and it makes my stomach hurt. But I understand why you feel like we should. Would a phone call work?"

Maybe. I don't know. I feel like it would be better if he saw us. All of us. We aren't his pack, and we couldn't ever make up for that devastating loss, but we did fight alongside him.

"Don't chew your lip off, Talia. I don't think a phone call would cut it," Alex says. "I don't like that motherfucker, but he did help us get out of that shit hole, so I've called to check on him a couple times. If we're going to go there to see his awful ass, we need to do it before you're any farther along."

Reid stands up and folds his arms over his chest, glaring at me and Alex. "We are not going to that facility. Talia is not going any farther than town. And she is absolutely not going anywhere near Seth fucking Pratchett."

Jasper nods his agreement, but doesn't say anything.

The kitchen is apparently divided. Jasper is standing between Reid and Corso, with Trent and Kaleb leaning against the counter beside them. Nathan is sitting on the opposite counter, and Devon and Alex are sitting with me at the table. Nobody actually wants a visit to the facility, but there are varying degrees of *absolutely not* scattered around the room.

Nathan blows out a breath and says something completely un-expected. "We should go. All of us. I can't imagine being in his position. I thought...I thought Devon was dead, and they were killing Trent and Kaleb, and they had Jasper... It was so bad, but I still have all of you. He doesn't deserve it, but I don't know what I'd do if I was alone like that after everything. And he's really alone. The only people he has are his shitty father and his weak mother. I don't want to see him, and I sure as shit don't want Talia around him, but maybe we could go for a short visit. Like, in one of those meeting rooms with the big tables. Besides, I have a couple questions that only he can answer and I don't want to risk an interception."

"No, Nathan. You're too fucking nice for your own good. I don't want you there, either," Trent says.

I agree. I really don't want to risk Nathan having a setback.

"That's what makes this so stupid," I lay my head over my arms on the table, "I know exactly why we shouldn't go. I know why I shouldn't go. I don't want Nathan or Jasper there. But it just feels wrong to leave him there with no support at all. Like I said, I won't go if you say no, and I won't go off the rails and go anyway. That's not how we treat each other. I just wanted to talk about it."

"We can do a video conference. If the facility will allow it. That's the only compromise I'm willing to make. I won't agree to her going there, pregnant or not. And Seth doesn't even get to breathe near her." Kaleb has put his foot down. "Your questions will just have to wait, Nathan, I'm sorry. I never pull rank, not ever, but I don't want you near him, either. I don't think he's a threat, but he doesn't deserve your empathy."

Four days later we have that video conference. We set up Kaleb's phone on the porch banister so that nobody has a view of anything but the woods behind us. We're paranoid enough that we don't want anyone seeing the inside or the outside of the manor.

He looks horrible. Gaunt. Dull. Pale. And the white, very-medical, eye patch over his eye just makes everything worse. The first several minutes of the call are very awkward, with everyone on either side of the screen staring at each other without trying to stare at each other. It's ridiculous. "Aren't you eating?" I ask. I should have probably gone with something a little more polite, but Seth and I are a bit past polite.

"I eat." He sounds like shit, too; his deep voice reduced to a soft rasp.

"You look like you don't. Do you sleep?"

"No."

A guard walks behind his chair to the other side of the room and I can tell Seth's fighting the urge to turn around and watch him. That was a shitty thing for the guard to do. He's not there as a prisoner, he's there to get the help he needs to overcome the shit he's been through. "Are all the guards there like that prick?" I ask, and he smiles a little, letting his eye finally drop to my stomach. You can definitely make out the swell, but it isn't horribly obvious in this sweater. The second he sees it, his face falls and his eye shoots to Kaleb.

"Can you get Talia a chair? She looks a little upset to be on a call with me. That's understandable, but will you please help her sit down? You guys are outside, maybe there's a blanket or a coat she could put on?"

"I'm not-" I start to argue, but Seth cuts me off.

"Please, Talia. I feel bad enough already. Just sit down, or go inside. I don't want you getting sick just to talk to me."

This is weird as fuck. Since when does Seth care so much about me getting sick? Strange as it is, I still sit in the chair when Kaleb puts one behind me. And I'd be a liar if I said having someone tuck a thick quilt around you when it's chilly outside didn't feel amazing. "Thank you, Kaleb," I say, and fight off a giggle when he kisses the tip of my nose.

"There," I go back to Seth, "I'm sat and snug. Now tell me why they're treating you like a prisoner instead of a patient."

He tries to smile, but it falls flat. "Some of the doctors here are great. I do counseling a few times a week, and I have a psychiatrist that listens to me bitch and moan twice a week. They even do scent therapy."

"That sounds fucking horrible. What the hell is with them and scent therapy?" I don't care if they can see and hear my distaste.

He explains it, but it still sounds horrible, and useless. It also reminds me too much of when nurse fuck-off put that box of bullshit on my bed when I was in the hospital. "That's not going to help anything. You need to eat. And sleep. Has anybody been by to see you?"

"Dad came by. We had a good talk. He apologized for so many things. I think it'll be okay, eventually. He said he tried to apologize to you, but Devon wouldn't let him."

"No, I fucking didn't," Devon says. "One look at him and she had a goddamned panic attack and that's your fault too, you piece of shit."

"Devon. Don't," I hiss, but he continues.

"Listen, I know you've had horrible shit thrown at you. But fuck you and your father. Do you know what he was saying to her at that auction? He was accusing her of going after her dad and her brother. And he goddamned knew what he was saying. He wanted to hurt her anyway he could."

"I'm sorry," Seth says softly.

"You can't apologize for your father's shit, Pratchett."

"No offense, Johnson, but I wasn't apologizing to you. I was apologizing to Talia. And I hope she never forgives me. I don't deserve it."

"Seth," I start, but he holds up his hand to stop me.

"I'm going to apologize to you every time I see you, Talia. Whether you want to hear it or not. I can't make up for it, all I can do is say I'm sorry. It's never going to be good enough."

"That's not why we called, Seth. We, I, wanted to check on you. You need to know that you're not alone. You were with us at the compound, and that's worth something. I just wanted you to know that you're not alone." I don't know what else I can say to him.

"I'll be alright. Do me a favor though, okay? Stay home. Stay wherever the fuck you are. Jasper, too. Don't go anywhere without your pack. Listen, Devon, Kaleb, don't let them out of your sight."

"We don't plan on it. Eat more than you're eating. And get some fucking sleep. We'll check in on you again soon. We're going to get Talia and Jasper inside now," Kaleb says, and ends the call with Seth staring a hole in me.

"That was fucking bizarre," Alex scrubs his jaw. "He looks awful. And why would he have a guard instead of a nurse. And why did he freak out over Talia? Something stinks."

Nathan opens the door for all of us to file inside, but I don't miss him visually checking the places where we have cameras. "Now I have even more questions."

Later that night Devon comes into my room and sits down on my bed.

"Devon."

"Talia." He pulls my foot into his lap and starts rubbing it. It feels absolutely glorious.

"Did you come in here just to rub my foot, which I appreciate very much by the way; or is there something else?"

He lifts my foot up and kisses the inside of my ankle. I'm very slowly getting accustomed to Devon's affection. He is every bit as affectionate with me as he ever was and is with Jasper. It was awkward for me at first, but now I love it. "Why did you have such a strong reaction when Seth mentioned scent therapy? We all felt how repulsed you were. You don't have to tell me if it's too hard to talk about."

"Oh, it's not too hard for me to talk about. It's just awful. And they need to stop doing it. I can't imagine something like that actually helping someone. When I was in the hospital a nurse came in with a box of foul smelling clothes. She said they were scent samples of alphas who could potentially help me through my impending heat. It made me so sick. I thought I was going to puke all over the bed. I couldn't breathe through my nose for hours and I ended up needing to get new bedding and everything. I still don't understand how people can go around stinking like that. The staff wasn't thrilled with me. I was very uncooperative."

Devon kisses the top of my foot, "I'm sorry, Talia." I try to pull my foot back but he holds fast. "You shouldn't have been there." He kisses the sole. "You should have been home with us." He starts kissing my toes. I think I might kick him in the face if he doesn't stop. My emotional ass can't handle this.

"It's fine, Devon. It's over and done. I'm good."

He kisses another toe. "We should have gone after you. I was too stupid to realize what was happening until you were too far away for us to catch up. I'm so sorry, Talia." He kisses my big toe. "I hate myself for letting any of that happen to you. You will never go through that again. None of it."

"You're going to make me cry."

"Don't cry, pretty girl. You've done enough of that, too. Just let me take care of you. I have so much time and bad shit to make up for. Let me love you, Talia. I can love you so well, I promise."

He really is going to make me cry. Devon is as serious about his promises as I am. "I know you can, Devon. We're alright. You want to sleep with me tonight?"

"Just you and me?"

I nod. It's strange to think about, especially with all the sex and togetherness that happens in this pack, but Devon and I have never slept together without someone else with us. "Go shut the door."

"Really?"

"Yep."

I didn't think Devon could be or look bashful, but there he is at the foot of my bed being bashful. He kisses the top of my foot again and goes to close the door and turn off the light. He strips down to his boxers and I hold up the blankets for him to get in the bed with me. Devon is warm and smells like springtime, and he's a damn good cuddler. Jasper and Alex are octopuses, octopi?

What a weird fucking word. Either way, they cling to you with every arm and leg they have. Corso and Kaleb are good sturdy snugglers. They both like being little spoons. Trent is a cover hog, and Nathan is a starfish. Devon is the perfect combination of all of that and he doesn't even snore.

The next morning I am jolted from sleep by what feels like an invasion. It takes me an embarrassing amount of time to realize that it's the baby moving inside me. Up until that realization I thought I had some sort of horrific stomach plague. I definitely should get everybody in here, but if I yell or move, the baby might stop moving. Shit.

Devon is on his side, so I grab his hand and put it over my stomach where I feel the movement. He doesn't wake immediately so I pinch him, just a little, and tell him to shh when he starts to talk. I put my hand over his and whisper, barely louder than a breath, for him to hand me my phone. When he hands it to me I blow up the group chat, telling everybody to get in here right now, but be quiet about it.

Devon is still confused, he might even think something is really wrong, then the baby moves again and he sucks in a breath. It actually does feel like a kick from the inside, I always thought that was bullshit. How could something feel like a kick from the inside, especially if it was so small? But it really does feel like he's kicking me. I look back at Devon to make sure he can feel it, too. He's looking back at me with this dopey grin and watery eyes. Then the other's start coming into the room, and we motion them over, emphasizing the need to be calm and quiet. They are all very concerned and confused, but then Corso notices mine and Devon's hands and he sits on the bed and spreads his hand beside ours. Jasper is next. It's just unfortunate that my stomach is still too small for everyone to touch at one time. It's okay, though, because the baby kicks again on the other side of my stomach this time, and Jasper claps a hand over his mouth to keep from shouting. Corso is openly crying when I meet his eyes, and I reach up to brush away his happy tears. Then they take turns trying to feel the baby moving around. I'm glad he's so active, it gave them all the chance to feel him moving around. The amount of pride and love flowing through my bond with all of them right now is overwhelming. I love it, but it's a lot.

I call Obi in the afternoon. After he finishes laughing at me, and Devon and the rest of them for getting implants put in just in time for me to get pregnant, he says he'll come by in the next few days to do a check up and a scan, and to bring by some equipment that will stay here until after the birth. He wants to know if I want a water birth. I would not. That sounds horrible and disgusting. I want to have my baby in the nest I'm building for us. It will be cozy and perfect. The main one will be in Corso's room where Jasper and I built our nest together; and I want to build another in Nathan's room where I like my own nest to be.

"I'll need to bring Jamie along for this, Talia. His baby sister is having a baby, after all. He gets to be an uncle again and you know how much he adores children."

"Okay. I'm sorry I asked you to sneak around so much. I can't wait for you guys to find your omega so you can have a bunch of kids. Jamison is going to be the best dad. You all are." And I mean that. My brother, Obi, Andrew, and Issac are all going to make wonderful fathers when the time comes.

"Does your mother know yet? Can I tell her? Oh my god, please let me tell her."

I laugh, "she already knows, but you get to tell Jamison. And I'll let you tell Daniel and Bianca if you want. Mother can handle the rest of them."

I thought he might wait until he got off the phone with me to tell him, but he goes straight to my brother and announces it. Whoops and whistles sound down the line as the entire pack gets the news.

"Congratulations, you hateful little brat. I feel sorry for the kid already with you as a mother." Jamison is always shouting, and always giving me a hard time. Maybe it's because he's losing his hearing in his old age. He is a few years older than Corso and Alex, and he's been on the wrong end of more than a few explosions, so it's a possibility. I'll tell him my theory about his senility next time I see him.

I hear the distinct sound of a smack in the background, then Isaac, who isn't my biological brother but who has been part of my family as an alpha in my brother's pack since I was a little girl, is putting Jamison in his place. "Oh shut up, Jamie. Talia is going to be a wonderful mother. I'm just glad Corso finally got what he's been wanting. Congratulations, little sister. I'm so happy for you."

"You always were my favorite, Isaac," I say sweetly, "I'll take you over Jamison any day. Where's Andrew?"

"Right here," he calls, "I'm so happy for you and your pack. I can't wait to start buying the most obnoxious toys the world has to offer." I do believe that Andrew is happy for us, but I also know how sad he is about his own pack's situation. They've tried for years to find the right omega for them, but nobody has been the right fit.

Any omega would be lucky as fuck to be with them. I have a working theory that they put so much effort into trying to make themselves out to be a great option that they lose track of what already makes them great. Jamison is also, as I said, loud, abrasive, full of shit most of the time. And Andrew is the exact polar opposite. Most of the young omegas at the meet and greets don't really know what to do with my brother's pack. It's very unfortunate.

~

Obi comes by with my brother and Isaac a few days later, just like he said. He didn't bring the big monitors that will stay here until the baby's born, just a small portable doppler that will confirm a healthy heartbeat. The only one of them who isn't watery-eyed right now as we're listening to the swooshy thunks coming out of the little speaker is Kaleb. Corso is openly crying, and Jamie isn't much better off.

"Everything looks good. Heartbeat is good, you're doing very well, measuring a little ahead, but everybody carries differently. You say you're eating enough, but I'm going to ask you to up your caloric intake since you're over the half-way point."

"Thank you, Obi. I'll try to eat more than I have been. When do you think you'll start bringing the other equipment in? How much room do I need to make?" I feel bad for taking over Corso's room, but I don't think he minds too much.

Obi shrugs a shoulder and starts putting his tools back into his bag. "Shouldn't need more than a corner. It's not all that much, and none of it will take up too much space. I'll be back in a few weeks with the larger machine to check the individual organs and things. Maybe try to see the sex of the baby if any of you are interested."

"I'm interested." Trent is staring at my stomach like it's a bomb.

It's hard not to laugh at him. He's so anxious. Intensely and comically anxious. "Trent, even if it's a girl, she'll be a tiny, small girl. There's nothing scary about that."

His eyebrows come very close to touching his hairline. "Talia. That's not helpful. *You* are a tiny small girl."

Alex snorts and pulls the hair tie off the end of my braid. "Fair point, Lancaster."

Chapter Twenty-Three

Trent

Nathan and I have been going to the nearest council building almost every day since Nathan got a line on those omegas. I'm tired of this shit. I'm tired of looking at computer monitors and asking questions and carrying boxes of disks and notebooks and whatever the hell else is in them. I want to be home. With Talia. I'm so jealous of Kaleb it isn't funny. He doesn't rub it in, or anything, but it's still hard not to resent him. Just a little.

I don't think I could take better care of Talia than he is, and fuck knows Jasper's all over her. I just feel like I should be home with her. I think we should all be there. Every second of the day. She'd hate that, though. She already feels like she's tripping over all of us half the time. She's patient with our questions and checking on her, and she's been very good about letting us help her do stuff. I just, I don't know, feel like I need to be there. And I miss Jasper, too. I miss going on a job every few weeks and being left alone most of the time otherwise. This shit of having to work with and look at these old fuckers everyday is getting tedious.

."You're sighing," Nathan looks up from his current screen, "a lot."

"Sorry. How much longer?"

Nathan looks back at the screen and drags his hand down his face. "Just a bit. You know how we thought Alpha Pratchett was in Alpha Crane's pocket? Well, if I'm understanding everything, Alpha Pratchett isn't very high up on the food chain. Jay and

Derrick were obviously plants, soldiers even, but there's no family records for either of them, not real ones anyway. Look at this."

Please, god, be actual words instead of lines and numbers. When I look at the screen, it's split between Derrick's and Jay's d-reg. Everybody has a designation form they have to submit to the council in order to register their designation and pack status. They typically have a chart that goes back several generations so the council can keep track of how packs and families align themselves. It's a fancy way to be able to pull rank, if you ask me. It also shows a criminal background that goes back a couple generations. The strange thing about Derrick's and Jay's registration is that it only goes back one generation, and their maternal lines are not listed on the registry at all. "Where are their mother's?"

"Exactly. And then there's this," he clicks around for a moment then points to a number where the location of their birth's should be listed. "What the fuck is that?"

"I don't know, Nathan. It looks like something that is squarely in your department." I stare at the numbers for a minute, then it clicks. "Coordinates. Like when we used to do that geo-cache stuff when we were kids."

Nathan's eyes light up and he does more clicking and tapping, then he starts whisper-yelling. "Holy shit, Trent, you're right! That's exactly what it is. I forgot about that." More clicking, then more quiet cursing. "On the coast. A few hours away. In the wilds, nowhere near a residential area."

"Who'd be stupid enough to leave this big of a trail? I mean, you're amazing for finding it, but this is pretty obvious. Who signed off on their registration?"

He goes back to that screen and starts shaking his head. "No wonder it was so hard to get into his files. That firewall was intense, and then everything is written in half-assed code. I'm saving this. I want to print it, but I'd rather do it somewhere else. Give me your phone." I hand it to him and watch him take a picture of the registrations with both our phones, and then do the same with the screen showing the coordinate locations. "That way there's more than just my phone with it on there, back up, you know?"

I nod. When Nathan hands my phone back I scan the picture of the registration to see who signed off on it. "Fucking Crane? How many more are there like this?"

"We're going to find out right now. As much as we can, anyway. Getting through the firewall he had in place was like walking through knee-deep mud. If I have to do that again it's going to take a while. And I never would have realized what those numbers were if you hadn't been here. It would have driven me crazy. Marcus is going to shit."

I want to groan. No. I want to throw an entire fit. I want to throw computers and desks and filing cabinets out the fucking windows. I might even want to start throwing secretaries and clerks out windows. I want to go the hell home, not stay here and help Nathan do smart shit. I'm glad I was here to recognize the geo-cache thing, but now we're going to have to be here even longer.

"I'm calling Talia to find out what's for dinner. And I want to ask Jasper what snacks he wants for the movie." I don't care what Talia makes for dinner, I'll eat it and probably love it. And I don't care about the movie, I'm sure it's going to be just as awful as every other movie he puts on. I just want to talk to them.

"I'm sorry, Trent. I know you're done with this shit. Thank you for being here with me. I do better when you're here. It won't be long before we can do all this stuff from home. Half the point of being here is so Marcus and Thaddeus can see how the other council members react to what we're doing. Once we get the go-ahead, I can do almost all of the computer stuff from home."

"It's okay. I know we need to do all this. I just want to go home." I pull out my phone and dial Talia. I've actually noticed a shift in all of us in regard to who we call first, we meaning me and Nathan, Devon, Kaleb. Corso and the others were already there. I don't know exactly when it started, but when we call home, we call her.

Before, we would have called Jasper. When something is wrong, or I get anxious, I want both of them fucking immediately, but now I say Talia and Jasper more often than I say Jasper and Talia. I'd feel shitty about it, but Jasper's the same. He's changing, a little more every day. It sounds stupid, but it makes me think of how the planets rotate around the sun, not exactly, but kind of. We thought Jasper was the sun, until Talia came. Now it's like she's the sun, and he's constantly making tight loops around her, and we're making bigger, slower loops around both of them. He's at the center as much as she is, but it's her that keeps the grass growing, even for him. Maybe I'm about to have a nervous breakdown or a psychotic flip. Comparing us to planets or some shit. I'm ridiculous. What the fuck.

"Hey," Talia answers a little breathlessly. "Are you alright? What's wrong?"

"Nothing. I just wanted to check on you. Why are you out of breath? You're not supposed to be doing anything that would get you out of breath. Where's Kaleb and Alex?"

Her laugh is a little husky. "Liar. You're worked up about something. And Kaleb is right here. He's why I'm out of breath. I swear I think I need to fuck twelve times a day. Alex and Jasper went to the store to get a few things for dinner. Pepperoni and olives are involved, but it isn't pizza. You probably have time to catch them if you need them to grab anything for you." Of course she's talking about grocery store runs and dinner ingredients while she's fucking Kaleb. He's probably laughing his ass off.

"I was worked up, but I feel better now that I've talked to you. If you were a sweet girl, you'd send me a fun picture to tide me over till I get home."

"I'm not a sweet girl, but I'll still send you a picture. Where's Nathan?" I hear jostling, and Kaleb laughing. Then my phone buzzes with a notification. I lick my lips when I see the picture. She's perched on the kitchen counter, with bowls of stuff and spices on either side of her. She's wearing my blue flannel shirt, it's unbuttoned and her gorgeous tits are catching the light in the best way. Her little rounded stomach is clearly and beautifully visible, and just below that I can see her thighs spread wide around Kaleb's hips. I immediately forward it to Nathan.

"Damn, darlin, just make my life hard, why don't you? Can I get some of that when I get home?"

She giggles. God, I love when she giggles. I'll never get tired of hearing it. "You can have whatever you want when you get home. Do you feel better now?" Her words are cut short by a gasp, and I can hear Kaleb murmuring something in the background that makes her moan into my ear.

"I do. I'm going to get back to work rushing Nathan so we can get home faster."

"Wait! You send me a picture. I know your dick's hard right now."

I groan into the phone. My dick is hard, but I can't whip it out in the middle of a council office.

"Pretty please?"

Fuck it, yes I can. "I hope your dad comes in here and catches me taking a picture of my cock to send to his daughter. You're a terrible influence on me, Talia. Just awful." I undo my belt and pull down my zipper.

"Fuck, I love that sound." She's panting on her end, and I can hear the sound of Kaleb's body meeting hers. It just makes me that much harder, which is good for the picture I'm about to take.

"What sound, darlin?" I angle the phone down and take the picture of my hand wrapped tight around me, there's even a drop of precum on the head. She's going to love it.

She moans again, "the belt, the zipper."

Good to know. I'll definitely be using that to my advantage. Then she gasps. "That's a hot fucking picture, Trent. I might cum all over Kaleb's dick while I'm drooling over a picture of yours."

"I'm going to go now. I absolutely do not want your dad walking in here catching me jerking off while I'm on the phone with you.

You're mine when I get home, baby. See you in a little while." Then I end the call with more giggling coming from her end.

"I can't believe you took your dick out in the council building." Nathan can totally believe it, though. He just wants to sound like he's clutching his pearls.

I shrug and do up my pants. "She said pretty please. What else was I supposed to do?"

Nathan ends up finding twenty-four more alpha registrations with numbers that link to that area on the coast. He says he wants to check back through the rest of the files we have on the people who were brought back from the compound before we take it to Marcus. I am back to being a petulant asshole who wants to go home, so it's good that we're finally doing it.

We're walking through the lobby when I remember something that bothered me about the registration. "Nathan, the mothers. Or the lack of them. What if, it sounds horrible, but what if females have been going missing for years. You know how Jay and Derrick were plants? They just came to training one day, with a story that they were transfers from other territories so nobody questioned anything. What if their mothers were missing girls from years ago? Like the omegas we're trying to track right now. They're taken, turned into a baby factory for whatever purpose, and then...I don't want to think about it."

Nathan stops right in the doorway and turns back for the elevator. "Come on." When we get back to our temporary office he turns all the computers back on and I have to aggressively fight the urge to rip all my hair out. I want to go the fuck home. "If I show you what to do, can you help me? I want all the files put on this hard drive, and I don't want to do it wireless. I only trust four people in this entire building, and two of them are us."

"Yeah, I can do it. Show me." He plugs two of the computers into a hard drive he takes out of his bag and shows me how to move things from one window to another. Then we get to it. It only adds another bullshit hour to the day, but I understand the urgency.

Marcus said we shouldn't make a big show of taking things in and out of the building, and to not say anything too important sounding enough for anybody to hear. I suppose my loud mouth did just that when we were in the lobby.

When we get back to the car, Devon's car to be precise, Nathan doesn't say anything until we're well out of the parking garage. We've both been quiet, just trying to get all the files moved over, so when he starts yelling it scares the shit out of me. "You figured it out! You got it! I can do all this internal stuff and digital digging and sneaking and backdoor shit, but you put it all together. That's got to be it. We've been hearing stories about omegas being taken our whole lives. And think about it, Trent. Every alpha that transferred from another territory was always such a prick, and aligned himself with the other transfers from almost the very first day. It was always a male, never a female alpha. And Crane or Tomas always took a special interest in them because they ran the transfer program. They've been taking omegas for years and years, and Crane was part of it the whole time. I'll just bet that's where the omegas we're tracking are headed to, the coast. And I know we can find proof in those files. I just didn't want to leave them there. Anybody could come in and destroy evidence, especially since Crane was so high ranking. Who knows who all is working under him."

"Yeah, alright, but who's his boss? Crane obviously didn't run the whole thing because it's still going. He's lower down than we thought."

Nathan's hands grip the steering wheel a little tighter while he thinks. "I don't know. Hopefully we'll find some answers now that we have a better idea of where to look."

It takes a million and eight years to get home, but we finally make it. My plan was to kiss Jasper and scoop Talia up and take her to my room, dinner or not. But when I get to the kitchen, she's sitting on the same counter from earlier, the flannel unfortunately buttoned to her collarbone, eating whole black olives out of a jar while Jasper is at the stove stirring a pan of something that smells like heaven. Alex is at the table with his laptop, and there's music coming from somewhere. It's very, very domestic. I love it.

"Those were supposed to be for dinner. You can't sit there and eat an entire jar of olives." Jasper's mouth is fussing, but his hands are snatching the jar and taking it to the sink to drain and dump in a bowl. He gives it to her and tugs on her braid then goes back to his stirring. So, so domestic. And so fucking wonderful.

I lean on the counter next to her and wrap my arm around her waist. When I turn to her with my mouth open she feeds me an olive and kisses me after she puts it in my mouth. I might have an emotional outburst. We've been feeling more and more like a family and this moment is what cements it for me.

"At least give me a handful before you two eat them all, this really does need just a few for the taste." Jasper's smiling when I look over at him, and I grab a few out of Talia's bowl and deliver them to the stove.

"In the pan?" There's some of the lot of stuff in the pan that I saw around Talia in the picture she sent. I see the pepperoni, but also zucchini, mushrooms, little tomatoes, and I can smell the onion and garlic.

"On a plate. I'll chop them up so they spread farther. Did you and Nathan have a productive day?"

Oh my god. He basically just said how was your day at the office, honey. This is too much, just right, and not enough all at the same time. "It actually was productive. We think we've got some things worked out. I'll let Nathan tell you when he's finished. I think I'm going to go take a shower real quick before dinner, unless you need me for anything."

"I think she needs you for a couple things. That was a fun picture, by the way. Dinner in twenty minutes, Devon and the other's should be home by then. So go quick if you're going."

When I turn back to help Talia off the counter all I see is an empty bowl.

Chapter Twenty-Four

Jasper

The more time Obi spends sliding the transducer across Talia's stomach the harder his expression becomes. I can hear the quick rushing of the baby's heartbeat, so that makes me feel a little better. He's turned the monitor away from us so I can't see what he's seeing. The only thing known for sure is that he doesn't like whatever he's seeing. Talia's eyes flick back and forth between my face and Obi's and I can tell how hard she's fighting to maintain neutrality.

Obi starts to make another pass across her lower abdomen and she bites his head off. "What the actual fuck are you doing? Why are you so goddamned worried all of a sudden? If you don't show me right fucking now I'm calling for every single alpha in this fucking house. Tell me what's wrong, Oberon Samuel Green. Now."

He pulls in a deep, slow breath and takes his time blowing it out before he turns the monitor toward us. For a minute it looks like just a grainy, swirl of dark chaos but then I see it. There is more than one black hole. More than one tiny, fluttering heart. I sit down in the chair beside the bed and recount the images on the screen. Three. There are three.

"Jasper," Talia whispers, and I drag my eyes from the monitor to her. She's staring at the monitor with the same pinched expression Obi is wearing. I pull her hand between both of mine.

"Are they alright? Are they all okay?" That's all I can think to ask. We were trying to have one, singular baby. None of us would have ever guessed multiples would be an option. Twins are so rare that they're not really a consideration, but three? It's unheard of. I have literally never heard of it happening in my lifetime.

"They look okay. I'm going to check each one individually as well as I can, but at a glance all three appear to be thriving."

"Look at them. Every detail you can see. Show us everything," I say, looking back at the screen. I can see each baby twitching and kicking their tiny legs.

"Do you see this dark area?" Obi asks and points at the larger sac, "these two are sharing the same sac. Do you want to know the sex of the babies?"

I look back at Talia.

She shrugs, "it's up to you, princess. It would make picking clothes and decorating the nursery easier, but I'm alright with a surprise."

"Tell us," I say. I don't like surprises. Especially not huge ones like this.

Obi slides the transducer around and presses just a little harder against her stomach. "There," he says, pointing at a set of little legs, "do you see that?"

"I don't see anything," I reply, and he smiles.

"Exactly. There's nothing to see because that's a girl. And this one," he presses in at a different angle, "is also a little girl."

Talia barks out a laugh, "Trent will be ecstatic. I can't wait to tell him we're having two girls."

"Let's not tell him. Let's let it be a surprise. And there might be three girls." I love the idea of the alphas not knowing the sex of the babies. I especially love the idea of Trent passing out when I start handing him multiple little girls to be terrified of.

"Let's see what we have over here," Obi hums. "You see that?" he points to the third little set of legs.

This baby is very obviously a boy. "So, a neutral color in the nursery."

"Are they okay? Hearts, skulls, and livers fully formed? All appendages accounted for?" Talia asks.

Obi nods. "Would you like me to print some pictures? Want to take a video with your phone?"

Talia and I both nod silently without taking our eyes off the babies. Three babies. *Three.*

Obi clicks the mouse and the pictures start rattling out of the printer attached to the cart. "Obi," I force my gaze away from the monitor, "can you deliver them. Will Talia be alright?"

Obi scrubs his jaw. "I can't see a reason why she wouldn't be. She's an omega. Omega's are built to have babies, single or multiple. If something happens and we need to quickly get them out, I am up to date on my certifications and licensed to perform that surgery. I will have any and all potentially necessary equipment onsite. I'd have it all here anyway, but Talia is essentially my sister. I will do every single thing I can to help her birth these babies."

"Thank you, Obi," Talia says, "I'll be alright. This is just very unexpected. I'm so relieved that they're all three alright. Fuck me, we've been having a hard enough time agreeing on a name for just one."

Obi laughs and hands her the pictures he printed for us. "My mother's name was Zetty, if that's any help."

We tell the alphas after Obi leaves for home.

"Motherfucking fuck. Shit. Goddammit. Fucking shitballs." Trent, for some reason, has climbed onto the back of the couch and is standing up there, stiff, a wild look in his eyes.

Talia is putting effort into not laughing at him. I am not. I am cackling. Nathan is also openly laughing at Trent's reaction.

"It's not fucking funny. She can't have three babies at one time. She can't carry three inside her for fifteen more weeks. Why did you get her that pregnant? This is too dangerous. It's a bad idea." Trent is very quietly shrieking.

I laugh even harder. Even Reid is starting to crack up. Devon isn't smiling, though. If I didn't know exactly how worried and afraid he is I'd think he was angry.

"What do you suggest I do, Trent? I can't just not have two of them." Talia's losing the battle, she's got her lips trapped between her teeth to keep from laughing.

"Fuck," he barks, "shit," he takes a few breaths in an attempt to calm himself, but he makes no motion to come down from the couch. "Are you okay, Talia? Do you feel alright? What the fuck do we do?"

Talia stands up and goes over to offer her hand to Trent to help him climb down. The idiot takes it. If he could see how ridiculous it is, a tiny, significantly pregnant female omega helping a big, terrified alpha down from a precarious location, he'd laugh his ass off.

"First, you're going to get your shit together," she tells him, "then, you and Alex are going to order some baby-proofing equipment. Out of all of us, you two are most likely to have been horrible children, so you will know what needs to be padded and locked and whatever else better than the rest of us. Then you're coming up to my room for the night. I might even let you sleep."

"Excuse me, sweet pea, but I was a perfect child," Alex says, trying to sound offended.

Talia rolls her eyes. "I'm sure you were."

"Do you think the two of them will be identical?" Corso asks. He's beaming. Joy is rolling off of him in waves. I don't need a bond with him to feel his happiness, it's flowing through the room and around everyone in it.

"We'll have to wait and see," Talia answers.

"Are they boys or girls?" Kaleb is his typical stoic self. All business, already planning, already making mental preparations. "Or two and one of each?"

We don't answer.

Kaleb's mouth twitches, "did Obi tell you?"

"Yes," I reply, "and don't you dare ask. It's unfair that you'd be able to smell the lie we'd tell you. You all get to be surprised."

"I like surprises," Corso says, a smile still taking up most of his face.

Talia doesn't let Trent sleep. And he only partially got his shit together. I stayed with them for about an hour, but her appetite for sex has surpassed mine exponentially. When I left her room for Nathan's, Trent was taking his time to work her to another orgasm. Hopefully this one wears her out enough to let her sleep for the night.

She's exhausted, but she says everything from her nipples to her toes is so much more sensitive that she spends half her day wishing she could hump somebody's leg. As much as she complains about that, she says that this kind of omega bullshit is still better than going into heat every few weeks because she's able to make the conscious decision to *not* hump anybody's leg. I think any of us would thoroughly enjoy her humping any part of us, but I didn't tell her that.

"You smell wonderful. A mix of all three of you. Like orange truffles with a mug of coffee, so rich, so decadent," Nathan says when I crawl into his bed. He pulls me into his body and I immediately feel so warm and taken care of. That's the thing about this pack, the dynamics between us all shift so easily. I'm not expected to be a needy omega every second of my life, but when I do feel like a needy omega someone is always there to take care of me. I can fluidly go from a level plane of dominance with Corso or Alex to soft and cuddly with Nathan or Devon and right back to whatever Talia needs me to be and nobody thinks anything of it. It's amazing to let myself be more than an omega being well cared for by my pack. Now I get to be the omega, but that's not my only role. Talia actually has a harder time of it. I have always been an omega, so being treated like an omega is normal and comforting for me. Talia is only just now letting herself try to be the soft omega that lets herself be taken care of, and I'm pretty sure she hates it most of the time.

"You smell good, too." Nathan always smells like a walk through the woods in the middle of fall. I needed his soothing energy tonight.

His arm tightens around me, "you okay, baby?"

I wriggle closer, enjoying the way his chest feels against my back. "I'm alright. I think I'm a little nervous. I've never heard of anybody having three babies at a time. And the only accounts I've read about are presented in a mostly vague and negative light. Obi isn't worried. He says all three are fine, and that Talia is doing amazing."

Nathan starts a gentle purr and kisses my shoulder. "It'll be alright. Everything's going to be okay. If anybody can have three babies at one time, it's Talia. We need more cribs. We need more of everything." He goes quiet, then after a few minutes he asks, "are you sure you're okay? We went from not considering kids, to having one, to having three pretty quickly. That's a lot for all of us to process."

He's right. It is a lot for us to process, some of us more than others. Trent is a nervous wreck. He's excited, but he's terrified something will happen to Talia. Devon and Kaleb are their usual solid selves, even though they're every bit as afraid as Trent. They will coast through anything that happens and keep us all from sinking despite the fear and anxiety. Not that we would sink in the first place with Corso's joy spinning around all of us, as well as Alex's excitement. Reid is stoic, but he's very quietly thrilled. The moment he registered that Talia would be having three babies a flood of pure happiness rushed down my bond with him. "I think we just need to get used to the idea. I'm alright, Nathan. I'm tired, though. Give me extra cuddles and sleep with me and I'll feel a lot better." He kisses the back of my neck and I fall asleep to the sound of his purr vibrating in his chest.

Chapter Twenty-Five

Nathan

We have to get these sideways fucks off the council. That's the only way to keep any of this shit from happening. I sifted through all the files. Every one of the alpha transfers came from either the wilds near the coast or from obscure places in other territories. All with numbers for birth places. None with mothers listed. And all signed off on by Crane. From a distance everything looks squeaky clean, but if you give it even a quick second glance you can see how off it is. Nobody thought to give it a second glance, though, because Crane put real effort into building a name and reputation that wouldn't lend to the idea that he'd be involved in anything nefarious.

Marcus and Thaddeus have said on more than one occasion that they stopped trusting Crane years ago, as far back as when Trent and I were kids. But there wasn't a tangible reason to request an inquiry, it was just a feeling they had and talked about. And now that he's dead because of all the backwards, dishonest, treasonous bullshit he put together, lined up, and executed, so many things are coming to light. We just don't know who else is involved. Yet. At least one other major player on the council is involved, hopefully no more than that.

The second I find out who it is I'll have to decide if it would be better to report them and go through the proper, slow-ass channels, or just lace up my boots and take Trent and Kaleb on a little road trip. The more I think about it, the more I think this is one of those better to apologize than ask permission situations. Then, there's no link to Marcus or Thaddeus that anyone can use to accuse them of plotting or sabotage or anything else. We need them in the clear. I've discussed it with Devon, Kaleb, Corso, and Anthony. I think Marcus, Thaddeus, and Anthony should take point on the East Coast Council. They wouldn't rule, obviously, but their seats would hold more weight than the others, and we'll need that weight when we eventually figure out exactly what the fuck is going on with all these missing omegas and mysteriously appearing alphas. It's all connected.

"Let's get them over here for a dinner. Her parents, mine. Our moms can have a blast talking about baby stuff and getting all over Talia's shit, and we can talk shop with my dad and Talia's dads. I don't know if they'll go for it, but if we can convince them it will go a long way when shit hits the fan." Devon is pacing the length of the main room.

Talia is at the piano plunking keys in a way that hints at an actual song, but her eyes are following Devon's path. "I think they'll do it. My dads already don't trust half the council. I can't speak for Alpha Johnson, but I like him, and he's been right and fair about a lot of things. But if you think I'm going to be trapped in a hen-huddle talking about baby stuff you're going to be disappointed. I can't do it. I don't care about the nursery, the babies won't be in it regularly until they're older, anyway. They're going to be in one nest or the other, or with one of you. The only thing I actually do care about is what we're going to do with them once I start having heats again. They can't possibly stay here while their mother loses her mind to heat. My parents either left for what they called their honeymoon cottage or they sent us packing to friends' houses. I don't know what they did when we were babies."

"You could always talk to them about that. Merris might even survive the conversation if Elizabet and you can contain your sarcasm and blunt honesty," Kaleb says as he throws his feet up on the coffee table.

Devon stops pacing and gives Talia a harried look. "I don't think my mother has ever discussed her heat with a person who wasn't my father, Arthur, or Steven. My family isn't like yours, Talia. My dad thinks you're wonderful, and he loves your mother's lack of bullshit, but my mother is almost painfully polite and private. Please don't give her a heart attack."

"I would never." Talia crosses her heart. I don't miss the smirks and mischievous glances spreading through the room.

I actually have a suggestion for the heat predicament, though. "So, I've been thinking about it, the situation with you and Jasper going into heat. Jasper's heat might not be that big of a deal because it's more infrequent, but we can be pretty loud." Snorts and chuckled agreement resounds. "If we can stand it, we could go to the farmhouse when they're in heat. We could take it in shifts or turns, or whatever. But the farmhouse is an option. I also talked to Becca. She said that she'd take care of any kid that was mine whenever I needed her to. She offered. She also offered to come help when it's time to have the baby, but I didn't know how you'd feel about that, so I told her I'd give you her number."

Talia sighs, and plunks a few more keys. "I think that's a sound plan, the farmhouse is a good option. I hate being apart, though. It feels wrong for us to be separated like that, in different locations that far apart. Just thinking about it makes me fucking anxious."

"We wouldn't separate. I'm not putting that much distance between us ever again if it can be helped," Jasper says quietly. "When they're small it won't matter, but when they're older we'll send them to stay a few days with any one of their grandparents or aunts and uncles. They have quite a few. I'll call Becca and thank her, but it would probably be good if you called, too. Actually, we need to have some kind of family thing here before the babies are born. You haven't met my parents, except overhearing them when I call. I don't think you've officially met any of their parents, except for Alpha Johnson."

"I agree," Corso claps his hands and rubs them together. "Let's have a gathering. We can do a big dinner and invite all the parents and whoever else. I might even be able to convince my parents to fly in. There will be a slight language barrier, but they already adore Talia, and they've met Jasper through video call." Corso loves a good party, and he loves the idea of a huge family gathering even more. My parents are the same.

But someone has to put a damper on things, and this time it's unfortunately me. "It's getting colder. If we're doing it, we need to do it before it starts getting icy. And please don't take this the wrong way, cupcake, but we should probably do it before you get much bigger. The belly, I mean. We're not trying to have anyone know there's three in there, and if you're much bigger than you should be somebody's going to ask some questions and there will be too many alphas around to lie. Another thing to consider is keeping it quiet. With all this shit going on with the council and the rogues, all we need is for someone to find out that we're having all our families over for a party. Which brings me back to the point, we need to have a meeting with your dads before we plan anything with our families."

"When do you want the dads here? I'm assuming we want the meeting here, since we know this is the only clean and clear location." I nod, and she takes out her phone. "I'll call all the dads. Mine and Devon's."

"I can call my father," Devon stops pacing, but then cocks his head to the side and raises an eyebrow. "Actually, cupcake, I think you should call him. If I call, he'll come, but if I don't say it's an emergency he'll come when he comes instead of when I want him to. If you call him he'll go out of his way to be here whenever you tell him to be."

"Six tomorrow evening?" When we all agree as she dials up Devon's dad. "Hi...Yes...No, I'm fine, we're all fine...No, really, we're okay...Can you come over tomorrow evening, around six? My fathers are going to be here. I know it's a drive, and I'm sorry, but it would be... Yes, I'll make the soup...You'll pick up rolls? Thank you...If she wants to come of course she can... I don't know, I hope not...You're sweet, but yes she is. She's been my mother my whole life, she's a lot to handle...I really am fine...Yellow or green, you don't get to know before Devon knows...I'm sure you can. I'll think about it...No, no hints. You're too smart for that, and I'm surrounded by people with big ears and bigger mouths right now...Okay. I'll see you tomorrow."

"See?" Devon smiles. "I'd still be on the phone with him explaining why I want him over. And he's bringing you rolls."

"He's not that bad. I'll text my mother about my dads coming over. It sounds like your mom wants to come, and for some ungodly reason Merris would be happy if my mother came over, too."

"I could say the same to you, your mom's not that bad. But she's, well, she's a lot to deal with, but she's someone you definitely want on your side. It must be a family trait," Devon says and winks at her. He's not wrong about that, on either point.

~

The dinner goes very well. Lots of laughing and talking while everyone was eating, but as soon as the dishes were cleared Talia took a deep breath, closed her eyes, and asked her mom and Devon's if they'd like to see the nursery. Corso and Kaleb finally convinced her to turn the sitting room on the other side of Corso's bedroom into a nursery instead of remodeling the walk-in closet in her bedroom. She says she doesn't care what color anything is so long as it isn't garish or harsh. We have bets going about whether or not that will remain true. Me and Trent are the only ones who believe she really doesn't care and won't mind if Jasper really does paint the walls that soft gray he keeps talking about.

Talia has been upstairs with Jasper and a pair of gushing grandmothers for the past fifteen minutes, and we're just now getting to the meat of this visit. We decided that we wanted Corso to bring it up and lay it out even though he doesn't have a familial tie to the council. Honestly, I think Corso would be perfect for the council, but he doesn't want anything to do with it.

"As much as we want this to be purely a family visit, there is a very serious matter we want to discuss with you. It is related to the bad business happening with the council and we knew discussing it here would be safer than discussing it at any official location." Corso walks around the room of gathered alphas handing out glasses and filling them with his whiskey. He sounds so sure of himself, like he could lead every one of us; and the way we're all watching him, even the grandfathers'-to-be, he probably could.

"Things must change, that much is obvious. With Crane being the traitor he was, Tomas's involvement, and Pratchett Senior being in the mix, it occurs to me that we need to investigate and relieve some council members of their seats and replace them with more honorable alphas. But even before we get into that, we'd like the three of you to consider stepping up and taking more weight. Crane has no descendant to take his seat, and thank the stars for it; and Tomas was barely holding onto his seat to begin with. We don't know how deeply Pratchett Senior was involved, but I don't like him and I won't respect his place because of the things he is responsible for as far as Talia is concerned." Marcus drains his glass as Corso finishes and taps it twice on the table. Trent, Alex, and Kaleb do the same.

"But," Corso continues, "after the events at the compound, my god, I can't believe I'm saying this out loud, I don't think Seth is a complete loss. I think he needs someone to mold him into what he could become. I see potential in him, I hate seeing anything good in him at all, but it's there. If he were provided with a decent and patient example, he could take his father's seat. I would like to motion for Pratchett Senior to step down as a decision-making member until Seth is recovered and prepared to hold the seat. I, we, think it would be the most beneficial thing for everyone in the territory if the three of you would absorb Tomas's and Cranes's seats, and essentially put Seth's on hold until he's ready for it. I am not on the council, therefore I cannot make true motions, but if I was, that is what I'd suggest."

Devon's father is the first to speak. "You could take Tomas's seat, son. You've been preparing for a seat your whole life."

"I don't want it, Dad. I'll take your seat when you're ready to hand it down, but that's not now. We need you to do this. I'm not handing my life, and their lives," he motions toward all of us, "over to the council. Even when I do take the seat, I will not allow it to rule my life. We already talked about that. I don't mean any disrespect, I just want to do like I said. I want to make my pack solid. I want to have a family. I want to follow you and Marcus and Thaddeus and any other alpha with a seat who is honest and just. When it's my time I'll accept the seat with every bit of honor it deserves, but not now."

"I'm proud of you, son. I couldn't say that to my father. My pack, my family, myself, all suffered." As the last word leaves his mouth I feel stress and anxiety leave Devon to be replaced with relief and peace.

"He'll be insufferable, you know." Marcus refills his glass and tips it toward Thaddeus. "Pratchett Senior will be an even bigger pain in the ass if we try to push him out. Think we can get the support to absorb Crane's and Tomas's seats? Unless, of course, Corso would reconsider. I've been after you for a few years, we could create a new seat in the stead of these two vacated ones and put your name on it. You're made for it. Hell, I'd support anything you put on the table. You sure you're not royalty or something?"

"I don't think I would enjoy it. I want to make my whiskey and love my pack. That's what I want my life to be. I am beyond honored that you have asked." Corso salutes Marcus, then everyone else.

Thaddeus sighs, "I guess that's that. I don't know how official we can make it until we get some of this other business sorted. Have you made any more progress with the files?"

"I have," I say, "they're going to the wilds near the coast. A bit outside of North Wisen to keep it quiet but convenient is my guess. The transfers that keep coming in are likely rogue offspring, produced with omega mothers that have been disappearing for years. I don't have clearance to send a COT or anybody else less official out to have a look, but I know we'll find omegas who have been missing since I was a kid. I've followed a paper trail like you wouldn't believe. I'm in the process of making my findings look presentable and understandable, but yeah. That's what I think based on what me and Trent have found. I'd like to wait until all the vehicles that I've tagged with omegas get there, maybe scope it out to see if it's another compound or individual structures, then get them all out. There's probably babies and young kids there, too. I have a feeling we'll find some seriously fucked up shit there. Maybe even bigger than the last compound."

"Let us worry about sending people to the coast," Thaddues says, "you have enough to handle with the little one half way to here. You've been overworking yourselves anyway. And Talia is likely a nervous little wrecking ball with you all away so much. Elizabet could hardly stand for us to leave the house in the last stretch." Then he eyes Corso. " I don't know if I agree with you about Seth Pratchett, but I've been monitoring his recovery. Something feels off about it, and I don't know if it's because of him or because of something else."

"See?" Trent exclaims, "I don't trust him, either. And Jasper still wants to kill him."

"You misunderstand me, fratello. I don't trust him. And I would gladly accompany Jasper to rid the world of him. But Talia wouldn't, and I *do* trust her. She feels very strongly that he is redeemable, and I am inclined to follow her lead as she is who he wronged. I also think that if he were to be rehabilitated, he could be strengthened into the councilman we need him to be with the proper guidance, which would be a huge improvement over his father. Pratchett Senior can, as Talia says, get fucked as far as I'm concerned."

I'd be happy to drop Seth where he stands, but Corso's right. Talia, for some fucking reason, doesn't hate the very air Seth breathes. And she doesn't want us to hand him to her a piece at a time. She wants him in rehab and for us to do video calls with him. Like, I get that he did what he thought was the best thing with the options he was provided, because I couldn't do shit to save those omegas at the compound at the time; but every single time I think about his fucking hands on her my vision goes a little red. Jasper can't even talk about it. He might kill Seth one day, regardless of the rehab, guidance, and molding Corso's talking about. And at least three of us will help him do it or at least help him dispose of the body.

The unofficial meeting adjourns with Talia stomping down the stairs yanking on the end of her braid and telling both her Elizabet and Merris that they can buy whatever baby shit they want because we'll use it all, and that they're welcome to get with Jasper and make a whole day out of painting and decorating. She plants herself on Reid's lap, taking him by surprise and quietly laughing, "help. I've had enough, and I'm tired. I don't want to hurt Devon's mom's feelings."

Reid doesn't do a thing but stand with her in his arms and offer a quick and polite goodbye before carrying her right back up the stairs. Reid doesn't give much of a shit about what happens with the council, so long as those omegas are found and we shut that entire operation down. He wants everything to work out, but he has made it clear that Talia and our pack is his main priority.

When I go up to check on her after everyone leaves, she and Reid are curled up in her nest in my room. I'll never be able to fully put into words how it feels that she keeps making nests in my bedroom, but I love it almost more than I love anything else.

"Would you like to be tagged in? I have something I want to work on for a while, but our omega is in need of cuddling." Reid hugs Talia to him, and raises his eyebrows at me.

Our pack bond is growing stronger as time passes. There are other packs who go through some kind of ritual, usually dealing with bloodletting, but neither of our packs felt the need for that before we came together and we don't need to do that now. The only thing we are going to do is alter the tattoo on our necks. Corso's pack never got pack tattoos, but they want to get them now. Reid has been working on a design that will reflect both individual packs coming together as one whole. He's going to work with the butterfly we already have to come up with something new.

"I do need cuddling," Talia says, snuggling back against Reid, "but if you two are switching out anyway, let's move to the bed." Then she winks at me and I know cuddling isn't what she's after. All the better for me. I would have been perfectly happy with cuddling, thrilled with it, to be honest. But if Talia wants more than cuddling from me that's exactly what she'll get because I want that, too. She points at me, "you, get naked." Then she lets Reid help her up and reaches up to tug his earlobe, "thank you for saving me."

"You're mine to save," he tells her and kisses her forehead. I know it's been months already, but sometimes I'm still thrown by how affectionate she is with all of us, but especially when I'm seeing it from the outside. Before we joined packs, she was affectionate with Jasper, but with the rest of us she was very hands off. She was playful and friendly, but there was still a distance. Those first bits of sweetness on the porch when she left with Corso and the rest after her first heat were wonderful, but still a little stilted because outside of sex there wasn't much physical interaction between us. Now she tosses around kisses and cuddles and everything else like we've always done it and it's the most amazing thing. Jasper has always been affectionate, very affectionate. Talia...not so much. Even with her family, I get the feeling that this side of her is reserved for us and only us and I love that as much as I love her nest in the corner of my room.

Talia's pulling off clothes and climbing into the bed before Reid makes it out of the room. We've switched to heavier quilts and blankets since it's getting so much cooler at night and the weight of them feels so good as Talia and I get settled against each other. I like to take my time when I get her to myself. It doesn't happen often, with her or Jasper. There's almost always another person with us, which isn't bad or unwelcome, but sometimes it's nice for it to be just us. After I get pulled into me and tucked under the blankets we just lay still and hold onto each other for a few minutes, then she pulls my arm around her a little tighter and softly says, "I'm really proud of you, Nathan."

I close my eyes against the sting and I swallow around the sudden thickness of my throat before I can respond. "You're proud of me?" It's lame, but I can't think of anything else I could say that won't have me embarrassing myself with an emotional outburst.

"I'm so fucking proud of you. You found those omegas, and you made the dads understand they had to step up and be more so we can get all this shit straightened out."

"Corso did that. I wish he'd take the seat they keep offering him. He'd be so good for the council." I mean that, too. Corso would be perfect for the council.

She hooks her foot around my calf and wiggles her ass against my crotch, another thing I love. "He wouldn't have if you hadn't been so adamant about it. Corso fucking hates politics. He wants to be left the hell out of it. If you hadn't made him understand how much weight his opinion held he would have let you, me, and Devon try to talk our dads into basically taking it upon themselves to dissolve two seats and absorb the power those seats held; which is pretty high handed. My dads love me, and value my opinion, but I wouldn't have been able to convince them to do it quickly enough to do any good. They would have considered it overstepping in an extreme way. Corso said it, made a solid argument for it, and they listened because they see him differently than they see me and Devon. Devon and I are their children, and as important as we are to them, we aren't leaders. Devon will be, but he isn't yet; and I don't fucking want to be. Not ever. Corso pushed them because you pushed him. You got this rolling, Nathan. And I'm proud of you."

"You give me too much credit, honey. Corso would have done it if you asked him to. He'd do just about anything you ask him to do." I can't accept praise for pushing for something that's the right thing to do. I do agree with Marcus, though. Corso should be on the council.

"He wouldn't suggest overthrowing council rule and procedure just because I bat my eyes at him. He's too honest and good for that, you know that as well as I do."

I breathe my answer to that into her neck, brushing my lips over one of our marks. "That's all it should take. I'd do a lot of questionable things if you bat your eyes at me." She gives me breathy giggles I'm after and everything feels lighter. I don't mind talking about serious, heavy, incredibly important things with her, but I spend most of my days neck-deep in serious shit. Right now I just want to lose myself in her.

I'm sliding my hand over her hip when she grabs it and puts it over her stomach. Talia doesn't bring attention to the babies moving around very often, but when she does it's a little bit of a race to get to her first. This time I got it all to myself. I don't feel anything for a few moments, then the little thunk of movement hits my palm. I stay perfectly still while I wait for the next little bump, and Talia whispers for me to spread my fingers out. When I do, my hand spans across almost her entire stomach, but I can feel the little rolling thumps. "I can't believe there are three in there. It's so amazing. Trent's terrified of them."

She laughs, "I know. It's so funny. I hope he'll calm down a little once they're here. I don't know what I'm going to do when they're bigger and in there moving around. It's strange enough now when they roll around. I'm going to be enormous."

"You're going to be beautiful just like you are now," I tell her and kiss her shoulder. "I don't think you're capable of being enormous, but if you do pull that off, I can't wait to see it. Jesus, I love the thought of you like that."

"Mmm, I can tell," she hums, reaching behind her to grip my cock that's trying to push between her thighs. She moves her hand up and down the length of me a few times, then guides me inside her.

I love how easy it is with her. I love how good it is when she lets herself be soft like this. It's everything to me that I can hold her and bury my nose into her hair while we move together. There's no urgency right now, only gentle rocking and her soft noises filling my ears. I drag my mouth across her neck and shoulder, grazing every mark our pack put on her skin. Through my bond with her, I can feel the warmth of her reaction flowing through her and that bloom is mirrored inside of me. I don't know what it's like for any of the others, but I feel things through my bonds so intensely; and Talia's want, her need, burns so hot sometimes that it takes my breath. She's not burning us up right now, though. Right now she feels so languorous and content.

"I love how you feel, Talia. So soft and warm and perfect." I run my hand across her hip and up her side to cup her breast and circle her nipple with my thumb. She sighs and covers my hand with hers again so we can both touch her.

"I feel the same with you. So safe." Hearing her tell me I make her feel safe, feeling the truth of it in our bond, rolls me with a dizzying sense of pride. It's the same when Jasper tells me he feels safe with me, but Talia is so much more guarded than Jasper. It's humbling that she feels safe with me like this.

I could spend the rest of the night like this, with these gentle touches and sweet sounds, but eventually my knot forms and I'm faced with a question I've been curious about for the past couple weeks. I never want to hurt Talia's body with mine, not ever. Not even if she asked me to. The others can give her that, it's not for me. It shouldn't, but I'm afraid of knotting her while she's pregnant. I've read that some omegas want it and others don't; I'll give Talia whatever she wants, but I need to know first. "Does it hurt?"

She gives me a soft, raspy laugh, "no, it feels so good."

"I mean the knot. Does it hurt? Since you're pregnant?"

"Oh," she pushes back against me a little more urgently, "no, it doesn't hurt. It feels right. I'd tell you if it hurts, I promise."

"Good. I never want to hurt you."

"I know." She pulls my hand up her body and presses it against her chest where I can feel her heart beating. That's how we finish together, with my hand over her heart.

We're asleep, but still locked together by my knot when Jasper comes in and lays behind me so that I'm pressed between him and Talia. "Go back to sleep," he whispers, and wraps his arm around my waist and tucks it between me and Talia. Sleeping between them actually is my favorite thing in the world. It's better than anything else. I usually try to stay awake for as long as I can just to feel the cocoon they create around me, but I'm a lost cause tonight. It probably takes me less than a minute to doze off.

I wake up a little while later when Devon comes in to pull the quilt back over us. "Stay," Talia whispers.

"You sure? I don't want to cut in." Devon asks.

"Stay," I say softly, and lift the covers in front of Talia. "You can be littlest spoon for the night."

Devon slides in and it immediately feels perfect. We have this new pack dynamic we're mostly settled into, but I've spent a lot of years following Devon. Sleeping in a cuddle puddle with him and our omegas is so relaxing. I hate to admit it, but I feel myself fully relax once he's settled in the bed with us. It's always been like that, though. There's always a part of me that stays alert, I'd be a shit alpha if I wasn't able to hang on to that; but Devon makes even that little bit feel lighter.

Chapter Twenty-Six

Talia

Corso's mother is even more aggressively affectionate than I remember. I don't think it even has anything to do with my being pregnant. She and Lorenzo, Corso's biological father, flew in over the weekend. They're staying at a bed and breakfast a few miles away but they've been here for everything but sleeping. I tried to convince them to just stay here, but Lucia was so excited about the bed and breakfast experience that I gave up. I've eaten so much food. Jasper has eaten just as much. I'm pretty sure Trent is planning to build Lucia a cottage on the other side of the garage.

Reid's mother and Aunty Josephine are driving up this afternoon, and Alex's parents will be here from the central territory by this evening. I'm probably most excited to see Alex's parents, if I'm honest. Likely because they're both betas. I just feel so comfortable around them. My mother and fathers are all coming, and once Jamison found out Reid's sister might come he was a pain in my ass until I told him he could come as long as he was on his best behavior. Nathan's parents couldn't make it, but they promised to come soon; and Kaleb's father will be coming. Trent's entire familial pack will be here, including his two younger brothers. There is about to be so many people in this house. I'm considering sneaking out the back before they all get here.

"The motor's still up on chains, cupcake. You're as trapped as I am." Devon bends down to kiss my shoulder. "You've been eyeballing the keys as hard as I have. If it gets to be too much give me a sign and I'll get us out of here. They'll never miss us."

"Yes they will. And if I try to leave the house again Corso's mother has threatened to use the spatula on me." She'll do it, too. She whopped my ass with it the first time I met her when I tried to pass a round of drinks to the alphas gathered in the main room for Corso's birthday. She didn't, and still doesn't, speak anything but the language of her people and I had no idea what I was getting a spanking for. I thought it was because I offered the tray to Corso before his father and earned myself another swat trying to rectify the situation. That was a super fun learning experience.

Kaleb looks up from his laptop and his coffee, "I'll use the spatula on you." Then he winks and goes back to his work.

"I won't let him," Devon whispers against my neck, "can't have him being so rough with something so tender."

Kaleb speaks again without looking up. "She'd enjoy it. Maybe in a few months we'll see how much."

I take a quick minute to mull that over, deciding pretty quickly that I would definitely like it if the sudden wetness ruining my panties is any indication.

Devon purrs into my ear and dips his fingertips just under the waist of my leggings. "Naughty girl. Of course you'd like it. You want him to lay you over his lap? Or across the bed? What about if I held you while he did it? How many swats would it take for you to be a wet, sticky mess?"

"I'm already a wet sticky mess. And there are too many parents here for me to drag you upstairs to clean it up." I'm sitting here pressing my thighs together and fighting the urge to grind my ass against him. "You're both assholes, by the way."

Lorenzo walks into the kitchen twirling an empty teacup around his finger and walks right back out, shaking his head. A few moments later Corso comes in pulling on the ends of his hair and muttering something under his breath in Italian, but two steps into the kitchen his nostrils flare and his eyes snap to me. "What fun am I missing in here?"

"Devon wants to hold me down for Kaleb to spank me with the spatula."

Corso tilts his head to the side and the corner of his mouth turns up. "That would create such a nice association, bella. We'd think about that lovely pink shade every time we use it. This is a wonderful idea. After everyone goes home, of course. Although, it does seem like you're in need of relief now, stellina mia. Will Devon be taking care of you, or would you like my assistance?"

Oh god. Can't I have both? I've never been with Devon and Corso at the same time, not that I can remember, anyway. No, I definitely can't have both, not with his mother's bat-like hearing. "Fuck. I can't have both. Damn it."

"Are you going to pout, cupcake?" Devon drags his mouth over Corso's mark on my shoulder and I release a flood of slick.

Corso comes to stand in front of me and leans down to lick over either Trent's or Nathan's mark on my other shoulder. "There's no need to pout. We can make you feel much, much better right now if you think you can keep quiet?"

If either of them fuck me right now I might scream the house down. But I feel like I'm on fire, my pussy is literally throbbing with my pulse. Maybe I don't care if Corso's mother walks in with me bent over the table for him and Devon. "I'll try," I whisper and reach behind me for Devon's zipper while I drag my eyes over Corso, licking my lips in anticipation.

Devon pulls my hand away from his pants and clucks his tongue. "No, no, cupcake. I can't fuck you in the kitchen with Corso's parents in the next room. That would be terribly, terribly rude. But I can do this." He pushes his hand down the front of my leggings and groans. "You're so wet. You really like the idea of us spanking you, don't you baby? What else is making you wet like this?" He slowly slides his fingers over my swollen lips, trapping my clit between them and pressing his palm against my pubic bone.

He cups me like that until I'm thrusting into his hand, then he switches to rolling my clit between his fingers and the only thing that stops me from moaning is Corso's kisses.

"Devon asked you a question, bella. You should answer him," Corso says into my mouth. His hands move up my ribs and under my bra so he can alternately pinch and pull my nipples, and my head lolls back onto Devon's shoulder.

"I need you to fuck me," I moan as quietly as I can, "both of you."

Devon's husky laugh just makes everything worse, "no time for that right now, pretty girl. Fairly sure somebody's pulling down the driveway." He's right, and based on the thrill that just rolled through my bond it's Reid's family that has arrived.

Kaleb's chair scrapes on the floor when he gets up to look out the window. He turns back to us and motions for them to hurry things along. Hurrying is just fine with me, so long as they don't stop.

Devon pushes his fingers inside me and latches into the mark on my shoulder and my knees give out. I'm gasping my pleasure, but Corso's mouth is suddenly covering mine, his tongue lashing my own as he rolls my nipples between his fingertips. Between Devon's fingers and Corso's kisses, it takes all of five seconds to push me over the edge into the unexpected kitchen orgasm in a house that is officially crawling with our families.

"I should be the one to take the spatula to both of you. Now I have to change clothes," I hiss as I try to collect myself. "I don't know if I can make it up the stairs now. My legs are wobbly."

I do climb the stairs, though; and after I've changed into a tank top, a pair of jeans that I haven't been able to button for weeks, and Trent's blue flannel shirt that I have no intention of returning, I head right back down them to the best surprise. I actually squeal, and I don't give a single shit about it. "Johnny made this, didn't he!? He carved every piece! And look! There's an entwined Z and J! I think I'm going to cry."

Reid's father is a carpenter. He made a cradle. There's a huge, old-fashioned cradle in the middle of the main room with daisies carved into the head and footboards beside our pack initials. And it's full of handmade quilts and knitted blankets in so many colors. I'm going to cry my fucking eyes out. I'm going to sob, actually. "Why couldn't he come? I need to hug him? Can we call him?"

"No, baby. He and Randall had to stay home with Zeri. Her heat started yesterday. She's so sad that she couldn't be here, but she says she'll come to help out after the baby's here if you'll have her. Randall, too." Reid's mother sits on the floor next to me and wraps her willowy arms around me so we can cry together. "Zeri knitted up the blankets, and Randall helped me and Joe with the quilts. He wanted you to know that he cut most of them himself."

"Maybe you all can come back?" I sniff, holding a green and blue quilt to my chest. I'm going to have to pull myself together. This is ridiculous.

Auntie Josephine kneels down on the other side of the cradle and hands me one of the knitted blankets, red and yellow striped one. "We'll come back as often as we can. Zeri will be able to come after the baby's born, even if her heat takes she'll still be just twelve weeks along. She's going to be so happy that she made the hard ass herself bawl her eyes out. She sent you some hard candy, too. Lemon ginger." She digs into the bottom of the cradle and pulls out a small brown paper bag of yellow candies dusted with powdered sugar, then she glares at Alex. "Don't let me hear that you touched that bag, Mister Rosen."

Alex throws his hands up in a feign of innocence. "I wasn't even considering it."

"Liar," I laugh, and wipe my eyes. "You and Trent would sneak pieces until the bag's empty."

"Oh, another one, I see. Lancaster, is it?" Auntie Josephine raises her brow in Trent's direction.

He grins and crosses his heart, "I promise not to touch her candy stash."

I laugh again because he's such a liar. I'm going to have to hide this bag.

The next day Lucia swats me with the spoon when I start helping make the huge dinner for everyone. Apparently I'm only allowed to sit at the table and sample bites of ingredients and finished dishes while she's here. I love it, but I'm also ready to have my kitchen back. When Alex's parents knock on the door I basically leap up from my chair to let them in. For some reason I want to drag his mother upstairs to see the nests I made. I didn't feel the urge to show anyone else, but nobody will mind. Besides, they all got to see me have an emotional breakdown. Cassandra lets me pull her up the stairs after she instructs Alex's dad to put something in the fridge and bring in the box.

I take her to the larger nest in Nathan's room first. I tucked and wove things that belong to all of them into both nests, but this nest is a little heavier on Alex than the other one. She walks all around the outside of it before she squats down and holds her hand over one of the corners. "May I? I've never actually seen an omega's nest before?"

I nod and smile when she runs just her fingertips across the pillow and surrounding shirts, one of which actually is Alex's. "I never thought...I'm so glad you came back to them. We didn't know what to do with Alex most of the time when he was little. He was so different from his brothers. When you left them, they weren't well. It got a little better over time, but they never let you go. And now you're an omega and that just makes it better. Now you're carrying their marks. Can I see the marks? Is it inappropriate for me to ask?"

I undo a few buttons of the shirt I stole from Kaleb's closet this morning and pull it to the side so she can see Alex's mark on the inside of my breast. I'd be shy about it if Cassandra and I weren't betas. Well, I've been a beta for most of my life so it still feels like we're both betas. We just don't get overly shy about things, especially about satisfying functional curiosities. Alex's parents are betas, his siblings are betas. He's the first and only alpha in their lines and there has never been an omega in their family. Cassandra has likely never seen a nest or an alpha-omega claiming mark outside of a diagram in a textbook.

"I thought it would look more like they took bites out of you. I've been sort of dreading seeing you in a mauled state. This just looks a bit like a strawberry birthmark." Her face is about three inches from my chest and she's looking at both Alex's and Kaleb's marks with a clinical eye. She isn't even seeing my partially bared breasts. I miss being a beta. I honestly think they're the superior designation sometimes.

"Corso's is a bit messy, but the other's are mostly clean." I pull the shirt off my shoulder and lean forward for her to look at Corso's mark.

She draws in a quick breath when she sees it. "Did he hurt you? I can't imagine Corso doing that on purpose."

I shake my head. "No. Well, I don't remember if it hurt. It was a terrifying situation until we figured it out. But he'd never hurt me on purpose. He felt like shit for a long time. He still does sometimes."

"And your omega? Where is he?" She drops back to sit on the floor while I do up my shirt.

"He, Devon, and Corso went to the distillery to check on one of the stills. One keeps giving them trouble, and Jasper likes the walk. They'll be back soon. I can't wait for you to meet him. He's so beautiful." I may or may not still gush over Jasper on occasion. I gush over all of them in turns, though.

Cassandra pats my knee, "I'm sure he is. Do you know if you've got a boy or a girl in there?" She looks down at my rounded stomach and smiles.

"I can't tell you. We said we wouldn't tell anyone until they're born." I clap my hand over my mouth. There's no way she didn't catch my slip.

She pales. "They? Talia. They?"

I nod. "Please, Cassandra. Please don't say anything. Nobody can know. Alex and the rest of my pack knows, and Obi, but we're not telling anyone else. Everyone will freak out and that will be overly stressful for me to deal with. I'm sorry to put you in this position, but please don't tell anybody."

She closes her eyes and takes a deep breath. "If Jake asks me I'll have to tell him. But so long as none of the alphas ask it should be fine. Can I know how many or if they're boys or girls?"

I shrug, she already knows that there's more than the customary one baby. "Two girls and a boy."

"Three!" she hisses. "Talia! Three? Are you alright? You look a little bigger than I expected, but everyone carries differently. Are they all okay? No troubles?"

"They're all perfect as far as we can tell. Obi comes once a week to check on everything. He says we're good."

A small smile starts to form and she tucks her hair behind her ear, glancing toward the door like a true conspirator, "I'll send some bottles. I wanted it to be a surprise for you, but I brought some of Alex's clothes from when he was a baby. I can't wait to shop for things for the girls."

"You brought Alex's baby clothes?"

She barely has time to nod before I yank her into a hug and start crying again.

A few minutes later Alex struts into Nathan's room. "Came to check on you, sweet pea. Felt heavy for a minute, now you're crying again. You're not supposed to make her cry, Ma."

"It's good crying. Wait till you see what she brought, Alex. It's wonderful." I really am going to have to pull it together. My eyes are getting sore from all this crying, and we still have more family coming.

"Would you tell me to get fucked if I suggested sending Nathan up to purr you into a nap? You seem like you need a bit of a rest, baby."

A nap actually does sound good. "I wanted to show your mom the other nest, though."

Cassandra pats my cheek, "that's alright sweetheart. I can see it later if you still want to show it to me. I agree with Alex. You look a little worn. I'll send up a snack with Nathan, was it?"

"Oh god, don't say my name and snack in the same sentence when you're near the kitchen. I've eaten so much food since Lucia's been here. It's amazing and I love every bite, but I'm trying to wait until dinner to eat anything else. I might actually explode."

"Okay," she laughs, "no snacks. You should lay down, though. Alex, help her up and tuck her in." She gets to her feet and stands in the doorway until she sees me properly tucked. Then she asks, "does that really work? Can they actually purr and put you to sleep?" She's eyeing her son skeptically as he leans down to kiss me before he leaves.

"It does. It's one of the few perks of being an omega," I answer.

"What are the other perks?"

"Nope. No. Negative. You are not answering that question. My mother does not need to know about any of the other omega perks, thank you very much. Come on, Ma. Let's go send Nathan up. Talia stole you away before you got to meet him. You're really going to like Nathan. He feels like being a little wine-drunk on a warm day and he smells like trees."

That is by far the best description of Nathan that I've ever heard.

Chapter Twenty-Seven

Kaleb

I have enjoyed spending time with every single one of the people crowded around the table in this dining room, but it's time for them to leave. I love Reid's mother and his aunt. I haven't met another female alpha that I identify with as much as I identify with Josephine. I adore every tiny inch of Corso's mother, and every crumb of food she has cooked. I think the world of Alex's parents simply because I can feel how much Talia loves them. I have even thoroughly enjoyed watching the friendship between Elizabet and Devon's mother, Merris, blooming. These are all wonderful things. And they all need to pack up their leftovers and get the fuck out of here.

I'd never say that aloud. Of course they can stay until Talia and Jasper have had enough of them. Jasper's being spoiled as much as Talia. Alex's parents in particular have gone out of their way to talk to him and ask him questions. But Talia is exhausted. I've exchanged several texts with the others and we all agree that this shindig needs to be wrapped up. I wonder what would happen if I just stood up and announced that my omega is too tired, overwhelmed, and emotional to continue the visit. They'd all probably feel like shit and trample each other to get out the door. Then Talia would be pissed at me.

"What are you over there sighing about?" Jamie asks as he pours Talia and Jasper tea from the fancy ass tea set Marcus rolled in here.

"She's tired, but she won't admit it. And she won't go up to bed because she knows that everyone will leave once she does."

Jamie hums and holds up a finger before he carries the tea to the couch Talia and Jasper are curled up on. They're listening to Reid's mother talk about when he was little, and they're not likely to break free of that spell until it's finished. When he comes back, he sits on the stair next to me and stretches out his legs in front of him. "It's a shame Joplin couldn't make it. I was looking forward to seeing her again."

"You were looking forward to getting laid," I snort.

"That too. I can see how tired my sister is, but I can't feel her the way you do. I do know exactly how goddamned stubborn she is, though. Want me to make an ass of myself and require more than Obi to escort me out of here? That would break up the party and keep Talia from blowing up at you."

I sigh for the hundredth time since dinner. "You're a good man, Jamison. I appreciate the offer, but she'll let us know when she's ready. I just have to exercise a little more patience than I anticipated."

Ultimately, I only have to exercise my ability to contain relief because Corso calls an end to the evening himself. He even announces it in such a way that dares Talia to argue. It's either that it's so rare that he actually puts his foot down or that she's just that exhausted, but she doesn't complain about sending everyone home. She frowns a little bit, but when people start making for the door she doesn't get up from the couch.

Once the door shuts for the last time she asks if she can't just sleep right there on the couch. Corso clucks his tongue and scoops her up, only taking pause at the foot of the stairs to tell everyone within ear shot that he thinks Talia would like it very much if we all slept in the same room tonight. That's just about what I had in mind, anyway, and we all end up sleeping piled on top of each other in the nest in Nathan's room.

"I wanted to show Cassandra the other nest," Talia yawns after Trent turns off the light once we're all settled.

"You can show her another time, bella. She'll be back often now that she knows what our pack is like together," Corso says before he begins to purr. I don't think twelve seconds pass before both Talia and Jasper are asleep to the point of snoring; which is funny and adorable and probably the biggest secret we'll ever keep from them.

~

Obi comes by at least once a week to check on Talia and the babies. She's only got four weeks left in the pregnancy and everything is progressing perfectly as far as Obi can tell. Her belly isn't as huge as I thought it would be while carrying three babies. She looks like any other pregnant omega that's nearly to term; maybe a little bigger, but not dramatically bigger like I expected. Obi says it's because the babies are smaller, but I think he's just as surprised as I am.

We're as prepared for them to be here as well as we can be. They'll all three fit in the big cradle Reid's family brought while they're tiny, but we've got cribs and pods and hammocks and whatever else ready to go for when they're bigger. The cabinets are full of bottles and formula in case Talia needs to supplement, which Obi says is a definite possibility with three babies. We've even got various grandmothers, aunts, uncles, and siblings lined up in case we need help. Everything is going to be okay. Everything is fine.

Until it isn't.

Seth fucking Pratchett is calling me at one in the morning. He's either terrified or delusional. Probably both.

"Kaleb. Hurry. Get her out of there. They know. I didn't tell them. I didn't say a single word, but they know. I tried to stall. I tried to lie, but they know. They're coming. You have to get her out of there, get her somewhere safe. Take her to Alpha Johnson's.

Go now." He's whispering into the phone so fast and frantically and I'm having a hard time piecing everything together.

"Who? What are you talking about? Who is coming?"

There's a jostling and the sound of him breathing into the phone, but after a few breaths he answers. "The rogues. They're the ones watching me. They were watching when we had that call. I snuck in here to call you so you could get her out. They know she's pregnant, Kaleb. They think the baby might be Jasper's and they want it. Some guy..." he stops talking and I hear some people calling to each other in the background. When he comes back on the phone he's even quieter. "I've heard the name Minos a few times, and the name Cobb. It doesn't matter right now. Just get her out. They're coming tonight."

I'm sitting straight up in bed now. I've got him on speaker and I'm texting Devon and Corso. Can't we catch a break? For fuck sake, Talia's just a few weeks away from giving birth, and Jasper is even less than that before his next heat. "How do you know they're coming?"

"They fucking told me. Taunted me with it while they beat the shit out of me. I wouldn't tell them anything, I didn't tell them she was or wasn't. I didn't say a word, Kaleb. I swear. Shit." The line goes silent for a few moments. I can almost hear his pulse thunking against the receiver, or maybe it's mine. I can't believe more people are coming after Talia. It's ridiculous. I don't know anyone with the name Cobb, and the only Minos I've ever heard of is some prick on the west coast council. I don't even think he's a major player over there, barely worth the mention.

"I've got to go," Seth hisses into the phone. "I have to move before they catch me. Get her out of there. They're coming. Hurry." Then he hangs up. Fuck.

"What is it?" Devon's expression is stark. He isn't surprised. He isn't angry. He's just ready to deal with whatever it is. Corso is right behind him, but a little less collected.

"Seth called."

Stoic or not, Corso lets out a line of curses before I can finish the explanation.

"What happened?" Devon begins his customary pacing in front of my dresser.

"He says to get Talia out of here. He says rogues are coming for her because she's pregnant and they think it's Jasper's baby." I get up and start pulling on clothes and shoes. Reid and Trent come in as I'm finishing up my laces.

"Of course he told them. But how did he know? Other than our families, we haven't really put it out there. And he's locked down in a fucking rehab facility," Trent rakes his hands through his hair.

Most of my weapons are in my closet and Devon helps me get them on the bed while I talk. "He says he didn't tell anyone anything. He told me the rogues have infiltrated the staff where he is and beat the shit out of him because he wouldn't tell them anything about her. He was hiding somewhere to make the call. He said to hurry. We can't take her out of here, I won't be caught out on the road. What's the plan?"

"How long?" Corso is grim as he pulls his hair back.

"Didn't say, just told me to hurry."

"Nathan's room. Where are the security feeds are. She'll feel better if she can see us. Maybe we can give her an earpiece or something and she can watch the screens and tell us what she sees," Alex says. I've only seen Alex being truly serious a handful of times, and this is the first time I've actually seen him angry. When he came with Talia and Jasper to get us from the compound he mostly looked like he was having his own little party with that flamethrower; but the cold rage burning in him right now is far from that.

Devon nods. "Okay. Her and Jasper in Nathan's room. Some of us in the hallway. The rest outside. Do you think we have time to get any COTs here? Or maybe one of Elizabet's teams?"

I shrug and shake my head, "I don't know. I'm going to say call them in but don't count on them getting here in time. Seth mentioned Minos, and somebody named Cobb."

"West coast Minos?" Trent asks.

"That's the only one I know of. You get Nathan going. I'll get Jasper and Talia."

Jasper and Talia are already up, dressed, and armed when I walk into his room. Talia is loading her shotgun and Jasper is checking the plethora of handguns lined up on the desk. "If it wasn't such a shit situation that would be sexy." Add a very pregnant woman dressed for battle and loading guns to my growing list of kinks.

"Who's coming? I'm so fucking tired of this shit. Every bond I have is so tight. How bad is it, Kaleb?" Talia lowers the shotgun to point at the floor and turns toward me.

"I don't know who's coming or how bad it will be. Seth called, losing his shit and told me to get you out of here."

"I am not going any fucking where." She plants her hands on her hips and glares at me.

"No, we're shutting you and Jasper up in Nathan's room so you can watch the screens. A couple of us are going to be in the manor and the rest will go outside to head anybody off."

Talia's face wrinkles in a snarl. "That's stupid. Going outside is stupid."

Jasper pins her with a look of his own. "Staying inside while they set the house on fire is even more stupid. Some of us will need to be outside. Probably Alex, Trent, Nathan, and Reid. Kaleb and Devon on the ground floor. Me and Corso outside Nathan's door."

"You're going to be inside Nathan's room with Talia." He can't possibly think he's going to be in this fight. I'm still not over the last fight he was in. Hot or not, Jasper fighting alongside us can't be an option.

"Fuck you, Kaleb. You're not shutting me in a room to keep safe when I can be better utilized. Besides, even if anybody got past all of you, you can bet your ass that they will absolutely not get through me and Corso. And then there's Talia and her armory to deal with." Jasper's tucking guns and knives into clips and belts like he's serious.

"Jasper, we can't let you –"

He barks out a laugh and a sound starts in his chest. It isn't very loud, but it's one of the most eerie things I've heard in my life and chills crawl up my spine and across every inch of skin on my body. "*Let*. Let me. You're not *letting* me do anything. I'm going to stand with my pack to protect our pregnant omega. *My* very pregnant mate. You'll lose this argument. The most I'll concede is being the last line of defense beside Corso. Talia will stay in Nathan's room and tell us every single thing she sees on the monitors. And she will not step a single toe across the threshold until one of us tells her it's safe to do it. Do you understand? If I have to make you do what I say I will. Even if you hate me for it, I will force you to let us keep you safe." He's talking to me, but those last words were for Talia. I half expect her to argue. She normally would argue for the right to protect him, but she doesn't. She's staring at him with wide eyes and pressing her free hand over her stomach.

"Do you understand me, Talia?"

She nods.

"Let me hear it."

"I'll stay in Nathan's room until you let me out. I don't like this, Jasper. What if you get hurt?"

He wraps his fingers around her arm and gives it a little tug. "Then I'll get hurt. Nobody will get past the guys that will be outside. And if they do, they have to deal with Trent and Nathan. If they manage that, there's no way they're getting around Corso to get to me, and both he and I will die before we let anybody get past us to you." He reaches up to stroke his thumb across her cheek. Their roles have reversed so completely, it's jarring. "Knives. Handguns. Not the shotgun, your off balance right now and the kick might throw you into something. Nathan will fix you up with a headset. You'll help us that way. Be our eyes, cupcake. You'll see things that we can't. Okay?"

Talia agrees. "Okay. But I don't like it."

"None of us like it," I say. "Devon's head is going to explode when he finds out Jasper's going to be in the fight. Just make that awful noise again and he'll see things your way. Come on."

This must be an alternate universe because Devon agrees that Corso and Jasper being the last line between Talia and whatever's coming is a good plan. He doesn't even question it. He just starts fitting Talia with a headset that's linked to the ear pieces we're all wearing. I think we all collectively feel like puking.

Chapter Twenty-Eight

Talia

I'm so fucking tired of people coming for Jasper, coming for me, and now coming for the babies that aren't even here yet. It's ridiculous. And tedious at this point. I'm tired of people attempting to kidnap us. It's becoming a little cliché. I'll sit here all night watching these screens and be happy if nothing happens, though. I want Seth to be wrong. I hope nobody comes for us. I hope the only thing I see tonight is the wind blowing the pine needles and leaves around and all this can be chalked up to a practice drill.

There's been nothing but trees and my own alphas on the monitors for over an hour when two SUV's pull down the driveway. They're not even trying to be stealthy. One stops halfway to the manor and a few people get out and disappear into the fields and woods, then it keeps moving toward the manor. Just so everyone knows, I let everyone know over the coms that four people are loose on the property and two vehicles approaching the manor. I get a series of confirmations, but Devon gives the order for everyone to stay put.

The vehicle in front stops as it's passing the garage and someone tries to get out. Kaleb is there immediately, shoving the person back inside the vehicle and shutting the door. I see him shake his head, then he steps away from the SUV to speak into the mic. "It's Pratchett Senior, Seth sent him. He's here to help. It's his people on the property. There are nine of them in total. Advise."

There's silence for a few breaths, then Devon and Corso both give the go ahead to let him help. I can see Kaleb talking to him, but I can't hear what they're saying. Pratchett himself gets out of the vehicle and points to the roof. Kaleb gives him a nod, but when he turns his face away I can see his scowl. I can also make out some cursing. "Kaleb," I say into my headset, "the fuck?"

"He says Seth called him after he called us and told him to get his crusty ass here in his place. Made him feel like shittier shit about everything than he already did. I couldn't smell any lies, he's here to help. He won't come near you. He swore he wouldn't unless there was no other option. I'm sorry he's here at all."

Well that's something. I guess I'll be glad for the assist, even if the thought of that asshole here at my home makes my skin crawl. There's still a sour taste in my mouth as I watch him climb up the corner of the house to get to the roof regardless of the fact that we need the extra support.

Everything's quiet again for a while, then I catch some quick movement at the northeastern corner of the property. I can't tell how many there are, it doesn't appear to be more than a handful, but they're dressed in dark camouflage and are carrying multiple weapons. There's more movement at the southwestern corner, with more people prowling through the cornfield back there than there are people sneaking through the trees at the front. I report every single thing I see, going so far as to mention the numbers on the screen just in case that's helpful to Nathan. I watch Devon and Kaleb become part of the shadows surrounding the manor and when the first of the intruders break from the trees my stomach drops and I can't breath for a second. Then everything starts happening almost faster than I can follow.

People start falling to the ground between the treeline and the lawn and it takes me a few seconds to realize Seth's father is on the roof picking them off before they can get close to the manor. Before they can get close enough to hurt Devon and Kaleb. At the back of the property I see the men who came with Pratchett, all wearing their own headsets, taking position and shooting into the corn when the intruders start coming through there. Gunfire is loud over the headset and it takes all I have to not scream into the mic when I see Pratchett's men in the back start getting overpowered. "They're coming from the back, around each side of the manor. Pratchett's guys are going down. Be careful." My heart is thundering in my ears. I can't do anything but watch as Kaleb and Devon either live or die.

Trent's voice comes through the headset. "I see them through the windows. They're almost to the back door and the side porch." Terrace. It's a terrace, but he can call it whatever the hell he wants as long as he's alive to say it.

"Let them walk. Don't give your position away. We need you in the house. Pratchett's still on the roof firing." Devon hisses, then I can't hear anything but my pulse again when he meets the men creeping around the corner of the garage. He doesn't seem to be struggling, he's dropping them one and two at a time. They must be betas. That many alphas at one time would be way more difficult for even him to handle.

I'm so busy watching Devon take down beta after beta that I don't see the veritable hoard of men crossing the lawn from the woods on Kaleb's side of the manor until they're on him. They didn't come from the front where Pratchett's guys are, they came from the side. Where the fuck did they come from? It's woods for miles, then it's fields. It takes every bit of willpower I have not to scream into the headset, destroying everyone's eardrums won't help this situation.

"Coming in from your side, Kaleb." I'm trying to count because I know he's going to ask, but there's no way to know.

"How many?"

I can't say anything. There's no way for me to tell him that there are too many for me to count without screaming.

"Talia," he clips. "How many?"

My voice is barely audible when I answer. "A lot."

"Copy." That's all he says. Then I see him begin checking his weapons.

"Alex. What's your location? I can't see you on the monitors."

A few seconds pass then his reply crackles through. "Coming in behind the assholes in the front. I got with Pratchett's assholes. I should have grabbed the flame thrower."

Corso's curses fill my ears. "Do *not* set the fields on fire."

"Unclench, Corso. I didn't grab it for a reason. Can you see Devon?"

"Between the terrace and the corner of the garden. Lot's of betas. He's good for now. Can you get to Kaleb?"

Silence.

"No. Not in time. Headcount?"

"Too many."

A round of *FUCK* resounds.

"I'm good." Kaleb's voice is solid, but my bond with him is the tightest it's ever been. Tight and becoming distant.

Jasper's voice comes through. "Don't you dare, Kaleb. You stay right with us. Clear?"

"I'll try," he says, but it's a lie. He's going to put up whatever block he can to keep Jasper and I from feeling the things he's about to feel.

"Coming through now. Do you see them? I see four, then five, then three, then a lot. They're moving in and out of shadows. Just on size, there are alphas, more than a few, mostly betas."

"I see them." I watch him take a breath, blow it out before he takes his stance. I might throw up.

Too many things start happening at once and I can't keep up. I can hear Jasper and Corso moving in the hallway outside the door, and I can feel Trent's and Nathan's anxiety. Devon is still standing, stepping over the literal pile of bodies around him on his way to meet another round of intruders, this time with alphas in the mix. Alex and Pratchett's guys begin to pick off the assholes coming for the front of the manor, and they're doing a damned efficient job of it. Reid...Where the hell is Reid? I haven't seen him since he left out behind Alex, and he's definitely not with Alex now.

"Reid. I don't see you."

His hushed reply doesn't make me feel a drop better. "You're not supposed to."

Then I have to watch in silent horror as Kaleb is swarmed. It isn't like the guys Devon's having to deal with, attacking in smaller waves. They all go at him at once. He did what he could to shoot them as he got clear shots, but there are too many. If they take him to the ground, he's done. Kaleb is throwing them off as quickly as he can, but it's becoming very obvious that there are just so many. This must have been what it was like when Devon was downed at the farmhouse. I should be able to hear gunshots and shouting, but I'm not registering anything but what I'm seeing on the monitor. There are too many. They're going to kill Kaleb.

"They're killing him." My voice sounds too far away, but I can't be alone in this.

I watch him waste time tapping on the mic on his chest. "Don't watch, Talia."

Then I scream.

Chapter Twenty-Nine

Reid

Talia's screaming is ringing in my ears and her complete despair is pouring down our bond. I don't see what she's seeing, but from my vantage point in this fucking tree I can barely make out Kaleb's foot sticking out from under the men attacking him. They were smart. None of us expected anybody to come through miles of country scrub, fields, then woods.

My original goal when I climbed this tree was to watch Pratchett, because fuck Jonas Pratchett. But then he consistently did what he said he was going to do and has done a damn good job helping our defense, so I've been watching him less and putting my effort into shooting people. Between the two of us we've significantly lessened the number that Alex is dealing with. Now Kaleb has fallen and Talia's grief is overwhelming and instant. I feel a similar pull from Jasper, but he isn't watching it in real time the way she is on the monitor.

"Please. Go help him," she's quiet. All terror, sorrow, and shock. "Go help him. Trent. Please. They're killing him."

They certainly seem to be trying to. Oddly, Kaleb hasn't been shot. That's what they should be doing. That's what I would have done. I would have immediately shot him in the head the moment he was taken to the ground. But they haven't. What could possibly be the purpose? They can't want to take him again. Then realization dawns. Leverage. They're going to use Kaleb, and Devon from the looks of it, to lure Talia outside. Omegas have been known to go to extremes when their pack members are in danger or hurt, and Kaleb is both. These intruders must be counting on Talia's instincts to go to her alphas aid.

"Talia. I need you to listen to me right now. Stay where you are. I've got eyes on Kaleb. They aren't going to kill him. Stay where you are." I already know she's not going to do what I say.

"They are. They're killing him. Trent, Nathan. Go get him. Please. *Please*."

"Stay put, honey. Reid's got him." Trent drawls through the earpiece.

"If you don't save Kaleb I will never forgive you. None of you. There are too many. Please go help him. There are too many." I hear clicks and jostling. Everyone hears it. Then I hear a door opening, and Jasper giving calm orders.

"Sit down, Talia. Not one toe. Just like I said. Reid is telling you he's got Kaleb, and he does. He's saying it for a reason. Alex is closing in, too. Didn't you hear? Look at me. Did you hear Alex say he was almost to Kaleb?"

"No."

"I'm almost there, sweet pea. Watch the trees." The strain in Alex's voice is enough to make my own throat tight.

Alex bursts through the treeline a few feet from the terrace, with Pratchett's guys right behind him, just as the sound of shattering glass comes across.

"Jasper." That's all Corso says.

"Do not leave this room unless one of us opens that door. Clear?" Even distorted by the earpiece I can hear Jasper's command. He might as well be an alpha in this moment. "Talia. Answer."

"Okay."

"It's going to be alright. Look at the screens. We're winning." Then I hear the door shut again.

Alex and Pratchett's team are working through the ones surrounding and pinning Kaleb down, but something is happening on the other side of the manor. I look through the scope just in time to see four big alphas and two betas close in on Devon. He's slow now, showing true fatigue. After several waves of betas, he's exhausted. He won't make it through this round without help, but the help is on the other side of the manor. And whatever happened to break the glass has to be on the back side because I can't see anything from here.

There's movement on the roof of the porch. It's Pratchett. He's shimmying down the goddamned lattice that was supposed to have been taken down weeks ago. I should have let Alex build the fucking moat. Pratchett drops to his feet and pulls a handgun as he rounds the corner toward Devon.

"Devon. Pratchett is coming around the corner." Talia sounds a little more solid.

"Betas in the house. First floor. A lot, lost count," Trent whispers. Damn. Why so many? There are only seven of us, plus two omegas. Granted, we're not doing too badly; but we've had help. Why send this many? We called for COT back up over an hour and a half ago. They should have already been here. With even one additional COT we'd be alright. There's no good reason for them to be taking so long to get here. This is the home of a future councilman and the pregnant daughter of two sitting councilmen. The place should be swarming with COT units by now.

I can hear the shooting that must be taking place inside the manor, but I can't tell what's actually happening with it being so dark inside. There's nothing I can do about that. Alex has tipped the picnic table on its side and dragged Kaleb behind it; now he and the men following him are filing inside the French doors. How did we not realize this place was such a disaster to defend? French doors made mostly of glass and without bars or even a deadbolt. They're gone now, busted in. And I will dig the moat myself.

"Stairs," Nathan barks, then more shooting. "Corso."

"Got it."

Not being able to see what's happening inside is hell, but I'm where I need to be. There are still men coming from the field and it is my job to kill every one of them before they make it to the manor. Pratchett is no longer shooting, he's fighting his way to the center of the fray to stand with Devon.

"Jasper. One your way," Corso says, and I'm genuinely shocked when nobody argues. Not even Talia.

"Copy." Jasper doesn't sound or feel concerned. If anything, our bond feels tranquil. Maybe even bored.

The three people emerging from the field take little more than a breath to drop, then my attention goes back to Devon. He and Pratchett are nearly facing each other now and are making quick and easy work of the rest of the intruders surrounding them. Pratchett is still shit, but I'm glad he listened to his son and came to our aid tonight. He and the men he brought have been the difference between life and death on two different occasions.

"Jasper. Sending another through." How many intruders are inside the manor for Corso to send now two threats to Jasper? I'm still catching people as they become visible, but I'm in the front.

"How many are inside the house?" Hopefully someone will be able to answer.

Nathan answers. "Ground floor is swarming, but it's mostly betas. We're going through them fast, there's just a lot of them. Any sign of the COTs?" A scream sounds in the background and it abruptly cuts off. "Jesus, Jasper. Fuck."

"What happened?" I don't want to panic, I can still feel Jasper through the bond, and I don't think that was him screaming.

Pride blooms through Talia's bond and it's apparent in her voice, "Jasper hung some prick across the banister by their guts. That was hot. We are winning."

"There's my girl," Alex croons.

"Of course you think it's hot. I'm killing people too, you know." Trent is grunting between words.

"I've been watching the whole time. You're hot, too. Two on the left."

Jasper's voice comes across, "Alex. How bad is Kaleb?"

"I'm fine. Just need to catch my breath. Devon?" Relieved doesn't begin to cover how I feel hearing Kaleb's response. Two more people come from the trees and they stop behind one of the stupid bushes somebody planted here at some point. I'm pulling them up. To make way for the moat.

"Coming in," Devon clips. "Pratchett, too."

Then something unexpected happens. Panic bordering on pure fear pours into me from Talia.

"Leave him outside, Devon." Jasper hisses.

"He'll help clear these assholes out." Devon's focus is more on getting every threat out and away than Talia's reaction to Pratchett being in the house. I know this because I trained with Devon. He eliminates threats by order of priority. In Devon's eyes, the men actually attacking his pack are a much bigger threat right now than anything Pratchett has done. He's right. Even I want Pratchett with us in this moment. The more help the better.

"If he steps into my home I will kill him. Understand that," Jasper says with zero emotion.

"Shit." Devon says into the mic, and I watch his jaw tick through the scope. I see him motion for Pratchett to stay outside, and Pratchett's chest rises and falls with what might be a frustrated sigh, but he nods. Devon steps through the door into the kitchen entryway and he's out of sight. I switch to check on Kaleb and shoot the lone runner trying to make it across the lawn. I hope that's the last of them.

"Nathan. The back door," Alex warns.

"On it," Nathan replies, then after a few seconds, "more coming in from the back line. I'll bottleneck. Why so many? It's ridiculous."

"Because we're a large pack with a reputation?" Trent offers to the sound of furniture breaking.

Kaleb gets to his feet, "coming inside. Don't shoot me." Then disappears into the house, leaving me to watch the property, and Pratchett.

"Not too many coming from the back," Talia says. "They look like betas. Nathan, are you ready?"

"I'm good."

I don't hear or see anything else for a bit, then the yelling and shooting begins again. It lasts for a few minutes then things go silent.

"What's happening?" I ask, holding my breath for a response.

"Nathan's shot, in the shoulder. Alex has him. Kaleb and Devon are beaten all to hell, but they'll live. Corso is pulling bodies off the stairs. Jasper is still upstairs, he's checking the monitors with Talia. I'm going to open the front door and start throwing these dead assholes out in the front yard as soon as you give me the go ahead. And where the fuck are the COTs? Devon called his dad directly. This is complete bullshit. Is it clear out there?" I usually enjoy Trent's petulant sarcasm, but at this moment, it might be one of the best sounds in the world. If he's okay enough to be more irritated than anxious, I can be ecstatic.

"There's been nothing out here for a few minutes. I think it's done. I don't know where the COTs are. They should have been here by now. I'm coming down." By the time I climb down from the tree, Pratchett has decided to walk around to the front door and is standing on the porch.

From inside I hear shuffling and Trent calling out, "wait, Jasper. Just wait a minute."

Jasper's laugh is sharp. "Why?"

Then the door opens and Pratchett turns to face Jasper, and I'm running. I don't know why, though, to be perfectly honest. I can feel determination and a hint of joy in my bond with Jasper, and an odd combination of violent aversion and tenuous hope in Talia's bond. I know what's about to happen, I don't mind in the slightest.

"Jasper." I can hear Pratchett from where I am. "Is Talia alright?"

"Don't ask about her." Jasper walks straight at Pratchett, crowding him off the front steps. I'm a few feet behind him when he leaves the bottom step. Jasper is still walking down them.

"Seth asked me to come. He wanted to come himself."

"I'm sure he did. Did you know she asked us not to kill him? She stood up for your piece of shit son after what he and his pack did to her? Get on your knees." There's a strange clicking sound coming through with Jasper's words. The hair on my forearms stands up as it intensifies the closer he gets to Pratchett. Devon, Trent, and Alex are rushing out the door and down the stairs. They might as well be standing still.

"Jasper." Devon quietly calls, but inevitability is heavy in the air.

"She's a good girl. She didn't deserve any of it. It was wrong. I was wrong." Pratchett's shoulders slump as he drops onto first one knee, then the other. "I made a mistake. I only wanted the best for my son. Talia would have been the best omega, but she wasn't meant to be his."

"You're right. She's mine." Jasper raises his arm, then blood and bits spray across my shins and shoes as the sound of the shot bounces off the front of the manor. Pratchett's body falls sideways onto the ground, but Jasper never sees it.

He turns around and walks back up the stairs between the others. "Where are the fucking COT units we called for? I thought we called your father directly. Now we've got to get several clean up crews in here. I'm calling Obi to come check Talia over, she's had two panic attacks in the last hour just because that mother fucker was on the property. And you know Jamison and the rest will come with him after they find out about all this. There's no good reason for there to have been so many for just us..." his voice trails off as he walks back into the house, and I look up to find Alex and Trent smiling down at Pratchett's body while Devon is scowling.

I expect Devon to be upset about Jasper killing a senior alpha and councilman on the front steps, but he says, "I did call my

father directly. The COTs should have been here a long time ago."
He pulls out his phone and after a second he's seething into it.
"Where are the COT units? We needed help, and fucking Jonas
Pratchett is who showed up. They were after Talia. They could
have taken her, there were enough of them to do it. Then what,
dad? We could have lost everything. Why didn't you send them?"

He stalks down the stairs and starts pacing in front of them.
"What do you mean? They never came. It's been my pack, Jonas
Pratchett, and nine of his men this whole goddamn time, against a
whole fucking army of bullshit. Now we have to deal with Pratchett's guys because he's fucking dead...Yes, dead..Jasper. He had it
coming. Everything with Talia and Seth was his fault...No, I don't
really give a fuck about Joyce, she's better off without him and she
has the rest of her pack. We'll contact Seth...I hope not. You'll look
into it, right? Nathan's been shot and we're getting Obi over here
to look over Talia, too... Fuck no, don't get Elizabet over here.
Talia will call her when she's ready...Yeah, alright. You, too."

Trent walks down the stairs to stand over Pratchett. After a few
seconds of silence he rocks back on his heels. "Sooooo, what are
we going to do about that?"

Alex has the perfect response. "I have some fireworks. Maybe
we can get Talia to make one of those refrigerator cakes with the
whipped cream."

Chapter Thirty

Corso

"It's a problem solved as far as I'm concerned. Now nobody has to convince him to step down until his boy is well enough to step up." Marcus says, with a yawn.

I agree with Marcus. I agree with my whole heart. The only unfortunate thing is that Seth is still nowhere near ready to assume a council seat and I have agreed to sit in his place until he is. I truly loathe politics. I just want to take care of my pack and my distillery, and now my children will be the ultimate priority. There's no way to keep the dramatics and scheming of the council away from them because Devon will eventually be a permanent member of the council and Talia is just as tied to it, but I had hoped that we could keep it in the far distance. Now it appears that I will be much more involved than I ever wanted to be.

"I'm just a placeholder, Marcus. Don't count on me to upend anything or make any major moves. I am only holding the seat until Seth is ready. I don't even feel comfortable voting on my own without at least discussing it with him. It is his seat, after all." I don't mention that the idea of speaking civilly with Seth Pratchett makes me want to pull my hair out. Talia sees value in him, and I trust her implicitly; but I would just as soon rip Seth's throat out than look at him.

Marcus waves his hand nonchalantly, which is usually a sign that he's got an underlying motive. "Sure, sure. We know, just until

Seth can manage on his own. How did he take the news? Kaleb called him?"

"I did," Jasper says. "I told him exactly what happened and why. I told him about Talia's reaction to just knowing his father was on our property, and about her much more intense reaction to actually seeing him. He was upset, understandably, his father is dead on top of losing his entire pack a few months ago. That's a lot to handle, even at the best of times; but he said he didn't blame me. He said that he'd have done the same thing, and that he knows he should be next on my list. I told him Talia doesn't want me to kill him and he laughed. I don't think he's well. I don't think he'll be okay for quite a while."

Talia's reaction to Pratchett's presence was violent. Her utter fear traveled through her bonds like an earthquake. I had to fight the urge to vomit right there on the stairs in the middle of an invasion, and that was secondary to what she must have been feeling. I have only felt that level of fear from her one other time, and that was the result of my own actions. I actively and vocally agree with Jasper taking Pratchett's life. It is both very interesting and completely expected that her trauma chose Jonas Pratchett as a focal point rather than Seth, who did the actual physical harm. I often wonder what would have become of Seth if his father had been more like Talia's or even Devon's.

"Seth has been moved to Mercy until a bed opens up at one of the other facilities. We've screened the entire staff as well as we can, but Elizabet has a permanent team in place to monitor him and the staff. Nearly a quarter of the staff at the last place he was in was part of the rogue operation. It's ridiculous, really. Doctors, nurses, councilors... not typically positions I'd associate with rogues." Thaddeus takes a sip of his tea, and gestures at Devon's father. "Any word on what the actual blue fuck happened with the COT units?"

We've been sitting in the main room watching five crews remove bodies, glass and bullets for the past two hours. Nathan has been properly stitched up and is currently in my bed being coddled by Talia. She didn't even want to come downstairs to see her fathers. She said she didn't want to see her home in disarray in person. She did well enough to let Obi check her over and do a quick scan to check the babies. All she's interested in doing right now is, in her words, "getting these fuckers, dead, alive, and otherwise, the hell out of our house so she can feel safe again". None of us enjoyed hearing that our omega feels unsafe in our home, not even temporarily. I have overheard two separate conversations that sounded too much like planning an actual moat around the manor, and Reid sent one crew for a different style of door to replace the French doors that lead to the terrace. I don't know how well Talia will take that, she enjoys the look of those doors. A moat is likely out of the question, as well, due to the potential drowning risk once the babies aren't babies anymore.

"Devon called me and I called the dispatch myself. Lawrence and Taylor never got the order. Protocol is a phone call directly to the COT lead, and those calls weren't received. Meghan was at the desk last night. I looked back on the feeds, she made calls, I even heard her telling them where to go, but she didn't speak with Lawrence or Taylor. We're looking into trying to find out who she spoke to, but I'm doing good if I send a text successfully so I'm hoping Nathan will feel up to checking up on it. I don't think I'd trust anybody else at this point, anyway," Anthony says. He's taking this very, very hard. He feels personally responsible for this because he heads the COT program. There's a disconnect somewhere in his department that could have caused the complete destruction of our pack. He's apologized countless times, but how was he to know the deception runs so deep?

"Minos," Kaleb says. "Seth said the name Minos. And Cobb."

Thaddeus rubs his hand down his jaw and across the scruff on his chin. "The only Minos I'm familiar with is an Alpha Minos on the west coast council. His family has held a seat for generations.

He's a bit of a bastard, but not in a treacherous sense. More in a pompous, arrogant fuck sense."

Trent snorts a laugh and shrugs when everybody looks at him. "Sorry, it's just hilarious when you pompous, arrogant fucks talk about other people being pompous, arrogant fucks. This asshole must be extra fun to be around if y'all think this much of him."

By the time the manor is cleared of people, corpses, and debris it's early afternoon and we're all exhausted. It took both Devon and I, but we finally convinced Jasper to go lay in the bed on the other side of Nathan and coaxed him and Talia to sleep with some intense purring. Talia and Jasper are perfect and beautiful, but when they're overly fatigued they both get deep, dark circles around their eyes and they're even paler than they usually are. Right now they both look like they could be sick with a plague. I hope they can sleep until dinner, which we will be making from the stores in the freezer. Trent suggested that he and Alex could go pick up pizza or any other take-out, but Talia handed him his ass and informed him that leaving the manor was just as unacceptable as having unknown and unexpected people here for the foreseeable future. Jasper agreed, and now we'll never have pizza again.

I get a call from Obi just as the sun is going down. He sounds pinched and thin. "Listen, I didn't want to alarm Talia, but you all need to be careful. She's only a few weeks away from delivery, and she'll likely go early because she's carrying multiples. No more excitement. None. Not even a scary movie, including the shit ones Jasper puts on. She won't do complete bed rest, you know she won't, and I don't have enough of a reason to justify it other than I'm scared to death. Don't tell her that. Just keep her as calm as possible for the next four weeks or so. I told her to keep calm and relaxed, and all she was worried about was whether or not she was still allowed to have sex. I don't have a medical reason to say she can't, but I'm telling you and you can tell the others. Nothing intense, nothing rough. Tell Alex to contain himself for the time being. If she wants and needs it, give it to her, whatever it is, just keep the rougher acrobatics to a minimum. After everything that happened last night I half expect her to go into labor any second. I'm well past tempted to sleep on your couch until it's time."

"You can if you want. Jamison might not be happy about it, but he'll understand." It's a genuine offer. I wouldn't mind at all if Obi took up temporary residence here until the babies are born. Trent would also be overjoyed, he'd give up his room.

"I might actually do it when we're down to the last two weeks. How are Nathan and Kaleb? They were well enough when I left earlier, but since I'm on the phone I might as well ask after them."

"When I last checked on Nathan this afternoon he was sleeping soundly between Talia and Jasper. I'll just go look in on Kaleb now. Dinner is almost finished anyway, and he won't want to miss that." I step over the board in front of my room that squeaks and make my way to Kaleb's room. He's laying on his bed staring at the ceiling. He looks horrible, but nothing's broken. He's just terribly bruised and swollen. "Kaleb. Obi is on the phone. How are you feeling? Do you need anything? Dinner will be out soon, would you like me to bring it up to you."

He lets out a breath and turns toward me. His face looks even more battered than it did earlier. Talia is going to have such a reaction. Kaleb may not be allowed to leave his bed until he looks a little better. "Thank you, but no. I'll be down. Tell Obi to worry about Nathan."

Obi clicks his tongue but I'm the only one to hear it. "How does he look?"

"Like a car crash survivor."

"I do not look like a car crash victim," Kaleb argues and rises into a sitting position with a wince. "I do feel like one, though."

"Unfortunately, Kaleb, you do look like you caught the wrong end of a lot of things. You look worse than you did this afternoon. Can you see out of that eye?" I don't know how he could, I can barely make out a sliver of space between his upper and lower eyelid; not mentioning how swollen his brow and cheek is.

"A little bit. I'll be alright in a couple days."

Obi clicks his tongue again. "Is it swollen shut?"

"Nearly completely. You're sure nothing's broken? It looks terrible." I watched both Obi and Trent finger Kaleb's cheekbone, brow bone, nose, and jaw and neither of them felt anything that felt like a break. Looking at him now, however, is making me question it.

"Just keep ice on it. And the ribs. Devon, too. He's probably a beauty queen right about now, too. I'm going to get back to work now, if I can get this paperwork done then I can get out of here. I'll check in again in the morning. If Talia so much as twitches in the wrong direction, call me, alright?"

"I will, Obi. Thank you." I end the call and turn my attention back on Kaleb. "Talia is going to lose her mind when she sees you. Prepare yourself."

"It can't be that bad." He gets to his feet and crosses to the mirror over his dresser. "Shit."

I slowly nod. "Yes."

Kaleb sighs. "She's still in there with Nathan and Jasper?" I give him another nod. "I'm going to go get some ice. Maybe it'll help it look better before she and Jasper come down."

I don't have the heart to tell him that there's no way in hell he's going to look like anything but a ruined punching bag. Devon looked half as bad as Kaleb when I looked in on him. Trent and Alex are a little roughed up, but honestly they were worse for wear after Talia's heat; so I'm not overly worried about them. Reid isn't wounded at all, but he's too good of a shot to have been wasted on hand to hand fighting. He argued when I made the call to put him up high so he could eliminate problems before they got to us, but it was the right thing to do. He's in the kitchen right now eating himself up with guilt because he didn't anticipate the number of intruders that would come from the far fields or the back line and there's nothing any of us can say to comfort him.

"I'll come down with you. Obi gave me a bit of news to share."

Reid is pulling a baking dish out of the oven when Kaleb and I come into the kitchen. I texted everyone but Talia, Jasper, and Nathan to meet us for a quick discussion and they come straggling in as I'm setting the table. I'll take three plates up to my room after I inform everyone we need to convince Talia that she might not need to be having the amount and types of sex she likes so much. I laugh to myself as I anticipate complete success.

"What's funny?" Alex asks when he comes in from the garage with Devon. "I like to laugh."

"You won't think this is funny. Let's wait for everyone else."

Once everyone is gathered and leaning against their counter of choice I drop the proverbial bomb. "Obi called. Talia is fine, that isn't the issue. Obi would be much more comfortable with the remainder of her pregnancy if she was on complete bed rest."

Trent snorts. "Yeah. That'll definitely happen."

"I had the same response. He amended his professional advice to encouraging her to engage in less intensely physical sexual activities; and for Alex, specifically, to contain himself. He says to keep her as calm as possible."

"Well what are we supposed to do when she drags us to the nearest flat surface by the dick with a list of demands?" Alex asks. I'd laugh at him if she hadn't done almost exactly that on more than a few occasions.

I shrug. "Our best, I suppose. Obi will probably want to stay here for the last few weeks until the birth."

"He can have my room. I'll bunk with Nathan," Trent says, just as I thought he would.

Devon sighs and glances at Kaleb. "You look like you were hit in the face with a shovel."

"It's not that bad," Kaleb argues. "So, to recap, little to no sex and a calm atmosphere for the next several weeks. That's not going to work. Jasper is due to go into heat in around three weeks, and we all know how that goes."

Alex and I exchange a look. During Jasper's last heat we were out of the nest with Talia. Jasper could probably get by with only three alphas because he's much less volatile during his heat than Talia is; but the problem is Talia herself. She won't let him be anything less than properly and fully cared for, which is a problem because she's due to go into labor the week after his heat. It is very unfortunate timing.

Trent speaks up before Alex or I say anything. "He won't leave the manor with her so close to having the babies, or I'd suggest taking him to the farmhouse. Talia wouldn't go for that, anyway; and she'd probably beat my ass for even suggesting it. Devon, Kaleb, and Nathan can handle him. Reid can tag in if he needs to. The rest of us will be out of the nest to make sure Talia is alright and she'll just have to be sour about it. And she's not allowed in the nest. I'll keep her out of it myself. Nathan's sisters said start hardcore nesting about two or three weeks before they have babies, and they do a lot of sleeping the week leading up to birthing. Hopefully Talia will be the same way. And hopefully Jasper's heat will be on the shorter side this time."

Trent has surprised me a few times since we joined our packs. I'm used to thinking of him as a younger version of Alex, complete with a food obsession and an affinity for the ridiculous. But there have been a few instances when Trent has taken charge and been selfless in situations where I'd expect him to add to one of his many lists of grievances. "I think that's a solid plan, Trent. I'm going to take dinner upstairs."

I grab the three covered plates of what was labeled a ham and cheese bake and put them on a tray with a bowl of diced apples and walnuts drizzled with honey and head upstairs. I stop short in the hallway when I hear Nathan choke out the words *oh god* in a way that doesn't suggest being in any amount of pain. If Talia and Jasper are happy enough to play with him and he's well enough to be played with I won't be the one to interrupt. I smile and turn around. When I get back to the kitchen with the tray still full of food, Reid's brows pinch together and he gestures toward the food.

"They're awake, and occupied."

"Well, let's light a candle for Nathan, then, because he's never been on the receiving end of both of them," Trent says and starts in on his food.

Chapter Thirty-One

Talia

"Oh god...fuck..."

I smile around the head of Nathan's cock. Jasper is sucking and licking his balls, and Nathan's got enough length that there's enough room for both of us to grip his shaft. The muscles that make up his thighs and stomach are twitching and clenching every time one of us sucks even just a little. Our poor, wounded alpha might be a little overwhelmed.

We woke up about half an hour ago when we smelled the ham and cheese bake I put up in the freezer and Jasper and I decided Nathan needed a little extra attention, after we made sure he was up to it. I also need the stress relief that making his toes curl provides. That's not even an omega perk, that's just something that I personally enjoy. Something about hearing him, or any of the others, wound up in their pleasure brings me and my ever-ready pussy immense joy. After last night I need all the joy and stress relief I can manage.

Jasper licks up the underside of Nathan's cock. When his tongue brushes against my lips, I slide my mouth over to suck on the other side of the swollen head and it quickly turns into Jasper and I kissing each other around it. Nathan's hips buck up off the bed and he makes a series of sharp little moans. I give him one last lick and pull off, letting Jasper continue. "How's your shoulder? Is it hurting too much? Is this too much stress?"

"What?"

I give his shaft a little squeeze, bringing my fist up to meet Jasper's mouth. "Your shoulder. Does it hurt right now?"

He has to think for a moment, but he eventually answers. "It's fine. Please, please don't stop. Will you do that again? What you just did? With both of you?"

I laugh and go back to giving Jasper sloppy, wet kisses with Nathan throbbing and leaking between our mouths. Nathan is making the most delicious sounds, and lets out a string of curses when I lower my hand to play with his balls.

Jasper pulls off of Nathan with a little pop. "You know what I like for Talia to do when she gives me a blowjob? None of you do it to me, which is actually pretty surprising."

"Oh god," Nathan says for the twentieth time, looking down his body at Jasper. "What?"

Jasper licks back down Nathan's length. "You're either going to really like this, or you're not. I think you'll love it."

Ah. I'm glad I insisted on a very careful shower before I dragged Nathan into the bed. I smirk up at Nathan, "put your leg over my hip, handsome."

"It's too heavy. It'll push on your stomach."

"Do what I said, Nathan." I bend my head and suck a mark over his hip. "Trust me."

He's hesitant, but he hitches his leg over my hip, being ridiculously careful to keep off of my stomach. Then he makes a sound that's close to a yip.

"Be still, baby," Jasper croons. "That was just air. I'm going to lick it soon. Tell me if you want me to stop."

"Jesus. Fuck. God. Fuck."

I'm trying to suck him back into my mouth, but I can't help giggling. Jasper absolutely loves it when I give his asshole extra attention when I'm working him over with my mouth. I don't even need to really lick him half the time before he's writhing all over the bed. And the sounds he makes, fuck I could cum just listening to him. I'm pretty sure Trent has gotten off listening to us on more than one occasion. "Tell me what Jasper's doing to you. Describe it for me while I suck your cock."

"Oh god, Talia. Please. I can't. Don't. I can't take it." Then he makes a noise that's a cross between a huff and a gasp.

"You don't want me to suck your cock?" Maybe I'm mean, but playing with Nathan like this with Jasper, teasing him, is probably one of the most fun things I've ever done. I give him a lick that's almost not there and run a fingertip up the side of his over-sensitive length.

"Yes. No. Oh, fuck."

Jasper lifts his head. "Which is it, baby? Do you want Talia's mouth or not?"

"Oh my god." Nathan takes a breath and nods. "Yes, I want it. Please."

"Such good manners for an alpha, don't you think so?" I hum at Jasper and give Nathan a long lick.

"He's the sweetest one of all of them," Jasper kisses the inside of Nathan's thigh, then lowers his head back down.

Nathan groans, and I ask him again if he can describe what Jasper's doing to him.

"I'll try," he breathes out. Then his hips buck a little and he lets his head drop back. "He licked between my balls and my asshole."

"Did it feel good?" I ask, and give him another swirling lick.

"God, yes." Then he's groaning again. "He licked it, my asshole. Why does it feel so good? Fuck." Jasper's rough laugh spreads just as much heat through me as Nathan's desperate noises.

Then I suck all the way down Nathan's shaft and bob my head a few times. He grunts and lifts his hips off the mattress as he sinks his fingers into my hair.

Jasper does something that has Nathan making the gasping, groaning, huffing sound again, and his fist tightens. "I can't describe it. I don't know what he's doing. It feels so fucking good."

I pull back so that I'm sucking and licking around the head and stroking up and down. I can see Jasper's head moving and I try to keep up with the pace he's setting.

"Fuck. I want to pull his hair. I need my other hand. Please don't stop. Oh god." Whatever Jasper does next has Nathan nearly jackknifing up off the mattress. "Gonna cum, gonna cum, gonna cum," he says over and over again until he does it, giving me his release and practically screaming when I give his knot quick, little strokes. Then Nathan goes limp. We've transformed him into a twitchy, gasping, puddle.

"How's your shoulder?" I ask. I hope arching up like that won't hurt him too much now that he's not in the throes of his pleasure.

"What?" he mumbles, not bothering to open his eyes.

"Your shoulder, Nathan. Does it hurt?"

"Nothing hurts right now. I'm spent, though; I'm sorry. I don't think I can even open my eyes. You'll have to fuck each other or call one of the others in."

Jasper rolls off the bed and stands up with his erection straining against his sweats, complete with a wet spot over the very clearly pronounced head. "We'll be alright. Stay here. I'll bring up dinner."

"How is your shoulder, Nathan? Tell me," I press. I know he wants to bask in the afterglow of that intense orgasm, but he was shot just this morning and we made him cum pretty hard.

A purr rumbles from Nathan with his answer. "It was just a little shot, barely a graze. I'll be good as new in a couple days. Do you really do that to Jasper?"

Graze my ass. The bullet went straight through, just under the ball joint. But he's right, he really should be alright in a couple days. "I do. He makes the best sounds for me."

"It feels fucking amazing. I'm going to do that to him during his next heat."

"Good luck," I say. "I don't think I could stand it during my heat."

Nathan laughs. "No, you definitely couldn't. You'd rip my head off and then demand to be fucked. You and him are so different when you're in heat."

I pull a few strands of his hair. "I'm not that bad."

He snorts. "Yeah, you are. I love it, though." He's quiet for a minute, then he whispers, "I was so scared this morning. I was so afraid we wouldn't be enough. And you were stuck in my room watching monitors. I know that killed you. Are you alright?"

"No." That's the blunt truth. "I'm not. But I will be. I was so afraid. I thought Kaleb was dying. He told me not to look and I kind of lost my mind for a minute. If Jasper hadn't come in and made that sound to pull me back together I don't know what I would have done."

"That sound makes my skin crawl. He's never made that sound before you became pregnant. I don't want to say it's the cause, but it's definitely correlated. What does it feel like? Is it like an alpha command?"

"The sound he was making at the table made him feel big, like he filled the room. I wanted to submit to him and it was a little unnerving. He never made that sound before you became pregnant. I don't want to say it's the cause, but it's definitely correlated. What does it feel like? Is it like an alpha command?"

The only alpha command that has really, truly had any genuine affect on me is when Alex told me to sit when we were testing out those ear pieces, but that was enough to let me know that I hate that shit and I don't ever want that to happen to me again. The sound that Jasper was making at the table had a similar effect, only worse. "The sound Jasper made is a lot more intense than an alpha command. I can still think and know what's happening around me with an alpha command. The sound Jasper made at the table caused me to completely lose myself. The tone he used when I thought Kaleb was dying wasn't exactly like that, but it stopped my panic. Could you guys hear it over the headset?"

He shakes his head. "No. We just heard him talking to you. Are you upset about Pratchett?"

"Fuck no. Fuck him. I'm so relieved. I don't know why seeing him and thinking about him being inside my home made me react the way I did, either here or at the restaurant Devon took me to. I'm just so glad that I don't have to think about seeing him ever again."

"What about Seth? Does he make you react in any kind of way?" Nathan is playing with my hair now, twisting the ends around his fingers while he talks.

I sigh. "Strangely enough, no. I have no reaction to Seth anymore, other than feeling sorry for him and worrying about him. He really will turn out to be good if he has the right kind of people guiding him. I know you all hate him, I don't blame you. Thank you for trusting me enough to give him a chance to change."

"Jasper wants to kill him," Nathan says flatly. "He might do it one day, Talia. Please don't hate him for it. He loathes every breath Seth takes. We all do. I don't care what his reasons were. He hurt you. Then he put you in a fucking cage to wait for him to do it again. If Jasper decides to kill him I'm going to help. Please don't hate us. I don't think I could take it if you hated me."

I lean over and kiss Nathan's cheek. "I won't hate you, I couldn't; but please try not to kill Seth. Corso really, really does not want a council position, and Seth can be turned into something good."

Jasper comes in carrying bottles of water with Corso behind him carrying a tray of food. "I warmed it," Corso says as he puts the tray on the foot of the bed. "Is Nathan going to make it? It sounded questionable for a minute or two."

"I'm going to make it," Nathan laughs. "Thank you for bringing food upstairs. I don't know if I could have walked down them."

I lose my composure, just a little, when I take the dishes down to the kitchen a while later; but I pull it together so that I don't launch all that stress and worry at Devon. He's at the table texting, with a very strong drink by the smell of it. He looks so awful. I haven't seen him since I laid down with Nathan earlier, and I think his injuries are the sort that look a lot worse before they start looking better. "You shouldn't be working. Have you been icing your face? For fuck sake, Devon, are you alright? I shouldn't have slept for so long. I should have checked on you." So much for being pulled together.

He attempts to raise his eyebrow at me, but the effect is ruined by the swelling on that half of his face. His lip is split so bad I think he needs at least a stitch or two on top of how ugly his eye is. He reaches for his glass to hold it to his cheekbone and I see how busted up his knuckles are. "I have ice, see?"

"That's a glass of watery, room temperature bourbon." I grab a bag of peas out of the freezer and hand them to him. "I think you need a stitch or two. What about the rest of you? How bad is it?"

He eyes me for a second before holding the peas to the side of his face. "I'll heal faster without the stitches. I can strip down and show you all my boo-boos, but it will just stress you unnecessarily, and that's unacceptable at this point."

"What do you mean unacceptable? If you're hurt I need to know how badly."

Devon sets down his phone and drains his glass. "Obi has given orders that you are to be kept as calm and level as possible for the remainder of the pregnancy. He also advised that sex needs to be limited and gentle. We all thought that was a pretty big ask on his part, but we said we'd try to convince you to be less...vigorous."

If I wasn't so worried about how many of Devon's ribs are broken I'd laugh. "We'll give it our best shot, but if I need to be fucked, one of you better do it or I might just pout. How many broken ribs do you have?"

"Miraculously, none. I'm just bruised. Reid has a theory that I agree with, especially after I saw the footage of how it was for Kaleb. The people who were attacking Kaleb and I weren't trying to kill us or they would have. They were trying to lure you out."

I nod. I had that thought earlier before I distracted myself with Nathan. "If Jasper hadn't come in when he did I would have. My vision even changed a little around the edges. I was so afraid for Kaleb and you, and angry with Trent and Nathan for not going out to help. I was taking off the headset to come out and shoot every one of those assholes who were hurting you."

"Did he make that sound again?"

"No, it was something different," I say, and start putting our dishes into the dishwasher. "I'm glad, but the way he was talking affected me almost like an alpha command. I'm glad he did it. It would have been catastrophically stupid for me to have left that room." I've been trying to process the changes happening in Jasper almost as hard as I've been trying not to think about them. I don't know what they mean. I didn't know it was possible for a male omega to make the sounds he's been making or to give what amounts to alpha commands. So far, I'm the only one affected by the commands, but I'm pretty sure we all get chills when he makes some of the sounds he makes.

"Agreed. Reid said he was making a new sound right before he shot Pratchett. His exact words were 'alarming throat clicking that crawled up his spine like a shot of ice water', so that's something. I wasn't there to hear it, but the others said that was a fair assessment."

I lean against the counter and try not to look like I'm scrutinizing every visible mark on Devon's body, probably unsuccessfully. He looks so swollen and bruised, I can only imagine how painful it must be. The longer I look at him, the worse I feel about sleeping for hours and then having fun with Nathan and Jasper.

"Stop it," Devon says. "Right now. You can't do anything for this," he gestures at his face. "You needed the sleep. I don't think you feel your emotions the way other people do."

"What's that supposed to mean?"

He sighs and puts the peas on the table. "It means that we can feel what you're feeling to a large degree through our bonds with you. You feel guilty right now; but when you feel other things, both good and bad, we can feel them. How did you feel when you saw Pratchett get out of the vehicle? How did you feel knowing he was close, that he could come into the manor if he wanted to?"

"Horrible. Angry."

"You had another panic attack like when we saw him at the restaurant. It was much more than horrible and angry. It was definitely those things, but it was a lot more. I can't speak for the others, but I felt fear more than anything else. Straight up terror, then aversion strong enough that it made me physically gag. That's what you felt like to me. If Jasper hadn't killed him this morning, I'd be out hunting him down right now."

Huh. It didn't feel like fear. It felt like I couldn't breathe with him that close to my home, and maybe a little like I might die if he actually entered it, but that isn't fear. Is it?

Devon steeples his hands under his chin. "What are you thinking about right now, this very moment?"

"How I was feeling when I thought he might come into the manor." Was I afraid of him being inside my home? I'm not afraid of Jonas Pratchett, but Devon is right. I had a huge reaction to seeing him at the restaurant, and I'd had another reaction to seeing him on the monitor. "I don't understand why I react to him the way I do. When I think about him I'm not afraid of him. He is nothing to be afraid of at all, just an awful man who does and says awful things. But since the auction, when he's been physically close to me, I don't know. I don't understand why it happens."

"It's a stress response, honey. You might not feel like you're afraid of him, you probably aren't, but your subconscious recognizes him as an intense threat and that's nothing you can control. Everything with Seth happened because his father pushed and pushed until Seth caved. Seth might not have ever bonded with Jay and Derrick if his father hadn't pushed him into it. Your brain chose Pratchett as the focal point for a trauma response. Close proximity to Pratchett, and Pratchett himself, are triggers for you.

It makes sense that you don't recognize him as a trigger because you've probably never actually had one before now. I hope knowing he's dead will help lessen your response to him."

So do I. I haven't had a reaction to anything the way I have reacted to a nearness with Jonas Pratchett. I didn't have that reaction to him at the auction, I was disgusted but I was still able to handle it. It wasn't until after I found out the role he played during my placement with Seth's pack that I had a panic reaction to him. I can't stand the idea of having an entire panic attack at the mere thought or mention of him.

"I'm going to check on everyone. Are you alright, Devon?" My plan is to make a round to check in on every member of my pack then drag Corso into my bed so I can make him read to me.

"I'm alright. I won't be up much longer. Everyone is scattered, though. Corso and Reid were going through the security recordings last I checked, Alex is outside somewhere doing whatever he's doing and Trent's with him. Kaleb is in his bed. I'd like for him to stay there as long as he can stand it. Before you see him, please know that he looks far worse than he actually is, but he's also a lot worse off than he wants to admit. And," he pushes away from the table and holds a hand out to me, "if you don't mind, I'd like to have you in my arms for a minute. This morning and today scared the hell out of me."

I smile and go over to stand between his legs. He wraps his arms around my waist and rests his head against my chest. His breath is warm and he smells like everything I like best about spring. I don't know how long I stand there letting Devon hold me, but when he pulls back from me, he feels so much lighter and I feel a whole lot stronger.

Chapter Thirty-Two

Kaleb

Talia is in my room. Her spicy scent is every bit as warm and comforting as the sound I've been listening to for the past little while. Talia's soft purring hum didn't wake me up, but the wonderful way it made me feel did. When I took myself to bed I felt really horrid, like my face might actually either explode off of my skull, or possibly ooze off of my chin, and I could barely breath with the pain in my hands and ribs. It might be a combination of things that are attributing to how much better I feel right now, but I'm giving Talia all the credit. Waking up to see her sitting by my bed reading in the dim lamplight is damn near perfection.

"You look so terrible." Talia's voice is so quiet, our bond full of worry.

"You look beautiful."

"How bad are you hurting? I'm going to go get you some pain meds and ice."

She starts to close her book, but I put my hand on her knee to stop her. "Stay. I'm okay right now. Read to me."

"Corso's better at it."

"I'd rather hear you."

She looks down at the book then back at me. "You won't like it."

"I will."

She takes a quick little breath that catches in her chest. "You were dying, Kaleb. I felt it."

"I'm still right here."

Talia isn't much of a crier, it usually takes things like being abandoned by the pack she was supposed to be part of or a hand-made cradle, but she's about to cry for me.

"Read to me, Talia."

She takes a much deeper breath and shakes her head a little, then she reads. It takes several pages before I realize why she said I wouldn't like it. It's one of the romances she and Jasper enjoy so much. I don't care. She could read me the back of a cereal box right now and I would think it was amazing. This story is apparently about an alpha who doesn't want to be an alpha so he can be with the girl he loves. Before I let sleep take me again I ask her if she's read this one before.

"This is one of my favorites."

Of course it is. "Does he get the girl in the end?"

She licks her lips and looks off to the side before she answers. "He does."

"Good."

~

Three days later I'm the happiest person in the universe because I can chew food. Soft food, but still food that is solid enough to require mastication. Talia made one of my favorite comfort meals, chicken and gravy over mashed potatoes, and I've eaten entirely too much. I think I may have actually given Trent's stomach some competition.

Talia and Jasper are at the sink finishing up the dishes while Reid wipes down the counters. It's supposed to be movie night, but we haven't decided what to watch that wasn't sappy or boring since action and horror is out. Talia very vocally thinks it's ridiculous.

"Washing the dishes is more stressful than any of the movies we watch. I can't go out for walks, I can't convince any of you to fucking rail me the way I want you to, Trent even took the spicy spices out of the cabinet; but nobody's volunteering to save me from my mother's multiple calls every day, and that shit is *actually* stressful."

Reid sighs and looks up at the ceiling. "I will take your mother's calls if they're really all that stressful. She's just excited. My mother and Alex's have also been calling regularly."

"No," she grumbles. "I'll take the calls, they don't really bother me. I'm just anxious and itchy and frustrated on a few different fronts."

"We could play a board game?" Jasper suggests. It's tempting, I haven't played a board game in years.

Talia and Reid both immediately veto it, though. "No," Talia says, drying her hands. "Alex cheats and, believe it or not, Corso is a sore loser."

Alex comes in at the perfect time to pretend to be innocent and offended. "Excuse me, I do not cheat. Corso is a sore loser, though."

Talia twists her mouth to the side and then her eyes light up. "Cards! We can play cards. There's a deck in the junk drawer. No spades, no gin."

Alex does cheat, almost as bad as Trent; and it turns out that Corso is, in fact, a sore loser. I never would have guessed Corso, with all his noble and just ways ideals, would pout over being the first to be down to his boxers. I am in no way surprised that Talia is not only fully clothed, but she has accumulated a pile of our clothes on the floor beside her chair. The only thing keeping Nathan and I in our shirts is our injuries.

"I should have known better when you were so happy about shuffling." Devon is side-eying Talia.

She throws him a saccharin grin. "I'm definitely happy with the result. It isn't my fault you guys can't keep your clothes on."

"I also appreciate how this is going," Jasper's eyes travel over all the exposed skin around the table. "How did you get to be so good at winning? It was Jamison, wasn't it?"

Talia pushes up from her chair and gathers the clothes she won. "No, well, Jamison did teach me the rules." She waits till she's nearly out the door before she says over her shoulder, "but Bianca taught me how to cheat." Then she escapes up the stairs.

"Did we let her win?" I don't feel like we let her win. I certainly didn't.

Trent starts cackling. "Hell no. I didn't, anyway. I thought Alex was supposed to be the one to look out for."

~

There's only three weeks left until Talia's due date. Jasper is winding up for his next heat cycle, but it isn't like every other time. He's needy and cuddly like he always is, but this time it's such a huge contrast from how he's been since Talia's been pregnant. He's changed. He's so much more, I don't know, dominant? Assertive? Borderline aggressive with some things? Jasper has been incredibly insistent about Talia's needs being met, all of them. He has also been very attentive to her, especially during this last small stretch; and every second he isn't being cuddly and needy he's been broody and angry. This is the first time I've seen Jasper be angry about going into heat.

I mentioned it to Talia and her face darkened before she told me how it was when we were trapped at the compound and Devon was at the hospital, when Reid had to create a bond with him that none of us expected to need. "He was so angry, Kaleb. He felt so, so guilty because you were all in danger and gone, and Devon was in such bad shape. But he couldn't stop his system from functioning any more than any other omega can. He was shutting down without you all. It isn't like going into heat and needing an alpha, it was so much worse. He couldn't feel any of you, and Devon was barely a flicker. Despite his connection with me, he was declining so fast without his alphas tethering him. Reid was perfect, though. He was exactly what Jasper needed. Jasper is angry right now for some of the same reasons I hate going into heat. You lose yourself. He's going to lose himself and almost an entire week when I'm only three away from delivering. He's afraid and angry."

I understand that, I really do. But I don't think there's anything that will make him feel better, or at least make it not so awful. The pressure and stress I feel in him is so heavy.

He and Talia are outside right now, discussing how hard they're going to have to fight Trent to put a tree house up in one of the massive trees on the lawn. They think Trent is the one to worry about, but hell might have to freeze over before Devon allows our kids to scale a tree. Not to mention Reid. Ever since the invasion, he, Alex, Trent, and Devon have immersed themselves in fortifying the property. Nathan has cameras watching everything covered from twig to pebble, but that isn't enough. The only thing stopping them from building a spiked wall around the place is Corso. He might go for the moat they keep talking about, though. Eventually. I thought they were joking, but apparently not because I caught the four of them looking at heavy equipment brochures.

Most of the leaves have fallen from the trees, with only a few shriveled, brown husks clinging stubbornly to their branches. The golden, late-fall sunshine is gorgeous, and my omegas look amazing standing in it. Then I remember something I wanted to do with Talia before she delivered. Trent is in the garage with Devon, tinkering with the disaster Talia calls a car. He's very conveniently wearing a blue flannel shirt. "Hey, Trent."

"Hey, Kaleb."

"Give me your flannel."

"What? Why? It's dirty."

Rolling my eyes, just a little, I hold out my hand. "Just give it to me. If you're chilly you can have mine."

He shrugs out of it and hands it over. "I'm fine, it's not that cold in here. What are you doing?"

"I'll show you later."

I head out to catch up with Jasper and Talia. They're still arguing under one of the bigger oak trees. "Hey. Come help me with something."

"Do you think this would be a good tree for a treehouse?" Talia asks, still looking up into the higher branches.

I want to laugh, but I don't. "Honey, you'll be doing good to convince us to tie a tire to the thickest branch. Let's go around back." The corn was harvested weeks ago, but there's still a corner of rows still standing for whatever reason. They're perfect for what I want. When we get back there I hold out Trent's shirt to her. "I know it's cold, but put this on."

"Over my sweater?" She glances at Jasper then back at me.

"No. I want to take your picture. Nathan's sister had pictures done of when she was as pregnant as you are. We're too antsy to have a photographer come, but I'm not horrible at it. Remember that picture of the sunflowers and the butterflies at the farmhouse? I took that. I thought about doing this with one of the barrels at the distillery, but the light right now is perfect."

Jasper smiles and starts helping Talia out of her layers. She's wearing her usual leggings and, so far, she's peeled off Reid's sweater and one of Devon's tee-shirts. There's a black tank top stretched over her stomach, only just covering her bellybutton.

"Are you too cold?" Jasper asks, fingering the hem of the tank top.

"I'm fine." Talia lifts her arms and lets Jasper pull off the last shirt. "Bra, too?"

"Leave it for now. Maybe we'll take some more fun pictures inside later." I give her a wink and hold out the flannel shirt. She takes a deep breath, mumbling about now wanting brownies, before she puts it on and starts to do up the buttons. "Wait, just one or two. Just to cover your breasts. I want to be able to see your stomach."

She snorts. "How could you miss it?" Then Jasper and I have what ends up being a truly wonderful afternoon posing Talia all around the back of the manor. I even convince Jasper to get in on one of the shots; I think that one will end up being Talia's favorite.

"These are really great, Kaleb." Nathan is helping me edit some of the best ones. It has been pretty difficult to choose the best ones. As sour-mouthed as she is, Talia takes a really beautiful picture. "There isn't a single bad one, even the one where she was making the face is good."

The face he's referring to is one of the last few I took. She was irritated that Devon, Trent, and Alex came back to watch what we were doing. It was alright at first, but when they started giving suggestions, Alex's being completely inappropriate, she was finished with all of us.

"This one, though. She's going to love this one." I point to the one of her sitting on the ground between Jasper's legs with both their hands spread out over her stomach. "It's going to be her favorite."

"I like this one more than the rest, I think." Nathan enlarges the one of her standing in front of the corn stalks. The distillery is far off in the background, and all the surrounding fields. It's a profile shot of her looking off into the distance. Her bare stomach is prominent with her hands resting on top, I can just barely see her fingertips peeking out from the sleeves. Everything about the picture is warm perfection.

"Yeah. Corso's going to love that one. I'm going to send that one to be blown up. She might kill us, but I kind of want to hang it in the big room, maybe over the piano. I'll have this one put in the nursery." He pulls up an enlargement of Talia's and Jasper's hands covering her stomach that he cropped from the other one.

"I think that would be perfect in the nursery. I think you're right about hanging the other one over the piano, it'll be worth the risk to life and limb." I glance through the rest of them again and bring up one of her laughing. Alex had just walked into a spiderweb that was between a couple corn stalks and he and Trent were trying to pull the webs and potential spiders from his hair after he did an impression of drunken karate. This one is a contender for being the best one because the focus is her, not the pregnancy. "Send this one to Devon. And Reid." They'll all likely pick through them and choose their favorites, but this is my project and I get to pick who sees what first.

"Corso might wallpaper the whole house with them." Nathan's only half joking.

"Not if he's smart."

Chapter Thirty-Three

Talia

Jasper's heat has been so strange. He's been building up to it over the past couple weeks, but now that it's here it's almost mild; and he's so angry between spikes and waves. Omegas just don't leave their nests once they're in heat, but when Reid made the mistake of telling Devon about my condition a little too loudly it was almost like a switch was flipped. Jasper left his nest to come see what was happening in mine and nobody knows what to think or say about that. He only stayed long enough to assure himself that I'm alright, but leaving his nest in the middle of a heat is a little beyond outside of the norm.

I really am alright, though. I'm just really tired. I can't seem to stay awake for more than a few hours, which I'm grateful for, if I'm honest. Any other time Jasper's in heat I want to be right in the middle of it with him, but not this time. I can't wait for it to be over. Then I can have him in my nest with me and we can rest together. My biggest problem right now is that I can't get the nest right. It was fine before this morning, but every time I wake up something new is wrong and I keep having to adjust it.

Corso has been a constant and comforting presence. He's so patient with me, even when I'm being a little short-tempered and more than a little irrational. Alex is also right here with me; bringing snacks, pushing fluids, stealing laundry so I can add to the nest. Earlier he brought me something from Jasper's nest that hadn't yet dried. It made me cry, then I was laughing because that isn't the kind of thing that should result in a sentimental emotional outburst. Sticky or not, that pillowcase is now part of the corner structure of this nest; and I'm not sure what that says about me.

"He's already winding down, I can feel it." Reid has been splitting his time between Jasper and me. He's being pulled by Jasper's heat to, at the very least, check in on him, and he seems very happy to watch me like a hawk. I know it isn't his, or any of their intention to make me feel like I'm a bomb just waiting to go off, but I'm starting to feel like one.

"It's only been two days," I yawn. "If he's able to will his heat to be shorter, I might kick him in the knee when he comes all the way out of it."

Alex's mouth twitches to the side, but he maintains his composure. "Oh, you will not. Well, you might. I don't think that's it, though. I think it's a subconscious, biological thing. Like, a mated pair thing. Kind of like he's your mate and those are his biological offspring and his system is somehow altering itself because you're about to have them. You're due next week, so that's a much more feasible possibility than him willing it to go away because he wants it to."

"You're probably right. I'm just grouchy because I'm itchy and tired. I wouldn't actually kick Jasper in the knee." I yawn again and curl back under my blankets. "The leg, I could kick him in the leg. Just a little bit. If he's able to make his heat go away on purpose. Come in here with me, I need you to snuggle me."

"Can we be naked? I'm feeling handsy." Alex makes a big show of wiggling his eyebrows at me.

"If we're naked I'll definitely be handsy, but I don't know if I'll be able to stay awake long enough to follow through."

He strips and crawls under the covers to help me pull off the little clothes I have on. "It isn't always about follow through. Hearing you talk, all you're interested in is my dick; and that's just hurtful. I've got a heart, too, and magnificent hair."

"I love your hair. It's very soft and warm, and it always smells amazing, like you."

He kisses my temple and curls his body around mine, cupping my breast in his hand like he does at night when he's sleeping. "What do I smell like to you, sweet pea?"

That humming purr begins in the back of my throat as I answer. "Like a fire, and burnt marshmallows. I love it so much. I'm going to sleep now." The last thing I hear before I drift off is Alex's purr matching mine.

I wake up the next morning to what feels like a pinch running up my abdomen, but I don't think much of it, especially since Jasper is watching me from about three inches away from my face. "You have to stop waking me up like this, princess."

He smiles and reaches over to tug on my earlobe. "You don't like seeing me first thing?"

"I love seeing you all the time. How are you feeling?"

Jasper's mouth pulls to the side and he hums. "I've never had a heat like this one. Only a couple days long and not overwhelming like usual. Not even a little. I've been needy like usual, but I haven't been drowning in it. And I think it might be over. How are you feeling? Something seems different. You've been sleeping so much."

I sigh and close my eyes again. It would be so easy to just go back to sleep, and it's more than tempting. "I'm alright, just really tired."

"I think it's almost baby time. I wish I had a bond with you like the others do. I've been leaning on Corso to tell me what he feels. He says you feel exhausted and tight."

That's a fair assessment. I am exhausted. Even sleeping makes me tired. And I do feel tight. Inside and out. My skin is stretched so tight across my stomach and my breasts feel humongous. Even feeling the way I do, it's been really wonderful not losing myself to a heat cycle. "I'm sure it'll be obvious when it's baby time. What's everyone doing?"

"Devon is doing something in the garage, mostly distracting himself from worrying about you. Corso and Reid went to check things at the distillery. They think it's baby time, too. So, they're doing a run-through before they're unavailable. Alex is working in his room, Nathan, too. Kaleb is reading. He's finishing the book you started him on a couple weeks ago. It's adorable to see him nose-first in a love story. And Trent is making a mess in the kitchen."

Warmth brings a smile to my face. Kaleb is finishing the book. I wonder how long it's going to take him to work out why I like it so much. "What is Trent trying to make, other than a mess? Do you know?"

"Bianca's soup."

Oh my god. He's going to ruin my soup pot. "Can you reach my phone?" He hands it to me and I call Trent. "Please stop everything you're doing. I'll be right down to help."

I hear water running, and the distinct sound of a metal ladle banging and scraping against the inside of my soup pot. "You don't have to come down. I've got this. I can follow directions. Besides, I can't stop now, there's bubbling."

"I"m coming. I want to watch you cook." What I don't say is that I want to come down there and knock him out with the ladle after I take it away from him for scraping the bottom of my pot.

The scene in the kitchen is....unfortunate. So unfortunate that I'm tempted to just walk away, but Trent really is pretty cute in an apron. "Where did you get an apron?"

"Nonna left it." Corso's mother is the only one of our parents who has officially and regularly been using her grandparent title, so we have also been using it. Some of us more than others, apparently. But the apron with the contrasted ruching around the top is just adorable on him.

"You're adorable. If you put that metal ladle near my pot again I'm going to beat you to death with it. There's a wooden one in the drawer by the stove. It smells good, though. Do you need help with the potatoes?"

"Oh," at least he has the decency to look sorry. "I didn't know there was a difference. Why do we have this one if we're not allowed to use it?"

"Fair point. I don't like how abrasive it is, but it's fine to use with the stock pots. What can I do to help."

Trent huffs out a breath and tongues the inside of his cheek. "Just sit at the table and look pretty while I finish making this. I can cook; I'm very capable. You can be the taster."

Giving up control of the kitchen takes a little effort, but I manage. I can let Trent cook in here, he's been cooking a lot more often since I've been so tired recently. They all have. I don't know why I'm so prickly about it right now. Jasper pulls out a chair for me and then goes to fill the tea kettle. As I'm sitting down I feel another of those pinches. I must make a face because Trent's eyebrows take over his face. "I'm fine."

"You winced."

I rub the stomach that has taken over everyone's lives and give Trent what I hope is a reassuring smile. "Growing pains. I'm alright." He definitely doesn't believe me, but he doesn't argue with me and turns to stir the soup he's been working so hard on.

I watch Trent add the diced potatoes to another pot of boiling water before he starts chopping celery in tiny slivers. I should do this more often. Trent working in the kitchen, barefoot, in a pair of soft jeans and an apron is entirely too sexy.

"Get your mind out of the gutter, darlin. You're too tired and I'm too busy to do anything about it," Trent says, his cocky smirk just makes him even more fun to look at.

Jasper brings over a cup of tea for each of us and we watch Trent finish adding things into the pot until the potatoes are finished. "Are you sure you're alright, Talia?" Jasper asks. "You look a little pale."

"I'm just tired. I think I'm going to go back upstairs. Will you walk up with me? You don't have to stay, you can just tuck me in."

"I'm staying with you. Are you finished with your tea? You barely drank half."

I nod. I did well enough to drink as much as I did. I feel another pinch when I push up from the table, but nothing significant. If I say anything about it they'll never leave me alone. I take the tea mugs to the sink and follow Jasper to the door, stopping on the way to pull the bow on Trent's apron loose. I'm stepping up onto the bottom stair when I sneeze. Twice. Just two little sneezes is all it takes for my water to break and I'm standing there, one foot on the stair, looking down at the growing puddle on the floor. "Shit."

Jasper whips around, his eyes huge, and joins me in staring at the water spreading across the floor. It isn't a lot, not the gush I had it built up to in my mind; but there's enough to thoroughly soak my leggings and socks. His eyes meet mine and I see him change right in front of me, even more than he already has. He goes from surprise, to fear, to an anchor in just a few seconds.

Then I sneeze again and I get the gush I imagined. "Shit."

"Trent! It's time. Hurry. Call Obi. Get the others here, fast!" Jasper yells.

Yes, those are definitely things we need to do, but more importantly, "turn off the stove! Do that first!"

We decided that me walking up the stairs is a better decision than Trent carrying me. It only took a threat or two. Alex met us at the top of the stairs, his eyes and hair wild, phone to his ear, and Kaleb was in the hallway behind him. Devon, smudged in all the right places with engine grease, came skidding into Corso's room right after Jasper helped me peel off my poor leggings; nearly knocking Nathan over. Obi somehow developed the ability to teleport or fly because he got here quicker than Corso and Reid. And now everyone is in here breathing too loud. "I need noise. Music, talk radio, a ball game, something."

Alex finds a classical guitar playlist and plays it loud enough to drown out the sound of all the breathing. Obi checks the monitor for the hundredth time, but I've got tough news for him. If he thinks I'm laying around waiting for contractions to get close together, he's sadly mistaken. I don't want to walk laps around the manor or anything, and the stairs are definitely out, but I'm not just laying here. I feel like I might start screaming if I have to lay here and be monitored another minute. "I'm taking this thing off. I need to move around. And you're all staring at me. We've got a while yet. The contractions are still about six minutes apart."

"It's going to go faster than it normally would with just one, and you're already a little early. You don't have to keep the leads on, but I'd rather you stay near the nest and equipment if you can stand it. I don't want you to be too far away if something happens." Obi really is terrified. If I thought Jamison could handle the situation, I'd invite him into the room to help Obi feel more at ease. Hopefully knowing that his alpha is just downstairs will help.

The next contraction takes my concentration and my breath. They're getting longer and more intense. "Help me take off the leads, I need them off," I grit out, pulling at the belt around my stomach that's supposed to monitor the contractions. It's ridiculous. I know when I'm having contractions. This is unnecessary and cumbersome. I can't move with all this stuff all over me. Hands start pulling things off of me, I don't know whose, I don't want to open my eyes long enough to look. It doesn't really matter, so long as they help.

The contraction passes and I can breathe again, so I talk while I can. "I'll try not to be hateful, but I'm probably about to be the worst version of myself. I'm sorry in advance. Please stay with me, unless it gets to be too much for you, but please don't leave."

Devon leans in so that his forehead touches mine. "Never. We'll never leave you. You can be as mean as you need to be. We can take it." I nod and close my eyes again to try to keep from crying with the relief and joy overwhelming me. I do not want to weep as I bring my children into the light. Devon said it so it's true. I won't be alone for a minute of this.

Things are harder once there are only a couple minutes between contractions. Trent is clocking them like it's his job, so I know that there were exactly two minutes and thirty-seven seconds between the last contraction and this one. I'm getting very tired now. And I have the sudden urge to hear my mother's voice. "Jamie!" I yell as soon as I can get a big enough breath to do it.

My brother is there before I finish calling his name. "I was in the hall. What do you need? Just tell me and I'll do it."

"Call mom. You talk to her, I can't. Hurry. Tell her I'm okay, keep her updated. Don't let her come yet. Wait till tomorrow. I just need to hear her. I don't know what the fuck's wrong with me."

Corso pushes my hair back from my face and starts twisting it up into another bun. They keep coming undone and falling down. My hair is hot and weighs a hundred pounds right now. I've been fantasizing about cutting it off to my ears for the past hour. "There's nothing wrong with you, tesoro. Are you sure you wouldn't like your mother to be here?"

"No, definitely not. I just want to hear her. I might cry. Hurry, Jamie. Before the next one."

I hear the dull ringing and my mother is on the line. "It's too late in the evening for you to call, my son. What's wrong?"

"It's Talia. She asked me to call."

My father, or one of them, grunts on the other end of the call and I hear a curse from one of the others. "What's wrong? Where is she? Marcus, it's Talia. Something's wrong." They were asleep, and now she's shoving them all out of bed for a phone call.

"No, no. Mom. Listen. She's alright. She's having the baby."

"Now!" she hisses, "I'm coming. Tell her I'm on my way."

"No. Mom. Wait. I'm here with her. I came with Obi. She just wanted to hear you. The contractions are a couple minutes apart now, so it shouldn't be too much longer. She wants you to come tomorrow. She just wanted you to know, she wanted to hear you. That's all. Go back to bed."

She laughs into the phone. "My silly, silly son. Go back to bed, are you kidding? Am I on speaker?"

"Yes," Corso answers.

"Good. Talia, honey, you're going to be just fine. You're the strongest person I've ever known in my life and I'm so proud of you. Your baby is the luckiest baby in the entire world because you're going to be his mother. Your pack is there with you, and they'll help you. Jasper, sweetheart, are you doing alright?" I'm so relieved that someone asked after Jasper. He says he's alright, and he's been helping me through every contraction that Croso hasn't. They've been taking turns pushing against my hips, rubbing my back, containing my hair.

"I'm good. Just trying to help Talia however I can."

"Push on her hips," she suggests. "Help her onto her hands and knees and rock with her. It'll help. That position is just as good at birthing a baby as it is making one."

"Jesus, Mother. Goddamn. I don't want that visual." Jamison is every bit as horrified as I am right now. It's wonderful.

"Stay in the room much longer and you'll have a far more detailed visual." Of course my mother is making crude remarks in the middle of my labor. It's perfect, and the exact reason I wanted to call her. "I'm going to make some tea and read a book until you call me with my new baby grandson screaming in the background. Don't get in the way, Jamie, and don't get on your sister's nerves. This is not the time to test her. I love you, my children." Then she hangs up. That was the phone call I needed. Short, rude, just what I needed, and ending just in time for the next contraction.

"Thank you, Jamie. Now, get out. Unless you want an eye-full of your sister's snatch."

"For fuck sake," he drags his hand down his face and walks out the door. "I'll be right out here if you need me."

Chapter Thirty-Four

Corso

The contractions have stalled at a minute apart, with no progression, for nearly an hour. Obi is concerned. I am a little past worried. And Trent is trying very hard to not climb the walls in his terror. I have never seen a man so afraid. He's also issued several death-threats to Obi if he doesn't 'get those babies out of his omega before they kill her'. I'm just about ready to issue a few of my own.

Talia is utterly exhausted. She's so pale that I can clearly see veins webbing beneath her skin. She's still working, though. She and Jasper are a unit. At this moment, she's leaning into him with her face buried in his shoulder, swaying with yet another contraction while I apply pressure to her hips. Jasper is making a quiet, altered version of the odd noise he made before that earned him a slap at the time, and it seems to be helping to relieve some of her pain and stress. Devon is driving everyone crazy with his pacing, and Kaleb is very literally wringing his hands. We are all useless and powerless right now and I hate it more than anything I've ever hated.

I've been trying to keep her hair back, feeding her chipped ice, rubbing and pressing any part she or Jasper points to, anything to try to help. But there's nothing. Talia is so stubborn. She is determined to have the babies without any interventions, but Obi sent out a secret text to me and Devon telling us that we may have to call it on her behalf. There are procedures he can perform here and medications he can give to help things along, but if she or the babies show another drop of stress he wants to carry her down to the sterile mobile clinic parked out front so he can get the babies out. I hope it doesn't come to that, she'll be so disappointed. Disappointed and no longer in this much distress with three healthy babies is better than the other alternative, though.

I keep feeling something tugging at me, something from Talia. Almost like a small sadness, but not like she's giving up. Just a small, nagging feeling of...loneliness? Being alone? We're all here with her, though. Encouraging her, purring for her, terrified for her. She must know that she's not alone. How could she not? I know omegas occasionally feel irrationally emotional, but... But Talia isn't an omega. Technically, biologically, she is, obviously. Inwardly, in her own mind's eye, deep inside her heart or hearts, Talia is a beta. She will always be a beta. And now she's surrounded by a bunch of alphas who don't do anything but react the way alphas do and a male omega who thinks and reacts like an omega. Obi is here, doing his job to monitor his patient and the infants she's trying to bring into the world, exactly as he should. He loves Talia like a sister, but right now he is being the best doctor he can be. He is doing his job. Talia is flailing and flagging because she's having trouble finishing her job, and that is the worst possible thing for a beta.

"Alex, get your mother on the phone." Everyone but Talia looks at me like I've lost my mind. I suppose it does sound like a ridiculous thing, since Talia isn't even asking for her own mother again. But I know this will help. "Just do it, alright. Trust me."

He pulls out his phone and makes the call on speaker. His mother answers after a few rings, sounding completely annoyed that he's interrupted whatever she was doing. "Alexander Rosen, do you have any idea what time it is? You better be on fire or bleeding out."

"Sorry, Ma. Talia is in labor. Corso said to call you, so I did." Alex sounds as pinched and worn as I feel.

"What's wrong? Is she alright? Are the babies okay? What do you need?" She said babies. She knows our big secret. That's trouble for later.

"She's so tired. And they're not coming, she's just having contraction after contraction and they just won't come out. We can't make it better, we can't do anything. Corso just said to call you, that's all. I don't know why."

"Are you alright, Alex?" Like most mothers, so goes from irritation to concern to worry within a few blinks.

"No. Corso, why did we call my mom?" He hands me the phone.

"I thought you'd have a suggestion. From a beta point of view. I don't know if there's a difference between a beta and an omega in labor, but I thought...I don't know. I thought you might know something that would help." It sounds completely stupid said aloud. Of course there's no difference between an omega and a beta having babies.

"Can she hear me?"

"Yes," Talia hisses.

"I know you're tired, but you've got to get three little bodies out of you. If you were in major distress, Obi would already have you out of there. How far apart are your contractions?"

"About a minute, for the last hour or so. I can't make anything move forward. I'm stuck." Her voice is watery and thin. It's horrible to hear.

I hear a tea kettle whistle in the background and cups clinking. "Stuck. Hmm. Would you like for me to tell you about when Alex was born?"

Talia nods and drops back onto her hands and knees, her fingers digging into the nest as she begins to rock back and forth again. I answer for her. "Yes, she's nodding. She's having another contraction."

318 THE BETA PART THREE

"You keep working, sweetheart. Just listen to me. We never joined a pack, so I didn't have any alphas there to get in my way and try to fix everything. That's what they do, honey. They don't know how to help, not in a way that's helpful to the work that needs to be done. They want to fix things. If they can't fix things right away, they tend to make things worse. That's one of the reasons I never wanted to tie myself to a pack, I don't have the patience to coddle them. I think that's what you're trying to do right now. Can you feel them through your bonds?"

Talia nods again, just once. Her eyes are squeezed shut and she's moved one hand to wrap around Jasper's wrist. He's sitting in front of her, breathing with her through her pain. I don't know exactly what their connection feels like to them, so I don't know how much of her pain he is actually able to shoulder. All I do know for certain is what I feel, and I know the others are sure to be feeling something similar. I want to take her pain into myself, but I can't. I was able to take on a little at first, I think we all were, but I can't now. What I felt through my bond with her when the first real contraction hit her took my breath and they just progressively got worse until I stopped being able to feel them at all.

"She can feel them," Jasper answers.

"You're bottling up all the pain. You're protecting them from it. That's what omegas do, and that's alright. But right now you have important work to do, so you're going to be a beta. I'm going to tell you all about Alex and his big head. He came in the middle of the night. Why wouldn't he? It was so hot that night, I couldn't get comfortable. His father had a feeling that it might be time, but I didn't worry about it because there's no planning that sort of thing. Babies come when they're ready." She pauses to hush Alex's dad and I hear the creak of the rocking chair that I know to be in front of the fireplace in their living room.

Talia sits back on her heels and reaches for Jasper. She has him sit between her knees so she can lean against him. "Did he take a very long time to be born?" She's quiet, a small tremble to her voice. I hate it.

"Yes and no. I got up to get a drink and my water broke, then I labored for almost the whole night before he came. We called the midwife to let her know how things were progressing, but since they mostly weren't, she told us to call her when the contractions were five minutes apart. She offered to be there from the beginning, but I didn't see the point in that because everything was going so smoothly. She and Jake both fussed about that, but, ultimately, I was the one giving birth so I made the choice. I got the idea that I wanted to get into a bath and that's where he was born. It felt so much better to be in the water, poor Jake had to keep warming it. Alex was born at sunrise in a tub of lukewarm water. His hair was black when he was born, it didn't start turning blonde until he was two. Can you imagine Alex with dark hair?"

I personally cannot imagine Alex with anything but a long, blonde mane. As Alex's mother continues talking about him as an infant, I begin to feel more of Talia's emotions, and more of her pain. I'm not the only one. Her bond with each of us is different; the function is the same, but what we feel through it is a unique thing between us and her. Based on Nathan's sharp intake of breath, he's feeling more than any of us.

"I like Alex's hair," Talia says through her teeth.

"Don't grit your teeth. Think loose thoughts. Think about water or a nice breeze. Relax your jaws. Alex didn't cry all that much when he was a baby, just when the occasion called for tears. He loved to babble, though. He would go on and on, for hours it seemed. He even woke up in the night sometimes to babble instead of crying. And he was always smiling." The longer she talks about baby Alex the more Talia shares the weight of what she's going through, if I could take it all from her I would. I'm sending Alex's parents on a vacation. A cruise. I don't care. Whatever they want.

Obi comes to check Talia's progress while Alex's mom keeps telling stories. He looks at me and nods, relief evident. "Almost time to push, Talia. You can do this. Lean on your alphas. Let them carry as much as you can. You're doing so good, honey."

I have never been present for a birth, but I have done enough research that I know it's almost time just from the feelings she is letting come across the bonds. Talia is turning inward now, she's not here with us anymore. Her focus is completely on what she needs to do next.

"Send me pictures once they're here, Alex. Hold her up, all of you. Do the purr thing. The omega part of her will respond to it. Don't distract her, don't be offended, and don't get in the way. Call me once everything is settled."

I end the call just as Talia makes the first vocal sound of pain I think I've ever heard from her. She gasps Jasper's name and he helps her raise up into a modified squatting position.

"Wait, Talia, just a second." Obi is moving fast to get the warmers and the cart laden with suction bulbs, surgical scissors, and a collection of other necessary things. "I'm almost ready. Reid, get ready. Devon. Hurry." The plan is for Obi to suction out tiny noses and clamp umbilical cords then hand the babies off to Reid and Devon to wrap and hold.

That isn't what's happening, though. Talia is ready, but Obi isn't. He 's still lining up equipment and blankets when she hisses Jasper's name again. "It's coming. I feel it. Fuck fuck fuck fuck fuck fuck." Jasper reaches down between them and he bites both of his lips between his teeth to keep from making whatever sound was about to come out of him.

"This one has hair. I've got you, Talia, I've got you. Obi, what do I do? I can't get out of the way."

"Just catch, Jasper. Talia's doing the hard part."

Then too many things happen at once for me to focus on any one of them until I hear a high pitched, very angry cry.

"Boy!" Jasper shouts, then he's frantically calling Obi's name over and over. "The cord, Obi. What do I do? Oh my god, fuck. Why does his head look like that?"

Alex bursts out laughing, and Obi swallows his own laugh. "He's been under pressure for about an hour, Jasper. Just hold onto him and let me take care of the cord, then you can wrap him up. Reid, bring a blanket from the warmer." Obi works quickly and soon Jasper has a little, screaming burrito in his arms.

"Let me see him," Talia says. Jasper holds him up to her, close to her face, and she smiles, then she calls for me. "Will you get behind me? I'm so tired. Can I lean on you?"

Every time she asks me to help her, my chest swells with what can only be pride, although I try hard to not let it show. I can't explain it. Talia is incredibly independent, she rarely needs our help and it's an even more rare occasion that she actually asks for it. I've already been on the verge of crowing about the fact that she chose my room to have our babies; I might not be able to contain myself now that she wants my physical help with the delivery. I kneel behind her and reach around to put my hands on her thighs. "Lean back, I'll hold you while you rest until the girls come."

When we were discussing and arguing over potential baby names, we picked names for both boys and girls; operating under the assumption that we with three, we would could have either sex. There were a few names that we all liked enough to call favorites. Dutch was at the top of the list with the most votes. Technically, he will be called Rowan Dutch Johnson. The girls will be called Iris Leigh-Anna and Zetty Rose. Obi doesn't know that one of the girls will have his mother's name. Talia has loved it from the time he jokingly suggested it.

Jasper's eyes shoot to mine. "How did you know they were girls?"

I give him a wink and a smile. "I may have overheard the conversation when you found out. I knew she wanted it to be a surprise, so I didn't say anything."

322 THE BETA PART THREE

Rest is fleeting and temporary. Sooner than I expected, Talia's body starts the work of birthing our daughters. Obi is kneeling in front of her as I help her to sway from side to side. After a few minutes she grunts and reaches out to clutch Obi's top. "Can we do it like before, with Jasper. I think I'd like it better if they caught them."

"Yes, if that's what you want and they're not squeamish. I'll be right here. Like I said, you're doing the hard part. We're here to support you." Obi doesn't look away from Talia, but his words are for us.

"Okay," she nods, and I feel a bit of her usual, assertive, all-business self flow back into her. She starts giving out clear, efficient orders. "Alex, I need you to hold on to my hands and pull when I pull. I'm too tired, you're going to help me get them out. Don't let me fall."

"I'll never let you fall. And Corso is right behind you."

I can feel her stomach tightening, one of the girls is about to make an appearance. "Nathan," she whispers, and he makes his way over; eyes huge and somber. He starts to get into place between her and Alex, but she stops him. "Just beside me, I need your scent." He probably doesn't mean to look as relieved as he must feel, but it is plain to see that Nathan is much happier to be beside her than in front of her. "Kaleb. Hurry. You catch."

"We're not playing baseball. This is serious. Obi's the doctor, he needs to get them when they come out." Trent is standing on my dresser, carefully not crushing my things. He does that, climbs the actual furniture when he's anxious. The more upset he is, the higher he needs to climb.

Kaleb gets into position just as Talia grips Alex's wrists and begins to bear down. She pulls him so hard he has to adjust his stance. She's pushing against me and pulling against Alex, and the world closes in on the three of us pushing, pulling, and rocking until Kaleb says, "that's it, honey. I can see her head. Almost there."

Talia lets out another string of curses, then Kaleb suddenly has a very small, very angry little girl in his hands. "She's so...tiny. And mad. You haven't known me long enough to be mad at me, little baby." Kaleb cooing at an angry infant is one of the better things I've witnessed. He's going to be absolutely foolish over them. We all are.

Talia falls back against me and closes her eyes. "Would you like to see her?" Kaleb asks and waits for Talia's nod. She doesn't lift her head from my chest, but she opens her eyes to smile when Kaleb lifts the baby up.

"Perfect," Talia sighs, and closes her eyes again. Her skin is more translucent than it was before, and her voice has taken on that far-away timbre that tends to alarm people in these situations. Which it does. Everyone in the room is at sudden and sharp attention. All eyes dart from Talia to Obi.

"You're almost finished, Talia. Only one more and you can rest. You're so amazing. You can do it. Just breathe for a few minutes, it won't be long. Then you're done." Obi touches Talia's forehead, then her neck.

It takes a moment, but I realize that he's checking her pulse; and that scares me more than anything. "Is she alright? What's wrong?"

"She's exhausted, Corso. Completely exhausted."

Everyone is quiet, even the babies who have been screaming their lungs out until just now. I'm watching Talia's chest rise and fall with her shallow breaths and trying to hold on to my composure. It won't help anything if I start screaming and begging whichever deity is close enough for help.

"She's coming." Talia whispers and tries to lift her hand to reach for Alex again, but she can't quite make it. "I don't think I can do it."

"You can," I kiss her damp temple. "You can. I know you're tired. I'll help you. Let's sit up a little. Would you like to try to stand up?"

She shakes her head. "Can't."

"That's alright, bella. You can do it. After this you can sleep as long as you need to."

"Here," Nathan says, taking her hand. "Hold on to my hand. I'll breathe with you. You're so strong, Talia. You can do this."

Alex crouches down and takes her other hand, and Jasper hands Dutch to Reid so he can come kneel beside me and murmur encouragement.

"Okay," she says, taking a deep breath and shaking out her shoulders. "Okay. Last one. Almost done. We can finish this." Then she begins pushing out the last baby.

This little daughter is determined to come out hand-first and I swear every bit of color in Obi's face drains onto the floor. "It's too late to reposition her. Talia, I need to help. This is going to hurt like a bitch. Are you ready?"

"No," she grunts.

"Tough," Obi says. "She's got to come out right now. I'm going to pull and you're going to push and we're both going to cuss. Ready, three, two, one, now! Push Talia! Right now!" She's pushing, but it isn't enough. "Lean against her, Corso, pull her knees up. Come on!" I pull her knees toward me and, finally, after a few collective efforts, Obi pulls the baby out and suctions her nose and mouth before he clamps the cord.

"Why isn't she crying? The other's cried." Trent climbs down from the dresser and gets on his haunches next to Obi.

"Give her a moment." Obi turns her over and starts aggressively rubbing her back.

"That's too rough."

"Hush it, Lancaster. Just give her a minute."

We all hold our breath until the tiniest little cry comes, not a scream like her siblings. Just a tiny, pitiful cry. Talia's relief rushes through me and she sags against my chest. Obi holds the baby up so Talia can see her. She's smaller than her siblings, much smaller. I don't know if she will be Iris or Zetty, but she's perfect.

Jamison suddenly screams from the other side of the door. "Three! You had three babies in there? My god, Talia. Mom's going to shit!"

A while later, after all three are measured, weighed, and washed, Jasper and Talia are sitting on my bed looking down at the babies sleeping in their blankets between them. Talia touches the larger girl's head and looks up at Jasper. "Zetty."

Jasper nods, and lays his hand over the smaller girl. "Iris."

Talia smiles, then Dutch complains that he hasn't gotten any attention. I didn't think that would be an issue until they're older. Talia laughs and picks him up. "Nobody forgot about you, sir. Trent, come here."

When he's settled beside her on the bed, she leans into him and runs her nose across his collarbone and pulls away with a little smile. "Here," she says, handing Dutch to him. "He's going to have your eyes."

Trent's head jerks back and his eyebrow disappears into his hairline as he shoves his hands into his armpits to keep from taking the bundle he is being offered. "How's that?"

"Smell his hair, and right behind his ear."

Trent pulls a face, takes Dutch gently from Talia, does as she asks, then nearly drops him. "What the actual fuck?"

Talia shrugs. "I don't know, but it happened. I hope he has your hair too. You've got great hair."

Trent looks from the baby, now cradled more securely in his hands after we all lunged toward him, to Talia and then to Jasper. His voice is a little high-pitched and that wild look he gets when he wants to climb the walls is back, but he remains on the bed with our son, turning him from side to side and smelling him every other minute. "But we have implants. I have an implant." He motions toward where Obi is cleaning up and putting away equipment, "he gave me an implant, just like the rest of you."

Talia looks over at Obi. He shrugs and keeps gathering things, "Maybe it was defective. I can cut it out and put a new one in. In fact, I need to do that or the next one will be yours too."

Trent growls a little but turns it to a purr when Dutch whimpers at the sound. "You are not cutting me open. I told you that you put it in too deep, now the fucking thing doesn't work."

Talia leans forward, into Trent's line of sight, and smiles up at him. "I don't care. I'm glad it didn't work. We have Dutch because of it."

Trent looks down into the sleeping face in hands. "Okay, but you're not allowed to act like me. And you can't be a sour-ass like your mother, either. Jesus, you're going to be such a little shit, aren't you?"

Chapter Thirty-Five

Reid

I live for my pack. I am utterly devoted to it. My heart belongs entirely to Talia, and if I have a secret within me, it is that I will always hold her higher than my pack. But I have never loved anyone or anything so completely, so immediately, as I love the three infants sleeping in the cradle. It is overwhelming. Devastating. Utterly terrifying. And wonderful.

Little Dutch is far more demanding than his sisters. If either of them fusses or cries and one of us doesn't immediately appear to console them he will scream his lungs out until we come to address the trouble. It could be that he doesn't like that they're crying, but my guess is that he's already starting to show his designation as an alpha and that's how he's able to help them. He also has big opinions about not getting attention every time one of the girls is getting attention; and even bigger opinions about being last to nurse.

The only physical difference between Iris and Zetty is their size. Talia thinks Iris's eyes might change color a little as she grows, but they both have little heads covered in dark curls, rosy little mouths, and pointy little chins. I think they look like elves. They already have distinctly different personalities even though they still spend most of their time sleeping. When she's awake, Zetty watches everything around her. She listens when we talk to her. Trent and Devon tend to talk gibberish to her, she mostly ignores that, but Corso and Alex talk to her like she's their equal. They have entire conversations with her, and I can practically see her mentally responding. I can't wait until she's old enough to talk back to us.

Iris, however, judges us. All of us. If you watch closely, you can see her weigh every word and action. I think I have even seen her tiny eyebrow raise on more than one occasion. Once she's mobile and able to communicate, we're all probably in for it. Dutch especially. I didn't know a child this young and small could throw a stink-eye, but Iris launches plenty of them in her brother's direction when he's being what Talia calls dramatic.

My quiet, alone time with the babies is interrupted when Alex whispers from the hallway. "Reid. Can you come down to the kitchen? We just got a call and it's a pack meeting sort of thing."

"Talia and Jasper are sleeping in his room. Should we wake them or wait until they're up?"

Alex pulls a face and says, "let them sleep. We'll tell them over dinner. They're going to be pissed, anyway, so waiting an hour won't matter. Maybe food will help."

I get the feeling that food definitely will not help, but I reach down into the cradle and pick up Dutch so I can hand him to Alex. "We'll take them down so Talia can rest a little longer. Can you manage two down the stairs?"

He rolls his eyes and reaches for Zetty when I lift her out. All three remain thankfully quiet until we get to the kitchen, where they all immediately start to complain. The kitchen is much brighter and louder than the peaceful cocoon that Talia has maintained in Corso's room. "What's happened?"

Devon motions toward Kaleb with the spatula in his hand. Devon doesn't typically do much cooking, both Talia and Jasper have forbidden him from touching anything that isn't made of cast iron, and he isn't generally allowed to touch any appliance more complicated than a toaster; but he makes an exceptional burger. Kaleb drags his hands down his face and gets to explaining. "Seth's mother called me. We, our pack, have been appointed to oversee

Seth's care. Joyce isn't in any condition to handle it, as much as she would like to. She's grieving the loss of his father, and also the loss of what could have been. Her pack is doing what they can for her, but she's not doing very well. She gave me the heads up about ten minutes before the lead doctor over Seth's care called. I'll be getting all the calls because I have somehow become the point of contact."

He sighs and continues. "Seth isn't doing well, either. He isn't eating, isn't sleeping. Isn't responding to care. The bed Thaddeus got him is at the best rehab on this half of the continent. He wanted to give Seth the best possible shot at recovery since we're all sticking our necks out for him. Well, for what we need him to become. But there are problems nobody expected. Seth cannot tolerate the presence of females, of any designation. Every time they try to send in a female staff member he has a legitimate panic attack and requires sedation. Someone on his care team suggested a visit from Talia might help, but —"

"No. Absolutely not. She isn't to be near him, I don't care. She can take it up with me if she needs to, but it isn't happening. And, for the record, I don't give an actual fuck if he recovers or not. I'd be happier if he never left that facility. He may have helped us at the compound, but we're not trusting him." What I don't say is that I know for a fact that Jasper still wants his heart in a paper bag and I'm more than happy to help him get that done. Seth Pratchett doesn't deserve Talia's empathy, and he will never get mine.

"He also risked his life to warn us about the attack; and sent his father here to help us in his stead." Corso hums.

He can play devil's advocate for anybody in the world except Seth. If he thinks I'm going to sit here and listen to him defend Seth, he's very wrong. "Corso, I love you. I respect you. You know I do. But if you say another thing in Seth Pratchett's defense, we're going to have a fight. There is nothing on any plane of existence that he could do to make up for what he's done. I don't care why he did it. I don't care that he thought he was doing the best he could. He hurt her, and he put her in a fucking cell after he did it. You carried her out yourself. That was his fault. He doesn't get forgiveness."

"We don't have to forgive him, and we won't. But we did give our word that we would do whatever we could to turn him around and make him the best alpha he's able to be." Devon's pointing at me with the spatula now. "Corso doesn't want the council seat for one second longer than he has to sit in it, and I will have to deal with Seth for the rest of my placement on the council...which will be a long goddamn time, especially if he's a shitty councilman. He respects Kaleb and he's probably a little afraid of the rest of us, considering the situation. And he knows that the only reason he's still breathing is because Talia has spoken for him. I don't trust him, but I do trust her. So, we're going to do what we can to get him in good working order so we can get on with our lives. He won't be there long if we can make him do the shit he's supposed to do. Then we can be done with him."

Done with him would be good.

"I'm not defending him, Reid. He doesn't deserve that. But I am trying to be fair and do what I said I would. Besides, maybe one day Talia will come to her senses and let Jasper off his leash, and he'll bring an end to it before we get the opportunity to be more annoyed than we are. I don't anticipate that actually happening, but it is fun to think about. It isn't like you to be so hot-headed about things, by the way." Corso gives me one of those smiles that lets me know he thoroughly approves of my display of opinion. I don't typically throw a tantrum, as Talia would call this, but I have an extreme aversion to hearing a member of my pack defending Seth. That might not be very fair of me, but I don't care.

"There's more," Kaleb says, and cocks his head toward Nathan.

Nathan rubs his chest. "They're going in after the omegas in a few days. I'm going. Trent, too."

"Talia is going to lose her shit," Devon says from the stove.

She is absolutely going to lose her shit. She hasn't been comfortable with any of us going farther than the distillery for months, there's no way she's going to be okay with Nathan and Trent going to the North Wisen on a rescue mission. She's going to forget all about Seth's rehabilitation after she finds out about this.

Talia makes her opinion about the rescue mission abundantly clear a little while later. We never get a chance to bring up the situation with Seth.

"Absolutely fucking not. You can't go. Neither of you. You're both going to stay your asses right here at home where I know you're safe. The COTs can get them out and give you a play by play. No."

Corso carefully intervenes on Nathan's behalf. He leans over to tuck a strand of hair behind her ear and touches her cheek. "Bella, be reasonable. He's been tracking them for so long, he deserves to see this through. Try to understand, Nathan needs to see them rescued with his own eyes."

"I need to see that he's okay with *my* own eyes." Her voice has gone from heated and sharp to watery.

"Wouldn't you want to see them be rescued if you were tracking them and searching for a way to save them? Nathan has worked so hard, and he's been so worried for them. I know you don't want anything to happen to Nathan or Trent, but Nathan needs to be there, and he will have Trent with him so they won't be alone." Corso tries again, and this time he's successful.

Talia looks down at the plate of untouched food in front of her. "I don't want them to go." She's quiet, her voice full of the thickness that comes before crying.

"None of us want them to go, stellina mia."

Talia takes a shuddering breath and nods. "Fine." She looks at Alex. "I need to nurse the babies. Can you carry those two up for me?" Alex nods and stands up to follow her.

Jasper touches her arm when she walks past him. "You haven't eaten anything, Talia."

"I'm fine, I don't feel very much like eating anything right now. You can bring me something later when you check on me." She leans over to kiss him on the cheek, then she heads for the door.

"Talia —" Nathan calls after her.

She responds without slowing down or looking back. "I said it's fine, Nathan."

After she and Alex have had plenty of time to get to the stairs, Devon's cheeks puff out as he blows out a breath. "That was three." At least they understand what the overuse of the word fine means. I was also keeping count after she said it the first time.

"She'll be alright, she's just worried. I am, too. It's been one thing after another for too long. And we have these new lives to care for. Not only are two of her alphas leaving her to do some dangerous shit that she doesn't want them to do; they are essentially leaving our home, our pack," he takes a little breath, "our children. They're not going to be here, which is its own problem, but them not being here is lessening our defense if something was to happen. She's scared, and no amount of reasoning will make her feel better about it because most of it is instinctual. Talia, herself, outside of babies and packs, understands that you have to go; you all know she gets it. But that Talia isn't driving right now. The Talia who just had babies, and who has watched and fought through fight after fight with us, is who just went upstairs without eating dinner."

I take her reheated burger upstairs after I think she's had time to finish with the babies. Nathan wanted to, but Jasper told him it might be better if someone else did it since Nathan is who she's mostly upset about. She's laying on her side on Corso's bed nursing Iris, with Zetty and Dutch cuddled close. I put the plate on the dresser by the door and pull out my phone. I'm not usually the one who takes pictures of her, but I don't think any pictures of her with the three of them have been taken and this would be a beautiful one. The others just take the picture, but I like to ask first because posing for pictures isn't her favorite thing. "Hey. I brought up your dinner. Can I take a picture before you get up?"

"I love you a little more for asking. You can take pictures of me, Reid. I don't mind. I'm not very hungry, though."

The soft lighting is just right and the way her face softens and warms as she looks down at the babies is so perfect. I put the phone away and help her get sat up and settled. Talia doesn't button the shirt she's wearing; she just pulls it mostly closed. There is a column of exposed skin from her neck down to her stomach. That would make for a nice picture, too, but I don't want to take another. "Will you try to eat just a little? I'm worried that you aren't eating enough to keep up with the demands on your body while feeding three infants. You're always beautiful, but you've lost more weight than I'm comfortable with since they were born."

Talia heaves a sigh, but she takes a bite and talks around it. "Maybe you guys could give one of them a bottle while I nurse the other two. We've got all that formula in the cabinet; we should use it."

My heart squeezes just a little. I have been looking forward to feeding them from the moment we decided to have them. I just didn't want to say anything that could potentially hurt or offend Talia. New mothers are touchy about milk supply and latching and anything else pertaining to feeding babies; I have been on the wrong end of a scolding on a few occasions for saying something insensitive to one of my sisters. I was trying to be helpful, but I chose the wrong words at the wrong time and it was a les-son-learning experience. "I would very much like to feed them. The others would, too. Corso especially."

"And Kaleb," she hums. She takes another small bite of her burger, then says, "I need to talk about something, and I think you're the only one who will understand the way I need you to understand."

"Alright." I send up a prayer to whoever wants to answer it that it isn't something horrible.

"Jasper is changing. More every day. It's my fault."

That...isn't at all what I expected her to say. "He is. He is so much stronger now than when I created a bond with him. Change isn't always a bad thing."

"He was a sweet, gentle omega before me."

"He's still a sweet omega." I have a different understanding of Jasper than she does. I don't think Jasper was ever gentle; not even before Talia came to him. He's certainly not gentle now. Jasper is quite possibly the most vicious of all of us, and he grows more determined to ensure our safety and position every day. I don't think Talia would believe me if I told her that, though. Considering she's describing him as a sweet, gentle omega.

She puts her plate on the nightstand. There's more than half her burger left, and all but two of the sweet potato fries. This is going to become unacceptable very quickly. "He executed Jonas Pratchett on the lawn."

"Does that bother you?"

Her nose wrinkles with a little snarl. "Of course not. I'm glad that piece of shit is dead. It's just...when I first came to their pack, there was an attack. The rogues from the compound came after Jasper. I killed most of them, but Jasper took one. I was there to protect him when the alphas were out on a job, like I was supposed to. That was good, I was comfortable with that. Now things have switched, and I'm the one being protected all the time. That's not what was supposed to happen."

Ah. I have been waiting for this conversation. I've felt it building for months. "Is that such a bad thing? To be protected by your pack? Jasper might be an omega, but he's your mate, as well. He can't help his need to protect you."

"Nobody protected me when I was a beta. I'm still just me. I do the protecting."

Careful. I'll need to speak carefully. "If you recall, we tried to protect you. But you were too stubborn and sour to let us. These changes in Jasper are good. He's better for it. And," I take a deep breath, "it's okay for you to be soft. It was okay for you to be soft when you were a beta, but you couldn't let yourself be. You aren't alone anymore, Talia. You have all of us to help you and take care of you. We need to take care of you, Jasper included. Would it be so terrible if you let us?"

"I'm trying, but it doesn't feel right. Not really. In my mind, I'm all beta. Until some omega bullshit takes over, but still. I'm just worried that it's too much change for Jasper. He's never been anything but an omega, he's always been treated like an omega."

I reach over and stroke down the shell of her ear. "The changes in Jasper are good for him. He's happy. He's strong. You don't have to change everything about yourself, or anything. I just wanted to tell you that it's okay to let yourself be taken care of. You've carried too much for too long. Give us some of that weight. And please try to eat more than you have been. I don't mean to nag, but I really am worried about you."

She brings my hand to her lips and kisses my palm. "I love you, Reid."

I lean over and give her a real kiss. "I love you, Talia. We'll be alright. All of us."

Chapter Thirty-Six

Alex

Talia isn't doing well. She isn't exactly sick, but she's in a lot of pain. Obi says it's a clogged milk duct; that it's supposed to be something that happens to a lot of nursing mothers. But I'm not buying it. Talia is miserable. She can hardly lift her right arm without wincing. And her breast on that side is mottled and swollen. Obi told us to keep her drinking water, to put ice on it, and to let the babies nurse on that side more frequently. How is she supposed to do that when it hurts her so much to let them? I called my mom to see if she had any advice, but she just said the same shit Obi did. Reid's mom has plenty more to say about it, though. She's on the phone right now telling us how stupid we all are.

"So, you're telling me, you bunch of silly asses are sitting around wringing your hands while your omega, the mother of your children, is up there in agony? When any one of you idiots could have already solved the problem?"

Corso closes his eyes and pulls down the ends of his hair; and Reid pinches the bridge of his nose. "We're doing everything Obi said to do, Mom."

"I thought he was supposed to be some amazing omega doctor. All you've got to do is pull it out. Draw straws and send the winner up there with a bunch of flowers and a shot of that whiskey y'all make and just pull it out."

"We can't touch the swollen area enough to try to dislodge the clog, and we certainly can't pull on it." Corso tugs at his hair again.

"You don't need to touch it to clear it, Corso."

Corso can take all the time he wants to politely work out what she means while Trent and I scream shotgun into each other's faces and beat the hell out of each other to be the first one off the couch and up the stairs. I may or may not kick him back down them. Just a little. He'll be fine. And I'll bring Talia all the flowers she wants and a whole bottle of whiskey later if she wants it.

Jasper and Nathan have the screaming burritos in Nathan's room so Talia can rest. She's in Corso's room, curled up on his bed under a ton of blankets. I carefully slide under the mountain of too-hot and kiss her forehead when she opens her eyes to scowl at me. "Don't be mad at me, not yet, anyway. I'm here to try to help. Reid's mom says we have to pull out the clog."

"If you try to pull anything from anywhere, I'll punch you in the face."

I swallow a laugh. I'm glad she's as dumb as the rest of us sometimes. "I'm not going to use my hands." I wiggle my eyebrows at her so she understands where this is heading.

"Oh...umm, I don't know about that, Alex. What if it hurts?" She starts to worry her bottom lip with her teeth.

Maybe I'm too lecherous for my own good, but all I can think to say is, "what if it doesn't?" and I give her an even more exaggerated eyebrow wiggle.

She presses her lips together and does a long blink. "Okay, then. What if it doesn't? And you get sprayed in the face with eighty gallons of milk?"

My dick fills with blood so fast that I'm surprised it doesn't hurt. "I don't think I'll mind if I get sprayed with milk."

"Are you sure?" she asks, but she's already throwing back blankets and sitting up.

I nod. "Let me sit against the headboard, and you get on my lap. I think it'll be better like that."

"Maybe you won't drown if you're sitting up." She undoes the top buttons of the flannel shirt she took from Devon's closet; and after I see her spilling over the cups of her bra, I firmly decide that drowning might be the way to go.

"New bras," I growl. "You need new bras. That might be what caused this in the first place." Then I'm hissing as she straddles my lap and gasps when she feels my erection. Her eyes shoot to mine, full of too many things for me to sort out. This isn't meant to be a sexual situation; well, it isn't meant to result in sex. It's too soon, and I don't want to be the first one to fuck her when she is ready. You'd think I, of all of us, would be dying to have her again; but I know it's going to be rough the first time and I absolutely do not want to fuck her with my dick knowing that it's truly hurting her. "Ignore it," I say. "We're not doing anything with it. Just pretend you don't feel it."

She laughs at me. "I can't ignore that, Alex. For one, it's too big to ignore. And two, I miss being with you. It's only been a couple of weeks, but it feels like forever."

I groan, and it isn't all pleasure from her pressing against me. "Don't talk about my dick right now, sweet pea. And don't talk about fucking. I can't take it."

"I'm sorry. I don't think I can take it, either. Not yet anyway."

I reach up and cover her mouth with my hand. "Don't say shit like that, either." She licks my palm, but it doesn't have the gross-out effect she's going for. All I register is that her tongue is sliding wetly against my skin, and it doesn't matter that it's just the skin on my hand. I reach around to unclasp her bra and it almost leaps off of her body. As soon as we're finished here, I'm going to order her an entire collection of nursing bras. Of all the things we bought in preparation, nursing bras weren't on the list. Talia didn't want to order any until she had a better idea of what size she'd need. If we order them today, we can get a rush on the delivery and have them here in a couple days.

She leans over and pulls a hand towel from under the pillow and laughs at my puzzled expression. "They leak. If I even think about milk or tits or babies they leak. If you're working on this one," she points to her right breast, "then this one will turn on like a faucet," she points to the left. My dick twitches and she laughs again.

My head thunks against the headboard when I look up at the ceiling. "Please stop talking." Talia manages to pull herself together and asks me if I'm sure about this. "Of course I'm sure about this. Now stop torturing me." Then the true torture begins.

She gently cups her engorged breast and lifts it up to me like it's an offering. I place my hands on her waist and remind myself to keep them there, then I lick her nipple before taking it into my mouth. She doesn't make a sound and when I flick my eyes up to her face her expression is pinched. I use my lips and tongue the way I normally would, but her expression doesn't change. "Suck with your whole mouth, not just your lips. Use your tongue."

It shouldn't be sexy, this is supposed to be purely therapeutic, but I'm hard as a fucking rock. I try to do what she says, and when I eventually figure out how to work my mouth the right way, I'm rewarded with a flood of the sweetest thing I've ever tasted. It's so fucking sweet. I don't know what I expected, but this isn't it. I'm an instant addict.

I roll my tongue and my eyes as the flow increases and Talia hums. Then she's gasping. "I feel it tugging. Don't stop."

I won't stop. I keep doing exactly what I'm doing, drawing more and more from her breast. She puts her other hand on the back of my head and holds me tight against her, groaning. "It aches and feels so good. Don't stop, Alex." She's rocking her hips, grinding against me. I don't think she realizes she's doing it, and I'm not going to stop her. I'm going to ruin these pants.

I know the moment the duct is cleared because milk actually gushes into my mouth, and I have to gulp it down or let it pour out all over us. She's still grinding her hips and holding me to her breast, so I figure fuck it. I wedge my hand between us and pull my cock out, tucking the elastic band of these poor pants under my balls. Then I start stroking it. I'll make a huge mess, but fuck, it's going to feel good to cum with my mouth full like this.

"Here," she says, pulling my hand away. "Let me do it." She's dropped the towel she was using to keep from leaking everywhere and I can just barely see milk dripping from her nipple and down her breast. Oh my god, why is this so fucking hot? She starts moving her hand up and down my length, twisting around the head every few strokes, I'm going to get off inside of a minute. I haven't been this quick to cum since I was a teenager.

She pulls my head away, much to my disappointment. I don't want to be finished, I don't know why this is so appealing to me, but I want more of it. I'm preparing myself for an epic pout, but she surprises me. "Fuck it," she says. "Switch." Then she pulls me to her other breast. Correction. I am going to cum all over both of us in the next fifteen seconds. I'm not an asshole, though. If she felt up to grinding on my dick, she probably feels up to letting me get her off. I reach between us again to cautiously brush my fingertips against her clit, and she moans. Good enough. Then we're both working each other over, desperately trying to get the other one off first.

Talia wins, and I'm not even a drop embarrassed. My cock erupts all over both our stomachs and chests. Our hair. We are going to need a shower. She's right behind me, though; groaning and yanking at my hair.

"God, you're so much fun." I kiss her and attempt to wipe away some of the sticky mess we created with the abandoned hand towel. "Shower?"

She nods and crawls off the bed. "Will you help me change the sheets? I feel a million times better already, but I'm still a little tender."

I nod. I'll help Talia do anything she ever asks for help with. She's finally, *finally*, starting to lean on us more. It's just small things, like it has been since she came back home, but it's a lot more of them. And for her to ask me to help her change the bedding, of all things, is a big fucking deal.

Over the next day or two her appetite picks back up and we all breathe a sigh of relief. She was well on her way to gaunt, but none of us wanted to force food on her. The plan, before Reid's mom told us we were idiots, was to give her stubborn ass two more days to try to work it out on her own before one of us, probably Jasper, made her eat more than three bites of something. I'm glad we didn't have to do that, because we all know how well that would have gone over. It's a fun thing when even Jasper isn't immune to her wrath.

I am enjoying watching Talia try to eat spaghetti without getting any on her mouth when Devon ruins dinner. It's always him. Whenever there's a perfectly good dinner to ruin, he's the one who usually ruins it. Kaleb might drag him across the table one day and suffocate him in whatever we're trying to eat.

"Dad called. They're going after the omegas tomorrow."

Talia puts her fork down and looks at Nathan. "When are you leaving?"

"Early," he says quietly. "Before sunrise."

She nods and picks her fork back up to silently finish her dinner. Everyone at the table is quiet after that. And it stays quiet when Talia and Reid start cleaning up after everyone eats. She leans on Reid most when she's upset. It used to hurt my feelings, but over time I started to kind of understand why she leans on him. He's quiet. He doesn't ask anything of her, outside of the odd request to eat some fucking food when she's being decimated by three adorable leeches. He just seems to know what needs to be done and does it. I have tried to be more like him, but the best I can do is to be more observant so I can try to anticipate what she might need; and then I usually end up getting in her way and on her nerves. I also can't be quiet. It's impossible. It goes against everything inside me.

"So.... are we going to just not talk until they get back? That might be a couple days. I can try, but I don't know."

Reid rolls his eyes at me, but Talia turns to face me and I regret making the joke. She's terrified. I couldn't feel it before, sometimes she's incredibly good at tamping that kind of thing down, but now that she's giving me her eyes, I can see and feel it. "They'll probably be home by tomorrow night. They're going to fly over, so it won't take long to get there, and then they'll go in and walk the omegas out the door and be right back home. They might even be home by dinner, especially if we have a late dinner."

"You don't have to do that," Talia says. "I'm scared and sad, but I'm not stupid. I know they need to go, and I understand why it's so important to Nathan. I can't help that I'm afraid. But Trent promised me that they wouldn't go in until the COTs clear out the rogues. It's going to be okay."

Chapter Thirty-Seven

Nathan

I have never been so torn in my life. Not when I abandoned the idea of Trent and me forming a pack with my cousin, Becker. Not when I had to watch my sister force a pack made up of my trainers and superiors make her submit to them. Not even when I traded a future of sleeping with females for a future with Jasper. I don't regret a single one of those things, but I might regret walking out the front door this morning. I feel gutted. Nothing has ever felt as shitty as Talia taking the hair tie off my wrist and putting it on hers when I bent to kiss her goodbye. Nothing.

"It's not that bad, is it?" Marcus yells. Trent and I are sitting across from him and Thaddeus in the astronomically loud little plane that's flying us to the extraction locale. "She'll be there when you get back to her."

I smile at him, but I don't have a productive answer. I know she'll be there; I just hate leaving her. Jasper's used to us going on missions. He has never been as distraught over it as Talia. Corso tried to make me feel better about it, telling me that it's because of the babies; but I know that's not it. Talia is going to burn everything to the ground if another, single, bad thing happens to our pack. She might be more inclined to be okay with us going on missions eventually, after things have been quiet and calm for a good, long time. Not now, though. Right now, she's on a precipice that requires complete and utter safety from every angle. And this trip is testing it.

True to his word, Trent holds us back until the last of the rogues have been escorted from the warehouse. A fucking warehouse. Cold. Empty. Unsecure. What the fuck. After all the shit at the compound we were held, they put all these omegas in a fucking warehouse. It doesn't make sense. It isn't even the facility we were thinking it would be. No older omegas, children or babies, no rogues in training.

There are thirty-seven omegas sitting in small, huddled groups. There is one male omega among them, in the center of the largest group. He can't be older than eighteen or nineteen, at the most. The girl with the purple hair isn't here, and I'm a little nauseous about it. I haven't been able to talk to any of them yet, the COT units wanted me to wait until they got all the omegas' names so they could work on getting them home. Some of the omegas look well enough, some look pretty shell-shocked, and a few of them look absolutely haunted. The male omega is an even mixture of haunted and livid, and he keeps making eye contact with me. He's the one I want to talk to when I'm given the go ahead, which should be any minute.

"You ready for this?" Trent asks. I nod just as Marcus gives me the signal to start asking questions.

The male omega doesn't wait for me to come to him. He must have been waiting too. He stalks over to me, and I feel his rage before I catch his scent. "You're the one who found us, aren't you?"

"I am. Where is the girl with purple hair?"

He glares at Trent, then snarls at me. "They had it worse than the rest of us, you know. Because they were different."

"They who?"

"Maddie and Ashe. Maddie had the purple in her hair."

My stomach drops. "What do you mean, had?"

"A few days ago, some new alphas came in here in gear just like that," he points at one of the COT units, "and took Maddie and Ashe away. I overheard them say Milos... no. Minos. And I heard them talking about some asshole by the name of Mister Owens, and how they were pissed that they had to use their own money to buy the girls coats. Why didn't you come sooner? You could have saved them."

"They are alive, though? The last time you saw them, they were alive, right?"

He nods, still glaring and snarling. I'd be angry, too. "Ashe tried to save me from them that day the compound was raided. She paid for it, too. That was you, wasn't it? In that cell? The computer guy."

All I can do is tell him I'm sorry, and it isn't good enough.

"Fuck your sorry. I know you're here now, and you're probably the only reason anybody found us in the first place. Don't think I'm not grateful, because I am really fucking grateful. But I'm so angry. None of this should have happened. And for what? So some douche can figure out what makes an omega and omega? So he can take a personal interest in the one set of twins he found? Everything that happened to us, *to me*, was unnecessary."

"I'm sorry."

He sighs. "Yeah, sure. We didn't mention it to those guys," he motions at the COTs again, all of them, "because they look too much like the ones who came to take Ashe and Maddie; but half of us are about to go into heat in the next week. Our diets are all fucked up, so we're, thankfully, not producing the right amounts of pheromones to make it obvious. We all kind of synced up and it's been a real party with the rogues. I'd appreciate it if you'd get us the fuck away from all these unfamiliar alphas before the collective bomb drops. It would also be a good idea to get us away from each other, as shitty as that sounds right now." Then he walks back to rejoin the group he was with.

"So fucking awful." Trent says one of the things I've been thinking. "That poor kid. If he can pull himself through this, he's going to be a force. Jasper would really like him."

My bottom drops out of my stomach again, and I get an intense urge to call home. "Remember me telling you about the squeaking? The male omega I thought was Jasper?" Trent nods. "That's him. I heard him being..." I rake my hands through my hair. "I'm calling home. I need to hear Jasper and check on Talia." I pull out my phone and call Jasper.

"What's wrong?" he answers.

I'm so glad to hear his voice that I forget to tell him nothing's wrong and he has to repeat himself. "Nothing, Jasper. I just needed to hear you for a minute. I'm glad I came, but I want to get the fuck out of here now. How's Talia?"

I hear one of the babies crying in the background. Dutch. He's very dramatic about things, I don't know who he could have possibly inherited that trait from, insert sarcasm as I cut my eyes at his father. "She's worried sick, but holding it together. She'll be glad to hear from you. Let me get her."

"No, don't," I say. I know exactly how disappointed and disgusted I sound, and I don't want to upset or worry her any more than she already is. "Just tell her I called and that me and Trent are alright."

"You sure?"

"Yeah. I'm sure. I know I sound like someone kicked my puppy. I'm going to see about an early flight home."

I listen to him shush Dutch for a minute, and even though the baby's screaming and I'm so far away, just hearing home makes me feel a little better. I catch Trent's eye, then flick my gaze to the door. He nods and glances at the phone I'm holding to my ear. I give him a nod of my own, our silent conversation concluded. We're leaving as soon as fucking possible, and everything is okay at home; and I couldn't be happier.

"How are the omegas?" Jasper asks, his tone stiff and cautious.

"Exhausted. Anxious. Angry. There's one I'd like for you to meet, when he's ready. I think you'd like him, and I think it would help him to meet you."

I hear the distinct sound of baby butt pats and Dutch finally quiets. Jasper lowers his voice to just a bit more than a whisper. "Whenever he's ready. If I can help, you know I will. I'm going to go put this little boy down with his sisters. I'm glad you're coming home early. Be safe."

Thaddeus arranges for a car to take us to the airfield so we can catch the flight he also arranged. I questioned a few more of the omegas while we wait, but none of them had any more information than the male, whose name is Aiden. I gave him my number and told him when he's ready, I'd like for him to meet Jasper. Apparently, he's already heard of Jasper and his entire attitude toward me changed once he found out I was Jasper's alpha. Then he really had a change of heart when he found out I was also Talia's alpha. It's a little jarring for me to be the possession, the acquired party. I'm so used to thinking of them in terms of being my omegas, but the opposite is just as true. I do belong to them. We all do, and that might be more accurate than saying they belong to us.

Trent let it slip in front of Aiden that we had babies, and Aiden had a less positive reaction to that information. "Are they yours, or theirs?" he whispered, glancing around the room to see if anyone was listening. I tried to answer, but he stopped me. "Don't tell me. Don't tell anyone. Especially if they're not yours. Nobody can ever know, not until we're safe. That's why they were so interested in Maddie and Ashe. Their parents are both omegas." I open my mouth to say something else, but he shuts me up again. "Don't. Just don't. Not here, anyway. You gave me your number. I'll be in touch as soon as I can. You need to know, but not here. We can't trust these people."

The fact that he included me in the *we* actually made me feel less at ease, and now that I'm watching the airfield markings grow smaller and smaller through my tiny window I feel even better. I can't wait to get home. I'll need to start digging and searching for the twins, Maddie and Ashe, but for now I'm going to be glad for the omegas I did save. That's big, it isn't enough, but it's more of a win than it could be.

"You'll find them," Trent assures me. "You found the others, and you'll find those girls. We're not going to tell anyone about ours, though. Not until it's safe. As far as the world knows, we only have a son. I hate it but protecting them is more important than making sure every person on the planet sees how beautiful they are."

"I don't know if we can keep Elizabet quiet about it." I don't know how she's managed not to tell everyone she sees about her three newest grandchildren, to be perfectly honest; but she hasn't. So far, I don't think Elizabet has told a single person about any of the babies, and it's very curious. Curious enough to call her and find out.

"What are you doing?" Trent asks when I take out my phone.

"Calling Talia's mother. Hang on."

She answers on the fourth ring, and I rudely don't give her time to be chipper and polite. "Why aren't you screaming about them from the rooftops?"

"The omegas? They'll be screaming soon enough themselves. I don't need to."

"No, not them. The set of heated blankets Obi delivered."

It becomes suddenly apparent that I've caught her driving when she starts cussing whatever 'slow piece of shit' that 'won't get the hell out of the fast lane if they're going to drive like it's Sunday'. I've never been in the car with Talia driving, but between her parents' temperaments, I don't think I want to. Kaleb and Reid do most of the driving, anyway.

"Sorry, honey. Some people shouldn't be on the road," she chirps, and I snort to keep from laughing. She might be the people that shouldn't be on the road, but I won't be the one to tell her that. "I don't think we should mention the blankets. Not until some other things get sorted. Maybe the blue one, but not the others. If it was me, I probably wouldn't tell anybody who made them if word does slip out, you never know how people will react, you know?"

"Yeah, I think so, too. Thanks, Elizabet. We just left Marcus and Thaddeus, they're good. We're going home. And I've got a new thing to look for... another set of blankets."

"Shit. Really?"

"Yes. So, if you have any leads on any manufacturers." God, I hope we're both smart enough to talk in this type of code, "I'd like their information." I don't know if there's anyone in first-class that might be listening, but it's safe to assume that anyone is a potential threat at this point.

"Will do, honey. Hug my daughter for me when you get home, okay?"

"I will. Bye, Elizabet."

Trent smirks at me, "I would have said burritos."

The house is dark when we get home, and the first thing I do is march straight up to Corso's room where I know Talia will be. She's on the bed between Jasper and Corso, with the cradle pulled up close to the side. Soon we're going to have to find a bigger place for them to sleep, or at maybe another cradle or cot or something. They're getting so big so fast; it's incredible.

I don't want to wake anyone, I just want to check on them, but Corso touches my arm when I'm bent over the cradle. "Get in on the other side of Jasper. Trent can come too, if he wants, but he'll have to squeeze in. They've been very worried."

Trent pokes his head in the door, and I motion for him to come in and be quiet, then I point at the bed and start undressing down to my boxers. He takes the hint and soon we're both snuggled in the bed. Trent somehow manages to wriggle between Jasper and Talia without waking either of them; and that's how we stay for the night. When the babies wake up for their middle-of-the-night meal, Talia and Jasper are completely horrified that they didn't wake up when we got home but are otherwise very happy to see us.

Trent and I help juggle the babies around until they're all fed and happy again, then we go right back to sleep, all cuddled together in the middle of Corso's bed.

Chapter Thirty-Eight

Talia

I have had enough. The babies are five weeks old. I need someone to fuck me. Alex is a pervert, which I adore, to be perfectly honest. Ever since he helped to clear my clogged duct, he has been very interested in making sure the ducts stay clear. I don't mind a single bit; it feels so fucking good to grind against his thigh or his cock while he's satisfying his interest. But all that grinding isn't fucking.

There is a silent understanding that Kaleb and Alex will be last in line to have actual penetrative sex with me. I'm so glad that there are no hurt feelings or pride about that. As much as I want them, I think it will be too painful to have either of them be my first bit of sex after childbirth. Somebody has to be, though. The more I think about it, the more I think it should be Corso or Jasper. Or both. Yes. Definitely both. And right now. Why not? The babies are downstairs with Devon and Kaleb. Devon likes to show them things even though they're too small to understand anything but his scent and the sound of his voice. Today's adventure is the garage. He's very excited about it.

Everyone else is scattered around the manor. Nathan is working in his new office downstairs, and Alex is sprawled across his bed working. I have no idea where the rest of them are, so a text message is in order. I send the same text to both Corso and Jasper. *I would very much like some attention, please. Whoever gets here first gets the attention.*

A minute later, Corso saunters into my bedroom. I haven't used my own bedroom in months, Corso's room just felt better. It still does, but I think being in my room now will be a nice change. "What sort of attention do you need, bella?"

"All of it." I strip off my shirt and unbutton my jeans. It's pretty amazing to be able to wear jeans again after months of being too huge or too uncomfortable. They look a whole lot better on the floor than my ass right now, though.

He gives me one of those smiles that makes me love him extra. "Are you sure you're ready? There's no rush, no pressure."

I crawl onto the bed and shoot him a look over my shoulder. "I'm under plenty of pressure." I drag my eyes down his body, "and I'm working up to a rush."

"These are terrible lines, amore." He's smiling, though. And pulling off his pretty, cream-colored sweater.

"Trent is a terrible influence."

Jasper runs into my room, skidding on the rug in front of the door. He looks from me to Corso, then back to me. "Shit. I was in the gym."

He certainly was. He's flushed and sweaty, and absolutely delicious. "I can tell."

"You don't want to do rock, paper, scissors, do you?" he sighs in Corso's direction.

Corso laughs. "I don't think that will be necessary, do you Talia? If we're careful enough, both of us can give you the attention you need, don't you think?"

"Yes. Definitely yes."

I end up on my back between them. I kept my bra on. Corso isn't opposed to the milk leaking everywhere, but Jasper is a little shy about it. It's a dark, plum color with what Alex calls easy access clips. He might be a little fascinated with the various kinds of nursing attire, especially anything with a little clasp or slit.

"I like this one," Jasper says, tracing the lacy fabric. "Alex did a good job picking them." Then he kisses me, one of those sucking kisses he's so good at that make my toes curl. Corso gently palms my breast and drags his lips up the side of my neck to purr into my ear, making my toes curl even harder. Corso and Jasper are every bit as good at teamwork as Nathan and Trent are. It's been so long since I've been with either of them that being with both of them might end up being almost too much for me to handle. Almost.

Jasper walks his fingers down my stomach and hardly makes contact with my skin as he touches my mound. I lift up, trying to get him to give me more, but he moves with me so he can keep that same barely-there touch. He pulls back from the kiss and starts a wet path down my body. Corso picks the kiss up where Jasper left it and changes it into something just as sweet but more demanding, gently biting at my lips and licking deeper into my mouth. Jasper's kisses seem to try to pull things out of me, and Corso's try to push things inside. The switch from one to the other is such a dizzying contrast, especially when they're working together to wind me tighter and tighter.

The harder I try to get Jasper to give me more pressure, more anything, the lighter his touch becomes. I reach down to grab his wrist to make him give me what I need, but Corso stops me and brings my hand up and holds it against his cheek. "Don't be so impatient, amore. Jasper always takes great care of you. It's been such a long time since we've been able to have you like this, let him play a little."

I don't want to let him play a little, or a lot. I want him to rub and pinch my clit and fuck me with his fingers until I'm trembling and screaming. And then I want him to do it all over again with his dick.

"Isn't this the attention you wanted, baby?" Jasper rolls his eyes up at me as he licks across my hip bone.

I groan in frustration and tilt my hips up for him again. He laughs softly and lays on his stomach between my legs. "Is this alright? Are you comfortable with my mouth on you?" Ridiculous. What a ridiculous question.

"Yes, Jasper," I try to keep the whine out of my voice. "I'm as comfortable with it as you are."

He smiles up at me and kisses the inside of my knee, then he hooks his hands under my thighs and around them. Then nothing. He's just hovering over me. I can feel every breath he takes brushing against my skin but that's all I can feel; and his tight hold on my thighs is keeping me pinned just where I am. Corso tilts my face to the side, exposing the side of my neck to his lips and teeth. My eyes flutter shut, and I roll my hips helplessly. I hope the marks will always be as sensitive as they are now.

"So many fun things to touch and taste, bella," Corso purrs into the place between my neck and shoulder. "So many ways to bring those wonderful sounds from you. And Jasper has yet to begin." He unclasps one of the easy access clips and pulls my breast free. The minute he touches my nipple I'm going to start leaking. I'm trying to decide whether or not I care when two things happen at once, almost like it was planned. Corso takes my nipple into his mouth and covers my other breast with his hand, gently kneading it and thumbing my other nipple through the material of the bra, and Jasper swirls his tongue over my clit before sucking it between his teeth. I can't do anything but bow my spine and rip at their hair.

I feel the familiar tingling that precedes my milk dropping and it's all I can do to keep from pouting. "Corso, stop. The milk. It's going to be a mess."

"I like to see it, Talia. It's beautiful to me. I'll take care of any mess, as you call it." He holds my gaze and returns his mouth, not letting a single drop escape. It feels so, so fucking good, with one hand buried in Corso's hair, keeping him at my breast, and my other hand gripping Jasper's curls, holding him still while I thrust myself against his mouth. It's a strange way to think of it but they're both taking from me right now, both taking *me* inside them. The thought brings a noise from my throat, and I hold them just a bit closer for just a moment. I could cum just like this. But they won't let me. Every time I'm almost there one of them changes tactic and I might start issuing threats soon.

Jasper's fingers dig into my thighs as he switches to giving every bit of me long licks, making sure to circle my clit with every pass. He's growling, groaning, purring, making so many delicious sounds. Of all the things I ever thought would happen when I walked into the kitchen at the farmhouse, being trapped and tortured between Jasper and Corso wasn't in the realm of possibilities. Not even close to the radar.

Corso releases my nipple and does up the clasp. "I love that you still give us access to your breasts. I was worried that you wouldn't." He kisses me again, letting me suck on his tongue, sharing the sweet taste.

"It feels too good to not let you," I say against his lips.

Jasper slowly drags his tongue back and forth across my clit, making me twitch and jerk with every movement. "I'm happy to have access to you again at all. It's been so hard to wait for you to be ready." Then he goes back to sucking and swirling wet circles around my clit and slides his fingers inside me, and I can't think anymore. He does it just like he did the first time, pushing them deep and holding them still until I'm shoving my hips at him and gasping.

Corso laughs into my neck and latches onto one of the marks just as Jasper crooks his fingers and begins to stroke that place inside me that makes my eyes roll back. "You're going to make me cum, princess. Don't stop." Then his laugh is vibrating against me and that's all it takes for me. I hitch my leg around his back, making sure he doesn't stop, and let loose a string of filthy words and phrases that probably make no sense.

When I let Jasper pull away, both his hand and his face are shiny with my release and he's smiling up at me. "Is *that* the attention you were after?" He moves up to press himself into my side and I try to answer him; but all I can do is nod and gasp because Corso takes Jasper's place between my legs.

He reaches between us and lines up the head of his cock with my entrance. "So wet, bella. Jasper is very good at pleasing you, isn't he? You were making the most wonderful sounds for him. Will you make those same sounds for me?"

I whine in response and unconsciously tip my head back, perfectly presenting my neck and throat.

"You never gave me that before you came back to me, Talia." He presses his forehead against mine. "I never would have asked it of you."

I comb my fingers through his hair and nuzzle his nose with mine. "I know. It just feels right to give it to you. You're my alpha, after all."

He growls and gives me another of his brutal, heart wrenching kisses. "Say it again."

Smiling, I wrap my legs around his hips and pull him down so I can purr into his ear. "You're my alpha, Corso. And I'm your omega."

His hips buck and he hisses curses I don't understand. "I knew you were. I always knew. Ours, Talia. You're our omega."

Jasper grips my chin and turns me to look at him. "Ours," he whispers, and gives me the sweetest kiss I've ever had.

"Are you sure you're ready, bella?" Corso nudges me with the tip of his cock again, careful not to enter me.

"Yes, oh my god, yes. I need you inside me." Corso is noble to a fault sometimes, and now is not the time. He slowly starts pushing inside me, so excruciatingly slowly, stretching me. Having him inside me is a little more pain than I expected, and I have to bite my lip to keep from snarling. It didn't hurt this much the first time he fucked me, and that was my first time ever.

"Too much? Do we need to stop?"

I lock my ankles behind his back. "Don't you dare."

Jasper puts his mouth over Devon's mark on my shoulder, sending chills across my skin when he says, "don't worry, baby. He's not going to stop. I've got you nice and ready for him, he's just too sweet to hurt you." He gives Devon's mark a sharp bite. "Sweeter than me. I'd already be fucking you into mattress." He licks the mark and rakes his teeth across it again, flooding me with heat.

Corso thrusts into me then, slowly and gently, as far as he can, stealing my breath when I feel his hip bones dig into the insides of my thighs.

"Yes?" he asks, the question bitten out through his clenched teeth.

"God, yes, Corso. More, I can take it. You won't hurt me." It's going to hurt, but I want it. After the hurt will come the pleasure and I need it so much.

He touches his forehead to mine again and snaps his hips. He pulls out of me slowly and I can feel my body clinging to him, trying to keep him inside. He murmurs something I can't make out and thrusts back inside me, with both his cock and his tongue. It goes on like that until Jasper turns me back to him and fucks his own tongue into my mouth. He's licking so deeply that I can't feel or taste anything but him and I can barely breathe because it's so good. It's what I didn't know I needed. I needed Jasper taking my mouth like this while Corso takes everything else.

Corso is giving me everything now. Everything but the knot I can feel beginning to swell. When we first started this, I wasn't sure if I'd want to be knotted, but I'm sure now. "Give it to me," I pant.

"I'll hurt you, bella."

"No, you won't. Please, Corso?" I run my hands up his sides and into his hair. "I need it. I need you."

He groans and drops his head onto my shoulder. "Tell me if it's too much, Talia, before it's too late." Then he pushes deep, and I close my eyes against the immense pleasure and the burning sting that comes with taking his knot. Fuck, it's so wonderful. I love being knotted. I didn't think it would be such an amazing thing, but it really, really is. It makes me feel so full and connected, a physical embodiment of not being alone.

"Jasper," Corso growls. "If you're going to, do it now."

I'm about to ask what he means, but I don't have to. Jasper takes my hand and wraps it around his length and covers my hand with his. "I was going to fuck your mouth while Corso fucked you, we talked about it, so we'd be ready when you were. But I want to kiss you while he makes you cum instead. We'll just have to get a little messy." Then he starts moving his hand, making us stroke him in time with Corso's thrusts while he matches that rhythm and pace with his kiss. Corso lowers his mouth to one of the marks on my shoulder and latches on to it with his lips and teeth, and that's what finally brings my orgasm thundering through me.

I vaguely register Corso's growl as his release fills me, or the way Jasper bites into Devon's mark on my shoulder when he splashes his own release across my hip and stomach. A little messy, indeed. We'll have to change the sheets, but not until I wake up. We'll just have to be sticky until then. The sleep that comes after being knotted is a definite perk right now.

Jasper does find something to clean up some of his cum, then we settle ourselves on our sides. I'm facing Corso with my leg thrown over his hip and Jasper is curled around me from behind. I'm falling asleep as they're getting the blanket over us, but there's something pulling at me that I didn't feel before. It's more of a soft, constant pull rather than the obvious tug that comes from my alphas. I sit up, eyes wide, gasping. "Jasper!"

"What? What's wrong?" He's looking from side to side, like there's a threat in the room. The gentle pull feels just a bit tighter.

"I don't know how it's possible. It shouldn't be possible. There's no way, right? I mean, how could there be?" I reach up to rub Devon's mark and when I bring my hand down to look at it, there's the thinnest smear of blood on my fingers. "Did you taste blood when you bit me, Jasper?"

His brows come together. "A little, I think. Are you hurt? I wouldn't think that would hurt you, considering."

"No, I'm not hurt. But," I take a breath and look back and forth between him and Corso, "omegas can't mark people. Not even mated omegas. It's impossible."

"Then why are you so worked up about it? Even I can feel how hard you're thinking." Jasper says. "Omegas can't leave marks. If they could, I'd have marked you months ago."

Corso's mouth turns up in a tiny smile. "You can feel how hard Talia is thinking? Really feel it, or you're just feeling how it makes you feel? Because those are two different things."

"I know the difference between my feelings and hers, Corso." He's full of snark and confidence until he realizes what he just said. Then he's grabbing my shoulders and staring into my face with wide eyes. "This isn't possible."

I nod slowly, but I'm smiling.

Corso laughs. "Elizabet is going to have a field day with this."

~

"You? Jasper. *You* are getting a tattoo?"

He sniffs and raises his chin. "Why not? They're all getting it. I want it, too."

I reach over and tug his earlobe. "I'm not saying I don't want you to, or that you can't. I just didn't think you'd want to. I didn't think Corso would either to be honest."

Reid has drawn up a tattoo design for our pack based on the one Devon and the rest already have. Omegas typically don't get the tattoos for whatever reason, and only a portion of betas get them. When I was a beta, I never felt inclined to want to get a pack tattoo; and now that I'm an omega I definitely don't feel the need for one. I couldn't begin to explain the thought process, only that I just don't feel the need to get one. I think it's probably because I carry seven bond marks and it would be unnecessary for me to get a tattoo showing pack unification; but who knows. Maybe it's one of those odd omega things.

Jasper's situation is unique, though. He is an omega who carries five bond marks of his own; but he is also a member of our pack without being an omega to them all and he wants the same mark as the rest of them. He can get whatever tattoo he wants, so long as he's absolutely sure he wants it.

"Yeah," he says, "I didn't think Corso seemed like the type to want a tattoo, but it's going to look good on him."

It's going to look fucking hot. Reid took the butterfly and drew it so that it looks like it's resting on a daisy. That's what our pack tattoo is going to be, a butterfly fanning its wings on the head of a daisy. It's beautiful and I love it. It's going to be gorgeous with all the other flowers Trent has, and the pretty wings and yellow center of the flower is going to be a nice contrast to the black ink Alex has on his arm. Nathan, Devon, and Kaleb will all just have the daisy added to the butterfly on their necks. Since Alex's is going on his shoulder, Corso's and Reid's will be on their shoulders as well. "Where are you going to have yours placed, princess?"

He thinks for a minute and then turns over his arm and touches the underside, just below his elbow. "There. I'll be able to look at it when I want to." That's actually perfect. It's going to look amazing when he turns up the sleeves of his dress shirts. "How long do you think we have before they wake up?"

They, being the babies. They're almost five months old now, starting to sit up and beginning to really interact with the world around them. That world doesn't know about the girls, yet. Only Dutch, and he seems to be very satisfied with his position as the public star of our family; not that we go out in public very much. There is no denying which alpha is his father as he is the spitting image of Trent. After everything that's happened to and in relation to us, I don't want the alphas or me and Jasper off the property, much less our dramatic little prince or his secret assassin sisters. They're going to be so much trouble when they're older.

"Long enough. Was there something you wanted to do?" I smirk and drag my eyes up and down his body.

"Well, I was thinking about putting you between me and Devon."

Interesting choice of words, considering that's exactly where I didn't want to be when I first met him. Now I can't imagine not wanting to be between them. "Is he in the garage?" He's always in the garage.

"Yep. In the brown coveralls. Without a shirt. And he's all smudged with oil."

My favorite. "Does he know we're coming?"

Jasper shakes his head, and I grin. "Think he'll run for us?"

"He will if he wants a sandwich."

Devon is wiping his hands with a cloth when we walk into the garage.

"You've been working all morning, Devon. Would you like a sandwich?" Jasper asks.

Devon throws down the cloth. "Yeah, I could go for a sandwich. I'm starving."

Jasper looks at me, I smirk at him, and Devon's eyebrows knit together. Then we turn devious, predatory gazes on our poor, confused alpha and give the same order.

"Run."

Chapter Thirty-Nine

The Alpha Part One
Releasing Early 2023
This is an unofficial transcript, so as the story is written this excerpt may differ from the final publishing.

How do they not see how much she doesn't want them? Even from my vantage point at the bar it is completely obvious that she is uncomfortable with the crowd of older alphas puffing out their chests at her. She doesn't care, she's too busy watching the twins at the other side of the bar. They're closer to her age, maybe a little older, and they are fucking livid. One of them is drinking something clear and the other is simply glaring across the room. Not at her. At the alpha who must be in his mid to late forties and keeps touching her hair. Why don't they just go over there? They're young and strong enough to stand in front of her. That's what I'd do. I don't mind causing a scene like that when it needs to happen. What are they waiting for?

The twin who has been nursing his drink turns his gaze on me. He watches me for a minute, never breaking eye contact when his brother leans into his ear to speak to him. He nods and holds my gaze long enough to ensure that I'll follow his when he moves it back to the omega across the room, then back to mine. He nods at me. I nod back. Then he and his brother are walking around the bar to sit on either side of me.

"We don't know you."

"I'm not from here."

"You don't know her."

"You do." I take a drink of my water and plunk the glass down.

He nods again and glances at his brother, who also nods. "You here alone?"

"For now. I only landed a few hours ago."

"Is your pack going to be joining you?" His eyes narrow.

"No. They couldn't make the trip."

"That's our girl. Our omega."

I look back across the room and meet the girl's eyes. She blushes and turns away. "Why are you over here, then?"

"Can't do much at one of these functions as a pack of two. Rules. Sanctions."

Ah. That's what it is. What horseshit. I'm only going to be on the West Coast for a few weeks. I don't know how much help I'll be for a few weeks, but she shouldn't have to suffer the attention of decrepit, pompous old men if she doesn't want to. Nobody will fault me for trying to help. "What do you propose?"

"Temporary alliance. You seem solid enough."

I sigh and look back over at the girl. She ducks her head the minute our eyes meet. "Deal. Let's go get your girl."

Made in the USA
Middletown, DE
13 November 2022

14871203R00215